PRAISE FOR LYNSAY SANDS!

"Lynsay Sands has just the right touch of humor and the perfect amount of mystery to hold you in her grasp. . . . *Lady Pirate* is a delicious treat."

—*Romantic Times*

"Intrigue and humor . . . that will make you laugh and turn up the air-conditioning. 4½ stars."

—*Romantic Times* on *Always*

"*The Key* is a happy surprise . . . a whimsical tale that never sacrifices smarts for silliness."

—*The Romance Reader*

"Lynsay Sands's strength lies in creating very light entertainment with elements of comedy."

—*All About Romance*

"Readers are swept up in a delicious, merry and often breath-catching roller-coaster ride that will keep them on the edge of their seats and laughing out loud. A true delight!"

—*Romantic Times* on *The Deed*

Other *Leisure* books by Lynsay Sands:
WISH LIST
BLISS
LADY PIRATE
ALWAYS
SWEET REVENGE
THE SWITCH
THE KEY ✓
THE DEED ✓

Lynsay Sands

The Reluctant Reformer

LEISURE BOOKS   NEW YORK CITY

For Melanie Jackson,
a dear friend who sees me through the worst times.

A LEISURE BOOK®

February 2002

Published by

Dorchester Publishing Co., Inc.
276 Fifth Avenue
New York, NY 10001

ISBN 0-8439-4974-0

Visit us on the web at www.dorchesterpub.com.

Chapter One

London, March 1815

Maggie shifted her feet slightly, trying to ease the ache her cramped position was causing in her legs. The small movement was enough to cause her to bang her knees against the door of the armoire she presently sat in, making it rattle. Wincing at the pain that shot up her leg, Maggie was busily rubbing the appendage when the cupboard door opened and soft candlelight spilled in over her.

"Stop yer banging about, or ye'll be givin' away that ye're in there."

Ceasing her leg-rubbing, Maggie managed an apologetic smile for the scantily clad young woman glaring in at her. "I am sorry," she began in conciliatory tones, then paused and heaved out a breath. She straightened and began to step from the small closet. "No, actually, I am not. Er, Daisy, is it?"

"Maisey," the girl corrected.

"Yes, well . . . Maisey, then," Maggie said. The girl's put-upon air was irritating, as were the wrinkles that Maggie was futilely trying to brush out of her gown. "This is all really rather silly, and quite beyond the information for which I was looking. All I really wanted was to—"

The sound of a rap at the door made Maggie pause, alarmed. The young woman before her stiffened, then steel seemed to enter her eyes and she shoved Maggie firmly back into the armoire. Maggie landed on her behind with a grunt.

"It's too late to be changing yer mind now, milady," she announced, bending to shove Maggie's feet inside the closet before she could regain her balance. "Madame says ye're to watch, and watch you will. Now keep quiet," she said in a hiss. The door pushed closed with a decided snap.

"Damn," Maggie said under her breath, then struggled to a sitting position. The door rattled slightly, nearly covering the sound of a bolt being slid home. Pressing one eye to the crack where the doors did not quite meet, she saw Maisey nod with a grunt of satisfaction and whirl away to answer the door. Frowning, Maggie lifted a hand to push experimentally forward, but the door stayed firmly shut. The girl had locked her in!

Well, this is just bloody beautiful, she thought irritably. *Brilliant! I do tend to get myself into fixes, don't I?*

Not that she could have gotten out now, anyway. Maggie considered herself a thoroughly modern young woman: highly intelligent, independent, and uncaring of what others thought of her—but only to a certain degree. Even she, thoroughly modern as she was, hesitated to deliberately draw the wrath and scorn of the ton down upon herself. Especially when she merely had to sit quietly for a short time to avoid scandal completely. Patience was not one of her natural virtues, but she had been attempting to cultivate it of late. Yes, she would simply have to look at this as a chance to develop herself. A learning experience, one might say.

She had barely finished that thought when it occurred to her that she was crouching down in a small armoire in one of the rooms of the infamous Madame Dubarry's—this was a brothel, for God's sake! What she would learn in this room . . . well, she just shouldn't know yet! What was more, she certainly couldn't write about it.

Good Lord, how had she ended up here? Madame Dubarry, of course. The woman had been slow to warm to the idea of allowing Maggie to interview her and some of her girls for a story for the *Daily Express*. Once the madam had agreed to the undertaking, however, she had become quite enthusiastic. The older woman had bustled Maggie from girl to girl, attending the interviews to be sure each girl told the juiciest stories; then she had rounded off this most peculiar day by offering Maggie refreshment in her own private drawing room. It was while the two had chatted over tea that Madame Dubarry devised this harebrained scheme. Clattering her teacup down in its saucer, she had sat up abruptly, her eyes on the clock in the corner.

"What time is it, nearly seven? Oh, really, this is perfect timing! You *must* witness this, Lady Maggie. Really, you must. You shall thank me for it, I promise."

So saying, the woman had stood quickly, grasped Maggie's hand and dragged her from her chair, then hurried from the room and along the hall. Before Maggie could even collect herself enough to ask what she must see and why, they had reached this chamber. Madame Dubarry shoved her inside, installed her in the cupboard with admonishments to remain quiet and see, then had instructed young Maisey that Maggie was to witness the night's proceedings. She had fled the room nearly as hurriedly as she'd ushered Maggie into it.

Maggie, stunned by the abruptness of the event, had remained still and silent for a moment before the cramping of her muscles had forced her to shift positions and draw the wrath of the shapely young Maisey.

Really, had she been a bit quicker, Maggie might have managed to flee the room before Maisey's customer arrived. Now it appeared she was quite stuck. She sighed irritably and tried to ignore the murmur of voices from the room outside. Maggie had no desire to learn anything more than she'd learned in her interviews. And I won't, she assured herself. I simply will not look through the crack to see who Maisey's client is or what they are doing.

She frowned as the voices drew closer. The man's slightly deeper-timbered voice struck a chord of recognition within her. It sounded amazingly like . . .

Her gaze slid to the crack despite her best intentions, and Maggie drew her breath in with a hiss. Good Lord, it *was* him: Pastor Frances. Her eyes narrowed on the man. She had just been discussing the fact that he was paying her court, and that she thought he might soon propose, when Madame Dubarry had rushed her up here.

Maggie was distracted from further thought by an odd question from Maisey.

"Who am I to be tonight, milord? Yer mother?"

Maggie's eyes widened in shocked dismay at that, but they nearly fell out of her head at Frances's answer.

"Nay. Tonight you shall be my dear Margaret."

"Sweet Lady Wentworth, is it?" Maggie was almost too shocked by Frances's presence to notice the irony in the young prostitute's voice. Almost. "The woman who personifies the very word 'lady'? The woman who never sets a foot wrong? Who is discretion herself?"

Maggie couldn't help but wince slightly at the pointy edges of Maisey's words. She also experienced a touch of alarm as she realized that, in her excitement, Madame Dubarry had addressed her by her real name when she'd brought her up to this room.

She forgot all such concerns when Frances answered, "Aye: my sweet Maggie. I have decided to propose to her. I arranged to take her to the Cousins' ball tonight. I shall propose to her afterward. I believe she will accept."

"Oh, 'course she will, guv'nor, a great, strapping man like yerself . . . ." There was no missing the irony in Maisey's voice then. At least, Maggie caught it; the gibe seemed to slip right past the rather thin and emaciated Frances.

"Fine. You be Maggie then, and I shall practice on you." There was a moment of critical silence before he murmured, "You had best put something else on."

"Something else?"

"Well, Maggie would never greet me so scantily clad."

"Not even if the house were afire," Maggie agreed

13

under her breath. Through the crack in the armoire doors, she took in Maisey's costume—what there was of it. Sheer silk and red, it covered absolutely nothing. It was scandalous.

There came a moment of uncertain silence; then Maisey heaved an impatient sigh. "Fine, then. Ye step on out into the hall, and I shall change. Give me five minutes; then knock."

"Why must I wait in the hall?" Frances whined.

"Well, ye want it to be as if ye were proposing to Lady Wentworth, don't ye? Would she dress in front of ye? Get on with ye. I'll only be a minute, and this will seem more real."

Through the crack, Maggie saw Maisey usher Frances out of the room as firmly as she herself had been shoved into the armoire. The prostitute closed the door behind the pastor with a snap, then locked it. She was a no-nonsense type of woman, it seemed.

"Thank God." Maggie burst out of the armoire as Maisey unbolted it. "I thought I should suffocate in there. Now get me out of here."

"You know where the door is," came Maisey's unconcerned response. The young woman was digging through her clothing, picking up and discarding gown after gown.

Maggie frowned and glanced from the door to the girl. "I can hardly exit *that* way. Pastor Frances is out there."

"Then I guess ye'll just have to get back in the closet, won't ye?" Maisey snapped, discarding yet another gown.

"Get back in?" Maggie was confused. "Did you not let me out to slip me from the room?"

"No. I let you out so I could find a gown suitable enough to play the likes of ye. I could hardly dig about with you sitting in my armoire just waiting to be discovered by the pastor, could I? Damn! I ain't got a single dress as drab as the one ye're wearing." Throwing her last garment down in disgust, she glared at her as if the lack of wardrobe were somehow Maggie's fault. Then a catty look came over her face. "You wouldn't consider letting me borrow yer gown fer a bit, would ye?"

"Certainly not," Maggie snapped. She looked desperately around the room. "There simply has to be a way out of here."

"There isn't," the girl assured her. "Unless ye can fly out the window."

"The window!" Maggie hurried over to it, then pushed it open and leaned out. They were on the third floor. The ground was a long way down. She was about to give up on the idea when her gaze dropped to the wall, and she saw a ledge a couple of feet below the window. It was just wide enough that she could walk it—if she were careful.

She would be careful, she decided.

"Here!" Maisey grabbed her arm as Maggie sat on the sill and made to climb out. "What? Are ye daft? Ye'll break yer bones jumpin' from here."

"I am not going to jump," Maggie said with a hiss of exasperation, tugging her arm free. "I am going to walk that ledge to the next room, climb in through the window there, and get away."

Leaning out, Maisey peered down, her eyes widening slightly in surprise. "Oh . . . well." The girl hesitated slightly, her gaze calculating; then she announced, "Well, that would be nice, wouldn't it? Except that Lady

15

X and Lord Hastings are in one of the rooms next door. Yer climbin' in on them would cause the scandal of the decade."

Maggie frowned at the news. Everyone, absolutely everyone, had heard of the infamous Lady X. She was the most famous of Agatha Dubarry's prostitutes, and as such, Maggie had not been allowed to speak to her—though she had caught a glimpse of the woman earlier while interviewing the others. From what she had spied, Lady X was a lovely blonde with a perfect figure, full lips, and deep, mysterious eyes. That was all she had seen.

Actually, it was all anyone ever saw. Her face was always covered by a blazing red mask that never came off. Men paid highly for the privilege of bedding her, each trying to discover her true identity, but no one had yet figured it out. It was rumored that the woman was actually a lady of nobility who worked thusly on the side to help shore her sagging family coffers. While many disputed the idea, claiming that surely no lady would risk being discovered in such an endeavor, there were enough men willing to dig deep into their pockets to try to find out, and Madame Dubarry was doing very well.

Maggie definitely did not need the scandal of walking in on the woman while she was entertaining—especially if she was with Lord Hastings, one of the most distinguished royal councilors.

"Which room are they in?" she asked.

Maisey smiled, the expression of a cat who has cornered a mouse. "Let me use your gown."

Maggie stiffened, then shook her head. "I shall find out for myself," she declared. Sliding her legs over onto the window ledge, she straightened slowly, clinging nervously to the sill as she fought to maintain her balance.

"Have it your way," Maisey said with amusement, watching. "But it does look a long way down. And I know I shouldn't like to make it all the way along that ledge to a window, simply to have to turn back and travel twice the distance to another." At Maggie's obvious uncertainty, Maisey pressed her advantage. " 'Tis just a gown. I'll give ye one o' me own to wear in its place. Then I'll send yers back to ye first thing on the morrow—once it's been cleaned."

Maggie took in the hopeful gaze of the prostitute, peered at the ground such a long way down, then shifted cautiously on the ledge. Her mind was made up by her jumping stomach. Cursing under her breath, she maneuvered back into the room and eyed Maisey unhappily. "The other room is empty, isn't it?"

The prostitute nodded solemnly.

"Fine. But—" A tap at the door cut her off, and both women glanced over sharply as the doorknob jiggled.

"Are you ready yet, my dear?" Frances cooed in a sickening tone. Maggie had never heard it from the usually dignified man.

"Oh, keep yer pants on. I'm hurryin' as fast as I can," Maisey snapped, then grimly turned to Maggie. "Well?"

"Oh . . . stuff!" Maggie huffed. She set to work disrobing as quickly as she could. Looking pleased, Maisey began to undress as well. The two worked in virtual silence until Maggie got her gown off. She handed it over, then crossed her arms, rubbing them as goose bumps began to form on her flesh.

"Yer shift and bloomers too."

17

"What?"

When Maggie stared at her in dismay, the prostitute rolled her eyes. "I'm supposed to be dressed like you. 'Sides, ye'll be caught fer sure if ye run around with those bloomers showing through my gown."

Maggie frowned at the transparent garment the girl held out, then shook her head in misery. "I will be recognized anyway if my face is seen. Oh, why did I leave my veil in Madame Dubarry's drawing room?"

Whirling, Maisey hurried to her armoire, returning a moment later with a plain red silk mask for Maggie to wear. "Here; put this on. With the mask, my clothes, and yer cloak, ye should escape all right."

Maggie glanced at it curiously. "Is this Lady X's mask?"

"Nay. Mine. Lady X's mask is far fancier." When Maggie continued to stare at her questioningly, the prostitute heaved a sigh. "Men like to play all sorts o' games. I . . ." She paused, scowling as there was another tap at the door, louder and more insistent this time.

"Maisey?" Frances sounded somewhat put out.

"Only just another moment, milord," Maisey called back. She shoved the mask at Maggie and said in a hiss, "Take it."

"Are you absolutely sure of this, Johnstone?" James Huttledon, Lord Ramsey, was finally moved to set aside the book he'd been reading when the Bow Street runner was announced. Carefully marking his spot with one of the many cloth bookmarks his aunt had made him over the years, he set the tome on a side table for later and sat up to give his full attention to this troubling turn of events.

"Aye, m'lord. I tried to find you right away. I knew you'd be wanting to know right prompt, but when I went by your townhouse, they told me you were at your club. By the time I got there, they said you'd left just moments earlier. I had to begin searching—"

"Yes, yes." James waved the explanation away and turned to stare out the window at the tranquil scene of the garden lining the back of his town house library.

Johnstone was silent for a moment, allowing Ramsey his thoughts, then pointed out gently, "It would explain where she's been getting the money to keep up the house and servants."

James jerked his head around to stare ferociously at the man. "You are not thinking that she *works* there?"

Johnstone appeared as surprised at the question as could be. "Well . . . what other business could a lady have at Madame Dubarry's?"

"For God's sake, Johnstone; she is a lady!"

"Aye, well, the claim is that Lady X is a woman of nobility."

James's mouth dropped open, but he quickly snapped it shut. "Good God," he got out between gritted teeth. He turned toward the window again.

They were both silent; then Johnstone said uncertainly, "I left Henries there to keep an eye out while I came to see what ye wanted me to do."

James remained quiet for a moment, then stood abruptly and strode toward the door of his library. "Hethers!" he bellowed as he stepped into the hall, relief filling him when he spied his valet approaching. "My coat. I am going out."

The servant hurriedly fetched his overcoat, hat, and gloves. As the man assisted him in donning them, James

19

added, "Have some things packed. I am leaving tonight."

"Tonight, my lord?"

"Yes. I shall be staying at Ramsey for a while."

"Yes, my lord."

Maggie peered in at the scene taking place in the room
next to Maisey's, and she groaned aloud. Her fingers
tightening on the cold wall, she leaned her head unhappily against it. After trading clothes, Maisey had helped
her climb back out onto this ledge, hissing that Lady X
and Lord Hastings were in the room on the left. She
had then left and hurried to attend the impatiently
pounding Frances.

Relieved to be out of her predicament Maggie had
immediately inched along the ledge to the next window,
expecting to find the room empty. Unfortunately, what
she had not realized was that Maisey had been referring
to her own left—which, of course, with Maggie clinging
to the wall facing her, was Maggie's right. Which meant
Maggie should have gone right. Which she hadn't. She
had ended up coming all this way for nothing, for while
curtains shrouded the window, making the images beyond blurred and foggy, the figures were discernible
enough to see two people engaged in the most energetic
round of ride-the-pony it had ever been Maggie's mis-
fortune to witness.

Resignedly Maggie turned to glance back along the
ledge, took a deep breath, then began the long return
the way she had come, clinging like a limpet to the wall
as she did. She was nearly back at Maisey's window before she realized that in her haste, the prostitute had

neglected to close it. Grimacing, she paused to the side and peered around its edge.

The time since she had crept from the room seemed like a century to Maggie, and while she knew that it was just the stress of the moment making it seem so, she was surprised to see that she must have indeed been gone for quite a length of time. A good ten minutes must have passed, at least, for Maisey—playing Maggie—had already served Frances a drink by a small table and chairs near the bed. Their refreshments finished and whatever passed for small talk between them done, Frances now knelt at Maisey's feet, the prostitute's hands clasped gently in his, heartfelt longing on the pastor's reverent face.

"I have known you for quite a while now, Margaret," he was saying. "Long enough to know that you are the woman for me. I would be most honored if you would consent to be my bride."

"Yes," Maisey agreed in a bored tone.

The pastor frowned. "Surely she wouldn't just say yes like that?"

"What would she say then?"

"Well, I don't know. Just . . . try to sound a bit more enthusiastic, please."

"Yes," the prostitute cooed.

Frances continued to frown, but apparently decided he wouldn't get much more out of the girl. Shrugging slightly, he surged to his feet, drawing Maisey up and into his arms with the same move. "You shan't be sorry, my dear. I shall make an outstanding husband—I promise you, we shall have a marvelous marriage." This he managed to gasp out between slobbery kisses across Maisey's cheeks and down her neck. When he reached the top of the prim black gown she now wore, he paused and pulled back to leer at her. "I love the proper little things you wear. They hide your lovely body from the eyes of other men, but there is no need to hide from me any longer." With that, he grasped the collar of the gown and ripped downward, rending it nearly to the waist before lifting wide eyes to Maisey's dismayed face. "Oops," he said lightly. "Now you shall have to punish me."

"Ye're damn right I will," the girl snapped irritably. "And ye'll be replacin' that gown, too. It weren't even mine."

"Then I, of course, shall replace it," Frances promised, unperturbed by her obvious anger. Releasing Maisey, he stepped back and began doffing his clothes.

Maggie turned away, unwilling to watch what would follow. She tried judging the space between where she stood and the other side of the window, wondering if she could traverse the distance quickly enough that she might not be detected. She supposed it depended on how distracted the two in the room were. Glancing back inside reluctantly, she saw Frances slide out of his top and drape it across the chair he had just vacated. Glimpsing welts on his back, Maggie paused in dismay, her gaze moving to Maisey to see that the girl had retrieved a long, wide leather belt from the armoire and was now eyeing Frances with a decidedly jaundiced eye. He continued stripping.

Staring in surprise at the pastor as he shed his trousers, Maggie saw that welts covered not just his back, but his buttocks and the rear of his upper thighs as well. She frowned in bewilderment. Was this what Madame Dubarry had wanted her to see? Did Frances really pay

Maisey to beat him with a belt? Some of the girls had told her such tales in their interviews: stories of men who enjoyed odd or even unhealthy diversions during their sexual encounters. Was Frances one of those? It would seem so.

She shook her head with a sort of pity combined with disgust. What would make a man turn to such games? Frances had seemed such a normal, well-mannered, polite sort. ·

The first crack of the belt across Frances's back dragged Maggie from her ponderings to the realization that she was perched on a ledge outside the third-floor window of a brothel, balanced delicately between breaking her neck and being discovered and ruined. This was no time to be reflecting on Frances's foibles. She should just be grateful she had learned of them ere he proposed. Imagine if she had accepted, never knowing that just hours before the man had been whipped, among other things, by one of Madame Dubarry's girls.

Would he have expected her to beat him once they were married? Maggie immediately pushed the question out of her head with a shudder. She had no time for such thoughts. She would *not* be accepting his proposal. On that determined note, she peeked into the room once more, relieved to see that Pastor Frances and Maisey were suitably distracted, then forced herself to move past the window and continue on toward the next window along the wall.

James stood uncomfortably inside the foyer at Madame Dubarry's, waiting impatiently for Johnstone to conclude his whispered conversation with the madam herself. Ramsey had already been approached by, and turned down the offers of, three of the madam's girls, one of whom had offered to do a thing or two that he had never considered trying before. He certainly did not wish to attempt it now, here in this place.

"It's done, yer lordship. Madame says Lady X is with Lord Hastings now, but you can have a go at her next."

"I do not intend to 'have a go at her,' as you so delicately put it," James said in a hiss.

A flicker of irritation crossed Johnstone's face before the runner controlled it. "I didn't think you would, my lord. But I could hardly tell her ye wished to kidnap the girl, now, could I?"

"I am not kidnapping her. I am rescuing her."

"Aye. Well, I'd guess that there is a matter of perspective, ain't it?" Pausing, the man shook his head. "Either way, it'll cost ye deep," he announced, then mentioned a shocking sum.

"You must be joking."

"I never joke about money, m'lord. But ye'll either be paying that amount or waiting till a week from Sunday to lay hands on her. She's booked full for the night—a different man every half hour. Dubarry was willing to bump everyone back, but she wants to be paid well for the trouble. What should I tell her?"

James considered walking out the door, getting in his carriage, and riding to Lady Wentworth's home to await her return there, but his conscience would not let him. He had made a promise to look after the girl—and looking after her did not mean glancing the other way while she bedded some two dozen or so men. Muttering under his breath, he pulled a bag of coins from his pocket and dropped it in the hand the Bow Street runner extended. "How long until Hastings's half hour is up?"

Johnstone's gaze slid to a clock in the hall. "About ten minutes. I'll just give Dubarry the money; then we'll go have a look around and see if there's another way out of here."

"Another way out?"

"Surely you didn't think to march out the front door with her, did ye? Dubarry ain't gonna like that. The girl is her golden goose."

"Ah, yes." James sighed; then he, too, stared at the clock on the wall. Ten minutes.

Maggie grabbed the edge of the window with relief and paused to rest her face on the cold glass. She was sweating. Amazingly enough, she was more terrified of falling than of discovery, which was surprising, because she could remember a time when the prospect of social ruin had been more frightful than anything. But that had been when she could afford such pretty concerns as her reputation, before she'd had the burden of so many lives piled on her shoulders.

"Damn you, Gerald, for dying, anyway," she cursed in a whisper, then immediately—if silently—apologized to her poor brother for cussing him so. Gerald had loved life. He had lived every moment of his short time on earth as if it might be his last. He had not complained when he was ordered off to fight Napoléon. And she had no doubt he had given his life in battle with as much passion and as little regret as with which he had lived. It was just too damn bad he'd been forced to leave her in such a fix.

As a woman, Maggie had been unable to inherit her

brother's title and estates. While he had bequeathed her his town house in London—a purchase he had made with money from investments before inheriting his title and station from their father—everything else had been entailed to some blasted second or third cousin . . . if they had found the bloody man. The only money Maggie had to live off of was a small investment she had made with her own inheritance from their mother.

It wasn't really that small an investment. In fact, she could have lived quite comfortably off of it for her entire life—had she not been saddled with Gerald's property and servants. It was a town house fit for a duke, with lots of rooms, and nearly as many employees in attendance.

The practical side of Maggie had ordered her to release the servants, close the house, sell it, and move to a small cottage in the country. There she might have lived very comfortably with one or two hired hands. However, sentiment had not allowed her to sell the property. Gerald had loved the place. He had rarely even bothered to ride out to the estate he had inherited with his title, but his town house—there his spirit seemed to linger still. Maggie simply could not part with his home; it was her last link to her now all-but-deceased family. And as for the servants . . . faced with closing up part of the house and releasing a large portion of the staff, Maggie simply hadn't been able to do it. Gerald's staff were hardworking, cheerful individuals. She hadn't been able to look a single one of them in the face and tell him he was no longer wanted.

Such being the case, she had been forced to find a way to support the large staff. The answer had come by chance. While sorting through her brother's papers,

Maggie had come across the knowledge that her brother had led a double life. He'd been Lord Gerald Wentworth, Duke of Clarendon, and also G. W. Clark—the adventurist writer who wrote columns for the *Daily Express*. He'd provided articles about the seedier side of London life: rumors, truths, stories of gaming hells, fortunes won and lost, affairs, everything. From Gerald's papers Maggie had learned he had met with Mr. Hartwick—the editor of the *Express*—only once, and then he'd been in disguise to protect his identity. Members of the nobility did not do anything so crass as to work.

She had also learned that he wrote the articles and dispatched them via Banks, his butler. Which was when Maggie'd had her brilliant idea: she would become G. W. Clark. She could do it—and she had for the last three months. She had gone to great lengths to continue her brother's column, going so far as to dress up as a young buck and travel to the seedier sections of London with Banks in tow to protect her—for all the good the elderly butler was.

All that was how she had ended up standing here on the ledge outside the third-floor window of Madame Dubarry's. The woman had apparently been a great friend of her brother's, at least according to his notes. Certainly Madame Dubarry had been privy to the fact that her brother was G. W. Clark, for when the column had started up again three weeks after his death, she had paid a visit to Maggie.

With a sense of adventure equal to Maggie's and her brother's, Madame Dubarry had arrived on the Wentworth doorstep dressed as a poor fruitseller. On being shown in to see Maggie, the madame had announced her true identity, revealed that Gerald had been G. W.

Clark, and complained that some "dastardly devil" had stolen his name. Maggie had been forced to confess herself the culprit. By the end of a pot of tea, she and Dubarry had struck up an unlikely friendship. They had been in cahoots ever since—although the woman had only recently given in to the interviews of her employees.

Amazing, Maggie thought. For the first time, she considered that perhaps Agatha Dubarry had been right when she had suggested Maggie come dressed as a man to this night's activities. Maggie had shrugged away the suggestion, thinking that the madam's girls might be more forthcoming with information while talking to another of their gender. It had worked, too. She had been introduced as the sister of G. W. Clark, sent to interview them, and the girls had responded very easily. And no one had known her true identity, not until Agatha had slipped up in Maisey's room. Maggie found she wasn't too concerned about Maisey, though. She had no doubt that Madame Dubarry could keep the girl quiet. Her real problem would be if some member of the *ton* saw her; then she would be recognized and ruined for sure. There was no way Agatha Dubarry could keep all of London quiet.

Yes, now would indeed be a beneficial time to be disguised as a man. And, she thought as she glanced down nervously past her long skirts, such a disguise would also have made climbing about on ledges more seemly.

"Lord Ramsey, we'll have to sneak her down the back stairs and smuggle her through the kitchen."

James nodded at Johnstone's suggestion. After he'd made a brief but thorough examination of the brothel, it indeed seemed the best bet to get the girl out. "Go have my driver move the carriage to the alley," he instructed, his eyes on the clock in the hall. "Hastings's time is up. I'll go see if he has left yet."

Nodding, Johnstone hurried away toward the front door, and James started upstairs. He was at the top of the steps before he realized that the runner hadn't told him in which room Lady X was supposed to be. He was about to return downstairs to ask Madame Dubarry when he changed his mind. He would recognize Hastings. Everyone knew of Hastings, if not in person, then by reputation. He was second only to the crown in power. Whichever room Hastings exited, James would enter.

He had just come to that conclusion when the thud of a door made him turn back around on the landing. A glance up the hall showed Hastings strolling jauntily toward him, whistling under his breath as he straightened his cravat. James almost cursed aloud. He had been too slow; he couldn't be sure from which room the man had come. There were several possibilities.

He would try them all, he decided resolutely. Giving Hastings a curt nod, he moved purposely past him to set about his work.

The thud of a closing door tore Maggie from her thoughts, and she glanced through the window into the empty room to which she had inched. If her thoughts had distracted her so long that this room was now occupied, too, she thought she might very well throw up. She did not think she had the stamina or nerve to traverse the length of the ledge again. It was with some relief that she saw that the room appeared empty. Letting her breath out, she reached down, opened the window, and silently slipped inside.

Now that they were on solid ground, her legs were more than just a bit rubbery. Ordering them to stand firm, Maggie strode quickly across the room, pausing at the door to take a breath and listen for sounds in the hallway. When she heard only silence, she eased the door open. About to step out of the room, Maggie recalled the mask Maisey had given her—she had shoved it into her pocket in her rush to finish dressing and escape. It would be better to wear the thing. So thinking, she turned back into the room and started to lift the flimsy red silk mask to her face. Her eyes fell on a bed and a woman gaping at her from the shadows within. The two females gaped at each other briefly; then the sound of footsteps in the hall reminded Maggie that she had to get out of here. She quickly finished raising the mask to her face, tied the strings of it in place, then slipped from the room without a murmur of apology.

She had just finished pulling the door closed when a hand slid around her from behind, covering her mouth and smothering her startled cry. She was lifted bodily, bundled in her cape, and carted swiftly down the hall.

Chapter Two

"Any problems, m'lord?"

The words came muffled through her cape to Maggie some few minutes after she found herself so abruptly abducted—minutes during which she had struggled uselessly against the iron arms of her assailant and attempted to scream through the wide, firm hand that covered the lower half of her face. Her struggles ended rather quickly, though. The hand covering her face was not just over her mouth, but also rested along the bottom of her nose, and though she didn't think it was her abductor's intention, she was very close to fainting from lack of oxygen. Her ears were ringing.

For a moment when she heard the voice, Maggie felt hope that the hand across her face would be released and she would again be able to suck into her deprived body some much-needed air. But rather than let go, the hand shifted, covering her more firmly as she was jostled and dragged into what could only be the dark interior of a closed carriage. In the next moment, the clip-clop of horses' hooves on the cobbled London street, and a jolt as the conveyance started forward, told Maggie her guess was right.

Her ears ringing more loudly, she prayed that her suffocation would end before it was too late. The hand remained firmly in place. Glancing around wildly, Maggie realized that, rather than adjusting to the dimmer light, her sight seemed to be dimming further. She would not get air in time to prevent fainting; she could only hope that she would get it in time to stave off death. With that, she slipped into the dark, soft cushion of unconsciousness.

"She's gone limp," Johnstone announced, squinting through the dim light at the woman James held across his lap. "I think she's faint—Damn, Lord Ramsey! You've got both her nose and mouth covered! She can't breathe!"

James removed his hand at once. Turning the woman's limp form slightly in his arms, he peered at her in dismay. The pallor of her skin was obvious even in the dim light, and he cursed as he tugged aside her heavy cape and lowered his head to listen to her heart. It was a great relief to him when he heard its slow, steady thud. Sitting up with a sigh, he peered down at the gown she wore as they rode under a streetlamp. The creation of sheer red material was not made to cover anything; her nipples showed right through it! The carriage moved past the light and its interior returned to darkness, leaving Ramsey's captive nothing but a pale bundle of shadows on his lap. He hurriedly tugged her cape closed again and sank back on the seat.

"Is she all right?"

James frowned at the huskiness in the runner's voice. Suspecting the sight they had just beheld was the cause, and unaccountably annoyed at the fact, he was a bit snappish when he answered. "Yes. She's just fainted, and shall recover."

"Good," Johnstone answered.

They both fell silent as they rode beneath another streetlight. This time both men peered at their capture's face, taking in the delicate features visible below her mask. James stared at that pale visage, so innocent in repose, and he felt bewilderment overtake him.

He had seen Margaret from a distance several times during the months since his return from war, and each time he had been struck by the delicacy of her features, the refined air about her. Even having discovered her in Madame Dubarry's himself, masked and all, it was difficult to believe that the delicate creature he held was the notorious Lady X. The name had been bandied about his club for weeks, along with descriptions he could hardly forget. So lovely, what one could see of her. She had a figure more perfect than a doll's, lips made for the licentious joys of the bedroom, a body that didn't stop. . . . She was a tiger in bed, giving each patron his money's worth—and with seeming relish. It was said that Lady X, nobility or not, was no lady.

Clearing his throat, James forced the thoughts away and glanced at Johnstone. The man was staring at their captive from the opposite seat of the carriage. "Well, do not just sit there," he said. "Find something for us to tie her up with."

The Bow Street runner's eyebrows rose. "Do you really think that's necessary, m'lord?"

"I intend to take her to my country estate and keep her there until we find an alternate career for her. Do you think she will come willingly?"

"No, I suppose not," the runner admitted with a grimace; then he asked, "What of her household?"

James's surprise showed in his voice as he asked, "What household?"

"Her servants. I realize she has no family left to be concerned about her disappearance, but her servants might raise a hue and cry when she doesn't return. What do you intend to do to prevent that?"

"Damn, I had not thought of it."

They were both silent for a moment; then the runner suggested, "Ye could write a letter. Tell them that you have invited Lady Margaret to the country to rusticate for a couple days and that she has taken you up on it."

"Do you think they would believe such tripe?" James asked dubiously.

"They are servants, m'lord. Servants don't question the word of the nobility—at least not out loud. Besides, you are a friend of the family. Well, at least you're a friend of her dead brother's. A letter should keep them quiet for a couple days at least, long enough for you to convince her to write something else to them, reassuring them she is fine."

James considered his suggestion for a minute, then sighed and nodded. "It will have to do. I will write a letter once we get back to my town house, and you can deliver it. In the meantime, we still need to tie her up." His gaze slid around the carriage, then to the runner again. "Perhaps we could use your cravat. Do you think it is long enough?"

Johnstone glanced down with surprise. "I think so, but . . . Oh, what the hell," he decided, setting to work on the garment, then he offered James a cheeky grin. "I'll just bill it to ye."

Maggie was slow to awaken. When she did, it was to find herself bundled in a darkened corner, her cape wrapped tightly around her—so tightly she couldn't move, she realized with dismay. *No, wait.* It was not her cape that restricted her movements, but her hands *were* bound. Her feet appeared to be as well. What the devil was going on?

Blinking in an effort to adjust to the blackness, she peered around at her surroundings. While she saw nothing, she could deduce that she was still in the carriage—the rocking motion of the seat she sat on and the steady clip-clop of horses' hooves made that obvious. Oddly, though, the noise of hooves was the only sound she could hear. The normal hustle and bustle of London's streets was missing. And she could still see nothing.

Then the darkness enveloping her was broken, the hood of her cape was tugged aside, revealing to her why it had been so dark. Without the material covering her face, Maggie could see the gray light of predawn creeping through the window.

Her gaze slid around the carriage, taking in the dark outline of a man seated across from her. He was the only other occupant of the conveyance. It was hard to see his features in the dim interior of the coach, but she could see his size, and that was enough to intimidate her.

"You are awake."

She blinked in surprise. His diction was perfect, his speech cultured. This was no street ruffian, but a gentleman. She had been abducted by a gentleman?

Abducted? Swallowing, she dropped her eyes to her lap to hide her confusion. She, Maggie Wentworth, had been abducted: dragged from Madame Dubarry's, suffocated to unconsciousness, and, apparently, carted off in a carriage. But why? For ransom? There was no money for which to ransom her, and even if there were, there certainly was no one from whom to demand it. Then, all at once, the answer seemed obvious. This was a mistake. She had been mistaken for someone else, one of Madame Dubarry's girls, of course. Perhaps even the famed prostitute Lady X, she realized with dismay. She still wore the red mask Maisey had given her.

"Oh, dear," she murmured somewhat faintly, drawing her abductor's attention. Forcing a smile, though she wasn't at all sure that the man could see it, Maggie sat up as straight as she could. Attempting an air of confidence, she explained, "There has been a dreadful mistake."

"What mistake would that be, Lady Wentworth?"

His address managed to knock some of the wind out of her sails, and Maggie couldn't hide her surprise. "You know my name?"

"Of course."

Well, that blew her theory to kingdom come, Maggie realized with distress. Good Lord, he knew who she was. There was no mistake. She had been deliberately kidnapped. But why, for goodness' sake? Before she could ask, her kidnapper, apparently noting her fear, tried to reassure her.

"There is no need to be alarmed, my lady. The secret of your exploits shall remain safe with me. I have no more desire to unmask you to the world than you yourself must have to be unmasked. In fact, if I have my way, there shall be no chance of anyone ever finding out the games you have been playing. But understand: your alter ego dies this night. You shall not be returning to your previous employ."

Maggie bit her lip, holding back any protest she might have wished to make about her lucrative career as G. W. Clark. There was no sense in annoying her captor until she knew his identity and just how much of a threat he was.

"Now," the man went on gently, apparently pleased that she had made no argument. "You should rest. We shall be traveling for several more hours." Having given that order, he raised a cane to rap on the ceiling of the coach, which drew to an immediate halt. With a nod in her direction, he disembarked from the carriage. Seconds after the door closed, the carriage rocked slightly, as if he were mounting it to sit beside its driver; then the coach jolted back into motion.

Once the conveyance had settled back into its previous monotonous rhythm, Maggie let out a small moan. She had been kidnapped by some madman who knew of her secret doings as G. W. Clark! Of course, there had always been the chance that someone might discover those pursuits, but she had never considered that up on discovering them, that someone might wish to kidnap her and force her to stop! Her real fear had been that they would reveal her and destroy her reputation.

She wearily leaned her head back against the cushioned seat. It seemed she had gotten into a true pickle this time. Not that such was strange for her; as a child her life had often seemed like one calamity after another. The fact had been something of a family joke. "Only you," her family had said. "Only you, Maggie, could end up in such a fix. Only you, Maggie, could land yourself in such a mess." And she had to agree. Just look at how she had ended up tucked into the armoire of a brothel. And how she'd been forced to climb out the window to escape an education she'd not been seeking. And now this kidnapping!

Maggie silently cursed herself for not allowing Banks to accompany her to Dubarry's. The butler often served as a bodyguard of sorts during her adventures, accompanying her and staying as near as he could without ruining her disguises. Old, thin, and fragile, the man wasn't really much of a deterrent to anyone wishing to do her serious harm, but his presence had always made her feel a little bit more secure—and she couldn't help now but wish he had been there tonight.

The butler had wished to accompany her, but Maggie had explained that, as she was simply going to interview women, she had no need of his protection. Madame Dubarry was a friend, she'd added, and thus Maggie would be perfectly safe. She found it ironic now that it had taken her some amount of persuasion before she had convinced him to stay behind.

"Idiot," she chided herself under her breath. Despite the fact that Banks probably would have been left to wait in the kitchens, and therefore would have been helpless to prevent her kidnapping, at least there would have been someone to notice her disappearance. Maggie wasn't at all certain that Madame Dubarry would think twice when she did not return. Men had already started arriving in search of evening entertainment when the brothel owner had hustled her up the back stairs to Maisey's room. The woman was likely now too busy tending to business to notice Maggie's absence. And who knew how long Banks would wait at the house before deciding to come in search of her?

Yes, she thought resignedly, she was in a fix all right. Now she just had to figure a way out of it. Getting untied would be a good start.

A new thought made her sit up abruptly. *Good Lord!* Her hands had been tied under the cape. Her captors would have had to open the cape to get to her hands. Which meant that they had seen the indecent scrap of red silk she was wearing! And what must they have thought of that? she wondered with dismay.

She peered around the dark interior of the carriage. Maybe they hadn't thought anything at all. Maybe it was dark enough here that they had not really seen what she was wearing. She had just started to nurture that hope when she realized that even if they had seen very little while binding her in the carriage, most likely they would get an eyeful when they arrived wherever they were going. With her luck, it would be bright as daylight when they decided to untie her, which would provide a lovely view of everything.

Damn Maisey, she thought irritably. If the girl hadn't insisted on the switch . . . *And damn Frances, too, for good measure*, she added, feeling peevish. *Heck*, she decided while she was at it, *damn Gerald as well!*

Groaning inwardly, Maggie let her head drop back again. This situation just got better and better. She really had to escape. Giving up relaxing on the cushioned seat, she began to struggle with her bindings. They were extremely well tied and very tight. They resisted being undone no matter how she tried.

All Maggie managed to do with her struggles was to tire herself out and rub her wrists raw. She gave up long before the first creeping fingers of dawn spread across the sky.

The carriage rolled to a stop in front of a manor house. Sitting up, Maggie winced at the pain the action sent through her now sensitive wrists and peered out the window, frowning at the immense structure. It was large—huge—obviously the home of a wealthy man, but the stone building looked awkward. It crouched rather than rose into the sky, and it cast dark shadows on the surrounding estate.

Frowning at the sight, Maggie tensed as the carriage rocked; someone was alighting from the driver's bench. She wasn't terribly surprised when the door opened and revealed the caped and hatted man who had been in the carriage with her when she had first awoken—not that she could see much more of him now than she had while he was in the dark carriage. While the sky was beginning to lighten, the coach now stood in the shadow of the mansion. She did, however, recognize the man's voice as he murmured an apology and leaned in toward her.

She understood the reason behind the polite apology as he quickly scooped her off the cushioned seat and out of the carriage. In the next moment she found herself hoisted like a sack of potatoes, the sudden impact of his shoulder in her stomach knocking the wind out of Maggie and effectively eliminating any possibility of her

shrieking for help. Not that there appeared to be anyone about to offer that help, she saw with dismay. Turning her head to glance frantically one way, then the
other, Maggie found there was no one in view but for
the man presently carting her toward the estate's front
door. Well, there was the driver of the coach, too, but
one glimpse of the man's amused expression suggested
that he would be of no assistance.

Deciding she had best save her strength, Maggie remained still in her undignified position, silently promising herself she would throttle her captor at the first
opportunity for this humiliating ride. Then her attention was taken up by the interior of the house they entered. A marble floor flashed by beneath her head, the
legs of a narrow table, too, then steps.

Maggie held her breath and remained as still as she
could; if the last thing she wanted was to throw off her
captor's balance as he ascended these stairs. She
breathed a small sigh of relief once the steps were replaced by the flat floor of a wide hallway; then she was
carted through a door and into and across a darkened
room. The Kidnapper's stride slowed, his hands shifted,
and he bent forward, dropping Maggie indelicately on
a soft surface in the still-dark room before turning and
exiting.

It took her a moment to realize that the soft surface
was a bed. Once she did, though, Maggie quickly tried
to scramble off of it—forgetting that her ankles were
bound together. She ended up crashing to her knees on
the floor just as light flooded in around her. Lifting her
head, she watched warily as her captor reentered with a
taper from the hallway, which he used to set a fire going
in the room's hearth. Then he carried the taper to the

table on the opposite side of the bed from her, the one nearest the door. He set it down carefully, then turned to eye her where she knelt huddled against the bed.

She returned his inspection, but was quite startled by the look of him. Her kidnapper was tall, with long, muscular legs and broader-than-average shoulders. His hair was dark and feathered, with gray at the temples, giving him a distinguished air. His face was handsome and strong, yet looked slightly hard, as if he didn't smile much.

The man gazed at her silently for a moment, taking in her wary state, then rubbed one hand wearily over the back of his neck and glanced fretfully around. "I am James Huttledon," he announced abruptly. When Maggie stared back blankly, he added, "I was a friend of your brother's. We fought side by side through most of the war."

Maggie felt surprise at this news, and some of her wariness dissipated as she made the connection in her head. Gerald had written to her often, long letters detailing his comrades, the battles they fought, the camaraderie they shared. There had been one man he had mentioned a great deal, and from his letters Maggie knew Gerald had respected and looked up to him. He had called the paragon James once or twice, but had most often referred to him as—"Ramsey," she said a bit breathlessly.

"Yes. I am Lord Ramsey. Your brother died saving my life, and his last request to me was that I see after you."

Maggie was silent for a moment. She had known Gerald died bravely—his commanding officer had written the details of his leaping in front of a musket ball to save a comrade. However, she had never known whom he had died to save; the name had been left out. Now she stared at the man who had kidnapped her, the man her brother had saved, and felt only bitter disappointment. Gerald had died in this man's place?

She couldn't help her suddenly tight expression or the tone of her voice as she snapped, "I see. Well, forgive me for pointing out something you may not wish to hear, my lord, but I doubt very much if smothering, tying up, or kidnapping me is what Gerald had in mind."

Lord Ramsey grimaced, but after a moment said sternly, "It was not what I expected to be doing when I agreed. However, I doubt your brother expected you to get up to the things you have done."

Maggie stiffened at his tone, indignant. "And just what is *that* supposed to mean?"

His gaze slid downward, drawing her attention to the fact that by half rising, she had revealed a good portion of the flimsy red attire she had on beneath her cape, as well as all the things it did not hide. Flushing bright pink at the view she was presenting, Maggie again hunched forward against the bed. Lord Ramsey's gaze immediately returned to her face. Feeling the mask she wore cold against her hot blush, Maggie felt an instant need to explain. Clearing her throat, she said, "This is just a disguise. I could hardly move about in there without one, could I?"

"Dear God, no!" the man agreed with sharp horror. Becoming stern again, he added, "You should not have been there at all. A lady of your standing has no business being in such a place, or working at such a . . ." When he paused, obviously in search of a suitable description, Maggie interrupted.

"Yes, well . . . I do have to earn a living, my lord. Someone must pay for the upkeep of that mausoleum my brother left me, keep the servants paid and fed." She pointed it out staunchly, but that only seemed to make the man's lips tighten with further displeasure.

Turning away, Lord Ramsey moved toward the door. "I am sure you did not rest much in the carriage. As for myself, I have not slept at all. We shall discuss alternate sources of income after we have both rested and refreshed ourselves."

"Just a moment!" Maggie cried in alarm. Her kidnapper stopped and looked back at her wearily, one brow arched in question. "My hands." She held them above the bed as if to show him the bindings. He hesitated, his eyes shifting warily to her face; then he shrugged and started back toward her.

"I suppose it will not hurt to untie you. There is nowhere for you to run, anyway. My servants are quite loyal to me." Moving around the side of the bed, Lord Ramsey dropped onto his haunches beside her and waited for her to turn so that he could reach her hands. When she hesitated, remaining positioned the way she was, the bed hiding her sheer gown, a crooked smile quirked his lips. "Suddenly shy? Is that not a bit like stirring the pot after the stew is burnt?"

Maggie felt her face flush but held her pose. He may well have seen all while she was unconscious in the carriage, but she was not offering any exhibitions now. Appearing to realize that, Lord Ramsey shifted to kneel closer to her and reached for her hands. Biting her lip,

Maggie tried to ignore the way his shoulder and hip rubbed against hers as he worked on her bonds, and the musky scent of him as it wafted up to her nose. He smelled of fine brandy and expensive cigars—a scent she had always found pleasantly drifting around her father and brother when they had just returned from the clubs. She idly wondered if that had been where he was before kidnapping her.

"There we are," he said. "Now your ankles." He turned slightly, shifting back a bit so that she could turn and slide her legs out for him, but Maggie remained as she was, unwilling to risk giving him an indecent view.

"I-I can manage those, I think," she murmured huskily, avoiding his gaze. She sensed his hesitation, but after a moment he stood and moved away.

"Ring the bell by the bed when you wake, and a maid shall bring you something more comfortable to wear." The bedroom door closed behind him on Lord Ramsey's last word, and Maggie slowly relaxed, realizing only then how tense she had been. His close proximity had caused her to tighten up like a snail retreating into its shell.

Shaking her head at her behavior, she shifted her position and reached for her ankles, untying them much slower than he had done. But then, her hands were somewhat numb from their confinement, and they gave her some trouble with the task.

Sighing in relief as the rope finally fell away, Maggie rose carefully and perched on the edge of the bed, then took stock of her prison. While the exterior of this estate had appeared stark and imposing, there was nothing of that inside. This bedroom was a cheerful light blue, its furnishings and coverings all nearly new, and expensive. Hardly reflective of its owner at all.

Grimacing to herself at the thought, Maggie glanced toward the door, briefly considering trying to leave, but just as quickly changed her mind. She could already hear the house stirring. There would be servants everywhere in no time. Besides, she had no way to return to town, or really even any idea which way London was from here. Nay, there was little sense in rushing off into the wilds of the country, especially dressed as she was.

Then, too, it didn't appear as if she were under any real threat here. If anything, it sounded as if Lord Ramsey were seriously trying to live up to his promise to her brother to keep her from harm. And apparently he felt her escapades under the name of G. W. Clark were too risky. Which they were, she had to admit. In fact, the whole situation had grown more and more precarious of late, for her readers were demanding more and more titillating articles. That was the reason she had risked entering the brothel—something she never would have considered ere circumstances had become so desperate, even with the heavy veil she had worn to hide her face.

Where was that veil now? Probably still sitting on the settee in Madame Dubarry's private drawing room. Maggie had taken it off after interviewing the last of Agatha's girls so that she and the madam might relax over tea. Both of them had quite forgotten it in the rush to Maisey's room. Which, in itself, showed the dangers of rushing about without planning. Nay, Maggie was best off sticking it out until she could convince Lord Ramsey to return her to her home, or think of a safe way to escape there on her own.

No doubt Lord Ramsey would offer her some sort of agreement when they met for their discussion later—a position as nanny to his children or some such thing. Yes, he looked the sort to be married with children. He was certainly old enough. Of course, she would have to refuse. Even if she dismissed the ignominy of being known to work for a living, no position as governess could pay as much as the *Daily Express*. No, when Lord Ramsey made the offer, she would be forced to regretfully refuse—then somehow had to convince him to return her to town.

Having settled the matter in her mind, Maggie stood and removed her cape and mask. She would have liked to remove her gown as well; it was terribly itchy. She didn't know if it was the material or a lack of cleanliness on Maisey's part, but the garment was insufferable. Unfortunately she had nothing to change into at the moment, and as indecent as the gown was, it was unthinkable to sleep in the nude.

Making a face, she crawled under the covers and settled herself in the center of the bed, unsurprised as she was overtaken by a yawn. Now that she believed she wasn't in any real danger, exhaustion was beginning to set in. This had been an incredibly eventful night, what with one thing after another. All she really wanted to do was rest.

Stifling yet another yawn, she glanced toward the bedroom door and frowned. It was all well and good that Lord Ramsey claimed a desire to honor her brother's last wishes, but really, she realized, she had no guarantee that such was the case. Actually, she had no guarantee he was even who he claimed. It was rather trusting of her to take the man's word for it like that. Naive and stupid, even.

"Oh, bother!" she muttered. Pushing the covers aside, she crawled out of bed once more.

"Here you are, milord."

James turned from a contemplation of the fire in his library hearth and smiled a vague thank-you at an unusually rumpled Webster. His butler at Ramsey came forward with a tray bearing warmed milk with whiskey—James's own personal remedy for an inability to sleep. It was something James had not thought he would need as he rode here; he had nearly fallen asleep several times on the hard bench during the journey. Crowch, his driver, had actually nudged him a time or two to wake him before he could tumble right off.

But that had been before he had carried Margaret Wentworth to the blue room and dropped her on the bed. That was before he had seen her in the candlelight, on her knees, her golden hair tumbled about her heart-shaped face, her soft green eyes glinting out from behind that damned red mask that lent such a seductive air of mystery to her and seemed to emphasize how sweet and soft were her lips. All that had been enough to give a man ideas. It had put images in his head: images of Margaret kneeling at his feet, her cape open to reveal all that blasted gown she wore revealed . . . her hands untied, reaching for the waist of his trousers, her glossy lips twisting as she pulled those trousers slowly down and . . .

Dear God! What was the matter with him? James gave his head a shake, relieved when the erotic imaginings dissolved. He could hardly believe he had been standing there fantasizing such things about a woman he was supposed to be helping. Hell, he could hardly believe he had been fantasizing at all. He just wasn't the sort to waste time on carnal pursuits. He prided himself on being a more intellectual sort. Oh, he had kept a mistress or two through the years, but it had always been more as a physical outlet—a sort of exercise, if you will—rather than from any real passion. In fact, James had always regarded the task as not dissimilar to boxing: Good for keeping the heart fit and the body in shape and a skill every man should have. And as with boxing, he had always considered the movements rather mechanical. In boxing it was jab, feint, uppercut as opposed to kiss, strip, fondle, and so on. Both were a step-by-step process leading to the final round and the ringing of the bell . . . so to speak.

Gerald and Robert had once claimed he was a bloodless sod when he'd revealed that philosophy. They had discussed many things while seated around the fire at night, and the subject of mistresses had invariably come up. Neither of his friends had understood, but James simply was not hampered by the carnal nature most men seemed led by. Or so he had thought. Yet here he was, lusting after the woman presently installed in a room upstairs, his mental processes as muddled as those of any brainless dog after a bitch in heat.

"Parliament canceled?"

James gave up berating himself as the last two words of Webster's question broke through his thoughts. Frowning, he glanced at his servant. "What was that?"

"I said you have quite taken us by surprise with this visit, milord. I did not expect you until the day after next at the least, after Parliament met. Was the meeting canceled?"

James stared blankly at the man for a moment, his brain slow to digest what he was saying, and slower still to accept that he had been so stupid. "Damn," he breathed at last, hardly able to believe that he had forgotten. He had long been a member of the House of Lords, and had made a concerted effort to attend each meeting. He had missed one or two, of course—illness, emergencies, life itself sometimes intervened—but just now there was a matter of some importance on the table and he really had wanted to be there. How could he have forgotten? Dear Lord, he had made a muff up this time.

Cursing, he set his untouched glass of warm milk and whiskey down with a clink and rose from his seat. "Tell Crowch to harness fresh horses to the carriage. We must head back at once. Then come to my room. I have to change, and I will give you instructions regarding Lady Wentworth while I do. Damn!" he added again.

"Lady Wentworth?" his butler asked in confusion as he followed James out of the library.

"She is in the blue room. A . . . guest. You are to be sure she remains one while I am gone."

Chapter Three

Sighing, Maggie shifted in her seat and again glanced toward the door. It was past the supper hour. She had awoken around noon to find a new gown lying at the foot of the bed in which she had slept so poorly.

Her lack of rest was no fault of the bed's—it had been as comfortable as a mattress of clouds, which was the only reason she had eventually fallen asleep at all. Nay, her inability to sleep had been due purely to her anxiety and nerves about her host's intentions. He claimed to be Lord Ramsey, and that his intentions were to aid her, but . . . Well, how could she be sure he was who he claimed? Or if his intentions were pure? After all, he *had* kidnapped her.

She plucked fretfully at the soft skirt of the light blue gown she wore and grimaced. Despite Lord Ramsey's telling her to ring the bell when she awoke so that appropriate clothing could be brought to her, Maggie had

not had to do so. She had risen to find this gown across
the foot of the bed. Someone must have slipped in while
she slept. But who? Had it been the man calling himself
her brother's friend or one of his servants?

One of his servants, she decided. Delivering gowns
didn't seem a likely task for a lord. Besides, the idea of
Ramsey slipping into the room while she slept was completely unnerving.

Maggie had checked the door this morning before
she'd tried to sleep, only to find that there was no way
to lock it. She had made a halfhearted attempt to barricade the portal with the chair she now sat in—the only
one in the room—but its back was too short to be
jammed under the doorknob. It was also too light to be
any sort of bar to the door's opening. Every piece of
furniture in the room had proven to be similarly too
small or too large and heavy to be used in such a manner. Maggie had been forced to resign herself to the
fact that there was no way to prevent anyone from entering. Which was why she'd had such trouble sleeping,
despite her exhaustion. Her unconsciousness during the
journey here had not, apparently, been restful. She was
as weary when she awoke at noon as if she had never
slept, and she'd spent the better part of this afternoon
nodding in this chair, waiting to be retrieved.

It was evening and she was still waiting. Was Lord
Ramsey never going to come? She shook her head and
almost managed a smile. First she had been trying to
find a way to barricade the door against his entry, and
now she was impatient for the rascal to come around.
Nonsensical, she supposed, but the waiting in itself was
driving her mad. Besides, she was growing quite hungry.

Nay, she corrected herself, she had *awakened* hungry; she was *growing famished*.

Her stomach rumbled as if in agreement, and Maggie suddenly thrust herself to her feet. Enough was enough! She could bear the waiting no longer. If the rude man had no intention of coming for her, she would go and confront him.

"He's probably a madman," she muttered under her breath as she crossed the room to the door. "Ready for Bedlam."

Such thoughts, she decided as she found herself standing before the bedroom door but hesitating to open it, were definitely not reassuring. She had just managed to shore her sagging courage and reach for the knob when a tap from the other side made her pull back with a squeak of dismay. Heart racing and mouth dry, she stared at the blank surface of the door with apprehension until a second tap came; then she swallowed and called out in a voice so high and squeaky that she hardly recognized it as her own, "Yes?"

Maggie scooted back several steps as the doorknob turned and the door swung inward. Her alarm eased somewhat, however, when a petite young maid stepped in.

"Oh, ye're up." The girl beamed approvingly. "I said to Cook as how I thought ye'd be, but he was sure his work'd been for naught and the meal he'd prepared would go to waste."

When Maggie merely stared at her, concern clouded the girl's eyes and she tilted her head. "Are you feeling all right, m'lady? Lord Ramsey said as how ye were exhausted from the journey 'ere and might sleep the day away, but ye're looking a bit peaked, too. Ye're not coming down with the ague, are ye?"

Maggie managed to relax somewhat, and even felt a smile spread her lips slightly in answer. "Nay. I am fine, thank you."

The girl brightened at once, again beaming at Maggie. "Good. Then I am Annie. I'm to be your maid while ye're with us. Anything ye need, ye just ask me."

"Very well. Thank you, Annie," Maggie said after the girl paused expectantly.

Nodding, the girl smiled wider. "Shall I show you down to supper?"

"I . . . Yes, thank you," Maggie agreed, then straightened her shoulders as she followed the maid out of the room. Annie led her along the hall, then down the stairs to the main floor. Maggie spent most of the trip distracted by her first real tour of the house in which she was imprisoned. It had been dark and gloomy this morning when they had arrived. Aside from that, her undignified position—hanging down her captor's back—had not given her much opportunity to look around. She did so now curiously.

Much to her interest, it seemed villains did not live in villainous abodes. Ramsey's home was lovely. His maid led Maggie down a hallway of soothing grays with furnishings that were expensive and round-edged. The soft color scheme continued down the stairs to the entryway where it became more muted with dark blue. Annie then showed her through another hall of neutral colors and into a large chamber with a long covered table—the dining room.

Lord Ramsey was conspicuous in his absence. Maggie felt her body relax slightly as she realized it, and thus took the time to appreciate the decor. The walls were painted a warm blue that could only encourage dallying over a meal. In the center of the room was a huge dining table covered with a pristine white cloth that barely allowed legs of a dark rich mahogany—matching the wood of the chairs surrounding it—to peek out from beneath. A sideboard of the same dark wood stood along the wall.

Maggie allowed herself to be seated, her gaze slow to move to the table itself. The maid had nearly left the room before Maggie took in the fact that hers was the only setting. "But . . ." she began, and Annie paused, peering back questioningly. Swallowing, Maggie managed a smile as she asked, "Is Lord Ramsey not to join me?"

The maid's eyes widened. "Nay, mum. He had to return to town. He left shortly after arriving and said— Oh!" She patted her skirts as if looking for something, then muttered fretfully, "He left a letter for ye. I was to give it to ye as soon as milady awoke. Now where did I—Oh, yes! Won't be a moment."

Whirling away, the girl fled the room, leaving Maggie to consider her words. Lord Ramsey wasn't here. He had returned to town. What did that mean? Well, she supposed that made it obvious he hadn't brought her here with the intention of ravishing her. *Not that I imagined for a moment that he did*, she assured herself. Though she did find herself feeling a touch deflated. There she had been hiding in her room all this time to avoid confronting a man who hadn't even been here. She sat up in her chair as the ramifications of that fact occurred to her. He wasn't here. Her captor wasn't around. There was no one to keep her here!

The thought brought her lunging excitedly to her feet, but before she could move away from the table, Annie came bustling back into the room with a self-satisfied smile on her face.

"Here it is." She presented a sealed message to Maggie in triumph.

Maggie hesitated, then accepted the note. She sank reluctantly back into her seat. Breaking the seal, she unfolded the missive and read, her consternation growing with every word.

Lady Wentworth—
My apologies, but I have to return to town to attend some business that could not be put off. Please consider yourself my guest for the next little while. Do not bother the servants with requests to aid you in returning to London. You will find no quarter there. It would do you well to take this time to reconsider your previous choice of career. You shall need a new one, and we shall be discussing possible alternatives upon my return.
—Lord Ramsey

"Arrogant ass."

"What?"

The maid's gasp drew Maggie's attention to the fact that she had just muttered the irrepressible thought aloud. Her mouth tightening, she forced a smile. "Just a glass," she lied blithely. "One glass of wine is all I shall have with dinner, I think."

"Oh." The maid stared at her doubtfully, but didn't question her veracity, then she nodded and slipped from the room with a murmur that she would inform Cook that her ladyship was ready.

Maggie folded the letter again with agitation, the words *arrogant ass* running through her mind again. What did Lord Ramsey take her for? An idiot? Did he expect her to simply sit here sweetly awaiting his pleasure? He must be mad! He had said that the servants would not aid her, but would they actually stop her leaving? Well, it might be too far to walk to town, but there had to be a village or something nearer than that, somewhere where she could rent a carriage or . . .

Of course, she didn't have any money to rent a carriage, she realized with a frown. In fact, all she had was the gown on her back—and that wasn't even her own. She scowled, then sat up a little stiffer to assure herself there was yet something she could do. She had two strong legs, a fine mind, and determination. Those together should be enough to see her well away from this place.

With that thought Maggie stood, then paused to glance toward the windows that lined the western wall of the room. They gave a lovely view of the setting sun. It would be dark soon. Which gave her pause. Did she really wish to traipse through the countryside in the dark?

Her stomach growled, adding its own protest, and she decided she really should eat before she considered leaving. She would need her strength if she planned to walk in search of a town or neighboring estate where she might find help—if that was going to be her plan. She hadn't really considered the matter yet. Perhaps it behooved her to actually determine a specific plan of escape. Perhaps she should learn how near or far away help actually was. Perhaps she should—

Her thoughts were interrupted by the arrival of dinner. It came served on a parade of trays borne by solemn-faced servants. One might have thought they bore the queen's jewels on those trays instead of suckling pig, roast duck, or the various other dishes she saw. Letting her plans to escape fade away, Maggie sat silently and—she hoped—stoically as each servant approached her in turn to serve her a portion from his tray. Rather than set the platters on the table and leave her to her meal, as her own servants would have done, each man lined himself against the wall, gloved hands clasped loosely before him, eyes staring straight ahead and expression blank.

Maggie peered at the servers uncomfortably for a moment, then decided they weren't going anywhere; she had best get to it if she wished to eat. Picking up one of her forks, she set to work on the food. It was an extremely odd meal. Despite the fact that the men were all staring blankly at the opposite wall of the room, she felt as if they were staring at her. And they must have been watching her out of the corner of their eyes, for, the moment she finished her wine, the fellow who had carried it in and poured her first glass stepped silently and efficiently forward to refill it. When she finished off the portion of duck she had been served, another servant, he who had carried that in, promptly stepped up to retrieve the tray and offer her more. Maggie found the whole process most discomforting and ended up rushing, waving away offers of seconds in her eagerness to escape the staff's stifling presence.

It was a great relief when she finished the last scrap of food on her plate. Setting the dish aside she stood, abruptly waving off the servant who jumped forward to offer her one of the lovely-looking desserts that were his charge. Managing a pained smile to soften her dismissal, she moved swiftly around the table and fled. She was actually relieved to find Annie awaiting her in the hall. When the maid asked if she would prefer a drink in the salon, a visit to the library, or a return to her bedroom, Maggie opted for the last. It was time to plan her escape.

"Damn." Maggie tugged at her skirt irritably, trying to pull it free of the log on which it had caught. This was only about the hundredth time that it had happened. The damn forest seemed inordinately full of fallen branches and the like, all catching at her gown and slowing her progress. It was as if the very woods themselves were trying to hinder her flight.

If one could really call it flight, she thought impatiently. This had started out as a grand escape, but it had foundered. Now she was merely lost in the woods. She managed to tug her gown free of its latest entanglement, then hesitated before dropping to sit wearily on the log that had previously been holding her back.

This was not going well at all. Oh, she had thought she was so clever with her plan. She had resolved to set out on the second day of her presence at Ramsey, directly after breakfast, but that had been before she realized that Annie was to be her "constant companion"— a much nicer description than the jailer that the girl really was. The wench hadn't left Maggie's side from the moment she arrived in her room the second morning to show her to breakfast.

Maggie had awoken that morning to find the blue gown gone and a yellow one in its place. Annie's work, no doubt, she had decided. Donning the gown, she'd found that it, like the first, was nearly a perfect fit. Nearly. Both gowns obviously belonged to someone who had a somewhat more generous bosom.

Maggie had no interest in deducing who the owner was. Probably a mistress of Lord Ramsey's, but Maggie didn't give two figs about that. Her mind had been solely occupied with her intention to escape.

She had followed Annie dutifully down to the dining room to eat, relieved to find that while supper had been solemn and attended by many servants, breakfast was a more relaxed affair. A selection of sausages, pastries, and such had been set out on the sideboard for her to serve herself. Maggie had taken that opportunity to store up on sustenance, eating a good deal, then slipping some serviette-wrapped goodies into her pocket for later, for her bid for freedom.

Once she was finished, she had exited the dining room to find Annie awaiting her. It was then she had realized that the woman would not be leaving her until she retired. It had been an unexpected crimp in her plan.

But Maggie had refused to give up easily. Pushing her irritation at this turn of events aside, she'd engaged the girl in conversation, trying to deduce the direction and whereabouts of the nearest village or neighboring estates, but Annie, while polite, had not been of much assistance.

"Oh, aye," the girl had assured her. "We have neighbors. Everyone has neighbors." But when asked how far away they might be, the girl had taken on a cagey look and shrugged. "I couldn't really say, m'lady. Not being nobility, I've never had much cause to visit them." She had been of equal use when it came to the direction and distance to the nearest village.

Given up on questioning the girl, Maggie had pretended to read a book, occasionally remembering to turn the pages as she pondered how to slip away. She had wasted the entire day that way and found herself subjected to another formal meal presided over by a bevy of servants that night, at last retreating to her room to consider and reject several other possibilities on how to escape.

In the end, it wasn't her own cleverness at all that had allowed her to flee. It was circumstance. Today had dawned gray and gloomy. Maggie had donned the rose-colored gown that had been silently set out overnight, followed Annie unhappily to the dining room to break her fast, then had opted for the library to glare blankly at another book and fret. Then, just before the noon meal, it had begun to rain—one of those slow yet steady, halfhearted drizzles that tended to last forever and cause a lassitude in everyone. Annie had yawned, and then Maggie had had her idea. She'd waited until after the noon meal, then had returned to the library, feigning a yawn or two to complement the real ones that were slipping from the maid. Then, as the girl had begun to nod in her seat, Maggie had closed her book with a snap that had startled the maid back to wakefulness.

"What a horrid and gloomy day," she had commented wearily, then added a yawn for good measure. "I think I should like a nap."

Much to her relief, rather than looking suspicious, the maid had appeared relieved at the announcement. Annie had escorted Maggie to her room without question, nodding when asked to wake her in time for dinner. After waiting what she considered a suitable amount of time for the servant to vacate the hall, Maggie had tiptoed over, grasped the doorknob, and slowly eased the door open enough to peer out. What she saw made her freeze at once. Annie had collected a chair from somewhere, positioned it to the side of her door, and settled in, looking as if nothing short of the Second Coming would move her.

Which verified her belief that the girl was a guard, Maggie supposed vexedly as she eased the door cautiously closed again and slowly turned the knob back before releasing it. Moving despondently away from the door, she had them peered about the room, stymied for a way to get rid of the girl. Something short of murder would be best.

Maggie considered sending the maid to fetch a beverage, or something to read or eat. But those options would have seen the girl return to find her missing, and Maggie wanted more time to get away before her absence was discovered. In her frustration, she started mumbling some not very nice words learned from her brother, before her gaze at last landed on the doors to the balcony.

Filled with hope, Maggie promptly hurried across the room and shoved outside. The balcony was on the second floor, of course, which was a problem in itself, but not one that was insurmountable. Maggie had been a rather adoring younger sister and had trailed her brother everywhere until he'd gone away to school. She had run with him, played games more fitting for boys, and had even climbed trees to keep up with Gerald. Which, she realized now, would come in quite handy.

There was a lovely tree growing right off this balcony, one large, sturdy-looking branch even reaching accommodatingly over the railing. This will *be a breeze*, she'd thought with amusement.

Of course, she hadn't considered the fact that it had been many years since she'd climbed trees with Gerald. Nor had she considered the problem of her great, hampering skirts, or the rain that made everything slippery. She had barely managed to get out onto the branch and start her descent before she'd lost her footing and tumbled the rest of the way. She'd landed with an "oomph" in the bushes below. They softened her landing somewhat, but not completely. The fall had been enough to knock the air from her lungs, and she had lain there in the drizzle for several moments, aware of nothing but her body's desperate need for oxygen.

Once she'd regained her breath, Maggie had eased to her feet and peered about, unsure whether to be relieved or unhappy that no one was around to note her bravery or her near calamity. Pushing such foolishness aside, she had moved quickly to the cover of the surrounding woods and slipped into them.

Making her way through the woods along the laneway had seemed the safest bet. She hadn't wished to take the lane itself and risk being spotted, but she also had wanted to avoid finding herself lost in the woods—keeping the lane in sight seemed the only option. Maggie had thought that as long as she kept the lane in sight, she would manage well enough.

"Ha!" she muttered now. Her plan had started out well enough, but then she had come across a river. There was a bridge over it on the lane that she had not realized they'd traversed. Worse, the bridge was still in plain view of the house, and her fear of being spotted had forced her to make her way deeper into the woods. Moving along the river in search of a place to cross, a shallow spot perhaps, she had not been concerned with getting wet. The constant drizzling rain and her fall into the damp bushes had already soaked her, so she had wandered along, moving farther and farther away from the lane, positive that soon she would find a safe spot to cross. Just a little farther. Just around this bend. Just around that curve.

A fallen oak had appeared across her path, reaching just to the river's edge, but not crossing it. She had been forced to make her way around, fighting with branches and brambles and moving deeper into the forest. Then she had pushed through a screen of underbrush . . . to find herself tumbling down an incline the foliage had hidden!

At the bottom, Maggie found herself not only wet, but mud-covered. She wasn't the sort to give up, though. *Stubborn* and *prideful* had been a couple of unattractive descriptions used for her in the past, and she admitted the designations were still true today. Determined to climb back up and continue on her way, she had found that the incline was impossible to scale. It was steep and slippery with mud from the rain, and her several attempts had only ended in lost footings and several behind-bruising falls. At last, she'd turned her determination to searching for an easier spot to climb. She had traveled an increasing distance from the river and the fallen tree, deeper into wilds, in search of that spot, following the curved and wending incline.

Maggie wasn't sure how far she'd journeyed before she discovered a place where the roots of a tree offered enough purchase to pull up out of the small ravine in which she found herself. She had barely reached the top when the snapping of a branch had alerted her to the presence of a nearby animal. Normally the stalwart, non-nervous type, Maggie had not been too alarmed at first, but slowly she became aware of the creepy silence of the rest of the woods. The hair prickled at the back of her neck as she stood listening to the sounds of something making its way through the underbrush from the way she had come. Finding her heart lodging itself in her throat, Maggie felt her body grow numb with fear. As she realized the sounds were drawing nearer, she broke, turning on her heel and making a mad dash in the other direction—running willy-nilly until her fear had eased enough to realize the mistake she'd made. The stupidity of running blindly in the wrong direction had been a hard enough admission, but the fact that she no longer knew the *right* direction was even more dismaying.

Maggie was now lost, completely and thoroughly. She was also soaking wet, muddy, cold, and miserable. Such were the results of her grand plan of escape.

Heaving out an irritated breath she peered at the surrounding woods, searching for something that might show her back the way she had come. Unfortunately, nothing looked familiar. She had not thought to note landmarks in her mad dash.

Her gaze rose to the trees surrounding her, and she briefly considered climbing one. Perhaps at its leafy summit she might glimpse the towers of Ramsey manor and, in that way, get her bearings. But the accident escaping her balcony was enough to change her mind; she was in no shape to climb trees anymore, was more likely to break her neck than anything.

She took a moment to wallow in self-pity, then forced herself to straighten her shoulders, stand, and get on with her escape. She had no intention of just sitting still until death by starvation or exposure overtook her. She wasn't the sort for such foolishness. Besides, wasn't she perfectly capable of taking care of herself? Else she would have sold off her brother's home and moved to the country, as any other woman would have done in her circumstances. Instead, she had taken up her brother's job and set about trying to support his home and servants. She could overcome any difficulty. She would simply head north until she came across something. But . . . which way was north?

Maggie pondered briefly, fairly sure she had heard that moss grew on the north side of trees . . . or was it the south? West? *Oh, dear.* Sighing, she decided she needed another manner of determining directions. Didn't the sun rise in the east and set in the west? Or was it the other way around? Oh, this was *damnably* irritating. She really should have paid more attention to such things.

At last, she simply decided that she would move toward the sun; in that way she could at least avoid walking in circles. The plan might have been a good one, if the combination of tree branches and gray clouds overhead had not obscured any possibility of finding the bloody sun.

It was beginning to appear that she was well and truly lost. Of course, it was all Lord Ramsey's fault. *The ass.* Had he not decided to stick his nose in her business and kidnap her . . . well, she wouldn't be *here!*

Satisfied that she had laid the blame firmly where it belonged, she wasted a moment attempting to shake some of the mud off her skirts, then straightened her shoulders and marched onward. If she simply kept moving, she would come across something. Eventually.

Much to Maggie's amazement, she hadn't been walking very long when the sound of rushing water caught her ear. Pausing, she listened to see which direction it came from, then moved toward it. Relief poured through her as she found herself stepping out onto the bank of the river. She had found it! Even better, she had come upon the waterway at a spot where it twisted and narrowed, one edge jutting out farther than normal and flat rocks making something of a path across. Some of her optimism returning, Maggie started over the stones, moving cautiously from rock to rock, until at last she leaped to the opposite side.

Buoyed by her success, she paused to debate her next move. Should she follow the river back to the land, back to where the Ramsey estate was in sight, then continue from there? Or should she simply move steadily away from the river and hope she came across the main road that led to Ramsey's drive?

The cautious side of her suggested that returning along the river was the smartest move, but that seemed to entail the loss of a great deal of time, and it was already beginning to grow darker. She had already wasted a good stretch.

The daring side of Maggie, that which had encouraged her to take such risks as donning the persona of G. W. Clark and visiting brothels or other unsavory spots in search of stories, was urging her to simply continue forward, away from the river.

She would likely come to the main road just as swiftly, but ages away from the Ramsey drive.

Maggie, as usual, found herself trusting the less cautious part of her personality. She pushed determinedly onward. It was only a few moments later that she found herself stumbling out of the trees. She came out on the side of a laneway, this one wider and—judging by its rutted state—better traveled than the Ramsey drive. Maggie fought free of the bushes, pleasure and relief just starting to wash over her when a carriage trundled past.

Her first instinct was to flee for cover, lest it be Lord Ramsey. Maggie followed that instinct and whirled about to dart back into the underbrush. She knew, even as she did so, that the action came too late; she caught a glimpse of a man's face through the carriage window as she spun away. Maggie didn't recognize the man. She *was* sure it wasn't Lord Ramsey. She was also sure that she had been spotted. Still, her survival instinct sent her crashing into the woods to hide herself behind a handy tree.

Pausing with her back against the old oak's rough bark, she pressed a hand to her racing heart and tried to listen over the sound of her own heavy breathing. Her alarm increased as she heard the man call out, the carriage slow to a stop, and then the telltale sound of the coach door opening and closing.

Damn! The man was coming to investigate. Maggie's mind was suddenly crowded with possibilities. He could simply be a traveler on the road, curious about a woman dashing wildly about the woods. But then, he could also be Lord Ramsey's cohort in crime. Or, perhaps he was simply getting out to stretch his legs.

Maggie snorted aloud at the last possibility and glanced wildly around, seeking escape. She had not managed to escape her prison only to be caught now! She considered her options. Running was one, but she had already experienced the difficulties of racing about the muddy woods with tree branches and bushes snagging at her skirts. That was out. Which left hiding. Dropping to her knees, she scuttled into a bush next to the tree.

Chapter Four

"Yoo-hoo! Hello? Are you in some distress?"

Maggie scowled and pushed a bothersome branch away from her face as she listened to the man's calls from her cramped hiding space. Wonderful! A knight errant thinking to aid a damsel in distress. If only I could be sure that was all he is, she thought with a sigh, then wrinkled her nose. An unpleasant smell was wafting up to her. She wondered briefly at its source, but was then distracted by the sound of snapping branches and the crunch of dead leaves as her "rescuer" moved nearer.

"Yoo-hoo! Can I be of some assistance?"

The racket the man was making as he pushed his way through the bushes drew alongside her, then continued past. Maggie sagged in relief and released the breath she had been holding. It was when she inhaled again that she recalled the odor she'd noticed earlier. It appeared to be growing stronger. Dear God, what is it? she wondered and raised a hand to wave the smell away. The stink increased tenfold, and it was then that she noticed the muck on her hand. She stared at it, slowly coming to a realization.

Horror rushing over her, she set her one hand back to hold her weight as she lifted the other. It, too, bore the stuff. Dear God, she had crawled right into, or through, a pile of animal droppings! Shudders rolled through her, and she suffered a sort of squirmy fit, her body twitching and jerking with disgust as she began frantically wiping first one hand, then the other, on the ground and surrounding branches and leaves in an effort to remove the squishy substance.

"Er . . . excuse me. Hello?" The words, spoken directly behind her, made Maggie pause and turn her head. She peered back through the foliage, only then realizing that the bush wasn't wide enough to hide her. It ended at her hips. Her derriere—covered by the yellow gown she wore—was sticking out. No doubt it had been thrashing around like some ridiculously huge canary just now. Which must have been a sight for this man to come upon, Maggie thought wearily. This simply wasn't her day.

"Are you in some distress?"

Maggie almost laughed at his tentative question. Reassuring herself that the reaction wasn't one of hysteria but amusement, and that surely it was a good sign that her sense of humor was still intact, she answered politely. "Not at all, but thank you for asking."

"I see. Might I ask what are you doing in there, then?"

This had to be the most humiliating conversation

she'd ever had, Maggie decided as she wracked her brain for an explanation that would both satisfy as well as get rid of the man. It was becoming unbearable to have him talk to her behind like this, trapped in the bush as she was.

"Only you, Maggie!" Her brother's amused voice echoed in her memory, and she silently cursed. She did not deliberately get herself into these messes. They just sort of . . . happened.

"I am bird-watching, and I fear your presence is scaring the birds away," she blurted.

"Er . . . might you not have more success with your bird-watching by looking *up?*" he asked.

Maggie promptly wished she could kick herself. It was obvious she did not think well under pressure. "Yes, of course. And I *was.* However, I . . ." She searched her mind for an acceptable excuse for her position, and was quite pleased when she came up with: "Dropped something. My . . . er . . . a hairpin!" she announced with triumph. "Ah, there it is. Thank you. Everything is fine now. You may go." She waited hopefully but was disappointed by the silence that followed. He wasn't leaving.

"I should be happy to assist you back to your feet now that you have found your hairpin."

Maggie sighed and considered her options. She didn't think he believed a word she'd said, and he obviously wasn't going to simply go away. Crawling backward out of the bush and facing the man was her only option. The very idea made her cringe, but taking a deep breath, she began to scramble out . . . only to stop as her hair caught on a branch.

"Is there something wrong?" came the man's concerned voice when she paused and gave an exclamation of pain. "Are you caught?"

"Yes, I fear I am," she answered, leaning on one hand and using the other to try to untangle herself.

"Perhaps I can help." She heard the words, then felt him grasp her hips. Maggie barely managed a startled gasp before he seemed to realize the impropriety of such a choice, and clasped her by the ankles instead. Which was not a better option, in her opinion. Her feet were pulled out from beneath her as he attempted to drag her out of the bush. She screeched in pain as her hair pulled free of the branch—or perhaps was yanked out of her head, she wasn't sure which. Then she was traveling backward, her skirt—apparently also caught on a branch—staying in place so that she came out of the foliage flat on her belly with her gown forming a sort of tent over her head.

"Oh, dear!" Her feet were dropped and the man rushed to her side, pulling the material free for her as she struggled to get off her stomach. Dear God, it would be just her luck to have been dragged through the animal droppings! Maggie scrambled to her feet.

Once upright, she raised her hand, intending to push her now wild hair out of her face. The sight made her pause.

"Oh! You've mud on your hands." Retrieving a handkerchief, her "rescuer" began to clean her fingers.

Maggie's mouth opened, then closed. What could she say? It was too late to stop his ruining the bit of cloth, so she remained silent as he tidied her hands. Her gaze moved over him. She had only caught a glimpse of him earlier, so really wasn't prepared for his attractiveness. Tall and lean with sandy-colored hair and a charming—

if, at the moment, somewhat alarmed—smile. She would place him at the same age Gerald would have been were he still alive. Which was, perhaps, two or three years younger than the man who had kidnapped her.

"I fear that is the best I can do," he announced apologetically, releasing her streaked hands and tucking the cloth back into his pocket. "Is there something wrong?"

Tearing her alarmed gaze from his pocket, she tried not to feel guilty about his waistcoat now needing cleaning. She was rather amazed that the man wasn't aware of what he had just wiped off of her, but then she couldn't smell it now so supposed he couldn't either. Likely, she had scraped the worst off so that what remained merely looked like mud.

Realizing that he was awaiting an answer to his question, Maggie shook her head. A clump of snarled hair immediately dropped into her eyes and reminded her of her ruined state. Having little choice, she pushed the tangled mess back from her face, then straightened with all the dignity she could muster.

"Thank you," she offered, then turned on her heel and pushed back through the bushes and out of the trees.

"Just a moment," he called, hurrying after her as she started up the road.

Maggie had taken several steps in her chosen direction before she realized that she should have gone the other way. She was now heading in the same direction that the carriage was traveling. This man was likely too polite not to offer her a ride.

"Might I assist you to where you are going? I should

not like to be unchivalrous," he added as if he had some-how read her thoughts.

"I thank you for the offer, kind sir. However, that is not necessary." Maggie didn't slow her step, but she did roll her eyes. Why were people so predictable? He would have done her a great favor had he been a rude boor and simply returned to his carriage and his journey. It would have been an even greater favor had he not stopped at all, she thought, glancing down at her hands with disgust. She really needed to find some water to clean up. A glance down showed that she had truly crawled right through the muck. The knees of her skirt were brown.

Her mother—were she alive—would have been horrified. Maggie was horrified. Creeping about brothels, and crawling on her knees through the woods!

She sighed miserably as she considered how low she had allowed herself to fall. I used to be such a proper lady, doing and saying the proper things—she mourned, then admitted—well, not always. She hadn't earned the refrain "Only you, Maggie!" by never setting a *single* step wrong. Still, she'd managed only mild mishaps in the past, and most of them due to clumsiness or inattention. Since Gerald's death, she had taken risks she knew she shouldn't have and—

"You wouldn't be headed for the village, would you?"

"Yes," Maggie answered distractedly, then clucked her tongue in irritation. She was sure she should have kept that to herself. She had no idea who this man was. He could be a bounder, or a—

"Then, I fear you are headed in the wrong direction."

That made her pause. She turned to face him.

"It is back this way," he continued, gesturing in the direction from which he had come.

Maggie peered up the lane, then sighed. She started in this new direction.

He fell into step beside her. "I should probably introduce myself. Lord Mullin, at your service."

She stopped again and faced him sharply. "Robert?" His eyebrows raised at the familiar address and Maggie flushed. "I apologize for the familiarity, my lord, but Gerald usually referred to you as Robert in his letters."

"Gerald?"

"My brother. Gerald Wentworth," she explained with reluctance.

It was his turn to pause. "Maggie?" he finally gasped, then shook his head and corrected himself. "I mean Lady Margaret?" He grinned. "Gerald often spoke of you. He . . ." Lord Mullin paused and frowned up at the sky as it again began to rain. "Come."

Before she quite knew what was happening, he had taken her arm and hustled her to his carriage. Ignoring her protests, he ushered her inside, then went to have a word with his driver. Extremely self-conscious about her less-than-pristine state, Maggie folded the sides of her skirt over the front, tucking just a bit of each side panel between her knees to keep the cloth there. The action hid a good deal of her soiled skirt, but did little to hide the smell.

Groaning inwardly, she offered a nervous smile to Lord Mullin as he entered the carriage and pulled the door closed behind him. Settling on the opposite bench seat, he didn't seem to notice the smell. He was busy grinning. "Gerald's sister. I can hardly fathom it."

Maggie offered him a pained smile. She wasn't surprised he could "hardly fathom it." She wasn't exactly at her best. That thought decided her to make an effort to repair at least some of the damage, and she set to work trying to return some semblance of normalcy to her hair. Unfortunately, it appeared that her lie of having lost a hairpin had become a reality. Several of her hairpins had been lost during her sojourn into the bushes.

"Gerald, James, and I were in the same unit. Lord Ramsey," he added after a moment. "He is my neighbor. In fact, those were his woods you were mucking about in."

Maggie stilled under his speculative gaze. This man and Lord Ramsey were neighbors? He had been on his way home from the village when he'd come across her, and from his reaction, he had not yet conferred with her abductor . . . Which meant her host's claims were likely true. Her kidnapper was indeed James Huttledon, Mullin's neighbor, and the Lord Ramsey her brother had mentioned so frequently. Recalling her brother's adulation of the man in his letters, she also supposed that Ramsey had been telling the truth regarding his reasons for kidnapping her. He probably *had* had the best of intentions.

Not that any of them mattered, Maggie decided grimly. She had escaped those good intentions and intended to stay escaped. Banks and the rest of her staff must be quite upset by now. She had to get home and let them know she was all right. Besides, there was surely nothing Lord Ramsey could do. She had been over and over her situation. Carrying on with her journalistic career was the only acceptable way to make the money she needed.

Of course, it didn't bode well for her escape that she had ended in the carriage of a friend of the man who had kidnapped her. That was rather deucedly bad luck. She was just beginning to ponder what it could mean to her plans when Lord Mullin spoke again.

"What were you doing—"

"You said Gerald spoke of me?" Maggie interrupted to distract him. It worked.

"Spoke of you?" Robert chuckled. "Yes. He spoke of you often. He, James, and I were thick as thieves, and he used to read your letters aloud to us around the fire at night. In fact, between his talking about you and our sharing your letters, I feel as if I already know you. Gerald was very proud of you," he added with a sad smile.

Maggie returned the expression. Her brother had always liked to talk. She had no doubt that he had regaled his friends with tales of their youth, and that he'd related them as vibrantly as he'd penned the articles for the *Express*. Gerald had always had a way with words. She hadn't been at all surprised to learn of his secret occupation; it had suited him.

Her gaze returned to Lord Mullin, and she stiffened. There was a perplexed look on his face, and he was turning his head slowly, sniffing as if seeking the source of some smell.

She flushed with embarrassment.

"I apologize for taking you out of your way," she said, hoping to divert him.

"Oh." He turned a distracted smile her way and shook his head. "Not at all. I am glad to have met you. I always hoped to. In fact, I have kept an eye out at the balls and routs, hoping to come across you."

"I haven't been attending many balls of late," Maggie said quietly.

"Ah, yes, of course. I should have realized." Mullin pulled his sullied kerchief from his pocket and raised it toward his face.

"Oh—" Maggie began, but it was too late. She knew that it had probably been a pleasantly scented kerchief when he'd left home that day, and that he'd likely hoped to use it to filter the stink presently invading his carriage. Instead, he got a noseful of the very scent he was trying to escape.

"Agh!"

She watched in alarm as he began gagging violently and tore the kerchief away. His horrified gaze shot to her hands, then to her innocent expression, then back to her hands. "Your . . . you . . . eh . . ."

"Yes, my lord?" Maggie wasn't surprised when he sank helplessly back in his seat without comment. It simply wasn't polite to tell a lady that her hands were covered with animal excrement. Which was rather silly. If such rules were made to prevent embarrassment, they didn't at all work, Maggie thought; they simply made it so that people suffered their embarrassment in shared silence.

She peered at Lord Mullin's face. At first alarmed at the growing ruddiness of it, she quickly realized that he was turning red because he was holding his breath.

It is a terribly unpleasant stench, she thought and she promptly began to fan herself. "Is it growing warm in here?"

Lord Mullin was not slow-witted. Looking relieved, he sprang up on his seat and quickly set to work opening the carriage window, inhaling deeply of the fresh air that swept in when he succeeded.

Not immune to the stench, Maggie slid along her seat to enjoy the fresh air as well, exchanging a wry look with her host as she did. She knew that was as close as they were going to come to acknowledging any difficulty.

They were both extremely relieved when the village came into sight. By that time the rain had stopped, and she and Lord Mullin were half-hanging out the window in companionable silence. The aroma now permeated the carriage, and seemed to grow stronger and more overpowering with each passing moment.

The situation had been beneficial in at least one respect, Maggie decided. Forced to hang out of the carriage to avoid the stink, with the wind slapping their faces, ready to snatch any words they might say, conversation between she and Lord Mullin had been impossible. She had been saved from the possibility of any awkward questions regarding her tramping about Lord Ramsey's woods.

Unfortunately, now that they were entering the village, they were forced to settle back into their seats.

"Gerald was a good man," Mullin murmured into the silence as they faced each other across the carriage.

"Yes, he was," Maggie agreed. A sadness settled over her. Gerald *had* been a good man. A good brother. A good friend. A good employer to his servants. Why did it always seem that the good were taken from the earth while the rotten sorts were left behind to trouble others? As she wondered that, she stiffened; her gaze had dropped to the bench seat she occupied. Her face flushed with guilt and embarrassment once again, for she saw that Lord Mullin's carriage would not just need an airing. Some of the muck from her skirts had transferred to the seat.

Mullin cleared his throat, drawing Maggie's attention away from her crime. One look at the determined set of the man's shoulders hinted that he was going to ask one of those annoyingly uncomfortable questions like, *"What were you doing in the woods?"* that Maggie was not eager to answer. There was the risk that if Lord Mullin discovered she was escaping his friend, he might well take her back. Which would be most inconvenient.

She briefly considered lying herself silly, claiming that she had been traveling to Clarendon, the seat of the family's title, when her carriage broke down, but there were a couple problems with that lie. The first was that she had no idea where Ramsey manor lay in England, and whether it was in a position to be on her way to Clarendon. The second was that this Robert might insist on gathering her things from her imaginary carriage.

Maggie was saved from prevarication and the risk associated when Lord Mullin's carriage began to slow, distracting both occupants and delaying the man's interrogation. She and he nearly bumped heads trying to peer out the window at the same moment, exchanged a slight smile, then glanced out in turns to see that they had arrived in the village.

"We are here," her host announced unnecessarily, then looked at her in question. "Where did you wish to go?"

"This will do," Maggie announced abruptly. Unwilling to give him the opportunity to ask those questions she could see swimming in his eyes, she pushed the carriage door open then rushed clumsily out.

"Oh, but I cannot just leave you here," Mullin called to her, climbing down from the carriage as well. "Are you staying at Ramsey? Did you—"

"Thank you ever so much for bringing me here, my lord," Maggie interrupted determinedly. "I appreciate your assistance. Have a good day."

Turning on her heel, she then hurried off along the street, not caring at all where she was going as long as it was away from Lord Mullin and his questions. Fortunately, he did not pursue or try to stop her. Still, Maggie stepped into the first shop she came across. She had no idea where to rent a hack, and she would need directions.

"M'Lord?"

James glanced up from the ale he had been contemplating to find Crowch at his side, hat in hand. "Is it fixed?" he asked the driver mildly. They had hit a rock in the road, and it had cracked one of the carriage wheels. Fortunately, the accident had occurred just a mile short of the village, and the wheel had remained intact until they could reach a shop where it could be repaired. James had left the chore to Crowch and settled himself in the pub, somewhat exhausted by his travels between his country estate and London.

"Aye, m'lord."

"Good. Get yourself a drink; then we'll be off again." The fellow's weary smile of relief was enough to remind James that he was not the only one who had made this trip back and forth and back again. He felt a moment's guilt, which moved him to add, "I appreciate your efforts these last few days."

The words sounded as stiff as James felt. They were an apology of sorts, couched in a compliment. He was not used to having to give apologies, but then he rarely worked his servants as hard as this. Crowch had been asked to drive through the night to take Lady Margaret to Ramsey, then, after less than an hour's rest at Ramsey castle, he'd had to turn around and drive James back to town for the meeting of the House of Lords. This morning, after the proceedings were finished, the man had been put upon for a return trip to the country. Last night's sleep was the only rest the man had had in two days. It was no wonder he was looking so weary. And the compliment was deserved, Crowch was a good man.

"We'll be staying in the country for a bit this time," James called as the driver settled with relief at a table for servants in the corner.

Crowch said little, but looked much happier at the news. He accepted the ale a wench set before him and drank thirstily. James waited as he did, idly pondering the arrangements he'd made regarding a Lady Margaret.

Lady. He grimaced slightly. Lady Margaret, Lady X—whichever she called herself, she wasn't deserving of the title. He could hardly believe she was the same woman that Gerald had prattled on about all those nights beside the fire. The Margaret Wentworth Gerald had described was brave, resourceful, smart, and beautiful. But above all, she was a lady. None of which seemed to match what James had learned about Lady X.

James had attended the meeting of the House of Lords that morning, but he had arrived back in London just before dinner last night. He had eaten, then found himself too wound up to sleep. Or perhaps he had been at that state of being overtired where sleep became elusive. Whatever the case, he had gone to his club to relax and await his weariness overtaking him. While there, he had sought out more information regarding the infamous Lady X. He had learned much. The courtesan was always a subject of gossip at the club, but James had paid very little attention ere now. Last night he had listened to the tales of her expertise with combined fascination and horror.

Lady X had arrived in London not long after Gerald's death. At least that seemed to prove it was circumstance that had led Margaret to take up such a disreputable career, James told himself. And yet, he had not been prepared for the degree of skill she was purported to have. Oh, he had heard before that the woman enjoyed her work, but until last night he had thought such words were simply the smitten boasts of her customers. But if half of what her marks claimed was true, she didn't just enjoy her work; she reveled in it like a pig rolling in muck.

From all he had learned, James was left wondering what on earth he was to do with the wench. Aside from the obvious, that was. He toyed briefly with the idea of offering her a position as his mistress. After all, he was between women at the moment; she was attractive and experienced, and might enjoy a break from her present position. Perhaps she would prefer one lover. It would be much less demanding.

The scheme was the briefest of daydreams, however. James would have liked to be able to claim that it was his fond memory of Gerald, and the fact that this was hardly what his friend intended when he'd asked James—on his death bed—to look after his sister, that turned him from the idea. But the truth was, it was his own responses to the woman that had quickly killed the fantasy. Just the thought of her had his body reacting like fire to an influx of oxygen. James was not used to, nor was he comfortable with, such passionate feelings in himself. He had always prided himself on his self-control and just thinking about Margaret shattered that. He did not know what it was about her. Perhaps it was the fact that she looked so sweetly innocent when he knew she was quite the opposite. Whatever the case, he had thought of little else but Maggie since taking her from Madame Dubarry's. And nothing he had heard during his visit to town had weakened his responses.

The girl was positively infamous. Every man in London was lusting after her. The only halfway sensible thing she had done was to wear her mask and insist on anonymity. But the game could not have continued for much longer. Sooner or later the girl's identity would have been revealed. Margaret was just lucky that he had been the first to discover it.

James was congratulating himself on that fact when the front door opened. He froze at the sight of Lord Mullin entering the inn. He'd bumped into his friend after leaving Crowch to see to the carriage repairs, and they had shared a drink together before Robert had left to continue home. The man's return now was wholly unexpected. Robert's troubled expression as he approached the table was concerning, too.

"Robert," James greeted his friend curiously. "To what do I owe your return?"

"You owe it to a certain lady of whose brother we are both acquainted," the man answered roughly. He settled on the bench next to James and said in a hiss, "What the bloody hell is going on?"

"What do you mean?" James asked warily, feeling himself tense. He had a bad feeling about this. "And which lady exactly?"

"Maggie."

"Maggie?"

Mullin made a face at his confusion. "Gerald's sister. Lady Margaret Wentworth."

James's eyes widened. "What of Gerald's sister?" he asked warily, already knowing he would not like the answer.

"What have you done to her?"

"Nothing. What would make you think I had *done* anything to her?" he asked, his mind beginning to work frantically. Had Robert stopped at Ramsey for some unknown reason on his way home? James hadn't considered that anyone might discover Margaret's presence in his home, or assume that . . . Good Lord, if she—

"Are you saying that she was at your estate without your knowledge?"

James winced. "You stopped at Ramsey?"

"Nay."

James was confused. "Then what would make you think—"

"I ran across her on my way home. There was nowhere else from which she might have come except your estate—and not by the normal route."

"What do you mean?" There was no mistaking the alarm he felt now.

"I mean, it was obvious she had left on foot and walked—or crawled, judging by the amount of . . . mud on her—through the woods to the road. So . . . Did you take her as your mistress? Have you had a lover's spat and she is now trying to run away on foot to teach you a lesson?"

"Of course not!" The fact that James had actually, however briefly, considered the idea of taking her as his mistress made his denial even more heated than it normally would have been. He saw the expression his emphatic denial inspired in his friend, and he scowled.

"Trust me, she is as pure now as she was when I met her." *Which isn't very pure at all,* he added to himself as he stood. "Come, Crowch," he called. "We must go collect Lady Margaret ere she stumbles into trouble on the road."

"I did not leave her there," Robert snapped, obviously insulted that James might think he had.

"You didn't?" James paused in his flight to glance back.

"Nay. Of course not. A gentleman would hardly leave a lady in the path of ruffians and ne'er-do-wells, even should it mean ruining the seats of his newly purchased carriage to whisk her to safety." The last was added on a somewhat pained note.

"I shall replace your seats," James said impatiently. "Where did you leave the wench? Is she in your carriage?"

"Wench?" Mullin echoed in dismay.

James gritted his teeth. "Where *is* she?"

Lord Mullin scowled, then said reluctantly, "Last I saw, she was headed for the livery stables. I think she meant to rent a hack." He paused. "Though she didn't appear to have a purse on her, so how she would pay for—"

James had heard enough. Turning on his heel, he burst out of the inn.

"Wait for me!" Lord Mullin cried, and James glanced back to see him nearly knock Crowch over in an effort to follow.

Shaking his head as he ran, James ordered, "Fetch the coach, Crowch, and meet us at the livery."

"Ye can't rent a carriage if ye don't have any coin."

"Yes, but you see, I do have coins—I mean funds," Maggie assured the surly, needle-thin man with whom she had been arguing.

"Well, then, show me the coins and we'll be off," the stableman said with obvious amusement.

Maggie ground her teeth with a frustration she tried not to let show. She reiterated: "I *do* have funds. Just not on me. I can pay you once I am returned to my home. My town house. In *London*." She added the last for good measure, hoping to impress the man, but knew at once that she'd had the opposite effect. His nose wrinkling with distaste, the man let his mean little eyes trail with disdain over her ragged and filthy form, then shook his head.

"Coin up front. 'At's how I do business. No coin, no carriage."

"But—"

"Margaret!"

That sharp call made Maggie turn in alarm to see whose voice it was. Her alarm did not lessen at the sight of Lord Ramsey striding forward, trailed by the younger Lord Mullin. James looked rather put out, she saw unhappily. As if *she* were the one who had done something wrong.

Silently cursing her luck, Maggie drew herself up and prepared to deal with this new problem. She had not walked, crawled, and fought through the rain and mud all day to be dragged back to Ramsey at its end. She would see herself to London or die trying. *Well, perhaps not die*, she allowed with a frown.

"Timmins!" Much to Maggie's irritation, at James Hattledon's brusque address, the stableman suddenly stood upright, a respectful expression covering his face that had been conspicuously absent throughout the duration of her conversation with him.

"M'lord." Mr. Timmins nodded at Lord Ramsey.

"My apologies if Maggie was bothering you," the nobleman said.

"Lady Margaret Wentworth," Maggie snapped, very aware that by calling her Maggie he was insinuating a lower station than she deserved.

"Oh, is it *that* game today?" Ramsey asked patronizingly.

Maggie whirled on him with dismay. Catching the meaningful glances he was throwing at Timmins, she snapped her mouth closed and turned to Lord Mullin. "I *am* Lady Margaret Wentworth. Tell him," she entreated, glaring.

When the younger noble hesitated, his gaze going to James, Maggie could have hit him. Any hesitation was enough to cast doubt, she was sure.

"I *am*," she repeated furiously. Then she added, "And this man has kidnapped me and is holding me against my will at his estate."

The move was risky. Her reputation would now be in ruins if this tale got out, but Maggie didn't see much choice. Besides, it wasn't as if she had any prospects to alienate. Frances had been the only man to show any interest in her since her brother's death, and she wouldn't marry him now if he were the last man on earth.

"Yes, and I have been ravishing you at every turn," Lord Ramsey said good-humoredly.

Maggie gasped. "You have not! He hasn't," she added for Timmins's and Mullin's benefit.

"Well, not recently, but I am sorry that I have neglected you so, my dear. I did have business to attend in town. I promise I shall be more attentive now that I am back."

Maggie was so confused by his words that it took a moment for her to realize that he had taken her arm and was leading her away from the livery. She recognized that fact at about the same moment she realized that his words would be construed as those of a man trying to soothe a neglected lover. She immediately tried to pull away from Lord Ramsey, but the arrival of his carriage right then aided him in preventing her escape; the way he bundled her up and thrust her inside could easily have been misconstrued as assistance rather than the brute force it was.

Unfortunately, while Mullin was close enough to tell the difference, his protest at such treatment was mild to say the least. Mentally Maggie named Robert a traitor as he murmured, "I say, Ramsey. Steady on. No need to manhandle her."

James's only response was to lunge up into the carriage behind Maggie and catch her as she tried to flee out the other door. He pulled her onto his lap, holding her firmly against his chest, trapping her arms with one of his own even as he covered her mouth with his hand when she opened it to scream. She was so busy struggling, she didn't even notice when Lord Mullin climbed into the carriage and took the opposite bench to glare at James.

"You had best explain this, my friend. I cannot allow you to treat a lady thusly. Especially not Wentworth's sister."

"I shall explain as soon as we arrive at Ramsey and she is dealt with," James snapped. He grunted as Maggie landed a healthy kick to his knee and bounced with restrained fury in his lap.

"For now, perhaps, you could just trust me?" he said in a hiss. Then his nose wrinkled and he glanced around with bewilderment. "What the Devil is that stench?"

Maggie paused in her struggles at the question and noted the way Lord Mullin's gaze slid to her.

"Dear God!" Lord Ramsey gasped. Banging on the wall of the carriage, he bellowed, "Home, Crowch, and fast!"

Chapter Five

James had rather hoped that Maggie would wear herself
out and give up her struggles by the time they reached
his estate. Such was not the case. She was still wiggling,
kicking, thrashing, and trying to bite his hand when the
carriage rolled up before his manor and stopped. He
didn't know where she got the energy. For his part,
James was exhausted from trying to hold her still and
prevent being neutered by her flailing legs and grinding
bottom. He was also heartily sick of the stench per-
meating his carriage, as well as the growing anger and
disgust on Lord Mullin's face.

With Maggie still clutched to his chest, James staggered out of the carriage and carted her through the
front door that Mullin hurried to open for him. Pausing
in the entry, he bellowed for his butler.

"Surely you can let her go now, James," Robert said

impatiently, his gaze decidedly sympathetic for the hell-cat.

"I will, as soon as someone explains how she got away."

"You could just ask her," his friend suggested dryly.

James turned to snap something unpleasant at him, but paused, his attention drawn to the top of the stairs by a gasp.

"But she's asleep in her room!" A maid stood, gaping down at them, and cried out, "I have sat outside her door all afternoon."

"My lord?" Webster rushed up toward them, shock on his face. James Huttledon was not the sort to bellow and stamp about.

He glanced from one servant to the other, then released Maggie, giving her a less-than-gentle push that sent her into the startled butler's arms. "See that she is bathed and given fresh clothes."

"I do not want to bathe," Maggie snapped, regaining her balance and pulling away from Webster.

"You enjoy looking like you just crawled out of the stews, do you?" James asked coldly. Her eyes narrowed on him in displeasure.

"What I would *enjoy*," she answered between gritted teeth, "is to go home. And if you will not take me, then I would appreciate Lord Mullin's assistance in the matter." She turned a stunning smile tinged with desperation on the other man. "Please, my lord. As a former friend of my brother's—"

"You can ask him after you bathe," James interrupted. He did not like the way Robert was swelling up in readiness to become the woman's protector. "Surely you

93

have ruined his carriage seats enough for one day? Besides, you will have to wait for his carriage and driver to be fetched. Both are still in the village."

Maggie hesitated, obviously shamed by the reminder of what her befouled state had already done to Lord Mullin's seat. Then her shoulders bowed with resignation. James was grateful to see that the hoyden wasn't completely unreasonable.

"Very well. I shall take a bath," she announced, turning to start up the stairs. Her attempt at dignity was ruined when she suddenly whirled back, transfixing Lord Mullin with her eyes. "Please promise you will still be here when I finish? If not for my sake, then as a favor to my brother?"

"Of course," Robert said quickly, his shoulders drawn up. "I shall be here when you return, and I shall help you in any way I can."

Satisfied with that, she delayed only long enough to toss a half-triumphant, half-furious glare in James's direction, then spun away to take her bath.

James watched her go, then glanced at Webster. The butler promptly straightened, a staunch look coming to his face. "Annie was told not to let Lady Margaret out of her sight until she retired. Also, the dogs were released at night as you requested."

"The dogs released?" Lord Mullin echoed in dismay.

Ignoring him, James rubbed his hands through the back of his hair with frustration. "If Annie was sitting outside her door, Margaret must have climbed off the balcony."

"The balcony?" Robert was goggling at the idea, but James continued to ignore him.

"Have the dogs released after you arrange for her

bath, Webster. And tell Annie not to let her out of her sight for a minute."

"Yes, my lord. Shall I arrange a bath for you, as well?"

The butler's question drew James's attention to the fact that a good deal of the mud originally on Lady Margaret had rubbed off on him. He grimaced, but shook his head. "Not right away; I need to talk to Lord Mullin first. We will be in the library. Send Lady Margaret there when she is ready."

Gesturing for his friend to follow, James led the way into the study, heading first for the sideboard and the liquor that waited there; he had little doubt that this was going to be at least a two-drink conversation. Fortunately, Robert followed him in silence, accepting the drink James poured and taking a seat to patiently await an explanation.

James paced between the chair Robert had chosen and the fireplace, searching for a way to begin his exposition, but nothing came to mind. At last he paused, turned to face his friend, and blurted, "Gerald's sister is Lady X."

The silence that followed was complete. Robert gaped at him and James waited, silently counting to twenty-three before the other man blurted, *"Lady X?"*

He certainly understood his friend's horrified disbelief, for he had felt much the same way when Johnstone had revealed the information to him. It was unbelievable. Gerald's innocent little sister, a prostitute? If James were to be entirely honest, he hadn't even believed the runner until he had actually captured Margaret leaving that room in the brothel in a mask—and then he'd had to see her without the mask to be fully convinced it was the right woman. The idea of Gerald's

95

sainted sister behaving so scandalously was untenable.

And yet he had seen the proof with his own eyes. Lady Margaret Wentworth, the sister of their late friend, was none other than Lady X. He doubted Lord Mullin would believe him out of hand any more than he himself had believed Johnstone.

"But—"

James raised a hand to interrupt his friend. "Let me explain before you start speaking your doubts—and I know you doubt me. I doubted this myself." Much to his relief the other lord fell silent and took a drink. Tugging at his cravat, James settled into the seat across from Robert, his gaze moving to the cold hearth before them. He supposed he should light a fire, or at least call a servant to do so, but he was feeling too weary at the moment to be bothered. Besides, the servants would be busy preparing Margaret's bath, not to mention preparing the evening meal. It was growing late in the day.

"As you know, Gerald's last request was that I watch after his sister," he finally began.

Lord Mullin nodded solemnly. "I was there both when he saved your life and when he gasped those words."

"Yes, well . . . as you remember, we were not released from service right away."

Robert nodded. Just because Gerald had died did not mean the whole unit was released; they had continued to fight old Boney until just a month ago.

"Well, by the time I returned, Wentworth's estate had been settled. The title and castle are going to some cousin or other who went off to make his way in America. At the time of my return they had not yet found the fellow, though they probably have by now. At any rate, while the estate's solicitors could tell me that much, no one seemed able, or at least willing, to give me Gerald's sister's whereabouts since leaving Clarendon—the seat of the Wentworth title—or in aiding me to find her. I had to hire a Bow Street runner named Johnstone to locate the girl."

"And you found her at Dubarry's?" Robert interrupted in outrage. "My God, lawyers are such cold-hearted bastards! To dump the woman out on the road without a second thought, leaving her to take up—"

"Nay," James interjected before Lord Mullin got too carried away. "Johnstone, the Bow Street runner I hired, did not find her at Dubarry's. Well, not at first." He heaved a sigh and shifted in his seat. "He found her at Gerald's town house in London. It seems that while he could not leave her the title and castle, he could and did leave her his personal property: his town house, a few small investments, his servants." James shifted again and took another drink. It gave Robert the opportunity to speak.

"But if she has the town house in London and money, why take up—"

"Greed, I suppose," James answered, staring into the swirling liquid in his glass with a morose expression. "Gerald's investments weren't enough to run the household for any length of time without the funds that are now going to Margaret's cousin. Had she sold the town house and purchased a small cottage in the country, then invested the money left over from the sale, she most likely would have been fine. But it seems such . . . rural living is not to her taste. Or at least that is what I must presume from the choices she has made. She settled in the London town house and, apparently, set to work at Madame Dubarry's to supplement her income."

"Good Lord," Robert murmured with consternation. "Who would have believed it of Gerald's sister? He always made her sound so sweet and naive."

"Yes, well, I could hardly believe it when Johnstone came to me with the news."

Robert's eyebrows rose slightly. "How did *he* find out?"

James shrugged. "He found her at the same time he learned the contents of the will. Which should have been the end of his investigation, I suppose, but it did not go unnoticed by me that financially she should be in a bad way and yet she had retained all the servants. I was . . . curious as to how she was managing, so I asked Johnstone to look into the matter."

"And he discovered she was Lady X," Lord Mullin finished.

"Aye." James took another drink. "I hadn't heard from him for a week or so; then he came to me the other night and announced, rather proudly, that he had sorted it all out. He'd had a man watching her, but the fellow hadn't come up with anything. Suspecting his comrade was slacking on the job, he had watched her himself and followed her to Dubarry's. I am ashamed to admit it was already his supposition that Margaret is Lady X, though he had no proof of it. Of course, the only way to find out if it was true was to unmask Lady X."

Robert stiffened. "You *didn't!*"

"What? Sample her favors and unmask her that way?" James asked sardonically, then shook his head. "Nay. I arranged a . . . er . . . meeting. But I never intended to sample anything, just to get her out of there and unmask her. Which I did. We smuggled her out of Dubarry's, got her in my carriage, and brought her here. Unfortunately, they convened the House of Lords this morning, so I had to turn around and head right back to London. I left Margaret here while I did. I headed back again directly after."

"No wonder you look exhausted," his friend commented.

"Yes."

They were both quiet for a moment; then Robert asked, "Did you hire someone to guard her?"

James shook his head. "I didn't think it was necessary. I told the staff that no one was to aid her in leaving, and that I would return as soon as possible. I ordered Webster to have Annie stick with Margaret all day, not to let her out of her sight until she retired. And I assumed the dogs loosed at night would discourage her from trying anything then. I even wrote her a note explaining that no one would abet her escape, and that we would discuss alternate career choices when I returned. I thought such a note would assure her she would not be harmed. I never imagined for a moment that she would still run."

"No. Most ladies would simply have awaited your return," Robert sympathized. Then he added, "Of course, most women in her situation would never have taken up the career she did."

Ramsey frowned. "You sound almost admiring."

"Well . . ." The fellow shrugged and smiled slightly. "I guess I do admire her a bit. You have to give her credit for at least attempting to take care of matters rather than sit about and cry."

James was scandalized. "Taking up as Lady X is

hardly an honorable way of 'taking care of matters,'"
he snapped. He scowled at the other man for even suggesting the thought, but Lord Mullin merely shrugged.

"Well, it is better than the poorhouse perhaps. Anyway, what was she supposed to do—marry? Most marriages these days are a form of prostitution, anyway. At least she is honest about it." Robert laughed.

Though James shook his head at his friend's argument, he had to admit he'd indulged a thought or two along those lines himself. Certainly every mistress he'd ever had had been like a wife: he'd paid for her home, her clothes, her entertainment, and her servants—at least for as long as they'd been involved. He supposed the only difference was that his mistresses were shortterm. Of course, Lady X's customers did not bother with manors or servants; they had only to hand over cold, hard coin for services rendered.

He didn't admit any of this to Robert, though. He would never allude to anything but dismay at her profession. This was Gerald Wentworth's sister, after all!

"So? What do you plan to do with her?"

James glanced up at that question and grimaced. He had been pondering little else since smuggling her out of the brothel. What *was* he to do with her? His promise to her brother would not allow him simply to let her go about her business as a notorious demimondaine. At the very least he had to offer her options, to attempt to talk Margaret into giving up this life of shattered morals. But how?

He was saved from admitting his bafflement by the crash of the study door slamming open and banging against the wall. Both men glanced with startled surprise at the woman now standing in the doorway glaring at them. She was a sight to behold. Bathed, powdered, and dressed in a fresh gown that almost fit, her fiery eyes snapped from James to Lord Mullin and settled on the latter with relief. She promptly pushed away from the door and rushed to Robert as he stood.

"Thank God you are still here, my lord! I was so afraid that you might leave."

"Of course I am still here," Lord Mullin assured her, looking terribly uncomfortable as he did. "I said I would wait."

"Yes, you did." She beamed at him, then clasped his hands. "I wish to leave. Surely you will see me rid of this place? You will not let *him* hold me here against my will? He is a madman. He kidnapped me."

Lord Mullin's obvious discomfort grew; he avoided her eyes and looked everywhere in the room but at her. "Ah . . . well, as to that, my lady, Lord Ramsey merely wishes to help you. He wants to allow you time to consider your options for a better life."

"Options?" Margaret Wentworth scowled. "What options? I was doing well enough without his interference. Surely, as a friend of my late brother's, you will not leave me here?"

Robert straightened his shoulders. "It is precisely *because* I was a friend of your brother's that I have to agree with Ramsey. Surely you do not imagine that your brother would approve of your present employment?"

She had the grace to look slightly ashamed at the question, but then her chin lifted defiantly. "He might not approve, but he would understand that under the circumstances—"

"And which circumstances would those be?" James interrupted. His dry words drew her irritated attention.

"Your desire not to give up the excitement of life in town? I suspect your brother expected you to sell his town house, purchase a cottage, and live in the country off the proceeds."

"Oh?" She turned, her hands resting on her hips. Her pretty face twisted with derision. "So you knew my brother better than I, who knew him all his life, did you? *I* think my brother never expected to die so young. He planned to see me married and settled happily. Unfortunately, such was not the case. Instead he died and left the town house and the responsibility of those servants to me. I could hardly sell the house and leave them all unemployed."

Robert touched her arm, drawing her gaze back to his amazed face. "Are you saying that you took up as a pr—*that* career to keep your brother's servants employed?"

Maggie scowled at Lord Mullin's shock. Writing articles for the *Daily Express* wasn't *that* shameful an occupation. The way these two were acting, one would think she had taken up prostitution! "What else was I to do? Every one of those servants was loyal to Gerald, and to my parents before him. Most of them have been in service to my family all of their lives. I could hardly see them on the street."

"Dear Lord," the younger nobleman said under his breath.

"You see?" Maggie smiled. He, too, was obviously horrified at the idea of such loyal men and women being left to fend for themselves. "I realize that it must seem a risky business, but it wasn't. Not really. I was always in disguise, or veiled, or masked—as I was when *he* grabbed me." She threw a disgusted look in Lord Ramsey's direction.

"Aye, but . . . I mean . . ." Lord Mullin gave a nervous laugh, then went on delicately: "Risk aside, surely you do not *enjoy* the work?"

She blinked in surprise at the question, then found herself reluctantly admitting what she had not yet admitted to herself. "Perhaps not always. At times . . ."

Both men leaned forward expectantly as she considered the matter, so consider it she did, forcing herself to be painfully honest about everything for a change—something she did not do often because she undoubtedly needed the money from her work. But if she were to be honest, she did not always enjoy being G. W. Clark. For instance, she had not liked climbing that ledge at the brothel. Though, now that it was over, it seemed just another adventure, at the time she had been nauseatingly terrified. And, in truth, she found some of the tales the women told her that night distressing. Some had even left her feeling tainted. The things those women did . . .

"Yes?" Lord Ramsey prompted, and Maggie met his gaze with some difficulty.

"Well, really," she admitted reluctantly, "sometimes it is frightening and unpleasant. But . . ."

"But?" Lord Mullin prompted when she hesitated.

Shrugging, she admitted, "But sometimes it is exciting, too."

"Exciting?" Both men echoed.

"Yes, of course." She shifted impatiently at their horrified expressions. Likely they were thinking of the gleaning of information for specific articles—such as the one about the gambling hells that cheated their customers, or the Four Horsemen's club, where young knobs went to race. She supposed those exposés had been a bit dangerous to write, but they had also been fun. Besides, both articles were about places these two had surely been a time or two themselves. Why should she be forced to remain ignorant of their particulars just because she was a woman? "Well, why should it be any different for me than for you?" she asked. "By all accounts you men certainly enjoy such pastimes. Why should I not?"

"Oh, dear." Lord Mullin tossed back the last of his brandy and set the glass down with a *thunk*, then he straightened and eyed Lord Ramsey meaningfully. "I wish you luck, my friend, but I fear you shall have a rough time rehabilitating her. Keep me posted on how you do." And with that the young noble rose to leave.

Maggie was horrified. Glancing at Lord Ramsey, she noted a similarly displeased look on his face. Why was *he* looking so resigned? *He* wasn't the one being left alone to deal with a situation with no way out!

"Surely you will not leave me here?" she cried, following Lord Mullin to the door. "I really do have to return to London. And you promised to help me."

"Yes, I did," the young man agreed. "But that was before I understood all the particulars. Now I realize that James is only trying to help. You will not come to any harm in his care."

"Perhaps not," Maggie allowed, then shook her head miserably. "But I *do* have to return. If for no other reason than that my servants have no idea where I am. They must be greatly distressed by my disappearance."

Lord Mullin took her hands briefly, then dropped them as though they were hot. "It is my considered opinion, my lady, that you exert far too much energy on your servants' behalf," he said stiffly. At her bemused expression, he added, "Really, this is for the best, my lady. Let Ramsey aid you in this matter."

Then he walked out, pulling the door closed behind him and leaving her standing alone and bereft in the house of her captor.

Lord Ramsey was silent for a moment, watching her obvious unhappiness; then he downed his drink and stood. The movement drew her wary gaze to him. As she watched suspiciously, the man gave an expansive sigh. She didn't trust him, and she never would. Kidnapping her had not been a propitious start, no matter his oath to her brother. He didn't try to explain himself, though. Instead, he paused several feet away and gave a slight bow.

"Please make yourself comfortable in my home, my lady. As Robert said, you are perfectly safe here. I have only the best intentions toward you." He spoke sincerely, but what was that glinting in the depths of his dark eyes? Maggie was taken off guard by his next words. "And you really have nothing to be concerned about when it comes to your servants. I had a letter delivered to them the night I brought you here, stating that you were coming to my country home for several days' relaxation. If you are concerned, however, you are welcome to write a letter to them and I will see it delivered on the morrow."

Before Maggie could answer yea or nay to that, he gestured to his muddy person and went on. "In the meantime, I am going to clean up, then will most likely retire. It has been a rather wearying couple of days. You may take dinner in your room or the dining room—as

105

you wish. I shall join you to break fast on the morrow, and we shall discuss then your situation and various ideas on how to improve it."

If he had hoped she would be seduced by his politeness, he was sadly mistaken. Maggie remained just as cold to him as before. She watched as he fought back an obviously annoyed expression; then she watched nonchalantly as he murmured good-night and left the room.

As he pulled the door shut behind him, Maggie felt frustration surge up within her like a fire. She could hardly believe this situation. Even more unbelievable was the fact that Lord Mullin had just left her here! Both of these men seemed to be of the opinion that they knew what was best for her. *Well, stuff that!*

Stomping to the library door, she tugged it open and stormed across the hall to the front entrance of the house. No one tried to stop her. No one even appeared. She should have taken it as a warning, but she was too swept up in her emotions. Pulling the front door open, Maggie stepped out on the front step with a feeling of triumph.

It died abruptly at the sound of barking. Turning her head, she glanced warily about until she spotted a pair of enormous dark-furred dogs racing toward her as if she were the fox in a hunt.

For a moment, Maggie couldn't move; then she gathered herself enough to whirl back into the house. She slammed the door just as the beasts raced up the steps, and there was no mistaking the way the wood shuddered a moment later from the impact of the excited dogs' bodies. Now she knew why Annie was no longer trailing her about, why Ramsey felt comfortable leaving her unattended. He had released the dogs.

Surely they were not trained to attack just anyone on the grounds, she thought unhappily. Unfortunately, she wasn't about to pop outside to discover if they had been racing up eager for petting and attention, or eager to bite her.

Mouth tightening, she listened to the animals bark and leap at the door for a moment, then eased slowly away, half afraid that they would somehow work the door open and come after her. Maggie had backed all the way to the stairs before they began to quiet. Swallowing, she spun about and hurried up the steps to her room. Once in that chamber, she looked frantically around, then rushed to the archway to the balcony. Bursting outside, she immediately heard the barking start up again.

The dogs had heard the slight squeak of the doors opening, and they were racing to position themselves beneath her balcony. Pacing back and forth beneath her, the beasts were leaping and barking excitedly. Maggie watched unhappily for a moment, then moved back into her room. Escape had been a foolish idea, anyway. She already knew she would never be able to rent a carriage to London; Timmins had proved less than helpful. And the chances of her coming across anyone willing to take her there themselves were slim. It appeared she was stuck.

As much as it galled her, she would have to see what her host had to say for himself at breakfast in the morning; then she would decide on her next move.

Closing the balcony doors on the still-barking dogs, she moved to the bed and lay down to rest until dinner was brought up.

Chapter Six

"My lady, first I wish to say that I do understand the necessity that drove you to this career choice. Truly, I do."

Maggie set her tea aside and raised her gaze politely to Lord Ramsey, her eyes taking in his chiseled face. He really was a handsome man. It was a shame they hadn't met under different circumstances. She would be interested in knowing if the arrogance he had shown her was his normal attitude, or if it was merely a result of the unusual situation that had brought them together.

She had spent the better part of the night before reconsidering that situation—partially due to the reaction of Lord Mullin. After she calmed down, it had been obvious to her, from the short time she had spent with him, that young Robert was a good man, and that he had considered her brother a friend whom he'd held in much esteem. She found that reassuring. After all, he

108

would hardly leave the young, innocent sister of his friend in the care of a man who might possibly put her in danger. She had also decided that Ramsey's motives were likely just what he had stated; to look out for her, as Gerald had asked. Which meant that James Huttle-don was misguided, but well-meaning, and also that she was perfectly safe.

Most important to her decision to tolerate Lord Ramsey was her brother's judgment; Gerald had written a lot about James in his letters, all of it good. He had considered him one of the most honorable men he had ever met and had given many examples: Tales of Lord Ramsey giving away his own food to starving women and children from destroyed villages they marched past, of risking his life to save others, of refusing advancement when it wasn't earned, but was offered because of his title. Gerald had admired, respected, and looked up to this man and—reading those letters—Maggie had come to feel much the same way. He was a good and honorable man trying to do his best for the sister of the man who had died saving his life. She would be patient with him and help him see that there was really very little he could do to help her.

Which didn't mean she didn't wish to get home. She had to get back eventually, and preferably sooner rather than later. She had things to do; she needed to return Maisey's horrid gown, and, more important, she had to finish her article on Madame Dubarry's brothel. Mr. Hartwick wouldn't pay her if she didn't get the article in soon. She had worked on it last night, and planned to finish it as quickly as possible.

She supposed that if she wasn't home by the time the article was done, she could always send it with her letter to Banks and have him turn it in. It wasn't imperative she be there; Banks turned her pieces in as he had done for her brother. She was rather hoping, though, that she could convince Lord Ramsey to return her before the article was finished.

Maggie very much suspected that the only way to convince her captor to return her to London was first to listen to what he had to say, then to explain in a logical, unemotional manner that while being G. W. Clark was risky, it was her only choice. He would be reasonable if she was reasonable; of that she was sure. After all, Gerald had never been one to suffer fools gladly. He wouldn't have considered James such a good friend or respected him nearly as much if he was as stupid as that ridiculous abduction of her from Madame Dubarry's had indicated.

Having decided all of this during the last restless night, Maggie had come down to breakfast fully expecting her host to start in at once. However, he had apparently thought it tactically preferable to wait until they finished eating. She could not say that it had been a poor choice. The delay had left her increasingly tense and unsettled as she had toyed with her food, waiting on pins and needles for just this subject to come up. Now she assumed an attentive pose, waiting to hear what Lord Ramsey had to say, prepared then to explain why he was wrong, in a calm and reasonable manner.

"I realize that there is very little for a woman, especially a lady of noble birth, to do to earn her way in the world," he continued, sounding quite reasonable. "But surely you see that what you are doing is not the answer? This profession will eat at your soul, steal your youth and your beauty. I have seen it many times."

Maggie felt her calm slip a bit and rolled her eyes at his dramatics. While it was true that researching her stories for the G. W. Clark articles sometimes saw her digging about in the underbelly of the beast that was society, the work was not as bad as all that. She didn't wish to argue, however, so she merely pointed out, "My lord, such worries are long past being a concern for me. I am five-and-twenty. What beauty and youth I had fled some time ago."

That put a frown on his face and had him observing her more carefully, at least what he could see of her from his position across the table. His eyes took in her golden hair in its prim style, then her face, her neck, and her breasts, covered as they were by her slightly oversized gown. The garment tended to sag a bit around her smallish bosom, Maggie saw with discomfort, and revealed more than she wished to display. She had to grit her teeth to keep from self-consciously tugging the neckline upward. When his eyes finally made their way back up to her face, she released a relieved breath.

"Why have you never married?" he asked abruptly.

"No one has asked me," she admitted through her teeth, feeling defensive. But her irritation immediately softened at his expression of patent disbelief. It was somewhat flattering that he did not believe her. "I am sure it is very kind of you to show yourself to be such a gentleman, but—"

"I will not allow you to return to your previous employment."

Maggie stiffened, the previous days' irritation at this pompous man returning in full force. "Unless you plan to hold me captive here forever, you really have no choice. You are not my father, brother, or guardian."

"Oh, but I am something of a guardian," he argued. "Your brother asked me to look out for you."

"I hardly think he meant for you to take me against my will and hold me captive in your home, my lord," she snapped with some asperity. The bolt struck home, and guilt covered his expression for a moment. She pressed her attack. "This is all really a dreadful mistake and waste of time. Please return me to my home and—"

"No." Lord Ramsey's discomfiture was gone at once, replaced with steely determination. "There are alternatives."

"Fine." She gave in gracefully. "Let us hear these alternatives."

"Well . . ." His expression showed that he had not expected her to be so open to discussion. Maggie waited patiently until the man had gathered himself together enough to plunge forward. She was not terribly surprised when he drew a piece of folded paper from an inner pocket of his morning coat, unfolded it carefully, then smoothed it out on the table. He looked over whatever he had written, then glanced up at her with a nod of apparent satisfaction. "I have taken the liberty of doing some figures, and, according to my inquiries, were you to sell the town house and add the proceeds to the monies you inherited from both your mother and the smaller sum from your brother, you should be able to purchase a good-sized house in the country and live quite comfortably for the rest of your days. That is, if you do not marry, of course. Should you marry, your investments will make a nice little nest egg, or be a supplement to your husband's income."

He glanced up from his notes, his pleased expression fading somewhat at the narrow-eyed look Maggie was giving him. Shifting uncomfortably under her cold stare, he asked cautiously, "Is there something amiss?"

"The money I inherited from both my brother and mother?"

"Aye." He frowned slightly, not understanding her displeasure.

"I suppose you have the exact sums there?"

"Well, yes. As far as I know. Are these not correct?"

He slid the piece of paper along the table until Maggie could reach it. She turned the sheet and scanned the figures. "Yes. These are correct. Might I ask how exactly you came by these numbers?"

"Johnstone—a runner—got them. Wills are a public record, you see."

"I do. Well, my lord. I am flattered beyond compare that you would take such trouble to dig out all my little secrets—my finances, my employment. My goodness, is there anything you do not know about me?" Folding the sheet of paper, she tossed it at him with an angry snap of her wrist.

Lord Ramsey caught the paper and set it carefully back on the tabletop, silent for a spell before carefully admitting, "I realize that you are not pleased by my having this knowledge, but your brother asked me to look after you. I did want to be sure you were doing all right financially."

Maggie felt herself soften again. As pompous as he could be, the man really was only trying to repay his debt to Gerald. "Yes, well," she allowed. "If you were able to find all this out, my lord, no doubt you also found that I am doing perfectly well on my own now. There is no need for your intervention."

"It would appear that you are handling your finances

113

well enough," he agreed reluctantly. "The money you invested is paying well, and you have not withdrawn any large sums to buy extravagances. In fact, you appear to be making steady deposits while at the same time paying your living expenses. But you *must* agree that the way you are earning this money is of some concern." When Maggie's only response was a thinning of her lips, Lord Ramsey frowned and looked down at his notes. "If you would just sell the town house and purchase a less expensive country home—"

"I am not moving to the country, my lord," she insisted. "Perhaps you cannot understand this, still having family, but I have nobody left. Therefore, I depend rather heavily on the few friends I have in town. I will not deprive myself of them simply to satisfy your desire to see me live a more traditional lifestyle."

On that note Maggie stood, slapped her napkin onto the table, and turned to sail out of the room before she did something silly like get emotional. *So much for logic and reason*, she mourned as she left the room.

James watched lady Margaret leave, his gaze dropping to the sway of her skirts as she went. She looked lovely in the deep green gown she wore today. The hue set off her coloring so nicely. Of course, the gown didn't fit as well as it might. His sister, Sophie, had left several garments behind when she'd married and moved away.

He had never noticed how generous Sophie's bosom was, but she was obviously larger in that area than Maggie. Overlarge, he decided, since Maggie's breasts had appeared perfect to him when he'd held her in his arms, the sheer, red gown of that first encounter revealing them fully to his startled eyes. Yes, they had appeared the perfect size and shape to him in that moment, so Sophie must be rather overendowed.

Grimacing at his less-than-gentlemanly thoughts, he peered down at the paper in his hand and the figures on it. He hadn't really expected her to agree to trading her brother's home for a less expensive life in the country. If that were an option, she would have done so long ago rather than resort to selling her body. He'd mentioned it only as the first of several ideas. Yet he hadn't considered the reason she was unwilling might be that she wished to stay near friends. He had rather assumed her reluctance was due to a wish to remain close to the excitement of city life. She had revealed a rather softer side of herself than he had expected. It was true, Gerald had been the last of her family. She had no one now but friends in the city. How could anyone expect her to give them up?

His eyes went to his notes, and he frowned slightly. He had one other option here that he would bring up at lunch. In the meantime, he really needed to try to come up with more. Which meant a visit to his library. James always found it easier to think surrounded by his beloved books. The very smell of the leather-bound volumes seemed to help him cogitate. Some time in the library, surrounded by the brilliance of countless ages, should help him find a solution that would please Margaret.

Maggie had just settled in a cozy corner chair in the library when her attention was caught by the sound of the door opening. Lifting her gaze from the book she had opened, she watched Lord Ramsey enter and close the door. The moment he did so, a change came over him. His very body language seemed to alter. The stiff, upright posture he generally practiced eased somewhat, allowing more graceful movement. His facial expression lost some of its severity, making him appear younger and more attractive.

Fascinated by this transition, Maggie was reluctant to make her presence known. She found herself shrinking into her chair in an effort to avoid detection as he walked to the far wall and ran his hands lightly over the volumes there. He picked one off the shelf, leafed through it, then set it back and chose another. After a quick perusal through this book, he let the hand holding it drop and—now clasping it behind his back with both hands—moved to the glass doors to peer outside. He stood there a good while, staring—blindly, she suspected—out over the gardens. He was rocking lightly on his feet, still holding that book, and Maggie found herself unable to look away. The pose was one she recognized as a common stance she herself took. She often stood, gazing out of the window of her own library in just such a manner, a favorite book clasped behind her back—more for its comforting presence than any other real purpose—as she wrangled with some problem or other.

Maggie had no doubt the conundrum he was pondering. Hers, of course, and what to do with her. She found it rather sweet. Not since Gerald's death had anyone been so concerned about her. Despite grieving the loss of her brother, part of her had enjoyed her new autonomy—few women knew what it was like to be truly free of male intervention in their life. Another part, however, had not. It could be terribly wearying to bear the weight of so many livelihoods, and extremely lonely knowing that ultimately there was no loved-one to care. In truth, Maggie mattered only to her servants now.

Or so she'd supposed. She now appeared to matter to Lord Ramsey as well, if only due to the duty he felt he owed her brother.

Maggie observed his troubled expression, for the first time considering that she was an added burden on his shoulders. She felt sympathy overtake her, but knew from experience that telling him that he needn't worry about her would help little. His conscience would insist otherwise.

Closing the book in her lap, she gently asked, "Am I such a problem?"

The man nearly jumped out of his skin. When her voice pierced the silence he gave a violent start and whirled, the book dropping from his hand. His eyes fell on her with astonishment as she got to her feet and moved toward him.

"I am sorry. I did not mean to startle you so. Was it damaged?" she asked with concern as he knelt to pick up the fallen tome.

"No. It is fine, I'm sure." He brushed off the volume, then lifted a rather wary gaze as she stopped before him. "I hadn't realized that there was anyone here. I shall leave you to your—"

"Oh, no, please." She caught his arm when he would have slipped past. "This is your library, my lord. I should be the one to leave."

"No. It's fine." He set the book on the corner of a nearby table and gestured vaguely toward the glass doors he had been standing before. I just—"

"You came here to think," Maggie finished for him.

His eyes examined her curiously. She felt moved to explain, "I recognized your pose there at the window."

She turned to peer out over the gardens. They were a far more lavish affair than Gerald's in London.

Mine now, she reminded herself sadly, then tried to distract herself from such melancholy thoughts by admitting, "I do the same thing at home. I tend to stand at the window, book in hand, looking out over the gardens as I ponder." She turned to him, vague amusement curving her lips. "Would I be vain in thinking that I am the problem you were considering?"

"It would be unchivalrous of me to call you a problem. A concern, perhaps."

"I see, well . . ." Maggie's voice died as her eyes landed on the book he held. "Pride and Prejudice."

"Yes." He lifted it for her to see.

"It is my favorite book in the whole world."

"Mine, too."

They shared a smile, then Maggie, finding herself oddly affected by his nearness, moved away to gesture around the library. "You have all of my favorites here, and many books I haven't yet read. This is a wonderful library, my lord. Gerald would be jealous. He prided himself on an extensive library, himself, but I think yours may surpass it."

"Do you think so?"

Something in his tone of voice brought her gaze back to James, and Maggie was astounded to find him grinning. She was helpless to prevent an answering smile as she nodded. "Yes. I do believe so."

He savored that for a passing moment, then his expression softened. "Books and our love of them are what first drew Gerald and I together. It was what we both

missed most while at war. The two of us bragged endlessly about the libraries we had at home, arguing over
whose was better." His gaze moved around the book-
lined room. "Being neighbors, Robert and I had been
friends for years, and he used to silence us both by
pointing out that my uncle's library could easily beat
both of ours. He was right, of course. Uncle Charles
collected books all his life. He was forever enlarging his
library to accommodate new acquisitions. It was three
times the size of this one, and he was planning on enlarging it again . . . much to my Aunt Vivian's horror."

"Was?" Maggie asked.

"He died before getting to it," James explained, a new
heartache entering his eyes.

Maggie was silent for a moment, respecting his grief,
but he next blurted, "Uncle Charles instilled me with
his love of reading. I . . ." He paused, looking suddenly
embarrassed, as if uncomfortable at having revealed so
much of himself.

Maggie regretted the end of these revelations; she had
begun to feel that she was getting a glimpse of the real
Lord Ramsey. Pretending not to notice his discomfort,
she glanced around the room of books and said, "It was
Gerald who taught *me* to love reading. It was the best
gift he ever bestowed on me, I think. He used to say
that books were treasures."

"And do you agree?" Lord Ramsey asked.

Maggie gave a laugh. "Of course. Books can take you
to far-off lands, occasion you to laugh or cry, and teach
you much about the world that you would never otherwise learn. Books are quite simply wonderful. They
even *smell* wonderful." She threw out her arms and

turned in a slow circle, inhaling deeply of the scent with obvious relish.

James didn't smile. His thoughts were far too serious. He was thinking that here was a woman perfect for him. It wasn't her beauty, for there were countless beautiful women in the world, many of whom he had met. None of them had captured his attention for more than a moment, and certainly never to this degree. But here was a woman intelligent and with a passion for the written word equal to his own. He allowed himself to imagine a life with her; one where the winter evenings were spent with the two of them cozy before a burning fire, reading out loud to each other and laughing over an amusing phrase. But then their laughter faded, their eyes meeting and reflecting the fire from the hearth. He took the book from her hand, reaching for her even as he set it aside. Their lips met, their mutual passion for language taking a carnal turn. Then the door opened and they broke apart, their startled glances finding Lord Hastings in the doorway.

"Sorry, darling," his dream-Maggie said cheerfully. "Time to get back to work." And James was left seated on the sofa, watching his wife walk away on the arm of another man.

Groaning, James closed his eyes against this vision. Could a woman who had known the life Maggie had lived really settle for one man?

"Did you say something, my lord?"

James blinked his eyes open just as Maggie turned to him. Her hands fell back to her side, the tips of her fingers unintentionally catching the corner of the book he had set on the table mere moments ago, sending it spiraling once more to the floor.

"Oh no! I am sorry, I didn't mean . . ." Her voice faded away. They had both instinctively bent to rescue the volume, and now they knelt facing one another, each holding an edge of the book. As in his daydream their gazes met, and James fancied that he did see a hint of fire flickering in her eyes. He knew there was flame in his own. They rose as one, each still holding the book as if it were a conduit for the electricity sparking between them.

James felt himself leaning toward her, his body following its own edict. He was aware when her breathing became shallow, and she too inclined toward him. He felt her breath, whisper-soft, against his mouth. Her eyes slipped closed, her lips parting the tiniest bit, and James was about to claim them when the soft click of a door closing drew his head around to the entrance to the library.

There was no one there, no Lord Hastings waiting to whisk Maggie away. The sound must have come from somewhere out in the hallway. But it was enough to snap James back to his senses.

Straightening away from her, he cleared his throat and turned to replace the book on the table. He risked a glance Maggie's way to see the confusion reining on her face, then searched for something to ease the discomfort of the moment. Reaching into his pocket for the slip of paper with his two suggestions for her future on it, he turned his back to her. He took a step away, then said, "It occurs to me that if you do not wish to move out of London and your brother's townhouse, another possibility is to close up the better part of the house and release most of the servants. You should be able to manage quite well with this reduced expense."

A long silence followed his words, but he waited patiently for her to collect herself.

She sounded weary when she responded. "Impossible. I will not turn out servants who have served my family faithfully and well for years when all I need do to keep them is a little bit of work. I fear you shall have to come up with something else, my lord."

He considered her words during the following return to silence and still hadn't come up with a response when the click of the door made him turn to see that she had left the library. He was alone. Letting his breath out on a sigh, he moved to the nearest chair and dropped into it with relief.

There was no way he could ignore the fact that Maggie was going to be a terrible problem. He had felt sure when he had stolen her from Dubarry's that he could find an alternative to her lifestyle. Now, as he considered the matter, he seemed to be drawing a blank. Unfortunately, there simply were not many opportunities for women to make money in this man's world. Most women just married for it.

That was an option, he supposed. Her previous employment was still a secret—no one would know unless he told—so Maggie was still marriageable, but he found himself resisting the option. He simply could not imagine her wedding any of the eligible men of the *ton*. Or, to be more honest with himself, he didn't want to imagine her bedding any of them. Again.

He did seem to like to imagine her bedding *him*, however. He'd found himself rather distracted with such images ever since bringing her home. Every time he had paused to think of an alternate career for her, he found himself imagining her in that red gown of hers, doing one of those things that the girl at Dubarry's had whispered in his ear. Which was damned distracting. And damned discomfiting, too. He had been walking awkwardly a lot of late.

He was finding it more and more difficult to control his physical response to her. Worse yet, his very mind was starting to follow his body's lead. For a man who prided himself on his self-control and who had spent some thirty years residing mostly in his head—with small safe forays into the occasional physical "bit of exercise" with his latest mistress—this was all rather disconcerting.

James had learned at an early age that loving people correlated with great pain when they were lost. He had done his best to avoid such grievous entanglements. It was safer to stick to more temperate emotions. Affection rather than love. A mild desire rather than an all consuming lust. Unfortunately, Maggie was bringing out intense carnal yearnings in him, and he feared he wouldn't be able to fight them much longer. Which was the problem. Had he kissed her just now, he very much suspected that it would not have ended with a simple kiss . . . or even just a passionate one. Even as he had bent toward her, his mind had been racing ahead to dragging her to the library floor and . . .

Feeling his manhood rise to make its presence known again, James killed his thoughts and closed his eyes. This was exactly the problem. The woman was driving him mad. His normally sane and controlled thinking was failing in the face of an almost continuous erection.

He considered his options desperately. Avoiding her

cropped up in his mind, but he dismissed that at once. Avoiding her, while possible, was not likely to help. Her presence did not seem to be necessary to affect his libido, he merely needed to think of her—and he seemed to do *that* endlessly. Perhaps, instead, he should try working her out of his system: Take her upstairs and bed her over and over and over until his fascination with her eased.

That idea had merit, he decided. His body certainly seemed pleased with it.

Grimacing, James stood and moved toward the door of the library. He needed to get away for a bit to think. It was obvious his brain dropped into his drawers whenever he was anywhere near the woman. Even in separate rooms in the same house she affected his thinking. His only respite was to get away for a while and hope to come up with a solution more acceptable. Not that he minded the proposition of taking Maggie as his mistress. In fact, the more he thought about the idea, the more he liked it. Unfortunately, it was the last thing his honor would allow.

"Robert," he decided as he stepped out into the hall. He would go visit his friend and neighbor, and see if the other fellow could help him. Lord Mullin had proven a brilliant strategist during the war; he should prove able to assist in this battle. Or so James hoped.

"I suppose you suggested she sell—"

"The town house and purchase a country house." James finished for his friend, and nodded. "Yes. That was my first suggestion, of course."

"And she did not like that?"

"She refused it, as I expected." He paced the length

of the other man's study. Lord Mullin had greeted him warmly on his arrival and agreed to lend his brainpower to the task. They were tossing ideas around now.

"What about closing up part of the house and releasing a portion of the staff?" Robert suggested.

"My second idea," James admitted wryly, "was shot down as quickly as the first."

"Hmm." The other man frowned. "I do not understand her refusing that. She hardly needs so many rooms for just herself. Or all those servants, for that matter."

"Don't you remember, Robert? She will not turn servants out who have 'served her family so faithfully,'" he quoted peevishly, and Lord Mullin gaped briefly before giving his head a befuddled shake.

"Well," the younger man said after a moment. "It would appear she suffers the same failing as most women. She is too softhearted for her own good."

"Too softhearted?" James spun on him in amazement. "The woman is bedding half of London rather than release some unneeded staff! That is a bit more than softhearted. Softheaded, more like."

"Well, surely not half of London?" Mullin argued with a smile. "Half of London is women, which means the other half would be men—and since she has not slept with either you or I, she cannot have slept with that entire half, either. Perhaps half of half of London. Aye, she may have bedded a quarter of the town."

"I am not amused, Robert," James said tightly.

"Sorry. I was trying to lighten the mood."

James ignored his friend's shrug. "I do not need the mood lightened, I need resolution." He began pacing again.

"Well . . ." Robert mulled the matter over. "Kendricks mentioned that he is looking for a nanny. Perhaps—"

James stared at him in horror. "You are not suggesting that we allow her to take a position where she would actually have influence over children?"

"Oh. I see what you mean." Mullin grimaced.

"Besides, the Kendrickses are, at present, a very happily married couple. Her presence in their household would put an end to that within a week."

Robert frowned. "I do not know about that. She may be a prostitute, but that doesn't mean that she would attempt to disrupt a happy marriage."

"She would not have to try. Her very presence would be like tempting Adam with the apple."

Lord Mullin's eyes widened slightly and a faint laugh slipped past his lips. "Oh, now she is charming I am sure, but Kendricks is quite taken with his wife. I hardly think—"

"Taken with his wife he may be," James swore, "but I guarantee you that one week with Maggie, and Kendricks would be blind with lust."

"Blind with lust?" Robert appeared doubtful. "She is attractive, but—"

"Attractive?" James interrupted again. "The woman is temptation personified."

Robert pursed his lips, the image of a muddy and bedraggled Maggie stumbling out of the woods coming to his mind. That was followed by a more presentable vision, her still-damp and inglorious appearance after she had had her bath. She was attractive in a sweet, wet sort of way, he supposed. But he wasn't seeing what his friend was ranting on about.

"She has nice eyes," he said judiciously at last, and James gaped at him.

"Eyes? Forget her eyes! She has the most delectable body I have ever seen. The woman is perfect. Nay, Kendricks wouldn't be safe from her. Oh, at first he might barely notice her, but then he would begin to notice her scent, become aware of it every time she entered or left a room, wafting around him, drowning his senses. Then every time her name was brought up, or he tried to think what to do with the woman, she would rise in his mind like Aphrodite, her lips full and sweet, her eyes mysterious behind that red mask, her skin pale and perfect in that see-through red silk gown she wears, the cinnamon-red of her nipples showing through its hazy gauze—"

"Cinnamon nipples!"

James stilled, blinking a time or two as Robert's exclamation recalled him to propriety. Just what had he been raving on about? Dear Lord, the woman was driving him mad! He despairingly quit his pacing to drop into a chair.

"What see-through red gown is this? And what the devil have you been doing over there at Ramsey with Gerald's sister? For God's sake, James! You are supposed to be reforming the wench, not—"

"Nothing. I have not been doing a damn thing." He bestowed a disgusted glare on his friend. "Get your head out of the gutter, Robert."

"Well, then, what is all this nonsense about a delectable body and see-through gowns?"

James shrugged unhappily. "She was wearing a see-through red gown when we snatched her from the brothel," he admitted. Then he shifted impatiently.

"Enough about that! I came here today hoping you would have some helpful advice for me."

"Yes, yes, of course. I will try to do better," Robert assured him, but James was already off on another tirade.

"I have been racking my mind and coming up with very little!" he was saying.

"Well, you have been rather distracted, what with rushing back and forth from town."

"But all I could come up with were the same damn things you just brought up. The same things she discounted when we first talked to her. I even considered finding her a position with a family as a nanny, but I cannot, in good conscience, suggest her to anyone."

"No, I suppose not," Robert agreed. "If she would even consider it."

"Yes. That is the other thing, of course. I doubt she would agree."

"Hmm." They were both silent for a moment; then Lord Mullin asked, "What else is there for a woman?"

"Very little." James grunted. "Which is my problem. But I cannot in good conscience allow her to return to Dubarry's either."

"No. That wouldn't do," Robert agreed.

"So, you see my problem?"

"Aye."

"That being the case, I have considered one last alternative," James admitted reluctantly. When his friend peered at him in polite inquiry, he hesitated, then added carefully, "Something more along the line of her previous employment, but not quite as disreputable."

"Her previous employment?" Robert frowned; then his eyes widened in incredulity. "Steady on! You are not thinking of taking her as a mistress?"

"Well, it would be a damn sight more respectable than working for Dubarry," James said defensively. "Besides, there is no sense in seeing her talents go to waste. And you yourself heard her say she liked the work."

"Dear God, James!" Robert's feet slammed to the floor with a crack. "That is hardly reforming her and seeing her out of the business!"

"She wouldn't be 'in the business.' And it would be a lot less risky. There would no longer be any worry of her identity being discovered."

"Oh no, everyone would *know* who she was—and that she was *your lover*," the other man pointed out.

"We could be discreet."

"Discreet? James, do you hear yourself? Think of Gerald, man!"

That gave James pause. Gerald, with his sweet stories about his sweet sister. His little Maggie with her sharp mind and pretty face. Gerald had left out mention of her delectable body, he thought bitterly. Perhaps, had he prepared James for—

"Gerald saved your life."

James grimaced at Robert's condemnation. He could have done without the reminder of what he owed Wentworth.

"He wouldn't want his sister to be your mistress."

"Not even to get her out of Dubarry's?" he asked.

"Of course not," Robert said firmly. "Use your head, Ramsey. You are supposed to be finding a solution to this problem, not becoming a part of it."

James accepted that, then glared at the other man. "Well, then I suggest you come up with something, because I am at a loss as to what to do with the woman. All I can think about when she is around is—"

"Her cinnamon nipples?" Lord Mullin inserted with dry amusement. "I shall give the matter serious consideration."

James grunted at the promise, but Robert ignored his pessimism.

"I will come up with something. In the meantime, it would appear that you are somewhat overly tempted by the girl. Therefore, you should avoid her as much as possible. In fact, why do you not stay for dinner? A little time and distance might help get her out of your system."

James hesitated, then nodded in agreement. It certainly sounded a better idea than sitting about gaping at Lady Margaret like some lovestruck pup.

Chapter Seven

Maggie stared out over the gardens. It was a lovely day. The sun was shining brightly on the multicolored roses along the path she was walking, but with her mind taken up with thoughts of her irritating host, she hardly noticed. She was beginning to believe another escape attempt would be necessary.

Unnaturally weary after their encounter in the library, Maggie had asked that her lunch be brought to her room. She'd wanted to avoid another tiring clash. Yet, by the time dinner rolled around, she'd recovered and been all girded for battle. The dratted man had muddled her plan by not showing up. She had eaten the meal alone—if one could call being surrounded by an army of servants, 'alone'—and, much to her alarm, Maggie had found herself missing the presence of the arrogant ass. Worse, assuring herself that her reaction was only due to restless boredom had not assuaged her fears.

The way her spirits had fallen this morning, when Annie announced Lord Ramsey would not be down to breakfast, had only exacerbated her annoyance. The maid had imparted, "his lordship returned quite late from Lord Mullin's estate." The girl hadn't said so, but the disapproving look she'd worn had made Maggie suspect the man had returned well sotted, which would explain his absence.

It did not, however, explain the unnatural attachment she seemed to be acquiring for her captor. She didn't understand it herself. She found James Huttledon irritating and arrogant. Yet there was no denying he was attractive, and there was a certain spice to sparring with him. Maggie felt alert and on edge whenever she was around him, much as she did during her escapades as G. W. Clark. It was as if she were indulging in something a little risky and dangerous just by being near him, and that sensation was intensely titillating. Which made her worry that her choice of employment was beginning to affect her adversely; perhaps she was becoming addicted to risk.

Maggie had found herself asking Annie questions about Lord Ramsey as the maid fixed her hair that morning. She'd learned that, much to her relief, the man was not married and never had been. He was the eldest of two children. His younger sister, Sophie, had been married two years earlier to Lord Prescott. Their parents had been lost at sea while both children were quite young, leaving them to be raised by their aunt and uncle. The uncle had died in his sleep while James was away at war, but his aunt Vivian, Lady Barlow, was still alive and well.

That had been the sum of what she had managed to learn, but the very fact that she had felt moved to ask was troublesome, to say the least. She didn't wish to like Lord Ramsey. Perhaps if he were not quite so obviously disapproving of her recent choices, if he weren't so stodgy and traditional, she would not mind so much. But there was really no sense in becoming attached to a man who looked down on her for working for a living. Once she convinced him that she did not need his interference in her life, Maggie doubted she would ever see the man again. They did not move in the same circles. Not anymore at least; she could no longer afford to.

Maggie wasn't one to yearn after things she couldn't have, so there was no sense at all in being the least bit interested in Lord Ramsey—she had repeated that to herself throughout her solitary breakfast. It was also what she was reminding herself of now as she wandered through Ramsey's gardens. She was a sensible girl and would behave accordingly.

Now all she needed was to convince the man to return her home so she could get on with her life.

"Would you care to break your fast now, my lord?"

James waved Webster's question away, continuing down the hall and out of the house, pausing only to snatch his hat and cape from the rack as he went. He had no interest in food this morning. All he truly wanted was some fresh air. He needed to clear his head. Avoiding his unhappy houseguest wasn't a bad idea, either. At least until Lord Mullin arrived with his promised solutions.

He recalled very little of the strategy session they had attempted last night after the fine meal Robert's staff had served. Most of what he remembered was that Lord Mullin still had the finest port in England. Unfortunately, that was mostly because it was having an unpleasant effect on him this morning. His hangover was the reason he felt a nice walk through the gardens was in order. Such exercise would serve to remove the last of the effects of the port pounding at his head, as well as keep him out of Lady Margaret's way until reinforcements arrived.

He would also keep Gerald firmly in mind, James decided as he walked along the garden path. That should help keep him from being tempted to seek out the girl. Satisfied with his strategy, he nodded to himself, then lifted his head just in time to keep from crashing into the back of the very woman he was trying to avoid.

Damn, was his impotent thought as she turned with a start.

His second reaction was to reassure himself that he should remain calm. It was broad daylight. They were out in the open. All he had to do was keep Gerald in mind, and he could keep himself restrained. He had not acted on his rather lusty thoughts ere this, and there was no reason to think he might now. Somehow, though, it seemed harder not to act on such thoughts now that he was admitting having them.

It wasn't as if there was the usual invisible barrier of the girl being pure and untried, some dark part of his mind pointed out, weakening his resolve. And she did look lovely in that delicate little white gown. It emphasized her false air of innocence. It even almost made James forget how she had looked the night he had swept her from Madame Dubarry's: her hair had not been piled atop her head then as it was now, but had tumbled about her shoulders in golden disarray as if she were fresh from bed. Which she had been, of course. And her skin had seemed lustrous through the gauzy red material of—

Damn! He wasn't supposed to be thinking of such things, James reminded himself. He wouldn't think of such things!

Maggie was a bit disconcerted to find the focus of her contemplation appear before her as if conjured by her thoughts. Taking a deep breath, she straightened her shoulders and prepared for a continuation of their previous struggles. She had no doubt there would be a continuation, the man was like a dog with a bone when it came to the matter of her career. One would think she were prostituting herself, the way he carried on. However, despite her attraction to him—or perhaps because of it—Maggie was determined that today she would convince him to give up this ridiculous task he had set himself, and make him return her to her life and home.

She opened her mouth to fire the first salvo, only to pause as she noticed the way the man was staring at her. The oddest expressions were flitting across his face. She was becoming quite uncomfortable in her thin white gown when he seemed to realize that he was gaping. Forcing a smile, he straightened and offered a quiet "Good morning."

Gesturing for her to continue walking he fell into step, and they walked in silence for several moments before he attempted to break it. "It is a chill day," he murmured finally.

135

Maggie felt herself relax. It appeared they would discuss the weather and refrain from butting heads. Clearing her throat, she managed a smile and a nod. "Aye. It is a bit chilly today, my lord. It was lovely just a moment ago, but now a cloud seems to have appeared to hide the sun. Thus it is growing a bit chilly." She realized the truth of it even as she spoke. The sun was hidden behind a large, fluffy cloud and, without it's warmth, the temperature had dropped several degrees. She began to wish that she had taken the cape Annie had offered her for this walk. Maggie had accepted the hat and gloves, but had thought a cape much too heavy for such a lovely morning. But then, the sun had still been shining.

"Hmm."

The sound drew her attention to her host. Noting the fretful expression on his face, she felt a smile curl her lip. That one comment on the weather appeared to be the extent of conversation that Lord Ramsey could manage this morning. The realization brought her some amusement as silence fell over them again. Crossing her arms and grimacing, she rubbed her hands lightly over her forearms in an effort to brush off the morning chill. It was a wholly unconscious movement, one she became aware of only when Lord Ramsey removed his cloak and draped it about her shoulders.

Maggie accepted the garment uncomfortably. When she then suggested they turn back to the house, he agreed in silence, taking her arm to lead her. They had nearly reached the doors to his library before he spoke again, the words bursting forth this time as if they simply could not be held in.

"How can you stand it?"

"Stand what, my lord?" she asked with bewilderment.

"What you do," he explained. "How can you *bear* it?"

Maggie turned to peer at him curiously, surprised at his true confusion and the almost pained expression on his face. He awaited her answer. Was he truly so perplexed that she could do what she did? She had to wonder a little impatiently what little lords were taught about women while growing up. Why was it so painful for him to consider that she willingly wrote articles for the *Daily Express*?

She forced herself to temper her irritation. After all, most of the ton would be shocked by a male member of the nobility writing such "rubbish." She supposed it was not so surprising that he would be horrified by the idea that a female member did. Sighing in acknowledgment of that, she turned to continue on toward the house. She had exited the manor via the doors to the salon, but he was steering her to the library, which was closer and more convenient.

"I can stand it because I quite like it, actually," she answered.

"You like it," he repeated not sounding at all happy. Maggie paused again to glance at him. He had stopped walking once more and was looking as miserable as he sounded. It was an exaggerated reaction, in her opinion, and she scowled before turning to stomp the last few steps to the glass doors.

"Aye. I *enjoy* it," she snapped. Tugging the door open with more force than was warranted, in her irritation, she strode inside and up to his desk. There she whirled to find him entering behind her, his expression verging on disgust. Maggie felt her chin lift defiantly as they faced each other. "I have always had a curious mind, and wondered about such things."

He continued to stare at her with that fascinated yet repulsed expression, and Maggie's mouth tightened. She would wager all the money she had been paid for her last article that he enjoyed pastimes like gambling and racing and such as well as talking about them afterward as G. W. Clark did in his article. Apparently a female such as herself admitting that she had enjoyed similar escapades was somehow grossly offensive to him however. *The hypocrite!*

"Oh, come now, my lord," she chided, tugging off her gloves with a series of impatient jerks on the fingertips. "I have heard a lot of puritanical types harp on about this, but I would never have taken you for a puritan or a prude. Surely you will not tell me that you have not had your own curiosities about such things? That you have not secretly enjoyed—"

"I will not deny it," James interrupted quickly, unwilling to hear Maggie actually voice what she had done in that brothel. He was already alarmingly excited at this vague discussion; should she start to describe the things she enjoyed in detail . . .

His gaze slipped over her figure in the soft white gown she wore beneath his open cloak. He had thought it very demure when his sister wore it. Unfortunately, on his guest it seemed subtly seductive. Or maybe that was the fault of the recurring images he kept having of her from the night he'd kidnapped her. It was hard to forget the curves he'd held in his arms, the breasts the gown had seemed only to emphasize in the gloom of the carriage. Even Margaret's innocent face had seemed seductive behind the red mask, framed as it was by her mussed flaxen hair. One's eyes had been forced to her sweet, swollen lips. While every single one of the borrowed gowns this woman had worn had only hinted at those charms, his mind filled in the blanks repeatedly and often, torturing him with that image and the knowledge of her lost virtue.

Feeling his sex harden at the thought, he straightened, his lips compressed. He forced out the words: "I realize that there is great pleasure to be found in such endeavors, but—"

"There, you see." She turned from setting her gloves on his desktop to beam at him. Her delight in eliciting such a confession from him was obvious. "There is nothing to be ashamed of in admitting to it, my lord," she went on gently, turning to move behind his desk. "My brother enjoyed it a great deal, too. I begin to think there may be a bit of the adventurer in our family blood. He was quite taken with the entire thing. I know."

James was shocked, and he asked carefully, "You mean with the brothel?"

"Well, as a matter of fact, he was quite well acquainted with Madame Dubarry," she admitted. "It was through him, indirectly, that I met her."

"Through him?" James repeated in horror as he followed her around the desk.

Maggie turned, startled when she found him standing directly behind her. She frowned. "Well, yes. Not directly, you understand. But she came to see me after he died. They had been friends and she—"

"Suggested you go to her brothel?"

"No." Maggie's expression grew distracted as her eyes focused on his mouth. He felt her gaze there as an almost physical touch. They were only inches apart, and

James became aware that he was crowding her, that she was leaning back slightly because of it, but he couldn't seem to move away. Her chest was rising and falling at an accelerated rate. Her mouth parted, and he nearly groaned when her tongue slid out to wet her lips. It appeared a wholly unconscious action, but knowing her career, James found that difficult to credit. She was a skilled seductress, and there was no question in his mind that he would be easily seduced.

"Uh . . ." Maggie cleared her throat suddenly, and gave a little shake of her head as if to clear it. Then she said, "Nay. She did not wish me to visit the brothel. She thought it was terribly risky."

"The woman has more sense than I thought," James muttered as the tension eased between them.

Maggie rolled her eyes before rushing on, "But I assured her it would be fine, that I would wear a disguise. No one would ever find out."

"But they did," James argued.

"Yes, well, I suppose it was bound to happen eventually," she admitted with obvious resignation.

Taking a deep breath, Maggie forced a smile, then shrugged philosophically and raised her hands to remove the silly little feathered hat that matched her gown.

Lord Ramsey still stood distressingly close, and showed no desire to move away as he asked, "And that is all you have to say? There is no shame?"

Maggie stiffened at the question, the hat half-off her head. "Why should I be ashamed? I realize that earning one's way in the world is frowned on by the ton, but then few of them *have* to earn their livelihoods. And many of them don't care what happens to their servants. Besides, I assure you my brother would not have been ashamed. I suspect the only reason he kept his own behavior secret was to protect me from any taint."

Lord Ramsey waved away her comment impatiently as he removed his hat and reached around to set it on the desk behind her. "It is different for a man," he said.

"Oh?" she asked archly. She drew her hands down between them, her hat clutched in her tense fingers. "How so?" Lord Ramsey frowned, but she continued, "You disappoint me, my lord. I hoped you would be different. That you would not hold men up to one standard and women to another. I thought you an intelligent man."

He squirmed at the rebuke, and Maggie was pleased to see indecision in his eyes, but then he gave a small shake of the head. "I am sorry, Margaret. I guess I find it hard to believe that you actually enjoyed your foray into the brothel."

Maggie caught her breath in surprise. This was the first time that Lord Ramsey had called her by her given name and the tone he had used while addressing her was almost gentle. Biting her lip, she confessed what she would have refused to before. "I didn't. Well, perhaps I did at first. But by the end, I just wanted to get out."

Surprise spilled across his face at the confession; then his eyes softened and he raised a hand, startling her with the gentle caress of one rough finger down her cheek. "And now you are."

"Yes." She swallowed hard, her eyes focusing on his lips as they drew nearer. He was going to kiss her. She knew he was going to kiss her. She also knew that she should stop him. A proper lady would stop him, but Maggie didn't want to. It was that damned curiosity of

141

hers. She wanted to know what it felt like to be kissed by a man like Lord Ramsey. Would his kiss be soft and wet, like Pastor Frances's tentative kisses had been? She didn't think so. She suspected they would be much different. They would not leave her wondering how to get the man out of the house without hurting his feelings. Maggie was positive they would make her toes curl. Actually, her toes were already curling in her slippers in anticipation, and her breath was coming in short, excited bursts. Yes, she was ripe for his kiss, so when she saw uncertainty flicker across his face and the way he hesitated, she took matters into her own hands. Stretching up on her curling toes, she pressed her lips to his.

Wham! She felt her heart slam into her rib cage, her body vibrating with excitement as she slid her lips uncertainly over his; then he took over the kiss with a sound somewhere between a moan and a curse. His mouth opened over hers, his head tilted and he began to devour her lips. Maggie's eyes popped open in surprise at the sudden hunger he showed. She saw that his own eyes were closed; then his hands slid up to cup the sides of her face, and he urged her mouth open. Maggie's eyes drifted closed again.

Pastor Frances had never kissed her like this! This was . . . carnal, sweetly sinful, and definitely delicious. Moaning into Lord Ramsey's mouth, Maggie inched closer, uncaring of the hat being crushed between them in her eagerness to feel his body pressed against her own.

Releasing her face, Ramsey slid his hands down to her arms and backed her around the chair until she bumped up against the desk; then he caught her in an embrace, drawing her close where his hands could slide down to curve over her bottom through her gown. He pressed her firmly against him and thrust forward. Maggie shuddered as she felt his hardness press into her; then she felt the first pangs of fear. She had instigated this kiss, had wanted it, but his arousal warned her she was playing with fire.

Raising her hands, she pressed gently against his chest, her face turning, but Lord Ramsey didn't appear to recognize it as an attempt to end their kiss. Instead, as she pulled away from him, his eyes opened and went to her chest. He raised a hand to cup one breast, and he spread his legs slightly, pressing her lower body more firmly between the desk and the proof of his arousal.

Maggie had begun to murmur an apology when his hand closed over her breast. Her mouth snapped closed, then a moan escaped as he brushed her borrowed cloak aside and lowered his mouth to the flesh revealed by the neckline of her gown. She felt his lips and tongue linger over the plump flesh there, then dip between her two breasts to lick that delicate skin. All at once, her breast was free of the gown and Lord Ramsey's mouth closed over the tender flesh of her nipple. Maggie experienced an immediate flood of fiery sensations pooling in her lower stomach.

Gasping for breath, she arched instinctively into his touch, her lower body grinding against his. Releasing her hold on her hat so that their bodies were all that held it between them, she reached back, pushing unknown items out of the way so that she could brace herself against the desk. She felt something warm and damp spread beneath her fingers, but cared little as he stirred her passions. Maggie let her head fall back, moans erupting from her throat as he tugged her gown down off her shoulders enough that her second breast spilled free. It was immediately enclosed in his warm hand, his thumb and forefinger replacing his lips on one nipple as he moved to lick and nip at the other.

Breathing something that might have been "Oh, God," Maggie lifted her head to peer down at him, her hands sliding into his hair and tugging unconsciously at the strands.

She wanted him to stop.

She wanted him to continue.

She wanted these feelings building in her to end.

She wanted the bliss they promised.

Her mind went fuzzy, confused by all her conflicting wants. Had anyone suddenly asked, she might have had trouble remembering where she was. Perhaps even *who* she was. All she seemed to be was a bundle of desire. And she wasn't even quite sure just what it was she wanted, but she wanted it badly.

Responding to her tugging on his hair, Ramsey released her breast, then covered Maggie's disappointed moan with his mouth, catching and turning it into a groan of shared desperation. Where she'd been uncertain earlier, this time Maggie responded to his kiss with unadulterated hunger. Sucking his tongue into her mouth, she nipped it gently as she gripped blindly at his cravat with her free hand. Somehow she managed to get the cravat undone, and she pulled it off, releasing it in a flutter to the floor.

Maggie turned her attention to his shirt. She wanted to feel his bare skin under her hands. It was a desperate mindless want and she pushed herself off the desk so that she could use both hands. Unfortunately, Lord Ramsey's nearness hindered her attempt to straighten so that she lost her balance. She grabbed at him to keep from falling, one hand catching in his shirt, and the other—the one still down by her waist—landing quite a bit lower. His sharply indrawn breath and the sudden swelling of the body part she had unintentionally grabbed, told her what she held. Maggie broke their kiss, mortification rushing through her.

"My lord," she began, then paused when he covered her hand with his own. Maggie had been about to remove her hold on him and apologize for the embarrassing mistake, but was now unable to. He didn't seem to want her to.

"James," he gasped in a strangled voice. "Dear heavens, Maggie, I think you can call me James, now."

"James," she breathed, squeezing him curiously. He had been hard when she had grabbed him, and seemed to grow more rigid by the moment. Despite the fear caused by treading on this dangerous ground, she found herself curious about his body. He seemed extremely large to her inexperienced touch. Maggie tentatively followed the length of that hardness, amazed when he gasped and shuddered against her.

"Oh God, yes, Maggie. Touch me," he exclaimed. Then he turned his lips to her throat. He alternated kissing, licking, and nipping at the skin there, with whispering heated words against her warm flesh. Maggie adjusted the pressure she applied, and where she applied it, curiosity and uncertainty battling within her.

"Oh God, you're so talented," he groaned, surging against her hand. Maggie bit her lip. Some of her passion had faded under her curiosity and her head was beginning to clear. She didn't feel talented. She also didn't feel terribly comfortable. She shouldn't be doing this, any of it. Before she could remove her hand, however, Ramsey was brushing it away himself. Claiming her lips with his own, he once again thrust his hardness against the very center of her through their clothing. The double assault had her forgetting her fears in no time. Within moments, her legs were weak, and moist heat was pooling where Lord Ramsey was rubbing himself against her.

Maggie clutched at his upper arms, dazed by her body's reaction to him as he insinuated one leg between hers, rubbing the material gathered there against her suddenly exquisitely sensitive core. Breathing heavily, she clung to him with her lips and hands. She rode his thigh, her body moving with his, then she shuddered as a breeze whispered past the burning skin of her leg.

She pulled her head away then, glancing down distractedly to see her crushed hat lying abandoned on the floor at their feet. Any guilt she felt at the abuse of the borrowed item was quickly displaced as she saw that one of Lord Ramsey's strong dark hands was tugging her skirt upward, his fingers sliding over the paler flesh of her thigh. A warning sounded in her head, but Ramsey's mouth had moved to her ear and was terribly distracting. It sent little tingles and shivers rippling through her. Maggie made little mewls of sound, then turned her head abruptly to catch his lips with her own.

His kiss this time was bruising in its intensity, but Maggie's response was just as passionate. Ramsey's fingers caressed their way onto her inner thigh. She cried out when they brushed against the swollen flesh of her excitement—more from the shocking tingling that shot through her at the caress than anything—then sucked desperately at his invading tongue, squeezing her legs around his caressing hand.

These delights were something Maggie had never experienced. She had never even imagined such waves of sensation as he was causing in her, and she was completely overwhelmed. Her chest heaving, her mind blank of all but wants, her body pressing closer, she rode the hand that promised such ecstasy. Then he ruined it by speaking. He dragged his lips from hers and nipped at her ear then moaned, "God in heaven, Maggie, you make me wild. I've tried to resist you but, God forgive me, I can't."

Maggie shook her head, his words piercing her passionate fog. He made it sound as if she were doing the seducing, but Maggie was quite certain it was the other way around. A good deal more of her ardor was snatched away in the face of sudden panic when she felt him invade her. She glanced down sharply, relief coursing through her when she saw that it was only his hand under her skirt, and she realized that it must be a finger he was inserting inside her. She wasn't certain she cared for the alien feeling, and certainly didn't like the panic it instilled in her. It suddenly came home to her that she was playing with a very dangerous fire.

"You're so tight," he breathed, sounding both awed and pleased.

Maggie wasn't sure what he was talking about, but did know she had to stop this. She squeezed her legs closed around his hand, trying to stop his movement. "My lord—"

"James," he reminded her, then silenced her with a kiss as he withdrew and inserted his finger again. The feeling was less alien this time, and he was again caressing her where it felt good—with his thumb, she thought—but Maggie resisted falling back into that mindless desire that had gripped her earlier.

"I want you to burn for me, too," he breathed against her lips, then licked her lower one and sucked it into his mouth.

"That is very nice, my lord," Maggie said a little breathlessly the moment her mouth was free again. "But . . ." She paused abruptly, because she had opened her eyes to find he had disappeared from view. She glanced down as his hands slid from between her legs and, instead, gripped her hips. He had dropped to his knees before her.

"Uh . . . yes. Well, I am quite flattered that youeeee!" She broke off on a squeal as his hands slid between her legs to caress her intimately once more. "Oh!" She swallowed, and tried to close her legs, but his body appeared to be in the way. "I . . . You really . . . Oh . . . It's nice that you want to make me . . . oh . . . yes . . . that *is* nice," she moaned.

"Yes. Burn for me, Maggie," he said. She shivered as his breath brushed against her thigh, her legs spreading farther of their own accord when he so urged. Then she went stiff as his head moved between her legs.

"What are you doing?" She jumped in alarm, nearly biting her tongue off as his mouth replaced his fingers. "Oh, no you mustn't!" Maggie grabbed at his hair and tried to tug him away. "You can't—You—Oh," she cried out as his teeth grazed her flesh, sending pleasure rippling through her. "Oh dear . . . that's . . . yes . . . I mean, no . . . no, you shouldn't . . . Oh, that . . . yes, that's nice too," she gasped. Giving up her hold on his locks, she curled her fingers around the edge of the desk and began to twist her head, her whole being centered on the sensations between her legs.

A knock at the door brought her back to earth with a thump. Stiffening and straightening, Maggie groaned as Ramsey again slid a finger into her. Legs trembling and chest heaving, she grabbed frantically at his head in a desperate bid to warn him, aware that he must not have heard the knock with her thighs pressed tightly to his ears. He ignored her panicked tug and grazed her again with his teeth. A gasp escaped her lips, for her body responded automatically with pleasure though her mind ballooned with horror as a second knock sounded at the door. Tugging viciously at his hair, she spread her legs farther to free his ears and opened her mouth to warn him.

Too late! She stiffened in horror at the sound of the door opening behind her. Panic like none she had ever before suffered raced through her, and Maggie abruptly released Lord Ramsey's hair. Brushing her skirts down to cover him, she quickly scooped the material of her gown back up over her shoulders, covering her breasts. Taking a deep breath, she turned to glance over her shoulder to discover who had entered.

Chapter Eight

"Lady Barlow," Lord Ramsey's butler announced, then blinked as he espied Maggie, seemingly alone. "I thought I heard voices. I just assumed Lord Ramsey was back from his walk and . . . in here," he said uncertainly. An elderly woman stepped into the room behind him.

"Ah . . . he, er, stepped out for a moment," Maggie murmured shakily. She straightened off the desk, and Ramsey, seeming finally to get the gist that they were no longer alone, eased away from her. He was still mostly under her skirts, and his position created an odd lump in the front of her gown, but Maggie was pretty sure that was hidden by the desk.

Glancing over to find the woman's eyes had narrowed on her, she raised a hand self-consciously toward her hair, freezing when it reached eye level and she saw that her right hand was completely black. Being a writer, she recognized at once what covered her hand, and her gaze

150

shot to the desktop in alarm. The overset inkwell and the puddle of black ink surrounded by lighter hand-prints on the desk's surface told their own story. Maggie grimaced, then had a brilliant idea.

"He overset the ink and went to change," she said brightly, gesturing to the mess on the desk. "No doubt he shall return momentarily," she added, when Webster and the newly arrived woman continued to stare at her. Then, realizing that she was being extremely rude by keeping her back to them, Maggie eased her leg over Lord Ramsey's head and turned. A flush colored her face as she felt him shift behind her. He was still under her skirts, his body brushing against the backs of her legs, his breath blowing lightly against her bottom. Closing her eyes, Maggie tried to ignore the sensation, to forget that he was under there, with his cheek pressed against one of hers. She managed a strained smile.

"I am—"

"Margaret Wentworth," the other woman interrupted, and Maggie stiffened in surprise.

"You know who I am?"

"My nephew pointed you out when we rode past in our carriage one day," the matron explained calmly. "It was your brother, Lord Wentworth, who saved my nephew during that nasty little war we had."

"Yes." Maggie yelped, kept by will alone from jumping as Lord Ramsey shifted behind her, his hands sliding up the backs of her thighs, grasping them lightly to help him keep his balance. She was quite positive he had not meant to reawaken the excitement he had been stoking earlier, but it happened anyway. The fires banked but not put entirely out by the arrival of Lady Barlow now danced once more along her nerve ends. Her nipples tingled.

Cursing her body for its complete indifference to the awkwardness of this situation, Maggie forced a smile, her mind working over the fix she and Ramsey were in. She had to get rid of the woman before James was discovered in this compromising position.

Dear God, what a scandalous discovery that would be! This woman would swoon, should she find her nephew under Maggie's skirts. Stuff it, Maggie felt rather like swooning herself. She could not believe she was in this fix. How had she got here?

"Only you, Maggie." The words echoed through her mind and she groaned inwardly. Then, her face began to redden at the vivid memory of James's head disappearing between her legs. Had she really allowed a man to do such disgraceful things to her?

Oh this was horrible! One visit to a brothel and she began behaving this way? This was too much even for her.

". . . and he died in so doing."

It took Maggie a moment to grasp what the woman was talking about. Oh, yes, her brother. His bravery. Gerald had always been a special . . .

Her thoughts died as she felt Lord Ramsey nudging at her legs, trying to urge them farther apart. Was the man insane? What the devil did he think he was doing? Surely he didn't think to continue their naughtiness with his aunt right here, crossing the room toward where Maggie stood! Fear of just that made Maggie's heart race in horror. Then her ankles were grasped firmly in two hands, and she gave a startled cry as she found herself slightly lifted, overbalanced, and dumped into the chair behind her. She caught a flash of Lord Ramsey's gray coat peeking out the front of her skirt; then the chair she sat in was tugged forward and she found herself tightly against the desk. Her skirt, with Ramsey still under it, was firmly under the desk.

"Are you all right?" Lady Barlow stared at her in amazement, and Maggie forced herself to smile.

"Yes. I, er, stumbled," she lied, then bit her lip as Lord Ramsey clasped her knees with his hands. She went still, waiting a moment before she was sure he had just been looking for a more comfortable position. No doubt it was crowded under there, and hot, and . . . She didn't even want to think about it.

"Where did my nephew go?"

Maggie blinked in answer to the question, then peered at Ramsey's aunt, her hands settling nervously on James's hat. "I am not sure, my lady. He did not say." Picking up the hat, she began to turn it slowly in her hand, then stilled as Ramsey gently pinched her calf. Apparently realizing he had her attention, he clasped her ankles and lifted and lowered her feet one after the other in a parody of walking. Obviously he was trying to tell her something.

Walking? she thought with a frown. *Walking. Moving.* "Leaving!" she cried.

"What?" Lady Ramsey regarded her blankly.

"I—It occurs to me that you must be weary and thirsty after your journey. Perhaps you would be more comfortable if we moved to the salon to await your nephew? We could have tea."

"That does sound lovely," Lady Barlow agreed. She turned toward the butler, who was already heading for the door.

153

"I shall arrange for it at once, my lady," Webster said.

Lady Barlow nodded, then turned back to Maggie. "Shall we?" she asked.

"Yes, of course." Pushing her chair back, Maggie stood, pulling her skirt with her away from Lord Ramsey. She didn't dare glance down at him, but simply started around the desk and across the room as Lady Barlow moved toward the door. The woman paused before opening it and glanced back, looking as if she were going to say something. She spoke then, amusement filling her eyes. "Did you intend to bring that with you?"

Glancing down, Maggie flushed. She still held Lord Ramsey's hat gripped in her hands. She was also still wearing his cloak clasped about her neck—which was probably the only thing that had saved her from being seen earlier tugging the top of her gown into place. "Nay. I shall just put it there on the desk," she agreed, turning to do so.

Hurrying back across the room, Maggie started to set the hat on the desk, then reached to undo her cloak, only to pause when she caught sight of Ramsey's hand waving from beneath the desk. Peeking over her shoulder, she saw that Lady Barlow was waiting patiently beside the door. She knew the woman couldn't possibly have seen the waving male hand, but Maggie cast her a nervous smile anyway, then turned back toward the desk, "accidentally" knocking the hat as she did. It tumbled off the desk, landing on the floor behind it. Muttering something about being clumsy, Maggie hurried around to retrieve it, and knelt out of sight.

"You mustn't speak of your work to my aunt," Lord Ramsey whispered to her. "She has no idea what you do."

Maggie spared him an annoyed glance for thinking she would be foolish enough to mention any such thing. "Of course I won't," she whispered angrily, then snatched up the hat. Holding it up for Lady Barlow to see, she started to straighten. "Here it is. No harm done," she called. The last word came out as a gasp, for James had grabbed her hand and tugged her back behind the desk.

"And if she asks what you are doing here, simply tell her that I invited you for some rustication—a thank-you for your brother's sacrifice."

"That was my intention, my lord." Maggie seethed, tugging her hand free and raising the hat to set it on the desk. Straightening, she forced one last smile for Lady Barlow and hurried around the desk and across the room to join the other woman. "Shall we?"

She started to urge Lord Ramsey's aunt toward the door, but Lady Barlow stood firm and gave her a narrow look. For a moment Maggie thought the woman had determined something was afoot, but then she merely gestured to the garment Maggie wore around her shoulders.

Glancing down, Maggie gave a nervous laugh. "Oh, my, the cloak. No, I shan't need this indoors, shall I? I shall just leave it on the desk with the hat."

She turned away, but before she could cross the room, Lady Barlow caught her arm. Then she called out calmly in an overly loud voice, "I shall just wait in the salon."

Maggie glanced at her sharply, alarm coursing through her at Lady Barlow's crafty expression. Pulling the door open, the woman called out, "Do not be too long, dear." Then she slammed the door.

Eyes wide, Maggie opened her mouth to say something, *anything* to warn Lord Ramsey of his aunt's trick, but Lady Barlow's hand was suddenly over her mouth. All Maggie could do was watch helplessly as the chair behind the desk screeched its way back across the floor.

"That was a close one," Ramsey murmured, brushing his suit jacket down as he straightened. Then he turned to look about for Maggie. He froze when he spied her and his aunt by the door. Maggie tried to convey her apologies with her eyes—just in case his aunt's hand over her mouth was not enough assurance that she had wished to warn him.

There was a bare moment of silence, then Lady Barlow removed her hand from Maggie's mouth. The woman propped both hands firmly on her hips and her disapproving eyes settled on her nephew. "I am shocked, James! Just shocked! And ashamed. How could you possibly take advantage of an innocent in your care? And she's the very sister of the man who saved your life then asked, with his dying breath, that you look after her. Is this how you repay his valiant act?"

"Oh, really, my lady, this is not all his fault," Maggie exclaimed, rushing to defend him. Lord Ramsey was presently squirming with guilt under his aunt's righteous indignation. Maggie's attempted defense obviously helped him past his finer feelings. Straightening, he nodded and said, "She's is right. This isn't as bad as it appears. She isn't as innocent as you may think."

Maggie's gasp was matched by Lady Barlow's. Both women gaped at Ramsey in horror at his unchivalrous words. He immediately attempted to soothe them. "I just mean that Maggie—er, Margaret—is not some young child who needs protecting," he said to his aunt, then started around the desk toward them. "She is a full grown—" He paused uncertainly when his aunt made a strangled sound.

Maggie glanced at the woman with concern, then followed her attention to James's fawn-colored trousers—mostly fawn-colored trousers, she corrected with mounting horror. Dear God! There was a very distinct handprint on his groin.

Glancing down, himself, James gave a choked gasp and promptly covered the spot with both hands. "I, er . . ." His gaze shot to Maggie, then away. "I spilled the ink," he excused himself, backing around the desk until it hid that portion of his body from view. Clearing his voice then, he asked, "Now, where was I? Oh, yes. Maggie. She is a full . . . er . . . grown, red-blooded woman.

"Blue-blooded!" Lady Barlow snapped, apparently recovered from her shock. "She is a full grown lady of nobility. She deserves more respect than this. In fact, she *deserves* a proposal."

Maggie supposed she shouldn't have been stunned by those unexpected words, but she was. And James appeared to be, too. He also looked horrified. The man had turned a sickly shade of gray-green she had never seen before, and Maggie felt her heart slip down into the vicinity of her borrowed shoes. She had told herself not be attracted to him. She had known that there could be no future with a man who thought so poorly of her career choice. But that was before their shared passion here in the library. To see him cringe now in such blatant aversion at the very suggestion of marriage to her . . . She felt shame overwhelm her.

"Oh, now . . ." James held up his hands and gave an

extremely nervous laugh. "There is no need to, er . . . You cannot expect me to . . ." He paused and turned to the door with relief as another knock sounded. "Yes?"

Lady Barlow's tug on her arm was the only thing that kept Maggie from being hit by the opening door. The older woman moved to the side, taking Maggie with her, then the butler addressed James from behind the door now hiding them from view.

"Oh, you are back, my lord. There is a man here to see you. He says it is quite urgent."

"Aye. It is," another voice interrupted shortly. "Very urgent, and very private."

"Johnstone!" James was shocked to see the man. And not entirely happy, either, Maggie noted with disinterest. He glanced from the visitor to Margaret and his aunt.

"Aye, m'lord," the other man said, then addressed Webster. "Ye see, he does know me, and he really needs to hear what I have to say, so ye can be back about yer business. A short, stout man's back appeared; apparently Johnstone was being forced to slide past the butler to get into the room.

"Very well," Webster said slowly, not sounding entirely sure of himself.

Sighing in relief as the door closed behind the butler, the other man turned to Lord Ramsey and promptly crossed the room. He obviously didn't see Maggie and Lady Barlow, and blurted, "We've made a terrible mistake, my lord. Just terrible."

"Johnstone, I do not think this is the time—" James began, furtively looking to where his aunt and Maggie still stood by the door, but the man didn't let him finish.

"You will when you hear this. Lady Margaret isn't Lady X after all!"

"What?" Lord Ramsey's startled yelp evidently covered the gasps of both women, and Mr. Johnstone didn't hear them. The man stopped before the desk, nodding his head. "It's true. She isn't. Lady X is still at the brothel, working. Lady Margaret wasn't there to 'ply the trade.' She was—"

"You thought I was Lady X?" Maggie shrieked. Her pain of a moment before turned to outrage.

Ramsey's eyes shot to her and widened, but Maggie started furiously forward, his outraged aunt on her heels. Apparently Johnstone's announcement had scattered James's thoughts; he gave her a look as if he didn't know who she was. Mr. Johnstone, of course, hadn't known she was there. The man turned to gape at her in horror.

"Oh, now, Margaret," Lord Ramsey began apologetically.

"You thought I was a prostitute?" Maggie repeated coldly as she stopped before him.

"Well, you *were* in a brothel," he pointed out reasonably. Maggie stiffened. She narrowed her eyes, then offered James a rather empty smile.

"Oh, of course. Perfect reasoning, my lord. And so were you. Are you a prostitute, too, then?" she asked caustically. Widening her eyes as if in surprise she cried, "But wait! I was in a men's club last week. Does that make me a man? Oh! And I fell into the river once. Does that make me a fish? And what if I go into the stables, does that make me a horse? Or a stableboy?" She screwed up her mouth with displeasure. It was the

159

only warning she gave before she yanked her skirts up and kicked him in the shin. Hard.

Cursing, Ramsey grabbed for the injured appendage with one hand and began hopping up and down even as he reached out toward her with the other. "I—"

"I do not wish to hear it, my lord. There is nothing to say. This explains *everything*." Turning on her heel, she sailed angrily across the library, only to pause abruptly at the door when Webster appeared there. Lord Mullin was at his side. Ignoring the butler, Maggie turned abruptly on Ramsey's unsuspecting neighbor.

"I suppose you thought I was Lady X, too?"

"Oh, well," Robert stammered, then fell into silent bewilderment as he realized the meaning behind her question. When Maggie propped her hands on her hips and began to angrily tap one foot, he managed to shake himself out of his stupefied state and ask, "You mean, you aren't?"

James could have told his friend that would be the wrong answer, but the other man learned soon enough; Maggie tugged up her skirts and kicked him in the shin. As she had done to him, she left Robert cursing and hopping about on one foot, then pushed past an amazed Webster to storm straight across the hall to the salon. She slammed its door behind her with a crack loud enough that James was sure it was heard in every corner of the manor.

He straightened slowly with a wince to stand on both legs again, and glanced at his aunt. She peered from him to the closed door across the hall, then back again, her expression one of gross disapproval.

"Now, Aunt Viv—" he began, determined to redeem himself in her eyes, but instead let out a curse as his relative, too, wrenched up her skirts and kicked him in the shin. Leaving him imitating a stork once more, the woman whooshed across the library to the door. Lord Mullin had learned his lesson by that point, and was quick to limp out of her way. She stormed out of the room.

"Are ye all right, m' lord?" Johnstone asked, moving to James's side with concern. James rubbed his abused shin in an effort to ease the pain there, then waved the man off. He limped around his desk to drop into his seat.

"Ye might want some ice on that, m' lord. They both gave ye quite a wollop. Shall I fetch yer butler back to find ye some?"

"Back?" James glanced up to see that Webster had apparently decided it behooved him to vacate the scene. Robert, on the other hand, had come up to the desk. He wasn't looking too pleased.

"No," James told Johnstone, waving away the suggestion of fetching Webster back with ice. Ignoring his friend's irritation for a minute, he felt below his kneecap with a wince. Damn; both women had managed to hit the exact same spot! And they hadn't held back in the kicking, either. He was definitely going to have a bruise from this business. Which reminded him of the matter in question.

He asked the runner, "If she isn't Lady X, what was she doing at the brothel?"

"She was there to interview Madame Dubarry's girls for an article," Johnstone explained. At Ramsey's sharp glance he added, "She is G. W. Clark."

"G. W. Clark!"

James gave up on his leg and sank back weakly in his

seat. His eyes went to Lord Mullin, who had just spoken, then passed him to settle on the still-open door of the library. His aunt was standing outside the salon, apparently hesitating to intrude on an upset Maggie's flight. Her delay had allowed her to overhear Johnstone's announcement, and she was now gaping at them in shock. Realizing James had spotted her, she turned abruptly and entered the salon, banging the door shut behind her.

"Aye." Johnstone's voice drew James's attention back. The Bow Street runner was smiling crookedly. "It took me by surprise, too."

"Are you sure?" James asked with a frown. "I mean, there is no mistake? You were so sure before that she was Lady X."

The runner grimaced apologetically. "I know, m' lord, and I apologize for me error. However, all the facts did seem to point that way, if ye'll recall, and even you believed it. Then, when you found her in that sheer red gown, her full, round breasts visible right through it—"

"I recall, Johnstone," James interrupted curtly. He also recalled that the man had been taken with the gown and all it revealed. "That did convince me she was Lady X. The mask didn't hurt, either."

"Aye. And she didn't even have any bloomers on. Her lower half was—"

"Johnstone!" James snapped, killing the gleam in the other man's eye. He then turned his wrath on a chuckling Robert, not appreciating his friend's amusement at all. Once the other man managed to curb his laughter, James turned back to the runner. "All of that being the case, how can you be so sure she is not Lady X now?"

The man shifted uncomfortably, then straightened his shoulders and reported, "Ah, well . . . the afternoon after you left for here with her, there was quite a titter about Lady X. It seems she had a rather nasty little tantrum and refused to see any more customers after Lord Hastings. I thought it was a cover for the fact that she was missing, thinking Lady Margaret was Lady X as I did. But then the news got out that Dubarry was able to soothe her by offering more money. X was back in business by that night.

"Well, I thought sure *that* news was wrong—since you were supposed to have her. So, I went to Dubarry's to see what was what." The runner grimaced. "The old broad wasn't pleased to see me, as you can imagine. It seems your not showing up for your allotted half hour was part of the reason for Lady X's snit. But I handed her some cash—it's in this bill here. . . ." He paused to retrieve a piece of paper and hand it to James, then quickly continued as James scowled at the amount in question. "Anyway, I greased old Dubarry's palm, and she let me talk to a couple of the girls. There was one named Maisey. I suspected she had some information I might use, and I took her up for a roundabout and learned from her that G. W. Clark had interviewed her and the other girls the night before.

"She was rather proud of the fact, really, eager to announce that G. W. Clark was a lady of the nobility. She said that a visit by the lady in question's betrothed made her sneak out the window in disguise, and that they had switched clothes. She showed me the gown Lady Margaret traded her, and I recognized it as the one Lady Margaret had been wearing when she entered the brothel. When I asked her what the lady had obtained of hers, she said one of her best sheer red nighties—and a red mask. Had anyone seen the lady, Maisey said, they would have been sure she was Lady X. She thought it a grand joke."

"You learned this last night?" James asked sharply. "Why didn't you ride out here at once with the news?"

"Well, after the last debacle, I wanted to be right certain, didn't I?" Johnstone shifted uncomfortably. "So, after I finished with Maisey I hung about hoping to catch a glimpse of Miss X, herself. I stood in the shadows of the hall forever. It wasn't until her last client left that I caught a glimpse of her. She *was* wearing a red mask, but it weren't plain like that one Lady Wentworth had on. It had fancy feathers and whatnot all over it." He paused to shake his head dolefully.

"I should have realized that someone as successful as Lady X would have more expensive duds. I'm usually good with such details." He heaved a breath at missing what he considered to be a telling detail, then continued, "At any rate, with the mask and all, I couldn't see her features—but I *could* see that she was definitely shorter than Lady Wentworth. She is also a lot . . . fuller." He gestured to his chest area. "Up top. Cannonballs, m'lord—in comparison to Lady Wentworth's apples, if ye know what I mean."

James scowled. He didn't care for the lady's chest being referred to as apples. Especially not when he'd had a taste of them.

"Apples with cinnamon, hmm?" Lord Mullin murmured with obvious amusement. It drew James's irritation away from the runner. He glared at his friend, greatly regretting the way he had ranted on about Maggie's nipples the night before. Dear Lord, he had been describing her in great detail, and she was a lady. *Oh, hell!*

Closing his eyes, he rubbed his forehead, frustration overwhelming him. This was the last thing he'd expected. It was bad enough when he'd thought he had promised to look after a lady of ill-repute, but now to have kidnapped, then ravished her, as he very nearly had, only to learn she wasn't a lady of ill repute at all . . . Why, it was scandalous! He had acted horribly. Gentlemen did not behave so.

"G. W. Clark," he muttered, his mind running over the conversations he'd had with Maggie earlier. Lady Margaret, he corrected himself sternly. She had said she'd met Lady Dubarry through her brother indirectly, that he himself had quite enjoyed the way she was now making her living.

At the time, James had thought she meant Gerald enjoyed the pleasures offered by the ladies of the brothel—just as he had thought she enjoyed plying the trade. This news cast a different color on things. He could recall that the man was forever writing letters, either to his sister or his man of affairs.

James had read G. W. Clark's articles with great interest and amusement before the war, but not during. He'd heard Clark had gone off to fight, too, and had continued writing, basing his articles on his wartime experiences. James had not been able to obtain those articles published while he was away, but he now suspected that if he had, he would have recognized many of the stories.

Maggie had obviously continued them after Gerald's death, effectively taking his place. What a clever little minx she was, he decided, his mind going over the scandalous articles of late. "A Night with the Rakehells," had been one of them. It had caused quite a stir among the men and women of the ton to have so many of their naughty little secrets published. How the devil had she managed that? Obviously she had either paid for the information, or she had disguised herself and infiltrated the clubs. The clever little puss.

Lord Mullin's sudden clearing of his throat reminded James that he had been seated, lost in thought, for a goodly portion of time. Gathering himself, he rose abruptly to his feet. Starting around his desk, he said, "I will settle your account in a moment, Johnstone. In the meantime, why don't you have a drink? You must be thirsty after your journey here. Robert, show him where the port is, please."

"Certainly," Robert answered. "But, James?"

Irritated with this delay, James paused in the door to glance back. "Yes? What is it?"

"I was just wondering why your aunt is angry? I realize Margaret is upset at our mistaking her for Lady X, but why did your aunt kick you? Could it be that you were caught red-handed . . . Or should I say black-handed?" he added, his gaze dropping.

James didn't bother to look down. He knew Robert was referring to the handprint on his groin and—despite the guilty flush now suffusing his face—he stood a little straighter. "I knocked the inkwell over."

"Did you?" Robert asked. For the first time, James realized Robert wasn't simply annoyed with him over the mistaken identity business; he was furious. Which became clear as the man continued, "I don't know, it looks like a handprint to me. A woman's hand. You are the investigator, Johnstone; what do you think?"

"I noticed Lady Margaret's hand was ink-covered," the runner answered quietly.

"So did I. She does seem to have a tendency to muck her hands up a bit, doesn't she, James? Oh! What is that I hear?"

James frowned at his friend's sarcastic tone. "I don't know. What is it?"

"Wedding bells, I should hope."

James winced at his friend's harsh tone, but merely turned away and crossed the hall to the library. It was the second mention of marriage in less than an hour. His aunt and Robert both seemed to think he should marry the girl. Marriage to Maggie.

He let that thought touch his mind, then quickly pushed it away to be considered later. First things first, he told himself. At the moment, he wasn't even sure she would speak to him. He suspected it was going to take a lot of swift talking to get her to that stage, and he supposed he had better get to it.

Straightening, he took a deep breath then opened the door and stepped into the salon. His mouth was already open, ready to spew the first "I'm sorry" as he glanced around the room in search of the two women. It closed just as quickly when he realized that the salon was empty. Both women were gone.

"Webster!" He called, turning away and starting to the hall. "Webster!"

Chapter Nine

Maggie was muttering under her breath. Most of that muttering was about Lord Ramsey, of course. He had thought her a prostitute, for heaven's sake! And so had Lord Mullin. They had thought her Lady X!

Well, all right, so she had been wearing a red mask and that horrid see-through red gown on their first meeting. And, okay, so that first acquaintance had taken place in the hallway, outside a boudoir of a brothel. Still, did she look like a prostitute?

Apparently she did.

And, she supposed, she had behaved no better than one today, allowing him to take such scandalous liberties with her. It was no wonder he'd been horrified at the idea of marrying her. She'd behaved no better than a tart and who wanted a tart to wife?

She flushed with a combination of shame and remembered passion as she recalled those heated moments in the library. His caresses had been liquid fire on her skin, and his kisses . . . Maggie could almost feel his lips moving over her breasts now, closing over her nipples, brushing up her thighs, nibbling at—

"You have gone quite flushed. Are you overly warm?"

The question was as effective as a pail of icy water being poured over her head. Maggie sat upright at once. Her expression stiffened, her eyes shooting to the plump, elderly woman seated across from her. Lady Barlow. Lord Ramsey's aunt.

Maggie had sailed out of the library, into the salon, and straight through, using the glass doors that led out onto the terrace overlooking the gardens to exit the room and the house itself. She had hurried for the stables, then—with every intention of stealing a damn horse if she must—to make her escape from Ramsey. Her only thought had been to quickly get as far away as she could from the site of this humiliation.

She had been so furious and caught up in her scattered thoughts that she hadn't realized that Lady Barlow—noting her absence from the salon and espying her furious flight for the stables—was hurrying after her. The older woman had caught up halfway between the house and Maggie's destination. When the woman had grabbed her arm, drawing her to a halt and asking anxiously where she was going, Maggie had not even hesitated to admit her intention.

Lady Barlow had hesitated, her gaze moving between Maggie and the house; then her expression had firmed. She'd turned Maggie around, urging her back the way they had come. But instead of marching her back into the salon, she had urged her past the glass doors and around the building to a carriage parked in the drive of

Ramsey mansion. The carriage they were sitting in now.

Lady Barlow's footmen had been in the process of unloading several large, ungainly chests from the top of her vehicle, but the woman had ordered them replaced, announcing that she would not be staying after all. They would return to London at once.

The panting, sweating men had goggled briefly between their mistress and the half dozen trunks they had just managed to heft down, then had grumbled as they set to replacing them. Satisfied, Lady Barlow had urged Maggie into the coach. The two had waited silently while the vehicle shook and rolled slightly as all the chests were returned to the top and strapped down. Neither relaxed until everything had been put back in place and the carriage set out, rolling away from Ramsey. They had ridden in silence until now.

"Thank you, no. I am quite comfortable, my lady." Maggie managed a smile for the old woman across from her. Lady Barlow *looked* like an aunt, she decided. One of those soft, round, sweet-faced older ladies who would spoil her nieces and nephews, children, and grandchildren equally. She was probably kind to everyone, Maggie thought and felt dismay rumble through her as she realized the woman had heard everything. Lady Barlow knew that James had mistaken Maggie for a prostitute, and not just any prostitute, but the infamous Lady X. It was anyone's guess what the older woman thought of this whole debacle.

Lord Ramsey's aunt cleared her throat. "Are you really really G. W. Clark?"

Maggie gave a start. "What? How . . . did you know?"

"I overheard that Mr. Johnstone person tell my

nephew so, just before I entered the salon and found you gone."

"I see." Maggie shrugged. She supposed Lady Barlow's knowing was no worse than James's knowing. "Yes. I am G. W. Clark."

"Oh," the older woman said happily, her face brightening. "I have read every one of your articles. They are marvelous. So interesting and entertaining and—" She shook her head. "I can hardly fathom that you are a woman."

Maggie's mouth quirked, though she told herself she wasn't offended by the comment. No doubt most people would be shocked to learn that the intrepid G. W. Clark was a woman. No one would expect the reporter who wrote exposés on several of the most popular men's clubs, gambling hells, and brothels to be a female.

"How do you get your information, my dear? My goodness, those articles on the experiences of war . . . Well, they were so detailed. So realistic. One would almost believe you had actually been there, in the midst of the madness and the fighting, smelling the stench of charred and rotting flesh, hearing the screams of the injured and the moans of the dying."

"Yes, well, my brother wrote those. He was the original G. W. Clark. I have only taken over since his death."

"Ah." Lady Barlow nodded. "You are quite good. I did not even notice a difference in the writing."

"I try to stay as close to my brother's style as I can," Maggie explained. "I did not wish anyone to be aware of the fact that any sort of change had taken place, so I studied his work carefully before I attempted to draft my first article. I even had to write and rewrite it several times before it was quite perfect. Actually, maintaining his voice is the hardest part; gathering the information is a breeze in comparison."

"Really?" Lord Ramsey's aunt asked with fascination, then beamed. "I must say, I quite enjoy the articles. Everyone does. They are quite the talk of the ton."

"Thank you," Maggie said with real pleasure. This was the first time she had received comment on her work. It was one of the problems with writing incognito: one did not receive praise for one's endeavors. Oh certainly one heard others' thoughts in a secondhand sort of manner, when one came across the topic at teas or such, but . . .

"Good Lord!"

Maggie focused on the woman across from her in concern. The matron's eyes had widened in a sort of horror. "Is there something wrong, my lady?"

"No. Yes. I just realized . . . That article, my dear, on what men get up to in the lesser gambling establishments, exposing the tricks and traps Drummond was using to rob them blind? It was published after your brother's death, but surely you did not—"

"Yes," Maggie interrupted with a sigh. "I did visit Drummond's establishment a time or two."

"But . . . how?"

"I disguised myself as a servant and slipped inside."

"They have female servants in those . . . places?"

"Certainly," Maggie informed her promptly. Then, beginning to feel a bit uncertain, she added, "Well, the two I went to did, at any rate." It had never occurred to her that they might not, and things had gone without a hitch—other than an unpleasant moment or two where clients had been overly friendly to the servant they thought her. She'd had to be quick to avoid the gropings and such, but she had handled it well enough. Her surprise at the rudeness of men in such places had quickly faded.

"So . . . how did my nephew come to the mistaken conclusion that you are the infamous Lady X?"

"You know her?" Maggie asked.

"Of her, yes. Everyone in London has heard the whispers." The woman tilted her head. "Is that what your next article is about? Exposing Lady X?"

"No!"

"Whyever not, my dear? All of London is a-twitter about that woman. Exposing her would be quite a coup."

Maggie frowned at the suggestion. "I do not like to go after individuals. I do not wish to harm anyone."

Lady Barlow's eyebrows shot up. "But, my dear, what was that article on Drummond, if not an attack on an individual?"

"Yes," Maggie agreed. "But that was because he was ruining the unsuspecting. He served them alcohol with laudanum, then robbed them blind with his crooked tables. He had to be stopped. Men were losing whole fortunes. But Lady X . . . well, she is hurting no one except perhaps herself. Besides, having to make a living in a less-than-approved fashion myself, I cannot look down on how she does it. Nay." She shook her head firmly. "Even did I know her identity, it would be safe in my keeping."

"Oh." Lady Barlow looked terribly disappointed. She had apparently rather hoped for such an article. She got over it quickly, though, and sat up a little straighter, a determined expression entering her eyes. "So tell me then, if you are not investigating Lady X, how did my foolish nephew come to the mistaken conclusion that you were she?"

"Oh." Maggie flushed. "Well, while I was not investigating Lady X, I *was* investigating brothels in general—and Madame Dubarry's ladies in particular. I thought it would be interesting to find out what men sought there and how the girls themselves feel about it."

Amusement curved the older woman's face. "Well, my dear, what the men seek there is really rather obvious, is it not? My, you are naive, aren't you?" she added when Maggie became flustered. "Five minutes in your company should have been more than enough to disabuse my nephew of his foolishness. Unless . . ." Her eyes widened incredulously. "Never tell me that you dressed as a servant and went to Dubarry's."

"Nay," Maggie assured the matron quickly. "Actually, I wore a black gown and thick black veil to interview the, er, ladies. But I fear there was some small difficulty getting out." Then Maggie reluctantly explained about Maisey hiding her in the cupboard and her own attempt to escape, only to be forced to hide by Frances's arrival, then Maisey's extortion of her dress.

Lady Barlow was laughing so hard by the time Maggie finished, there were tears in her eyes. "Oh dear. Well, I suppose James can be forgiven his initial mistake. Still, it should not have taken him long to sort it out once to Ramsey. And I must say, my dear, you took a horrible risk with your reputation."

"Yes," Maggie agreed. "I am always taking horrible risks with my reputation for these articles. However, I . . ."

Lady Barlow seemed to guess her dilemma. "Surely your brother left you well settled?"

Maggie grimaced. "He willed me his town house in London and enough money that, combined with what my mother bequeathed me on her death, if invested carefully, I could live the rest of my life quite comfortably. Frugally, but comfortably. Unfortunately, it is not enough to keep all the staff, and when it comes to deciding who to let go, I simply cannot do it."

"Ah, yes, that can be difficult." Lady Barlow nodded sympathetically. "In the end, that sort of decision comes down to necessity."

"I rather thought so, too," Maggie admitted. "So I cannot get rid of any of them."

The older lady blinked. "How so, dear?"

"Well, Banks—he is the butler and man of affairs, and he has served our family forever. He is too old to find work elsewhere, yet too young to retire. His job is very necessary to him, so I cannot release him. And Cook, well, she has children to support. She is a widow, you see, so I cannot put her out. The housekeeper is alone as well. Her job is very necessary to her well-being. Then there is Mary, my maid, and . . . Why, we grew up together! She is planning on marrying John, the stable lad. Well, I suppose he is too old now to call a lad, but they depend upon the wages, and as they plan to marry, I could not possibly put either of them out. And of course there are Mary's sisters, Joan and Nora. They are housemaids. I could hardly keep Mary but throw her sisters out! The three were orphaned around the same time as I was and must rely upon me now. Their little brother, Charles, works in the stables with John, and I can hardly release him and split up the family, you see?

So it is all a matter of necessity. They all need their jobs. And it falls on me to be sure they each have one."

Lady Barlow stared, aghast, through her explanation, then blurted, "But, my dear, if you cannot afford them—"

"That isn't *their* fault, and they are all excellent workers," Maggie announced firmly.

"Well, yes . . . But you could give them a good reference. Perhaps help them find alternate positions."

"Oh, I could not do that," Maggie exclaimed with horror. "It would be like splitting up a family. These servants were all originally at our country estate. When our parents died, Gerald purchased the town house and decided to spend most of his time there. He handpicked the staff he would take with him. I grew up with all these people. Why, Banks was our butler in the country. He used to trip over my toys when I was a tot. And Cook used to sneak me sweets. And . . . Well, I grew up with Mary. They are family."

"I see," Lady Barlow murmured. Her forehead crinkled in agitation.

"Yes. I must keep them all together. And writing for the *Express* has allowed me to do that. It is the only way," Maggie said with certainty.

Lord Ramsey's aunt eyed her consideringly, then asked in a gentle voice, "Your brother was the last of your family, my dear, wasn't he?"

"Aye. Other than my cousin."

"Your cousin?"

"Victor. He inherited Gerald's title and Clarendon, the country estate, since it was the seat of the title," Maggie explained.

"Ah." Lady Barlow nodded, then asked delicately,

"Could he not assist you? Perhaps he could take some of the servants back to the estate."

"Hmmm. I have thought of that. And he might be able to help. If they ever find him."

"Find him? Is he lost?"

"He went to America to make his fortune. The solicitor has men out looking for him, but it takes a while, you understand."

"Ahhh," Lady Barlow mused. Then she asked curiously, "If he isn't found, or isn't interested, or is found to be dead, would you inherit?"

"I am not sure. The title has always gone to the next male."

"Yes, but that is rather antiquated, my dear. After all, Elizabeth ruled the English throne for fifty years some two hundred years ago."

"Aye, but she was an exception. She never married and so was able to keep her power. Had she married, most of the power would have gone to her husband."

"It didn't go to Mary's Philip."

"He was a foreigner. We could hardly have had a Spanish king of England," Maggie pointed out. "Had she married a solid English cousin, things would have been different."

"Well, perhaps," Lord Ramsey's aunt conceded. "Men are so foolish with their laws."

"Hmm. Terribly greedy about power, are they not? I often wonder what they fear will happen when we gain it."

"That we should prove ourselves smarter than them, of course."

Her eyes wide, Maggie swallowed a bubble of nervous laughter that Lady Barlow did not miss.

"You doubt me? It is true. God gifted men with greater physical strength, but balanced it out by granting us greater intelligence." Spotting Maggie's doubtful expression, she asked, "Which creature would you say is physically stronger—the cat or the dog?"

"The dog. Well, most dogs."

"Which is smarter?"

"The cat."

"Just so."

"Oh?" Maggie felt uncertain. "Are you saying that men are dogs and women are cats?"

"Basically, yes, dear. Men are big, dumb creatures who lope about with their tongues hanging out. Nothing more ambitious on their minds than sniffing any likely bitch's behind."

Choking with scandalized amusement, Maggie covered her mouth. "And women?" she got out after a moment of struggling with her intense need to laugh.

"Well, I don't know about you, but I have encountered some pretty catty women in my time," Lady Barlow confided.

They both burst out laughing. Their mutual amusement faded after a moment; then the two sank back in their respective seats with small sighs.

Maggie eyed the older woman with fascination for a moment, then asked, "Do you count your nephew as a stupid dog, too?"

Lady Barlow's mouth puckered sourly. "The man who thought you a prostitute?"

Maggie was silent for a moment, then, much to her own amazement, found herself defending him. "That was not entirely without good cause. I was rather dressed up as one, and in a brothel, when he met me."

Lady Barlow made a face. "Oh, yes. No doubt he could be excused for it at first, but you were in his home for . . . How long was it? Two days?"

"Four days, actually, but only two with him in attendance."

"Plenty long enough for him to have realized that there was something wrong with his assessment. Of course, he might have been investigating further from what I saw."

"You saw?" Maggie echoed in a squeak of alarm.

The older lady smiled wryly. "I saw enough to know what was going on. Your hair was disheveled, your lips swollen, your eyes slightly glazed, and your gown off your shoulder . . . It was gaping open in front when Webster opened the door to the library to announce me! You recovered with commendable aplomb, though," she added to ease Maggie's mortification. "But did you really think that I wouldn't notice that my nephew was skulking around under your skirts . . . Or that I might believe it was for some *good* purpose?"

"You knew that, too?" Maggie asked in horror. She had rather hoped the woman thought he'd been skulking under the desk, not her skirts.

"Your state of dishabille and horrified glance downward were rather telling, my dear. Then, of course, when he crawled under the desk, I could see his feet and ankles." There was a brief pause, then the old woman finished, "I won't even mention that you left your fingerprints behind . . . quite literally."

Maggie bit her lip and glanced down at her knotted hands. She glanced up again only when Lady Barlow reached over to pat those hands reassuringly. "There is nothing to be ashamed of, my dear. It is obvious to me

179

that, despite your adventurous career as G. W. Clark, you are quite naive when it comes to men. Your reactions have convinced me that you are still quite innocent. James, on the other hand, is anything but. He is quite experienced, and old enough to know better. Then again, he is a man, and men, like dogs, are easily distracted."

"Distracted?" Maggie asked in confusion.

"Yes. They can be the best of guard dogs one moment; then a pussy goes streaking across the lawn and off they go—tongue hanging out, ears flopping, caught up in the chase."

Maggie was silent for a moment as the image of Lord Ramsey rose in her mind. He was on his knees before her, his head burrowed between her legs. Then he lifted his head and smiled up at her, his features pointed and canine, his tongue lolling, his ears suddenly floppy dog ears.

"Dear God," she said under her breath; blinking her eyes open to see Lady Barlow's amused expression.

"I can tell that you have noticed the resemblance. Never mind, my dear. He shall behave himself from now on. I shall see to it. After all, I too am grateful to your brother for saving my nephew's sorry hide, and I feel I owe it to him to look out for you."

Maggie smiled a little uncertainly at those words. It seemed she suddenly had no end of people wanting to look out for her.

She wasn't at all sure that was a good thing.

"It would appear that your aunt decided not to stay after all," Webster announced, his face expressionless. "She had her trunks reloaded and left. Lady Margaret went with her."

"Damn." James plopped into his desk chair at his butler's announcement. He had set the servants to the task of finding Margaret as soon as he'd discovered her missing. He had not been as concerned with his aunt's whereabouts. Now he knew where they both were, and his heart sank. Either woman was trouble enough on her own; together, the Lord alone knew what they might get up to.

Wincing at the possibilities, he considered the matter briefly, then stood. "I am returning to the city, Webster. See to the arrangements," he ordered.

After the man left to do as he was told, James turned to Johnstone. "You had best tell me everything you have learned about Lady Margaret. And about her writing as G. W. Clark."

Chapter Ten

The day was gray and gloomy, the overcast skies threatening rain. *Suitable*, Maggie thought irritably. It matched her mood. She should have been rather pleased with herself. She had entrusted her article on the brothel to her butler, Banks. He had delivered it to the *Daily Express* the day after her return.

As usual, Mr. Hartwick had read the article at once so that any editorial comments or revision requests could be returned via Banks. Much to her pleasure, the butler arrived home with the news that Mr. Hartwick was well satisfied. No changes were necessary, and the article would be in the next installment of the *Express*. That did gladden Maggie; however, it was the only thing that was going right of late.

It had been four days since she had returned from her imprisonment at the Ramsey estate. Maggie had spent most of that time alternately doing her best to avoid

Pastor Frances and visiting every dress shop in London in search of a replacement for the sheer red nightie that Maisey had loaned her.

Much to her consternation, Maggie had thoughtlessly left the item behind when she had fled Ramsey. This was the second fruitless day she had spent trying to replace it: a terribly embarrassing effort. Snickers and wide-eyed looks of disbelief had been the general reactions as Maggie had tried to describe the frilly see-through outfit to various modistes. With each shop she chose, she became more disheartened—and less sure that she would ever be able to succeed in the quest.

The shop she had just left, however, was the worst. The proprietress had at first been indignant upon hearing the description of the article of clothing; then she had become angry and rude. She had finally interrupted Maggie's stammerings to announce that she didn't need her "sort" in her store. The woman had then shown her out. Which was enough for Maggie. She was finally willing to concede defeat.

Perhaps it was for the best, she decided as she headed home; the garment would likely cost more to replace than she had readily available at the moment. With luck, Maisey would agree to call things even. Maggie would not request a replacement of her gown—the one Pastor Frances had torn off of the young prostitute—and she hoped that Maisey would forgo requesting the return of hers. She suspected Maisey would agree readily enough. The girl could use the money Pastor Frances had given for replacing Maggie's garment to replace her own!

Unless she's already used it to buy me a new gown.

The thought popped into her head from nowhere, and Maggie fretted over it. Maisey really was not asking too much to wish her garment returned. Surely there were special shops for such items, ones of which she was unaware.

Perhaps there was an article for G. W. Clark there, she considered as she began to cross the street. But on second thought, while she herself found the subject interesting, her readers were likely looking for subjects of a racier nature.

With her thoughts distracted as they were, Maggie didn't see the carriage coming at her. It was a shout from somewhere off to her right, toward her town house, a warning, that made her glance around. She froze in horror upon seeing the vehicle bearing down on her. Maggie could practically feel the hot breath from the horses' noses and mouths before she was grabbed forcibly and pulled out of the way.

"Are you all right?"

"Yes, yes. Thank you. I—" Maggie released a gusty breath as she turned to her rescuer, then froze. It was none other than Lord Ramsey. Wonderful!

She hadn't seen James since fleeing Ramsey manor. She had received several letters from him since her arrival home; each had been sent back unopened. She wasn't ready to read what he had to say. She could have forgiven James the insult of his mistaking her for a prostitute, after all, the circumstances surrounding their first meeting *had* been unusual. However, that humiliation had been compounded by shame at what she had let him do to her, and mortification over his reaction to the idea of marrying her. On top of that, while Maggie had defended him to his aunt during the journey to London, that was before she'd had the opportunity to mull the matter over. It had occurred to her, once home, that while Lord Ramsey had been spouting all those fine sentiments about finding her an alternate career, he hadn't passed up the opportunity to take advantage of the situation himself. She may have behaved shamefully, but he had behaved no better.

And, why hadn't he realized his mistake in believing her to be Lady X once he'd spent some time with her? Lady Barlow seemed to think he should have, and now Maggie did, too. The worst part was, despite her anger with the man—despite the insult, the shame and humiliation—just thinking about him was enough to send her pulse racing. And she couldn't stop thinking about him. The things he had done to her had been like nothing she had ever experienced. Her body had tasted ecstasy, and wanted more . . . Maggie wanted a man who had insulted and humiliated her and who, she was sure, was only now attempting to apologize because it was the "proper" thing to do and he wished to please his aunt. Which simply engendered even more shame in her. At the moment, her overriding feeling for the man was a burning resentment.

Realizing that her mouth was hanging open, Maggie closed it with a snap. "Oh, it is *you*." Turning on her heel, she rushed across the street, leaving Lord Ramsey staring after her. As she expected, it did not take long before he collected himself and hurried in pursuit.

"Maggie," he began, grabbing at her.

"I did not give you leave for such familiarity, sir," she snapped, tugging her arm loose and picking up her skirts so that she could hurry along without tripping.

"Very well, Lady Margaret, then." He sounded a bit impatient—or was it shortness of breath as he chased after her? Not that Maggie cared much.

"I fear we have not been properly introduced, my lord, and ladies do not speak to *gentlemen* to whom they have not been introduced."

James winced at the acidity of Margaret's tone as she said the word *gentlemen*, then realized that he'd paused and she was getting away. They had reached the town house she had inherited from her brother. Even now, she was pushing through the gate and starting up the short walk to the door. He rushed after her. "Very well, my lady. Please allow me to introduce myself and—"

He stopped abruptly as she sailed into her town house, slamming the door in his face with a resounding crash.

"Apologize," he finished softly. Straightening his shoulders, he rapped determinedly on the door.

It wasn't answered promptly, so he rapped again, a bit harder, then forced a pleasant smile to his face. The door opened, and out peered an elderly gentleman— one with the arrogant look of inquiry that could only be mustered by a butler of many years' experience.

"Yes?"

"Lord Ramsey to see Lady Margaret Wentworth," he announced calmly, producing his card.

The butler accepted the token but smiled blandly and murmured, "Lady Margaret is not in." He started to close the door on Lord Ramsey then, but James stuck his foot in the door.

His smile slipping, James said, "You had best check again, my good man. I know she is home. I just followed her here."

The butler's eyes narrowed superciliously, and he

shook his head. "Nevertheless, she is not *in*," he insisted, glaring at James's offending foot.

James opened his mouth to force the issue, then decided against it. He removed his foot, allowing the door to again be closed in his face. Scowling, he turned away and was pleasantly surprised to find his carriage waiting on the street outside the Wentworth gate. He had been on his way to his club when he spotted Maggie. Ordering the driver to stop, he had leaped out to approach and had nearly reached her when he noticed the runaway carriage headed her way. It was just a matter of good fortune that he'd been there at the exact moment needed to pull her out of its path. Not that she was appreciative of his saving her from being run down. The woman had made it more than clear since returning to London that she wanted nothing to do with him. She had rejected a plethora of invitations from both him and his aunt, and not responded at all to his letters.

It was obvious that Lady Maggie Wentworth had no intention of allowing him to apologize. At least not in a forthright manner, he amended, walking to his carriage.

Once there, James commended his driver for having the sense to follow him without being so ordered; then he directed him to his aunt's. As they drove away, his gaze moved over the Wentworth town house.

If she would not agree to speak to him and allow him to make amends in a forthright way, that meant he would have to use trickery. To get a few words with the woman, he would have to be devious. Much to James's amazement, he was looking forward to the challenge.

* * *

Maggie paused impatiently on the corner to allow several hacks to pass, annoyed despite herself. The day was lovely. The sun was shining, flowers were blooming, and a gentle breeze was blowing away the generally unpleasant smells of London. All of which had combined to make her decide on walking to Lady Barlow's rather than waste the money on a hack. Fortunately, the older woman's home wasn't far from her own.

She'd been invited to a ladies tea party by Lord Ramsey's aunt. Maggie had agreed to this invitation after politely making excuses to avoid the others for three reasons. First, James Huttledon might be many things, but he was not a lady; so she could be pretty sure he would not be in attendance. The second reason was quite simply that Maggie rather liked Lady Barlow. Ramsey's aunt was a charming woman, with a wonderful sense of humor, and Maggie had felt quite bad refusing her earlier invitations. The third reason Maggie was attending—despite the small risk of running into James before or after the tea—was Lord Barlow's library. James had first mentioned this colossal collection to her, but Aunt Viv—as the woman had insisted Maggie call her by the end of their journey together—had described it much more thoroughly when Maggie had shown an interest on the way back to London. The noblewoman was not as enamored of the written word as her husband had been, and still referred to it as "Lord Barlow's library," but had still shown a good deal of pride in the collection. She had described it in vivid enough detail that Maggie had been dying to see it ever since. And in a very few moments, she was going to get that opportunity.

Squelching down the excitement the thought raised

in her, she glanced along the row of townhouses, idly noting the house numbers. It was then Maggie realized that she couldn't recall Lady Barlow's address. Fortunately, she had thought to bring the invitation along. Lifting her bag, she pulled the folded piece of paper out to check. She had just started to refold the invitation when she felt a hard knock in her back.

A choked cry of surprise slipping from her lips, she threw her hands out, trying to regain her balance or grab at something to steady herself—but there was nothing there. She glanced around wildly as she found herself crashing forward into the road. Maggie spotted the oncoming track at the same moment that her foot twisted beneath her.

She fell forward and to the side, her fingers clenching instinctively around the invitation to Lady Barlow's as she thrust out her hands in an effort to break her fall. Those efforts were too slow and her fall was too hard; her head slammed down, cracking smartly on the road. Pain exploded in her head, almost but not quite blinding her to the fact that she was about to be trampled to death. As she tried to roll clear, the last thing Maggie saw were the oncoming horses rearing and kicking. The last thing she heard was their panicked screeches. Then she slid into darkness.

The murmur of voices drew Maggie from unconsciousness. Unable to understand what was being said, but vaguely recognizing that she knew at least one of the speakers, Maggie moaned and slowly opened her eyes. She winced against the pain the light caused her. Everything was blurry at first, and she closed her eyes again instinctively in an effort to clear her vision.

". . . She 'ad this 'ere invite clutched in her 'and, and I didn't know where else to take 'er. I figured leastwise you'd know 'er people and where she belonged." Maggie didn't recognize the voice that was speaking.

"Yes, yes, you did the right thing," another voice said. There was no mistaking it, and Maggie opened her eyes again slowly, confusion clouding her mind as hands gently brushed her hair from her brow and a dark face came into focus above her.

"James?" she murmured, positive she was dreaming. Or perhaps having a nightmare, she decided as she became aware of the vicious pounding in her head. She was forced to close her eyes again, for the bright daylight pouring into the room was unbearable.

"Yes. It's me. Are you all right? How is your head? You appear to have taken an awful knock."

"I did?" She couldn't recall. Squinting up at the man, she noted the concern on his face with some surprise, then glanced around as another voice spoke up.

"Yep. Ye sure did, ma'am. Near to knocked yer good sense out all over the road."

Maggie grunted and wearily closed her eyes. The speaker was not within her present field of vision, and she really didn't have the energy to sit up and search him out.

"Here you are, my lord." Maggie started at this third voice, her gaze finding a new figure looming anxiously at Lord Ramsey's side. A servant, she saw, for he wore a butler's vestments.

"Thank you, Meeks." She saw James take a cloth from the man, dip it in a small bowl, and wring it out. He turned toward Maggie. She instinctively closed her eyes as he reached to lay it gently on her forehead.

What had happened? Maggie wondered, her mind taken up with trying to understand her surroundings. *Near to knocked yer good sense all over the road*, the man had said. Reaching up worriedly, she attempted to feel her forehead, but her hand encountered only the cool, damp cloth, then was grasped in what she was sure was James's own large, warm hand. It pulled hers gently away. "Just rest for now."

"Am I bleeding?" she asked, feeling suddenly weak.

"No. But you have a nasty bump."

"What happened?"

"Do you not remember?"

"No."

"Oh, well . . ." James hesitated long enough that Maggie squinted over at him with concern, only to find that he wasn't looking at her; he was exchanging glances with the man out of her sight. Maggie tried to see the room's other occupant, but the moment she moved her head, a stabbing pain shot through it. Lying still seemed a more intelligent present course of action.

"It seems you fell while crossing the street," James volunteered.

"I did?"

"Nay," the other man spoke up then. "She didn't fall. She was pushed, I think. Right out in front of me carriage. Struck 'er 'ead real good, too, when she 'it the road. Knocked 'er right out. It's just luck, m' lady, that I was able to stop me 'orses. You were a hair away from being trampled. Still and all, ye knocked yerself something nasty. Nothing was waking ye up, neither. 'Ad you not been clutching this invite 'ere,"—he raised his hand slightly, and by tilting her head just a fraction Maggie was able to spot to her right a crumpled and muddy piece of paper: the remains of the tea invitation she had been reading when she'd been knocked into the road—"well, if it weren't for this, I don't know what I would 'ave done with ye. Couldn't just leave you there like that. It's lucky the coal man can read and saw that you was 'eaded 'ere."

Maggie managed by several small twists of her head to peer at the man speaking, her eyes widening as she recognized him and remembered. "I fell into the road." She gasped, trying to sit up, only to have another wave of pain convince her to lie still a bit longer.

"Just rest there, Maggie. It is better, I think," James said.

"Maybe for a moment or so," she agreed.

"So," James said, staring at the carriage driver. "Did you happen to see who pushed her?"

"Well . . ." The man's mouth twisted doubtfully. "It all 'appened right quick."

"You just said she was pushed. Surely you saw who pushed her?"

"Well, not really. It was the way she stumbled out into the road what made me think she was pushed. Her upper body sort of flew out, dragging her feet behind, and she looked startled and alarmed, like she wasn't happy to find herself there."

"Surely you saw something? Think, man," Lord Ramsey ordered impatiently.

The fellow's face crinkled, his eyes closing in concentration. "There were three or four people directly behind 'er, but there was one fella . . . sort of criminal-looking, if ye know what I mean. 'E had these mean eyes and a nasty scar on 'is cheek. 'E was big. Strong-looking. And 'e disappeared right quick, too.

Didn't stay to 'elp me carry 'er 'ere, either."

"Big, strong, mean eyes, and a scar," James repeated with obvious dissatisfaction.

"Aye. 'E 'ad dark 'air, too. Needed a cut in my opinion."

"Do you know anyone like that, Maggie?"

"No," Maggie said, but couldn't keep the uncertainty from her voice. She *had* seen a man with a scar somewhere ... perhaps at one of the gambling hells of which she had been writing the exposé? There were a lot of men with dark hair, though. And scarred faces were not so uncommon. . . .

"A scar on his cheek, you say?" she asked.

"Aye. A big, wide one. Looked like a burn, maybe. It was kind of a square patch a little smaller than me 'and. It covered a good portion of 'is cheek."

Maggie frowned as a face flashed in her memory: a laughing man, placing a bet, then turning so that she saw just such a puckered scar on his cheek.

"What is it?" James asked sharply, taking in her expression. "Do you know someone like that?"

"No ... I know no one like that. But I have seen someone fitting that description before, I think."

"So have I." When Maggie turned to him questioningly, James added, "The man driving the carriage that nearly ran you down two days ago was rather large and had dark hair and a scar."

Maggie stiffened. "Surely you are not thinking it was the same man? That either incident was on purpose?" When Lord Ramsey merely frowned, avoiding her eyes, alarm made her sit up despite the pain that stabbed through her brain. "Why would anyone wish to do me harm?"

James hesitated briefly, then met her gaze. "You *have* exposed a rather dastardly character or two with your artic—" His mouth snapped closed as Maggie's horrified gaze shot to the curious hack driver. He cleared his throat, then smiled widely at the man.

"We would like to thank you for your assistance in this matter, Mr. Lawrence. It was kind of you to bring Maggie to us. I realize we are taking you away from your business though."

Gripping the hack driver's arm, he led him toward the door.

Maggie watched them go and was sure she saw Lord Ramsey hand the man some money as they went. Wondering how she was to find out how much and replace it—she didn't want to be beholden to James for any reason—she slid her feet to the floor and sat up gingerly.

"Oh, my lady, maybe you should stay lying down for now," the butler Lord Ramsey had called Meeks exclaimed, catching the damp cloth as it slid from her forehead.

Forcing a smile, she started to shake her head, then breathed in sharply and hesitated. Perhaps the man was right.

"That's it," the butler said with relief as she sank back down. She glimpsed him dipping the cloth in the bowl of water, then closed her eyes. She heard him wringing it out and raised a hand self-consciously to her forehead, wincing as she brushed the lump forming there. She had barely removed her hand when the cloth was laid in place.

Opening her eyes, she glanced at Meeks, noting that his gaze had moved down her body with a small frown.

Lifting her head the tiniest bit, she followed his eyes the length of her gown. She, too, grimaced in dismay. Her head wasn't the only thing that had been damaged in the fall; her gown was ripped and covered with filth. It had been her best gown, but was now quite ruined. With the one Frances had ripped off of Maisey, her wardrobe was dwindling at a rather rapid rate.

"My lady has a tincture for headaches," the butler announced, drawing Maggie's attention away from her disrepair. "Would you take some if I got it for you?"

"I . . . Yes, I think I should be very grateful for it," she murmured. Her head really was throbbing rather fiercely. She could hardly think through the pain.

"I shall be right back, then," he assured her. She heard a rustle indicating he had left. In the quiet that closed in around her, Maggie could hear the murmur of voices from somewhere outside. She supposed it was Lord Ramsey talking to the coachman, grilling the man on every single detail of what had occurred. Concern drifted through her at the thought. As befuddled as she was, it was not very difficult to put together that he thought the other day's near-miss was connected to this accident. She personally found it a bit hard to believe. Accidents happened all the time. She, of all people, knew that.

Only you, Maggie. Only you could get yourself into such a fix.

A soft footfall warned her that she was no longer alone, and Maggie opened her eyes. Espying Meeks moving to her side with a bottle and spoon, she removed the cloth from her head and eased into a sitting position. The butler opened his bottle and poured a quantity of its contents into the spoon. When he moved it toward her lips, Maggie automatically opened her mouth, feeling like a child. A second spoonful of Lady Barlow's tincture followed, and Maggie took that as well, then offered a slightly embarrassed, if grateful, smile to the man. "Thank you," she said as he recapped the lid.

"You are more than welcome, my lady. Shall I freshen that cloth for you?" he asked, setting the tincture aside.

Maggie hesitated, then shook her head. "Thank you, no. I think it has done all it can."

For a moment she thought he would insist, but then he nodded and held out his hand. When Maggie handed over the cloth, he set it down beside the bowl, then looked toward the door. She suspected he didn't wish to leave her unattended, and was touched by his concern. It was surprising that Lady Barlow herself hadn't yet come to check on her, but Maggie supposed she was busy with the guests of her tea party.

She peered down at her ruined gown and sighed inwardly. A cup of tea would be heavenly now, something sweet to settle her nerves. She seemed to be all a-tremble after her calamity, and knew that chamomile with extra honey would help. However, she could hardly join Lady Barlow and the other guests looking the way she did at the moment.

"You said that you saw that man before. It wouldn't happen to have been at Drummond's gaming hell, would it?" Lord Ramsey's voice rang out.

Maggie turned her attention away from her ruined gown to watch as the man returned to the room, his expression grim.

"I am not sure," she admitted slowly. "It was at one of the gaming hells, I think."

He nodded, as if he had expected that answer, and she saw he was putting two and two together. From the look on his face, he was coming up with his own version of four. James certainly seemed to like to think the worst of her. First she was a prostitute, and now she was the sort to engender murder in the heart of some nasty scarred man.

Maggie scowled at him. Meeks's tincture was taking effect already, the ache in her head slowly receding, but unfortunately her irritation with the know-it-all before her was rising. What the devil was Lord Ramsey doing here, anyway? This was supposed to be a ladies' tea. And he was definitely no lady—the proof of which had been pressed against her quite intimately in his library in the country.

Grimacing at her thoughts, she turned abruptly to the butler. "Could you ask Lady Barlow to join us for a moment?"

Meeks turned a blank expression to her. "Lady Barlow?" he echoed.

"Aye. I should like to offer my apologies for having to miss her tea party before I leave."

"Tea party?" the man murmured, obviously at a loss.

"It is all right, Meeks. You may get back to your duties," Lord Ramsey butted in.

Maggie turned from the confused man to James, but waited until the servant had left before speaking again. "Lord Ramsey," she said shortly. "Where is your aunt?"

Chapter Eleven

"Lord Ramsey."

James didn't answer at once, but glanced a bit wildly around the room, wondering how he was going to get himself out of this one. It had seemed such a good idea to trick her into coming here with that fake invitation to a ladies tea. Unfortunately, he hadn't considered that Maggie would be no more pleased by his deception than she'd been with any of his past exploits involving her. Now that he had her here, what the devil was he to do with her? His intention had been to apologize for his past transgressions, but James somehow didn't think she would be any more willing to listen to him now than she'd been in the past.

"I understood I had been invited to a *ladies* tea," Margaret said, drawing his gaze reluctantly back to her face. Yes. She was angry.

"Aye, well . . ." Feeling the hot flush of guilt creep up

over his face, he grimaced, then confessed: "My aunt is not here. This is her bridge day. I took advantage of that to—"

"There is no tea party," she interrupted. It wasn't a question, but he answered it as if it were.

"Well, no. At least, not one others will be coming to attend . . . but I had to talk to you, and since you are never at home when I call . . ." He paused to glare at her—he was not at all used to anyone not being *in* to him—and could still hardly fathom that she had chosen to disregard his attempts at communication. She should be grateful that he had taken the trouble. Apparently she didn't see it that way, however. Even as he stood there, she was making impatient noises and getting to her feet. His eyes widened in alarm, and he rushed forward as she wavered unsteadily.

"You should not be up. You should be resting," he said firmly. She impatiently shook away the hand he used to try to steady her.

"I should not be *here*. And I am fine—that tincture has done wonders for me." She snatched up her crumpled and slightly muddy hat from where it lay on the floor beside the settee, and James admitted reluctantly to himself that it was true. His aunt's remedy had apparently been efficacious; Maggie was no longer pale or frail-looking. In fact, she had quite a bit of color about her right now, though he suspected some of it was due to temper. In fact, as he watched he became more certain that her quick recovery was due entirely to her building ire.

"I am leaving."

James watched helplessly as she arranged her hat so that it would not irritate her head wound, but when she started toward the door, he was moved to action. Rushing forward, he pushed it closed and then positioned himself firmly in front of it, arms crossed over his chest. "You can't. Not until we talk."

"I have no interest in speaking with you, my lord," she said stiffly, trying to grab at the door knob. James immediately shifted to cover it, and she glared at him impatiently. "Pray, stand aside."

He did not mistake the order as the request it was couched as, but James shook his head. "Not until you have heard me out."

"I see." Her eyes narrowed on him. "Then you are holding me against my will? *Again?*"

"No, of course not. But—"

"Then please stand aside," she repeated pleasantly.

He glared at her in frustration, then stepped out of the way. She immediately moved to open the door. Desperate to make her listen, James blurted, "I will tell everyone that you are G. W. Clark if you do not at least give me a moment of your time." That threat made Maggie pause, so he pressed his advantage: "And I believe that my past behavior proves that I am the sort to do anything I must to get what I want."

Turning from the now open door, she sniffed and peered at him with distaste. "All your past behavior has proven is that you are a fool, my lord. I have no intention of talking to you."

She turned to flee, but he stopped her with a hand on her arm, demanding, "Do you not fear my revealing your secret?"

"Ha! Hardly, my lord! You are too much of a gentleman to do such a thing."

James felt a spontaneous smile burst out on his face.

Despite his shabby treatment of her, Maggie still thought him a gentleman. It gave him hope that with a little time and the right words he could repair things between them.

Apparently reading the renewed confidence on his face, Maggie muttered in vexation and whirled away to storm out into the hall. James followed on her heels. "Maggie, if you would just allow me a word with you . . ."

She paused at the front door and turned, a tight expression on her face. "And what exactly would you wish to say, my lord? That you are sorry that I am not Lady X?"

"Yes!" He started to smile, then saw her eyes narrow and—recognizing that he had said precisely the wrong thing—quickly shook his head. "I mean, nay! I—"

Maggie didn't listen to what he had to say. She'd heard enough of Lord Ramsey's nonsense. It had been humiliating enough to have the man take advantage of her while thinking she was a prostitute, and to know that she still recalled the way his arms encircled her, the way his lips pleasured her . . . Now, to listen to the man's attempts at explaining himself was unbearable.

Dragging the door open, she hurried out and down the front steps. She had walked here and would walk home if necessary, though she would have preferred hiring a hack. Anger was carrying her forward, but Maggie knew she couldn't count on it to get her all the way home—especially not after her injury. Unfortunately, there didn't appear to be any hacks about just then. She considered sending for one, but the sight of Lord Ramsey rushing down the steps after her changed Maggie's mind. She turned and started walking. It wasn't so far to home, really; if she cut through the park, she could be there in a trice.

Bolting across the street, she started along the tree-lined pathways, doing her best to ignore the curious stares of people gaping at her muddy and torn gown. Lord Ramsey's chasing after her like one of Lady Barlow's "dogs after a pussy" was not helping her to be inconspicuous, either, she suspected.

She hadn't gotten far into the park when a sharp cracking sound made her start and glance around. It sounded like a branch snapping—a heavy one.

She paused, a frown sliding over her face as she raised a hand to feel carefully at her hat. In the next moment, her headgear was forgotten and Maggie was squawking in amazement as she was tackled from behind and thrown to the ground. Before she could quite grasp what was happening, Ramsey had thrown himself atop her and was rolling them both under the bushes that lined the path. Finding herself clasped close in his arms, his body pressing intimately down into hers, Maggie had to brace herself against her body's eager response.

"My lord!" she screeched in mingled embarrassment and anger. She pushed frantically at his chest in a vain effort to remove his bulk.

"I am not trying to attack you, Maggie," he said with annoyance. Leaning away, he peered back out through the bushes. "Someone took a shot at you."

"A likely story," Maggie snapped. "Gerald neglected to mention your penchant for prevarication, my lord. First the tea party. Now someone trying to shoot me. I think not!"

Taking him by surprise, she shoved him away and got quickly to her feet.

"Maggie!"

Margaret plunged back through the bushes, tugging at her skirt when he sat up and caught at her hem. Hearing the tearing material, she cursed impatiently and hurried onward, refusing to look down at the damage. Maggie's one thought was to escape the man now blundering out of the bushes after her, hissing her name in a voice she was sure people could hear at the other end of the park.

When he grasped her elbow and tried to drag her back to the bushes, she turned on him abruptly, swinging her bag and koshing him on the side of the head. Maggie knew she hadn't hurt him, but his surprise at the attack made him loosen his hold long enough for her to pull free. Before he could quite regain himself, she flew down the path and joined the throngs making their way on the London streets.

Maggie nearly convinced herself that she had lost him in the crowds as she hurried along, so when she reached her home and hurried inside, then turned to close the door, only to find him blocking her from doing so, she stepped back in surprise. That gave him the opportunity to slip inside. She glowered at him fiercely as he shut the door then moved to the window, shifting the curtains aside to peer out into the street.

Tapping her foot in a furious tempo, she propped her hands on her hips and tried to set him aflame with her eyes. When that didn't work—he didn't even turn to appreciate her wrath—she drew herself up and hissed. "You were not invited in, my lord. Pray, remove yourself ere I have to call my servants to help you on your way."

Turning, James goggled at her briefly in disbelief, then snatched her ruined bird's-nest hat from her head and shoved it under her nose. The feathers tickled. "There," he said. "See that? Someone took a shot at you."

Maggie opened her mouth to say something nasty, then paused, her mouth dropping to her chest. There was a round hole right through the center of her bird that she could have put a finger through.

"Well, finally! Something has left you speechless," he muttered.

Snapping her mouth closed, Maggie glared at her nemesis. "Did you hire someone to do this? To make me soften toward you? Because if you did, my lord, I can promise you that you will be replacing this hat!"

"What?" He was flabbergasted by the accusation. "Why the devil would I do a thing like that?"

"I do not know, my lord, but why would anyone shoot at me? No one has reason."

"So you assume that *I* set it up? To what purpose? To get into your good graces by saving your life? Fat chance, that!" He snorted, then drew himself up to peer down his nose at her. "How could you think such a thing of me?"

Maggie felt herself tensing as everything that had happened rushed over her. She felt herself adrift in emotion, and everything she'd bottled up inside her exploded outward. "How could I think such a thing of you? How could *you* think what *you* thought of me?"

James indignity seeped away like water off fastmelting ice at her obvious pain and outrage. Regret flashed in his eyes, and she felt herself soften. Then he shifted uncomfortably and tried to explain: "Well, you must admit that what you were wearing that night—" He paused as she flushed, her cheeks burning almost as red as the gown in question. "And then you were at Madame Dubarry's," he added.

Maggie had heard enough. Turning abruptly away, she stomped into the parlor and directly to the bottles of liquor in the sideboard. She poured a generous quantity into a glass, downed it, then poured herself another full measure.

"May I have a glass as well?" James asked, joining her at the counter.

"Get your own," she barked testily, then relented. Pouring him a glass, she pushed it toward him along the counter, then turned and walked over to one of the two overstuffed chairs by the fire. Dropping into it with relief, she stared bleakly down into the dark liquid in her glass for a moment. Then she glanced up into his wary face. "Why are you here? Why did you lie in wait at your aunt's? I presume you set this all up to see me?"

"Yes," he admitted slowly. Moving to sink onto the chair opposite her, he considered his own glass briefly, then admitted, "I wish to apologize—"

"Apology accepted," she interrupted. "You may leave now."

James's jaw dropped. He was not at all used to being dismissed. It didn't appear that he liked it much. "Your brother—" he began determinedly.

She interrupted again. "My brother is dead," she reminded him. Then, bluntly, she went on: "I release you

205

from any promises or vows he elicited from you on his deathbed. You may go."

"I *do not wish* to go."

They both blinked at those blurted words. James looked both sheepish and horrified at the depth of emotion that had sounded in them. Maggie found herself feeling simply stunned. Swallowing nervously, she tore her gaze from his. "I think you had better—" she began.

"Please don't ask me to leave again." His voice was soft and weary and, despite herself, Maggie felt her anger begin to ease. She gave the barest of nods, but he saw it and relaxed in the chair as he confessed, "I quite enjoyed your company in the country."

She felt herself tensing again. "You mean, when you thought I was Lady X? When you thought I was a prostitute available to the highest bidder?"

"*Despite* thinking you a prostitute available to the highest bidder," he began carefully. "Yes. I enjoyed your company immensely, and that confused me. I felt it in my duty to reform you, but was also attracted to you physically," he admitted with a self-deprecating twist of his lips. "I found my honorable side constantly struggling against baser instincts. And then, as I came to know you, I found I actually liked you." He shrugged helplessly.

Maggie stared at him in wonder. She had known he was attracted to her. The little incident in the library had made that clear. She had never dared hope, however, that he might actually like her, too. Somehow, that seemed more important. Not that the other wasn't, but Lord Ramsey was the first man who had ever done more than kiss her. He was also the only one who'd ever inspired a desire in her to do more. . . .

Pastor Frances had never gone beyond a few sloppy swipes of his lips on hers, which had been just fine. She'd been more attracted to the idea of a solid, good man than by any overwhelming desire. No, that emotion was something she'd experienced with James alone.

"Is there anyone who may wish to do you harm?" she heard him ask.

Maggie stared blankly, confused by the sudden change in subject. Still, she tried to answer his question. As Frances had been the last thought to pop into her head before James had asked his question, Frances was the first person to pop into her head in answer to it.

She frowned as she thought of the other man, then winced as her furrowing brow caused pain to shoot from the bruise on her forehead. She forced herself to let the skin there smooth out again so that she could think.

The pastor had been someone she'd wanted to avoid as much as Lord Ramsey since returning, but, as he was the head of her church and Sunday was creeping closer, she had decided that it would do little good to continue avoiding him. Yesterday she'd invited him to dinner.

As expected, he'd proposed.

She, of course, had refused. What else could she do after witnessing that little scenario with Maisey? Frances hadn't accepted her refusal as gracefully as she'd hoped, and had pressed his suit. She had remained apologetic, yet firm. He'd appeared confused as she explained she did not harbor "wifely feelings" for him; then he had become cold. He'd even, before he left, pointed out that she was well beyond the age of youth and beauty, and that she was not likely to get a better offer. He'd even said she would regret her decision.

She considered now just how far he would go to ensure that she did regret it, then shook her head. *No.* Pastor Frances was not the sort to do her injury just because she refused to marry him. It would be silly and even egotistical to believe such might be the case. Still, she would be uncomfortable around the man until he found someone else to favor with his attentions. Which was terribly sad and unpleasant, but not deadly.

"No," she said at last, then shook her head. "I know of no one who would wish to harm me."

"The irate subject of one of your articles, perhaps?"

Maggie started shaking her head before he finished the question. "I thought of that, but no one knows who G. W. Clark is. Well, except you and your aunt, and Madame Dubarry."

"What of the women you interviewed?"

"I wore a very heavy veil during the interviews."

"What of the girl who gave you her mask?"

"Maisey?" Maggie opened her eyes wide with a mixture of surprise and amusement. "No. Maisey saw my face briefly, but"—she shook her head—"she is not the sort to be rushing about shooting at me. Besides, why would she? I did not even mention her name in the article. I didn't mention any names at all." She shook her head again. "No. There is no reason for anyone to wish me harm." When he frowned at her words, she shrugged. "Mayhap it was a stray bullet, James. Or a random act. I really do not feel I am under any threat. It is more likely that someone was aiming at you and missed."

"Me?" He looked insulted at the thought, and Maggie nearly laughed. *Good.* Now he knew what it felt like to be maligned.

"Well," she said mockingly. "Of course you are right,

my lord. Why would anyone want you dead? After all, you are such a pleasant sort."

The man started to be offended, then he noticed the twinkle in her eye and seemed to realize she was teasing. He relaxed with a wry smile. They were both still for a moment; then he pursed his lips in thought. "I might be more willing to accept that it was an accident or some such thing if it weren't for the accident today—and for the other the last time we met. Those make me worry that bullet was aimed at you."

Maggie made a face. "On the other hand, one might consider the fact that all these things only ever occurred with you around. . . ." She paused at his dismayed expression, then rolled her eyes. With a sigh she said what she should have said before. "I must apologize for not thanking you for that, James. You may very well have saved my life that day."

He waved away her words, though he was obviously pleased by them. "The point is, if this were just a random shot, it would be one thing. But—"

"Oh, now you cannot truly imagine that wagon driver was deliberately attempting to run me down?" Maggie protested.

"Well, I had not considered the possibility at the time . . . but now that a similar-looking man pushed you out in front of another carriage, and someone is shooting at you—"

"We do not know it is the same man," Maggie protested. "You said the driver of the wagon was dark. Did you see a scar?" When James hesitated, obviously reluctant to admit that he had not, she added, "Besides, it was one stray shot in the park. Why did they not fire again if they were truly trying to kill me? I leaped back

209

up and charged out of those bushes, making a perfect target of myself . . . yet a second shot never came."

He conceded that fact with a nod as he got to his feet. "I can see that I am wasting my time trying to convince you that you are in danger. At least promise me that you will take care in future?"

"I promise," she murmured, rising as well but feeling a trifle awkward. She wasn't sure where they stood anymore. Her animosity appeared to be gone, but where did that leave them? After what they'd done, what could they be? Friends? Acquaintances?

"I would also appreciate it if . . . I mean, now that we have reached something of a . . . Please stop refusing my aunt's invitations," he blurted at last. "She quite likes you and is holding me wholly responsible for your snubs."

Maggie nearly grinned, but caught the expression back and instead solemnly nodded. "I liked her as well. I would be pleased to accept any future invitations."

Sighing at Maggie's words, James exited the salon, aware that she was following as he moved to the front door. Opening it, he paused to glance back. "And do try to be careful. Make sure that the servants lock the doors at night, and take a carriage whenever possible."

"Aye, my lord," she murmured.

James frowned at her easy agreement, suspecting that it was given only to soothe him, but there was little he could do to make her listen without alienating her again. Nodding, he turned away and left the town house, his mind already working on ways for him to tend the matter as he pulled the door closed behind him.

He would hire Johnstone again to look out for her. The runner could also investigate whether the three incidents were linked attempts on Maggie's life or mere accidents. She wouldn't like it if she found out, but he *had* made a promise to her brother, to look after her. Which was the only interest he had in the girl, he told himself as he started toward the park. Margaret Wentworth was a respectable young woman, and what he'd done to—with—her was reprehensible. From now on he would treat her only with the respect that was her due.

He just had to push away his memories of her naked flesh, and the rest would be tea and crumpets.

Chapter Twelve

Maggie cursed as her hair slid from where she had secured it atop her head and tumbled around her shoulders. Again. Heaving out her breath in irritation, she glared into the oval dressing table mirror she sat before.

"I should have asked Mary to fix my hair before she left," she admitted to the room. There was no one around to comment, no one at all; the entire house was empty. Which meant there was also no one to help her with this task, either. Worse yet, she had no one to blame but herself, she admitted in aggravation, making a face at her reflection in the mirror.

One of the fairs had come today. It was a much smaller fete than St. Bartholomew's, which was held in August, but it was one of the first of the season, so had caused a great deal of excitement among her staff. Their excitement had infected Maggie, too, and in a moment of largesse she had decided that every one of them should take the afternoon off.

At the time, she'd believed she wouldn't need them. As she was attending a ball this evening with James and his aunt, there was no need to make her meal, or clean up after her, and really there was little enough for the servants to do when she *was* around. With her plans to be out tonight, it had seemed silly to keep the servants in. She had convinced them all, against their somewhat meager protests, to take the afternoon off and enjoy the fair. Even Banks had gone, agreeing in his gruff old voice to Maggie's suggestion that an older, wiser influence might be for the best.

Of course, when she had given them all the day off, she had forgotten she would need assistance getting ready for the ball. Her maid Mary had brought it up and offered, with a pained smile, to stay behind and assist, but Maggie had not had the heart to keep her; it was hardly fair for everyone else to go while Mary alone had to stay behind and miss the fun. No, Maggie had refused to allow her to stay—despite her concerns about being able to do herself up properly.

It couldn't be that hard, surely? she'd thought. She could prepare herself. She was a perfectly intelligent young woman. She *had* managed to dress herself, though it hadn't been as easy as she'd expected, what with all the buttons in the back and such. Still, with some ingenuity and twisting and turning, she had mastered the situation.

Her hair was another matter entirely. Mary had always been swift and assured at the business, managing to perform miracles in moments with the unmanageable tresses. They seemed determined to defy Maggie's attempts. She was not feeling terribly intelligent or clever at the moment. In fact, she was feeling rather panicky and incompetent. The hour was growing late. James and his aunt would arrive any moment.

She felt herself blush. James and his aunt. She had seen quite a bit of the pair since the day of her injury. Lady Barlow had invited her to tea several times in the week since, and Maggie had accepted each invitation. James had been in attendance for all of them. He had behaved beautifully during each visit, a perfect gentleman. Nor had he brought up any nonsense about someone trying to kill her again, thank goodness. In fact, he had not tried to kiss her or do anything untoward—not even looking as if he had wanted to.

Maggie found herself looking rather purse-lipped at that thought, and she forced the lines out of her face. Surely she wasn't disappointed that he hadn't kissed her or anything else, was she? He was treating her like the lady she was, and that was only appropriate.

She wasn't fooling herself. Now that her fury at him had been resolved, she found herself recalling those decadent moments in his office. She had even relived them in a dream or two since, awakening as shaken and aroused as when it first happened.

Maggie's thoughts were interrupted by the sound of a door closing below, and she glanced abruptly toward the entrance to her room. Relief coursed through her. She hadn't expected the servants to return so early, but she was relieved that they had. Perhaps she could prevail upon Mary to help with her hair. She simply could not attend the Willans' ball with Lady Barlow and James if she did not look her best. She wouldn't want to embarrass them. They were taking her as their guest, after all.

Mary can fix my hair in a trice, Maggie thought with relief, standing and heading for the door. *If it is Mary*, she considered with a sudden frown. It could be that young Charlie had eaten too many sweets and one of his other sisters had returned with him. That would be all right, though; both Joan and Nora knew how to do hair, each of them had stepped in to take their older sisters place as lady's maid a time or two. They practiced on each other and were quite skilled.

Or, she considered as she stepped out into the hall, if it was old Banks, weary and returning early alone, she would even be willing to let him have a go. Which showed the degree of her panic and frustration, she thought with amusement as she reached the landing and peered down into the dark and silent foyer below. There was no sign of movement or activity that she could see, but the servants would most likely stick to the kitchens or their own rooms. They would probably assume she had already left.

In fact, she decided as she noted the fact that night was falling, leaving the house shrouded in gloom, it appeared late enough that she should have already left. Lady Barlow and James were late. Picking up a three-tiered candelabra from the table at the top of the stairs, she lifted her skirt slightly and headed down. One of her servants had returned early; she had only to find out which.

Reaching the bottom of the stairs, Maggie walked along the hall toward the kitchen, her concentration taken up with doing her best to prevent the candles she carried from going out and leaving her in the dark.

With her hand and arm out to shield their delicate flames, she opened the door to the kitchens by pushing against it with her hip. The action stirred a slight breeze that threatened to damp her candles, and, distracted by this concern, Maggie stepped into the kitchen before realizing that the room was in near darkness. Seeing that fact, she knew at once that no one had returned from the fair. Building a kitchen fire would have been the first act of any of her servants.

She stood, stymied for a moment by the realization, then stiffened. The hair at the nape of her neck was suddenly standing on end, prickles of electricity racing over her skin. Turning instinctively, she gaped in surprise as her candles illuminated a figure standing behind the door that had just swung shut.

Both of them froze for a moment as if posing for a portrait, the man blinking as his eyes strained to adjust to the candlelight splashing over him, and Maggie's breath catching in her throat as she absorbed the details of the intruder. He was tall and bulky, with wide shoulders and thick, strong arms. His hair was long and dark, his smile cruel, and a square and puckered scar deformed his cheek. She took all that in, then felt horror race along her nerves as he started forward.

Crying out, Maggie rushed backward, but she jarred her hip against the table Cook used to prepare food. Instinctively she swung the candelabra at her attacker. The makeshift mace made a satisfying impact as it struck her assailant's head, stopping him briefly and sending the candles flying. Two of them flickered out as they fell, but one managed to remain lit as it rolled across the floor. Still, the room descended into the gloom of dusk, and Maggie spun away, stumbling through the near-darkness, knocking against unidentifiable objects as she sought escape.

She was in a panic at that point, her only thought to flee and get help. Maggie knew without a doubt that this man was the one who had nearly run her down with the wagon, and the one the hack driver had said had pushed her out before his carriage. There was no longer any possibility to deny that someone was after her. James's voice rang through her head, telling her not to go anywhere alone, to be sure that the servants always locked the doors.

Maggie cursed herself roundly for sending the servants off and leaving herself alone and vulnerable. She hadn't given a single thought to his warnings, so sure she was that no one could be out to harm her. *I am an idiot and deserve whatever I get*, she thought viciously as she slammed into a counter, her hands knocking several items to the ground. A hand caught the back of her gown briefly as she tried to straighten, then released its hold to grasp her neck. Fingers closed around her throat from behind, squeezing viciously and cutting off her air.

Maggie's first instinct was to score the hands at her throat with her nails. When it had no effect, except to have the man slam her into the counter, his body pressing along the back of her own, she gave that up. Eyes closed and gasping for air, she felt frantically around for something, anything, to use as a weapon. Stars were starting to explode behind her eyelids when her hand fell on something hard. Fighting off the unconsciousness threatening to overwhelm her, she closed her fingers desperately around the handle of the heavy item—a pan, she thought—and, using all the strength she could muster, she swung it behind her, slamming it into her attacker.

A grunt by her ear and the loosening of the man's fingers told Maggie that she had hit her mark. Coughing and sucking in air, she staggered blindly away, but managed only to take a very few steps before she was again grabbed. This time the man caught her by the shoulder. He whirled her around.

Maggie opened her eyes in time to see the room explode; a heavy object slammed into the side of her face. The world seemed to tip inside her head, and she knew she was falling. Something caught her temple as she fell—the corner of a table, perhaps? Maggie cried out at the sharp pain, but hardly felt the impact of the floor when she hit it.

Moaning at the agony in her head, she let it fall weakly to the side and found herself staring at the flames in the fireplace. At least, that was what she'd at first thought they were. Her eyes had started to close when some part of her brain told her she'd made a mistake. Forcing herself back to consciousness, she stared at the dancing flames, frowning when her attacker suddenly knelt before them. He picked something up, and Maggie frowned as she realized that the flames came from a candle. What she was looking at wasn't a fire in the fireplace at all. One of the candles from her candelabra, the only one that had stayed lit, had rolled up against a sack of grain that Cook had left out and set it ablaze. Her house was now on fire, she realized.

Her attacker moved around the table and out of sight.

Alarm bells started tolling inside her head, and Maggie summoned strength enough to respond to them. Gasping in pain, she struggled to her hands and knees, swallowing the bile that rose in her throat as she did.

Getting to her feet seemed an insurmountable task, but she grabbed at the edge of the table beside her and managed to pull herself to her feet; her only clear thought was that she needed to find something with which to put out the fire. *Water*, she thought muzzily, leaning against the table. A sound drew her eyes to the opposite side of the room and her attacker. She frowned slightly, not sure at first what he was doing. He stood with his back to her, fiddling with something. Then light bloomed around him and he turned, a lit lamp in hand. The man seemed surprised to find her standing; then his mouth twisted and he hurled the lamp forward.

Crying out, Maggie threw herself to the side, tumbling to the floor as the lamp sailed past. She heard it smash against the wall, and a whooshing sound made her glance weakly over to see that oil had sprayed everywhere. The fire was quickly following.

The flames seemed alive, like fingers of some monster hungry to consume her. Her last thought before darkness claimed her was that she was going to die.

"We are late."

Lady Barlow peered at her nephew through the growing gloom inside the carriage and bit her lip to keep from smiling. The man was quite put out. He had arrived at her town house a good hour ago, earlier than she'd expected, and she hadn't been ready. Neither was she ready by the appointed hour, and she had left James cooling his heels in her salon while her maid had fussed over her. By the time she had made her grand entrance into the salon, the man was seething.

Far from being impressed with all the work her maid had put into her appearance, James had turned from his pacing with relief, snatched his aunt's hand, and nearly dragged her out of the house without her cloak or gloves. She had rebuked him quite firmly for the unseemly behavior, taken her time donning the items, then walked out to the carriage at a dignified pace. The whole while he'd pranced about her, almost begging her to move quicker.

Vivian had nearly burst into laughter at his antics, but she hadn't thought he would appreciate her amusement. She'd managed to stifle it behind a stern expression.

The boy was terribly eager to collect little Lady Margaret, which Vivian saw as terribly encouraging. James hadn't shown the least bit of interest in any of the other available ladies of the ton in years. She had despaired of his ever settling down and presenting her with a little grandniece or grandnephew.

She sighed to herself at the thought. *Babies.* She did love babies. Unfortunately she had not been blessed with any of her own. It had been both a tragedy and a blessing when her dear sister had died at sea and left her young children in Vivian's care. As much as she had grieved the loss of her sibling and brother-in-law, she had taken James and his sister to her bosom with love and devotion, treating them as her own. Without those two to look after and chase, she felt sure she would have grown into a bitter old woman. Any babies either child produced would be a further blessing. And now Vivian was becoming rather hopeful that Lady Margaret might be the one to lure James to the altar and begin producing such added wonders.

Her gaze slid to her nephew, and she smiled a little

slyly at the normally calm and dignified man's fidgeting. Then, forcing her expression to a more serious mien, she murmured, "This shall be good for Margaret. Having the child at the opera with us should raise a lot of curiosity about her, and then the Willans always have a lot of eligible bachelors at their balls. Perhaps we can find her some suitable husband material."

She was not disappointed at the sharp way James glanced at her. "What?"

"Well," she murmured comfortably, "her brother *did* die saving your life. It does behoove us to find her a good, strong, well-set husband to take care of her."

"She doesn't need a husband," he protested at once, looking put out by the idea. "She can take care of herself."

"Nonsense. Once she is married she can give up writing those dangerous articles. She is taking too many chances, as it is."

James stared at her in horror for a moment. It had obviously not occurred to him that his aunt might take it into her head to see the girl settled. It was also obvious he didn't like the idea. At all. *Good*, she thought as she watched him shift. There was no reason for him not to want to marry the girl off unless he was interested himself. Oh, yes, she would see the stubborn cur married by the end of season, or her name wasn't Lady Vivian Jean Barlow.

"Dammit! I told Crowch to drive quickly. What is he doing?" James grumbled, drawing her attention. She glanced at him in time to see his head disappear out the window to address the driver. "Crowch? What is the holdup here? We are nearly at a standstill."

"Sorry, m'lord. There appears to be some problem

up ahead. A fire, I think. There is smoke filling the road, and gawkers are holding up traffic."

"A fire?" Vivian asked, catching the man's explanation and leaning curiously toward the window.

Her nephew went as stiff as a board. "Can you see where it seems to be coming from?" he asked.

Vivian felt anxiety strike her at the dread in James's voice.

"I'm not sure, m'lord. It looks to be coming from somewhere near Lady Wentworth's. It could be one of her neighbor's homes, or hers. . . . I can't tell from here."

James was out of the carriage before Vivian had even digested Crowch's words. Leaning out the window of the door her nephew had just pushed closed, she peered up the street in concern. A black cloud of smoke was billowing up into the darkening sky.

James ran. He ran so fast his heart was thumping violently and loudly in his chest, deafening him to the startled gasps and complaints of the people he was pushing and shoving past in his desperate effort to reach Maggie. The fire couldn't be at the Wentworth town house. It couldn't be. But even as he tried to reassure himself, he knew that he was wrong, and cursed himself for not preventing this somehow—for not doing more about the danger she was in and seeing her safe.

He stumbled through the last of the onlookers, crashing against the gate separating the town house from the street. His hands clenched on the pointed metal spears as he gaped in horror at the burning building. Smoke was billowing out of several broken windows in the house and rising to merge into one large cloud that blackened the already inky sky.

"Maggie," he said under his breath. He had already started to pull the gate open when a hand settled on his shoulder.

"M'lord?"

James started to shake the hand off, but the man's next words made him pause.

"She ain't in there, m'lord. She's all right."

Turning sharply, James stared at the speaker, not recognizing him for a moment. "Johnstone?"

"Aye, m'lord." The man's expression showed some concern.

"Where is she?" he asked sharply, grabbing the man's coatfront in agitation.

"My man got her out." When James looked blank, the runner raised a soothing hand. "Ye remember? Ye said to put a man on her until we discovered whether someone were after her or not." His gaze slid grimly to the burning house and the brigade working to put it out. "Well, it looks like someone is after her after all."

"Where *is* she?" James repeated, his voice harsh. He didn't care about anything else at that point but seeing for himself that Maggie was safe. Seeming to finally realize that, Johnstone tugged free and started to lead his employer back through the crowd.

"This way, m'lord."

"James?" a voice called.

He hesitated in the street, then paused to rush back to meet his aunt. She was hurrying breathlessly through the crowd toward him. Frowning up the road, he saw that his carriage was still some distance back, and realized that his aunt had followed him on foot.

223

"Perhaps you should go back and wait in the carriage, Aunt Viv," he suggested as he reached her side.

"Is Maggie all right? Is that her town house?"

"Yes, it is hers."

"Is she all right?" his aunt asked again with growing alarm. James hesitated. He wanted to insist that his aunt return to his carriage and wait there, but he knew she would merely argue and delay him. Unwilling to waste time convincing her, he took her arm and hurried over to where Johnstone now stood leaning into a hack.

Reaching the runner's side, James released his aunt to step up and peer past the shorter man's shoulders into the carriage. It took a moment for his eyes to adjust to the dark interior. When they did, he found himself staring at a crumpled female form in the arms of a large, dark shadow.

"Jack says she was unconscious when he found and dragged her out of the house. He sent a lad to fetch me at the office and waited with her on the front lawn until the fire got too hot. When I got here, I had him get her in the carriage. I was going to take her to yer town house, but by that time the gawkers had clogged the road. We couldn't get out of here," Johnstone told him apologetically, stepping aside to allow James to fill the open door. Then he added, "She hasn't regained consciousness yet."

James didn't hesitate. Leaning into the hack, he lifted Maggie out of the other man's arms, then straightened with her. "Come," was all he said. It was enough; his aunt, Johnstone, and the man named Jack all trailed obediently back along the street to his carriage.

"Can you get us out of here, Crowch?" James asked

grimly as the driver leaped down from his bench to open the carriage door.

The coachman hesitated, his gaze moving over the vehicles now ahead of and behind them, then he considered the empty half of the road where carriages should have been traveling in the opposite direction, but weren't. He nodded determinedly. "Aye, m'lord."

"Good man," James said. "Take us back home."

"Your home or Lady Barlow's?" the driver asked.

"My home," his aunt promptly answered. When James frowned, she explained, "It is closer."

James's gaze dropped to the pale, smoke-smudged face of the woman he held; then he nodded and stepped up into his carriage. His aunt followed, settling on the bench seat across from him. James settled Maggie carefully in his lap, her head against his chest, her lower legs and feet taking up the rest of the seat. Johnstone paused long enough to order his man to join Crowch on the driver's bench, then clambered in as well, murmuring apologies as he settled next to Lady Barlow.

They were all silent as Crowch maneuvered the vehicle's horses, turned it on the lane, and headed them back the way they had come.

It was a very short ride back to his aunt's house, and James leaped out of the carriage—Maggie cradled to his chest—as soon as Crowch opened the door. He was grateful to see that Johnstone's man had already rushed ahead to announce their arrival. Meeks opened the door just as James reached the house, his eyes goggling at the sight of Lady Wentworth in James's arms.

"Another accident, my lord?" he asked in alarm, quickly stepping out of the way so that everyone could enter.

"*Another* one?" Lady Barlow echoed sharply.

James grimaced, but shook his head. "Not an accident, Meeks, and we will be needing a doctor this time. Send someone for Lord Mullin."

"Are you sure he is back?" Aunt Vivian asked with concern.

James nodded. "He returned yesterday," he responded, then breathed a heartfelt, "Thank God."

Robert had always been fascinated by medicine. That fascination had led the younger man to train in the field despite there being no necessity for him to work for a living. That training had been put to use when he was called to war. Robert had been the medic for their platoon, and James had watched him save many men he'd been sure were lost. James would trust no one else with Maggie's life.

"I shall see to it at once, my lord." The butler moved off down the hall to see to the matter as James carried Maggie into the salon. He laid her gently on the very same settee he had placed her on the day of the faux tea party. The room was dark for several moments, but then Johnstone thought to collect a candle from the hall. He used it to light several more tapers in the room, and within moments the salon was filled with a soft glow.

James almost wished it weren't. Up until that point he had thought her merely smoke-smudged; now that he was seeing her in the light, he could see that a good deal of what he'd thought were smudges were really bruises. The side of her face was one large welt, her lip was cut, one eye was blackened, and there were bruises around her throat.

"She fought," Johnstone commented approvingly, moving to peer over James's shoulder as his employer brushed the hair away from Maggie's forehead to reveal a nasty cut at her hairline. Then, apparently noting the blood that had soaked into her hair and ran back along her scalp, the runner added, "Landed on her back after the blow."

"I shall go fetch some water and a cloth, and be sure Meeks sent someone for the doctor," Lady Barlow hurried from the room.

"What happened?" James glanced toward the runner Johnstone had called Jack. The man stepped forward at once, his gaze going to Lady Margaret with a frown.

"I was watching from across the street. The servants all left in the early afternoon. She was alone in the house, far as I knew. Then, just before sunset, I noticed a sort of glow coming from some of the windows on the lower floor. I knew it wasn't candlelight, and thought I smelled smoke." He shrugged, his expression grim. "Had a bad feeling. Decided I'd better take a look-see. I tried seeing in the front windows, but all I could learn was that the light was coming from the back of the house. She didn't come to the door when I knocked, so around I went. I saw someone runnin' out into the gardens as I came around the corner. I was gonna chase after him, then saw that the back door was partway open, and that the kitchens were on fire—so I headed for the house instead. She was lyin' in the center of the kitchen floor."

He shook his head. "Everything else in the room was afire, but it hadn't reached her yet. 'Twas just nipping at her skirts. I ran in and pulled her out, then carried her around to the front of the house. I stopped a passin' boy and gave him a couple coins to fetch Mr. Johnstone here." The man frowned, looking regretful. "I should have given him a couple more and had him fetch the fire brigade, too."

"Ye did fine," Johnstone said. He patted the larger man on the shoulder. "The brigade came right quick. How's ye hand?"

The question drew James's attention to the fact that Jack hadn't gotten away without injury. His right hand was red and blistered. He had rushed into a burning building, but James hadn't considered what that entailed.

"Oh, dear." The murmured words drew his attention to the fact that Lady Barlow had returned. How much of the man's words she had heard was anyone's guess, but now she rushed to Jack's side with the bowl of water and the cloth she had brought.

"Fetch more water and cloths, Meeks," she ordered, then urged the injured Jack to a nearby chair. Once she had cajoled him into sitting, she set the bowl on his leg, picked his arm up by the wrist, and plopped his hand into the water. Seeming to think that took care of the immediate problem, she turned to where James and Johnstone still hovered by Maggie and eyed them like two misbehaving children. "Now, you had better tell me about this previous incident Meeks mentioned . . . and why exactly you still have Mr. Johnstone in your employ . . . and why you had this poor man watching Maggie!"

"He was keeping an eye out—just in case something like this happened." James answered the last question first.

"And Mr. Johnstone?"

"Lord Ramsey asked me to look into who was causing all of these accidents," Johnstone answered with a shrug.

Lady Barlow nodded, then speared her nephew with

her eyes. "What about this 'other incident' Meeks mentioned?"

James winced. It was a question he really would have preferred not to answer. He had sworn Meeks to silence about that day, so his aunt was not aware of the little incident at all. She knew nothing about the faux tea party, the invitation to which he had signed her name, or anything else about that day. Answering her now would definitely get him in hot water. She wouldn't be at all pleased to learn he had used her in such a way. Nor, probably, that he had used blackmail and lies to get Meeks to go along with him. Nor that he had put Maggie in a compromising position by tricking her into traveling somewhere to be alone with him.

Fortunately, he was saved from having to answer her immediately by the arrival of Lord Mullin, "Robert!" James said with relief. "Thank you for coming."

"Not at all." The younger man shed his overcoat as he crossed the room, Meeks on his heels. Pausing at James's side, he exchanged the garment for the bag Lady Barlow's butler had been holding for him, then turned his attention to Maggie. "What happened? I gather there was a fire? Was she burned?"

"I don't think so, but she has a nasty head wound," James said. "She's been unconscious for at least several minutes."

Nodding, his friend nudged him. "Let me have a look at her, then."

James stood at once and moved. He watched Robert poke at the wound on her forehead and lift her eyelids one after the other. When he started to look her over for other injuries, James turned away. Leaving his aunt and Robert to tend to the wounds of both Maggie and Jack, he urged Johnstone from the room.

"Have you come up with anything, yet?" James asked as he led the Bow Street runner into the library and closed the door.

Johnstone shook his head. "Not much," the man admitted regretfully. "I found a couple of people who witnessed the incident where she was pushed in front of the hack. A couple people remembered it happening, but couldn't say whether she had been pushed in front of the carriage or just bumped. No one remembered a scarred man being there except for that driver. I've nosed around to see if there's any ill will toward G. W. Clark, but no one's rushing forward with information. I'll keep at it, though."

"Aye. You do that," James murmured, rubbing a hand wearily along his neck. "This has to be connected to Lady Margaret's articles. There is no other reason for anyone to wish her harm."

Johnstone shrugged. "There doesn't appear to be. Usually such murderous attempts revolve around some sort o' monetary gain, but there doesn't appear to be anyone to gain from her death—except for her cousin, perhaps. He would probably inherit the town house and the money she invested if she died, but I looked into that and the lawyers still haven't located him. No, I believe ye're right, m'lord. It has to be connected to her articles."

"Did you look into Drummond?"

"Aye. It's not him. He's dead."

"Dead?" James glanced over in surprise and the runner nodded.

"Aye. Got his neck stretched. Rumor is that the judge

230

who tried him was one of the victims of his flammery."

James frowned. "Then it must be because of one of her other articles."

Johnstone nodded. "Well that's the problem: it could be one of the articles she wrote, or one her brother wrote. Anyone who discovered Clark's identity now wouldn't necessarily know her brother was the writer before his death, and would blame *her* for it. Do you know how many articles they have done between them?" he asked in disgust. "The suspects are in the hundreds."

"Damn."

"Aye," Johnstone agreed.

"Well, my main concern is to keep her safe. Which might be easier now that her house is gone. She never would have agreed to leave it ere this, but now it shouldn't be too difficult to convince her to stay with me. I—"

"She will stay with me." A stern voice resounded through the room.

Both men turned to peer at Lady Barlow. She stood in the door to the room, and they had been so caught up in their discussion that neither man had heard her open it. They exchanged vexed glances.

"It would be improper for her to stay with you," Aunt Vivian pointed out. "She will stay with me. But someone must be sent to wait for and collect her staff. She says that they went to the fair. I imagine they should be returning soon. They won't have anywhere to go, and Margaret is quite worried about them."

"She is awake?" James started for the door, only to pause when his aunt remained blocking the entrance.

"Robert is still with her. He has finished with Jack,

however." Her gaze slid to Johnstone. "I sent him to the kitchens for something to eat and drink."

"Thank you, ma'am. He is a good man."

"Yes, he is. He saved Lady Margaret's life. But he needs to rest for the remainder of the night, at least, before he will be any good as a guard again, so you may wish to arrange to send someone to relieve him."

"Yes, o' course. I shall see to it at once," Johnstone assured her. As he moved forward Lady Barlow stepped out of the way; then she closed the door behind his departing back and eyed James as she'd done when he was in trouble as a child.

"Now, James Matthew Huttledon, it's time you told me about this 'incident.' Meeks is looking bedeviled and guilty, and avoiding my questions. Obviously, whatever occurred includes your convincing him to behave against his instincts."

"Against his instincts?" James echoed with feigned surprise, trying to stall long enough to think of a way to explain without it sounding quite as bad as he knew it would. He already knew that his aunt wouldn't be pleased that he had used her name, her home, and her staff in an effort to get Maggie alone—even if his only intention had been to speak to her, not ravish her. His aunt wasn't of the belief that the end justified the means; he had learned that long ago. She preferred honest, aboveboard tactics in everything.

"Yes. Against his instincts. Even as a boy you were always able to twist that man about your finger. Meeks is as soft as pudding where you and Sophie are concerned. Now, tell. I am losing patience."

Chapter Thirteen

"Thank you, my lord." Maggie said, watching Lord Mullin return his implements to his bag.

"You are more than welcome. It's the least I could do for Gerald's sister." He closed his bag with a snap and stood. "Now, I had best go find James and Lady Barlow. I wish to have a word with them on your care. You just rest, Maggie. I know your head must be paining you. The tincture I gave you should help with that soon."

Maggie instinctively started to nod, then caught herself and merely watched him leave. He was right, of course, her head was pounding something awful, and her face felt as if someone had taken a cricket bat to it, but she was alive. That was something, she supposed. She wouldn't lay odds that she had much else left to be happy about. The last thing Maggie recalled before waking up here on Lady Barlow's settee, *again*, was lying helplessly on the floor of her kitchen as the fire spread around her.

Sighing, she closed her eyes and tried to get the image out of her head. The hum of voices from the hall told her that Robert had found James and his aunt, and was, no doubt, giving his diagnosis. Battered, bruised, and aching should about cover it, she thought wryly.

Reaching a hand up to feel her face, she found it swollen and deformed. Still, it was little enough to bear. Considering what might have happened . . . she'd been lucky and knew it. Maggie was not alive and well now due to any action on her own part. If anything, her foolish refusal to believe that someone might be out to do her harm had nearly cost her life. She should have listened to James. Any injury she had sustained was her own bloody fault. Even so, she could still hardly believe someone hated her enough to wish her dead.

A rustling made her start and peer around nervously, but she relaxed at the sight of Lady Barlow, Lord Mullin, and James entering the room.

"How are you feeling, dear?" the older woman asked, moving quickly to her side.

"Much better than I should, all things considered," Maggie admitted softly. She eased to a sitting position, ignoring the pain the action sent shooting through her.

"Are you sure you should sit up?" Lady Barlow asked, but her questioning gaze went to Robert.

"Yes," Maggie answered before Lord Mullin could comment. "If I continue to lie here, I will fall asleep . . . and I know I should tell what happened while it is fresh in my mind."

"Surely that can wait until morning . . ." the old woman began, but James interrupted.

"No, she is right. She may forget something important if we wait. Best to get this out of the way. If you feel up to it," he added gently, ignoring his aunt's narrow-eyed gaze.

She wasn't pleased with him at the moment. Aunt Viv had not taken the news of his faux tea party well. Fortunately, before she had been able to lambaste him about the ordeal, Meeks had tapped on the library door to let them know that Robert was finished with Maggie. James was rather hoping that tonight's events would see to it that his aunt never got around to that lambasting.

Aunt Vivian was the only one who could make him feel like a naughty five-year-old. He supposed it was a mother thing, and the woman had certainly filled that role for him.

A sound from Maggie drew James's gaze to her pale, battered face.

"Yes. I can manage," she assured them with quiet determination, then paused, seeming to try to organize her thought. Her eyelashes fluttered, and her eyes rose to him. "I suppose I should start with an apology." When he looked startled, she admitted, "You were right, of course, about the scarred man."

James's gaze sharpened with interest and he settled on the couch next to her, covering her hand where it rested in her lap with one of his own, he said, "Start at the beginning, Maggie."

She tried to nod, then paused abruptly, pain flashing across her face. She held still for a moment, then took a deep breath and began. "I let the servants go to the fair," she admitted regretfully. "It was opening day, and I was to attend the opera and then the Willans' ball with the two of you, so I saw no reason not to let them all go."

"Of course you didn't," Lady Barlow murmured soothingly, taking up a position on Maggie's other side. She reached out to squeeze her free hand. "It was kind of you to let them go."

"It was stupid of me, actually." A smile that held little humor twisted her mouth as she admitted what James was thinking. It *had* been incredibly foolish of her. He had warned her not to go anywhere alone, and here she had released her entire staff and left herself vulnerable at home. At least she now realized the danger she had put herself in, he thought, gratefully. Then she spoke again.

"I neglected to consider that I would need help getting ready," she admitted to a sympathetic Lady Barlow. "With everyone gone, I had no one to help me with my hair or dress."

James rolled his eyes at the complaint. *This* was why she thought she had been stupid in releasing her staff? Nevermind that it had left her vulnerable to attack; she'd had to dress herself! Dear Lord, wasn't it just like a woman to be more concerned with matters of vanity than her well being. He exchanged a speaking look with Robert, who had taken a seat across from them.

"And then, too," Maggie continued, "had I kept someone behind I should not have been all alone when that man came. He might not have broken into the house had the servants been there."

Relieved that the fact had at least occurred to her, even if only as a secondary consideration, James nodded and prompted her to continue. "You let the staff go and were preparing for the ball . . ."

"Yes. I heard a noise below and thought one of the servants had returned early. Which I thought was grand. I was in terrible need of someone to aid me with my hair. I took a candelabra and went to find them." Maggie frowned as the memory washed over her, clearly frightening.

"He attacked me when I entered the kitchen. We struggled and . . . I lost." She sighed wearily.

"He set the fire after you were unconscious?" James asked.

"Yes. No. I was still conscious, and he didn't start the fire, but he did spread it."

"Spread it?" Robert echoed in surprise.

"Yes." Maggie explained, "When I hit him with the candelabra, the candles went flying. One landed against a sack of grain. It started a fire. He used the candle to light a lamp, then smashed it against the wall. I tried to stop him but . . ."

James's hand squeezed hers tighter.

"Who pulled me from the fire?" she asked after a moment. Her gaze went to him. "You?"

"No. You were already out by the time we got there."

"A fellow named Jack pulled you out," Lady Barlow added. "He had you in Mr. Johnstone's carriage when we got there."

"Johnstone?" Maggie murmured. She frowned.

"The Bow Street runner who thought you were Lady X," Lady Barlow reminded her. James didn't think his aunt sounded at all impressed with the man.

"I asked him to hire someone to keep an eye on you," he explained. "Jack was to watch over you—in case something like this happened. I knew you did not believe anyone would want to hurt you and wouldn't take

237

the proper precautions. He smelled smoke and went around the back of the house just as your attacker fled."

"Did he catch him?" Maggie asked.

"No. He went into the house after you, instead," James explained.

She looked disappointed at the fact that her attacker had gotten away.

"He'll try again," she said faintly, then met James's concerned gaze. "Thank you. I really did not think anyone could be out to harm me, but I guess you were right."

"I wish I had not been," he assured her, concern eating at him as her shoulders sagged and her head drooped. Her eyes had grown sleepier and sleepier for the past several minutes, and she looked quite done-in now.

"The draft I gave you is starting to take effect," Robert commented guiltily.

"Yes." Maggie roused herself enough to nod and say, "I should go home and . . ." She paused, a frown plucking at her brow as it occurred to her to wonder if she had a home anymore. She had no idea how much damage the fire had done.

"The servants are preparing a room for you here," Lady Barlow informed her.

Maggie glanced over with surprise. "But my staff—"

"I had Meeks send one of the footmen to wait for and collect your servants. When they return from the fair, they too will stay here tonight. If necessary, we can make alternate arrangements on the morrow, after we see what is what."

Maggie felt gratitude rush over her at the matron's firm announcement. Such decisions were quite beyond her at the moment; she was more than grateful to leave them up to someone else. It was nice not to be the responsible one for a change. She had missed that since Gerald's death. Responsibility could be a heavy weight when one was alone.

"I shall just go see if your room is ready; then James can carry you up."

"There is no need. I am sure I can walk," Maggie protested.

"But why bother when I am here and can carry you?" James asked gently as his aunt left the room.

"James is right, you should save your strength for mending," Lord Mullin concurred, getting to his feet. "And I suppose I should let you all be and head home."

"No, don't leave, Robert," James said. "Johnstone should be returning shortly, and we are going to discuss . . . things. I'd appreciate your input."

The other man nodded and sank back in his seat.

Maggie knew she was the "things" James had alluded to; she hadn't missed the way his glance had dropped meaningfully to her as he'd said it. She supposed he wished to discuss how to find and capture the scar-faced man, but she remained silent, her gaze dropping to where her fingers were entwined with his. She was vaguely surprised at the sight, unsure when she had taken his hand, or if he had taken hers. She watched as his thumb brushed over her knuckles. Oddly, she felt safe and comforted.

"The room is all ready," Lady Barlow announced, returning.

Determined to get there on her own, Maggie quickly gained her feet, then paused, swallowing as bile rose in her throat. The room spun. She made no protest when James scooped her into his arms; instead she caught her arms around his neck and leaned her head wearily against his shoulders, breathing in the scent of him as he followed his aunt out into the hall.

Maggie stayed silent as he carried her up the stairs to the second level, the feel of his strong encircling arms reminding her of the intimacies they had shared that day in the country. Remembering his arms around her then, his hands moving cleverly over her body, his lips warm and demanding on hers . . .

Reaching the top of the stairs, James glanced down, his face lowering as he did, so that their lips were a bare breath away. For one brief moment, Maggie thought he might kiss her. She felt her heart speed up a bit, some of the weariness dropping away from her, but then he lifted his head again and nodded at a comment from his aunt.

Her breath coming out on a small sigh, Maggie turned to see that they had arrived. Lady Barlow was holding the door open for James to carry her into the room that was to be hers. He crossed the room to the bed—pausing as his aunt rushed forward to pull the coverlets back—then bent to set her gently down on its soft surface. The moment he released her and stepped away, Maggie missed his arms around her.

"Out you go, James. Go talk with Robert," Lady Barlow ordered as he straightened. Lord Ramsey left the room without protest, pulling the door closed behind him. She turned back to Maggie and smiled. "He thinks I am put out with him and is walking softly now, else he would have resisted leaving."

"Why would he think you are angry at him?" Maggie asked curiously.

The older woman moved to the bedside and urged

her to sit so that she could set to work at unfastening the back of her dress.

"Your buttons are mismatched," she announced with a chuckle, undoing them quickly. She helped Maggie to her feet to remove the gown, then answered her question. "He thinks I am angry about the faux tea party. I just learned of it tonight."

"You do not sound very angry with him," Maggie said when Lady Barlow paused to consider her in her shift. It had gone undamaged in the fire, but carried the distinct odor of smoke. Both women wrinkled their noses.

"I am not. In fact, I am delighted," Lady Barlow admitted, then she said, "I think we had best remove your shift as well, my dear. That smoky smell might give you nightmares."

When Maggie nodded in agreement, James's aunt helped her remove that last article. The older woman clucked in dismay as the various bruises Maggie had gained during her struggle were revealed. While her face had taken the worst damage, her hip was not far behind, and there were several other contusions across her body. The moment the shift was gone, Maggie slid into the bed, self-consciously pulling the sheets up to cover herself.

"Wait here, I shall fetch you something to wear," Lady Barlow began, then paused at Maggie's weary face and hesitated, before saying, "Well, perhaps you can do without tonight."

Maggie felt relief course through her. She didn't think she had the energy to don anything. She was having difficulty even keeping her eyes open. She watched the caring woman bustle about, collecting the discarded clothes, then asked the question that had been nagging her for several moments: "Why are you delighted that James tricked me into coming to tea?"

"Because I want grand-babies." Lord Ramsey's aunt frowned then added, "I mean grand-nieces and nephews."

Maggie stared at the woman, unsure what one thing had to do with the other. None of this was making sense to her, but she was far too weary to figure it out. She closed her aching eyes.

"My room is just next door," the older woman said quietly as she prepared to leave. "Just call out if you need anything."

"Thank you," Maggie whispered on a yawn.

"You are very welcome, dear. Sleep well."

Maggie didn't answer. She was already asleep.

It was an extremely rough night. Plagued by nightmares of being beaten and burned alive, Maggie struggled toward consciousness several times, only to relax as she dreamed she was held in strong, protective arms, and that James was murmuring comforting words to her.

A soft weeping drew her out of sleep the following morning. Opening her eyes slowly, she peered around the soothing green room she'd slept in until she spotted the source of the misery. Her maid Mary sat in a chair by the bedside. Obviously Lady Barlow's footman had brought her staff last night as promised, Maggie realized. But that didn't explain why the girl was sobbing.

Concern overtaking her, Maggie struggled to sit up, drawing the girl's attention. "Oh, m'lady, ye should rest," Mary cried, leaping from her seat at once and trying to force her mistress back down.

"Nay, let me up. What is the matter? Was someone hurt? James? Lady Barlow? Banks?" She started to run through the names of everyone on her staff, but Mary shook her head for each.

"Nay, m'lady. Everyone's fine. Except for you, o'course," she added, biting her lip and turning away.

Frowning in confusion, Maggie tried to understand what had the girl crying, then nearly kicked herself when she realized it must surely be the town house itself. It had been home to all of Maggie's servants too, of course, and every last possession they had had been destroyed in the fire along with her own. In fact, she realized as she noticed Mary wearing the same gown she'd donned for the fair yesterday, they had been left with only the clothes on their backs.

"Do not worry, Mary. There is no need to cry. I shall see that your clothes are replaced. In fact, you can all go today and purchase what you need. Just have everything put on my account."

"Thank ye, m'lady, but that isn't why I was crying."

"Then why *are* you crying?" she asked in exasperation.

The girl hesitated, her eyes returning reluctantly to Maggie's face. Then she cried mournfully, "Oh, m'lady, yer beautiful face!"

Fear touching her at the girl's horrified expression, Maggie struggled out of bed. Stumbling to the dressing table, she let a gasp slip from her lips as she saw herself. The entire right side of her face was a swollen mess of mottled red, black, and blue. If the left side of her face were not nearly untouched, she wasn't sure if she would have recognized herself. Her own eyes brimming with tears, she sank to sit on the dressing table chair.

She stared at herself for several minutes, her hands raising to touch her injured face, then Mary stepped up behind her holding out a robe. "Lady Barlow sent this up for you to use."

Maggie met the maid's reflected gaze in the mirror as she slipped the robe on. Her expression was pitying, her eyes full of sympathetic tears. The girl was about to burst into loud sobs again, Maggie realized and stiffened her spine.

"Well, that shall teach me to use my face for a club when next I fight off an attacker," she said with determined cheer. All it managed to do was cause Mary to lift the skirt of her apron to cry into it. Heaving herself up from the bench, Maggie moved to her side. She patted the girl's shoulder soothingly. "Oh, Mary, do not cry. It will heal in time."

For a moment, Maggie thought her words had worked. Mary paused and lifted wide eyes to her, but then she wailed, "Oh, m'lady, ye're so brave!" Then she set to sobbing even harder.

Maggie was still trying to soothe the girl a few moments later when the door opened and Joan and Nora entered carting a chest between them. Their sister's sobs brought them to an immediate halt, and they both stared with alarm.

"What's the matter with . . ." Nora paused midquestion as she spotted Maggie's face. Her eyes widened in horror, then, and she dropped her end of the chest with a thump. "Gor!"

"Blimey, he pummeled ye right ugly," Joan said as she, too, caught sight of her mistress. Letting the other end of the chest drop to the floor as well, she followed her sister over to get a better look.

Maggie shifted with irritation. There was just some bruising and swelling. It wasn't as if she were permanently disfigured. They were all overreacting terribly, she thought impatiently.

A rustling made all four women glance around.

"Is there something wrong, Banks?" Maggie asked with concern when she spotted the old retainer dithering in the doorway.

"No, my lady. I just thought to have a word with you . . . If you have a moment?"

"Of course." She glanced at the three maids who promptly started for the door. Maggie called out, "Collect the others together please, Mary. I should think the sooner you get the trip to the shops out of the way, the better."

"Aye, m'lady," the girl answered as she followed her sisters into the hall.

Banks waited until their voices had faded before crossing the room toward Maggie. "I wished . . ." He paused, wincing as he got near enough for his old eyes to focus on her brutalized face. Then, he drew himself up and said, "I wished to apologize."

"Apologize?" Maggie asked with confusion. "Whatever could you have to apologize for?"

"You. Your face." The butler's expression was tragic. "Your beautiful town house. All your—"

"Banks," Maggie interrupted gently, closing the last few feet between them to clasp his hands. "You have nothing for which to apologize. It is hardly your fault that someone broke in and—"

"But it is!" he protested. "I never should have left you alone. The only thing Master Gerald asked of me before he went bravely off to war was that I look after you, and—"

"You, too?" Maggie exclaimed, bringing confusion to

245

the butler's wizened face. "Good Lord, Gerald put everyone in charge of me. He must have thought me a complete ninny . . . or dicked in the nob."

"My lady! Nay!" Banks cried. "Master Gerald did not think you crazy. He loved you and wished the best for you." The man's shoulders slumped, then he forced them back up. "I failed him, and I failed you. But I vow to you here and now, I shall not fail either of you again. I shall look after you as I promised."

"Banks," she began, torn between affection and concern. "I do not—"

"Maggie?"

Margaret stiffened at that voice. Banks stood between her and the door, but she didn't need to see James to know it was him; she would recognize that voice anywhere. Her stillness ended when Banks started to turn to face the door. Recalling Mary, Joan, Nora, and even Banks's reaction to the sight of her face, she turned the opposite way, instinctively hiding her hideous bruises.

"Maggie?" She could hear the concern in his voice as Lord Ramsey drew nearer, and found herself glancing around in a panicky fashion, seeking an escape. Her earlier thoughts that it was "just bruising" and that it would "mend with time" flew out the window at the idea of him seeing her. But there was nowhere to hide, even were there time to do so. Trapped, she dropped her head, letting her hair drape down to obscure her face, and waited.

Banks excused himself, and Maggie heard the soft rustle of clothing as he left the room. The quiet click of the door being pulled closed told Maggie that she and James were alone. Then, he touched her shoulder, urging her to turn.

"Are you all right?" he asked when she kept her head bowed. "I know you had some nasty nightmares."

Maggie glanced up, her eyes wide. "You know . . . You mean I wasn't dreaming?" she asked in surprise.

Confusion covered his handsome face. "About what?"

"I was having nightmares, but I also dreamed that you were holding me," she admitted, before she could think better of it.

He smiled at her words. "Yes. For a little while. It seemed to soothe you."

She gave a shy nod, then stiffened as she realized he could see her face. She whirled away, ducking her head again. "Was there something you wanted?" she asked.

He was silent for a moment, then his feet came into view as he moved around to stand in front of her. "There is no reason to hide," he said quietly, forcing her face up with one finger.

"I look like a monster," she complained, trying to turn her back to him again. "Just the sight of me had Mary in tears."

"You do look pretty bad," he agreed honestly. When she lifted her face to glare at him for such an unchivalrous comment, she found his eyes twinkling.

"It will heal, Maggie," he assured her, then leaned forward to press a tender kiss to the corner of her lips.

Maggie inhaled, breathing in the scent of him as his lips brushed hers. The smell and taste of this man were familiar and exciting and took her right back to the their passionate moments in the library at Ramsey. It seemed like a century had passed since then, and Maggie couldn't hold back a moan of protest when he started to draw away. His mouth returned at once, and she could feel his smile before his tongue slid out to lave her lips.

Maggie moved closer, her arms creeping around James's neck as his slid around her waist. He pressed her tight against him until there was no space between their bodies, then he drove his tongue into the moist depths of her mouth. Pleasure rippled through her, and Maggie groaned. All her aches and pains, all her worries and fears dropped away. She felt safe and warm. She felt as if she had come home. Then he eased their embrace so that his hands could slip between them. He undid her robe with one tug at the sash and eased it open, then paused.

"Oh, Maggie," he breathed, and the regret in his voice made her peer down. She had been so horrified at the sight of her face, she had not even noticed her other bruises. Now she gazed at herself with amazement. There was one on the side of one breast, another on her ribs, and then a rather nasty one on her hip. There were more contusions on her legs, but Maggie was suddenly self-conscious standing there revealed and tried to draw her robe closed.

James caught her hands to stop her and bent to give her another kiss. It was unlike the ones they had shared in his library. Where those had been carnal, this one was sweet, slow and gentle; his lips and tongue were soothing her rather than invasive. The kiss stirred a lazy desire and sent a sluggish warmth flowing through her.

Maggie sighed into his mouth and relaxed in his embrace, then opened her eyes as his lips left hers. She watched his head duck, and caught her breath as he pressed a light kiss to the bruise on her injured breast— a feathery caress she barely felt as his hand closed over the other. Biting her lip, she watched him palm then squeeze that breast before shifting his hand to a more supportive hold as his mouth closed over her nipple.

"James," she breathed as he drew the cinnamon-colored flesh into his mouth and suckled. He barely seemed to have started, when he stopped and moved down to brush his lips over the angry discoloration on her upper ribs. The caress began as light as a butterfly's wings but ended with an erotic lick of the underside of her breast. Then James sank to his knees and his mouth whispered over the angry wound on her hip.

Maggie sighed again, then gasped when he moved his lips to the inner curve of her other hip. Her stomach jumped at the action, and she gripped the top of his head, as her legs went suddenly weak. His mouth moved to her stomach and he pressed a kiss there, his tongue delving briefly into her belly-button. He started to move lower, but his hands shifted to the back of her hips, and Maggie couldn't keep from crying out in pain.

James's head lifted at once, then he moved her robe aside and shifted on his knees to peer at her injury there. It was nearly as bad as her face, and she saw his sympathetic wince, then he stood, drew her robe closed and took her into his arms.

Holding her tenderly he said, "I am sorry. I didn't mean to add to your pain."

"You didn't. Well, I mean, I know you didn't," Maggie sighed.

Drawing back, James smiled at her, then pressed a quick kiss to her uninjured cheek. "I should go. I am meeting an agent from your insurer at the town house. He wishes to assess the damage and make arrangements for repairs."

Maggie opened her mouth to assure him that she could do that, then recalled her damaged face and changed her mind. She had almost forgotten how to accept aid since Gerald's death. This time she would take the offered help. "Thank you."

"You're welcome." James's smile widened, then he hugged her briefly and released her to cross the room. He paused when he came abreast of the chest Joan and Nora had carted in. "These are some of my sister's old gowns," he explained. "She and Aunt Viv are both pack rats. Neither of them ever throw anything out. See if you can't find something decent in here to wear, then come below. You can tell me what you wish me to say to the insurer before I leave."

Maggie nodded and watched him exit the room. Her body was still tingling. She also felt warm and . . . soothed. She had never felt like this before.

Chapter Fourteen

Maggie placed another stitch in the gown she was working on, then set it in her lap so that she could flex her hands and rub soothingly at her neck, which was beginning to crick. The last several days seemed made up of working endlessly at the task of altering James's sister's old gowns.

James and Lady Barlow had wanted to bring a dressmaker in to make new clothes for her—both of them offering to bear the expense of such an undertaking—but Maggie's pride would not allow her to accept such a generous gift. She was already terribly beholden to them, and she found it difficult to even accept these castoffs without some repayment. But neither Lady Barlow nor her nephew would hear of remuneration, so Maggie was forced to accept their generosity. She needed clothes, after all, and she was hoping that at some point she would be able to find a way to repay them.

Though, she supposed, she should be thinking of James's sister. It was that girl's old clothes being given away so freely.

Sighing, she picked up her needle and the green gown she was working on and again returned to her efforts. The day after the fire, Lady Barlow had spent a good deal of time helping her pin and sew the gowns so that the bodices fit. Maggie had sent her servants out to purchase clothes to replace their own lost wardrobes, and had appreciated the older woman's assistance, in their absence, but once the maids had returned and been available to help her, Maggie had convinced the older woman to return to her usual daytime activity of calling on friends.

While her female servants had assisted Maggie in sewing upon returning from their shopping trip, her male servants had gone with James to inspect the damage to the house, to see what—if anything—was salvageable. They had returned with the comforting news that the fire brigade her insurance company ran had arrived in time to ensure that most of the fire damage had been confined to the kitchens and the room above. The rest of the house had merely suffered smoke damage. While most of its furnishings needed reupholstering, and the linens and clothing needed replacing, the house itself was sound and would be quite inhabitable in no time. The work was, thank heavens, covered by the insurance Gerald had always insisted she keep.

Unfortunately, while James almost convinced her with his reassuring smiles, Maggie's butler, Banks, was a lousy liar. She had seen right through the tale. The way her butler had twisted his hat in his hands and avoided her gaze had made it clear that James was lying through his teeth. And the fact that, even several days later, the servants still returned each night to Lady Barlow's after spending the days helping to clear the town house seemed to confirm her fear.

At first it had just been the men leaving each morning to help out at the town house, but this morning Maggie had sent the women along, too, keeping only Mary back to help her with the last of her gowns. It had been cowardice that made her do so. With all of her maids sewing, they had been running through the gowns quite quickly, and Maggie had wanted to slow their progress. She was afraid that once she finished with all the alterations, Lady Barlow would insist on Maggie's accompanying her on social calls, and while Maggie's face was slowly returning to normal, it was still slightly swollen and an unattractive yellow. She was not vain by nature, but had no wish to be seen as she was.

Besides, she had some thinking to do. If, as she suspected, her brother's house was more damaged than James was letting on, she doubted if the insurance she'd purchased would cover the repairs. Which had her fretting. She needed money. Desperately. In fact, she had the gloomy feeling that her financial position was more precarious than ever.

Maggie scowled and jabbed her needle into the cloth she held, knowing that she shouldn't be wasting her time sewing extra garments. She should be out researching another story for the *Daily Express*.

Fortunately, Hartwick had long ago assured her he would take as many stories as she could write. Up until now, she had only ever supplied one article every two weeks; it wasn't so easy to keep coming up with fresh ideas, and biweekly articles had been enough to keep them afloat. Now she would have to squeeze out more. The only problem was, with her mind on all the many trials and tribulations in her life, she couldn't seem to think of anything good to write about.

Frowning, she considered the matter, thinking up and discarding one story line after another. One was too boring, another too similar to an article she'd already done. She was almost relieved when Meeks coughed at the doorway, drawing her attention from her rather hopeless thoughts.

"Yes?" she asked as the man came forward. He held a small silver tray in his hand, bearing a folded piece of paper.

"A letter for you, my lady."

"For me?" Her eyebrows shot up in surprise, but she set her sewing aside and took the note. "Thank you." Nodding, the man turned and wordlessly left the room.

Maggie opened the unsealed note and read the letter with growing surprise and relief. It was from Maisey, an answer to the letter she had sent more than a week back about their traded gowns and the possibility of calling it even. The subject had quite slipped her mind, what with everything that had happened since. The delay was clarified at the beginning of the letter; the girl explained that she had been away at a private house party during the whole of this last week.

Maggie grimaced slightly, knowing as she did the girl's occupation, then read on, relieved to find that the girl thought it more than fair that they call it quits on the gowns. She would keep the money Frances had offered to replace the ripped gown, and Maggie need not worry about replacing the red one.

It was one worry off her mind, but Maggie's relief knew no bounds when the young woman then mentioned that she had come across a certain club in which G. W. Clark might have some interest—a club in which it was said dastardly things took place. Maggie was to write back at once and let Maisey know if she was interested, then the girl could set up a time when it was convenient for Maggie to attend. The prostitute was even willing to go with her for a fee.

"Meeks," Maggie called, refolding the letter.

The man must have been waiting outside the door, because he stepped back into the room at once, not looking the least ruffled or surprised.

"It says here that the boy who brought the note would wait for a reply. Is there a—"

"I sent him to the kitchens to wait," Meeks answered calmly. Seeming to feel it necessary to explain, he added, "I could not leave the little urchin alone in the entry while I delivered the note; he might have pocketed something. And the neighbors would have complained had I left him on the stoop."

Maggie bit back an amused smile. She didn't believe his claim for a minute. The man was as soft as a raw egg. No doubt he had ordered the cook to find food and water for the "urchin." He had a kind heart.

"Yes, of course. I understand," she murmured, setting her sewing aside so that she could get up. "Do you think it would be all right if I used some of Lady Barlow's paper and ink to write a response?"

"Of course, my lady. Lady Barlow has said that I am to get you anything you require. If you follow me, I will show you to the library and supply you with all necessities for your correspondence."

"Thank you." Ignoring Mary's curious gaze, Maggie followed the man to the library, working out her answer in her head as she went. This was too perfect. She desperately needed a story, and Maisey, the dear girl, was giving her just that. It was the first stroke of good luck she'd had since that fateful night at Madame Dubarry's. Perhaps things were starting to look up.

James stepped down from his carriage and walked jauntily up to his aunt's house, a smile on his face. He had spent the day overseeing work on Maggie's town house and was pleased with how things were coming. The house had nearly been gutted before the fire brigade from the Union Assurance company—Maggie's insurance company—had arrived to put it out.

Of course, he hadn't told her that. The fuss she had raised over accepting a couple of cast-off gowns of his sister's, and her absolute refusal to allow him or his aunt to assist by purchasing her new gowns to replace the ones she had lost in the fire, had warned him she would be too proud to accept any help in repairing the town house. He had also realized, after a conversation with her insurer, that her coverage would not fund all of the necessary repairs, nor the replacement of her furnishings. So he had lied.

He knew without a doubt that Maggie wasn't completely fooled by his fabrications, but he was also quite sure that there was nothing she could do about them. He had brought in droves of workers and even her own people to ensure that the repairs and rebuilding were done quickly, and it was moving along nicely. Another day or so and her staff would even be able to move back in. By the time Maggie got to see it, she wouldn't be able to tell how much damage there had been or how costly it had been to set right. He would lie about the money, and she would not be able to prove otherwise. He was quite satisfied with his handling of the matter.

Reaching the door, James rapped lightly with his cane, then whistled lightly as he waited for it to be opened, enjoying the anticipation building within him. He had visited Maggie and his aunt often since the fire, usually playing cards with both ladies, though on occasion he had played chess alone with Maggie in the library while his aunt entertained friends in the salon. The doors had been left open on these occasions, of course, as was proper and expected.

James enjoyed those visits best. Maggie relaxed more around him when his aunt wasn't present, her smiles and soft laughter enchanting.

Tonight his aunt was having a small gathering of friends. James had not planned to attend—he'd expected to be meeting with Johnstone for an update on Maggie's attacker—but he had received a letter from the runner just moments ago and learned the man was rushing out of town tracking a clue and would miss their meeting. James had promptly ordered his carriage and headed for his aunt's—for Maggie.

He had no doubt she would be easily culled from the herd of females and lured to the library. It had not escaped his notice that despite the fact that her bruises were nearly gone, she was still shy about displaying her face in public. He had every intention of taking advantage of that.

The door was opened by Meeks. The old man's eyes

widened in surprise upon seeing him. "My lord, I thought you had a meeting and were not to be present tonight."

"My meeting was canceled," James announced cheerfully. He stepped inside.

"Oh, I am glad you are here, my lord."

"And I am glad to be here." James handed over his hat and cane to the man, his gaze straying to the salon door. He could hear the muffled murmur of female voices coming through it. "Is Maggie in there with the rest of the women?"

"Nay, my lord," Meeks answered grimly.

James paused on his way to the door to turn back questioningly. "Where is she then? Up in her room?"

"Nay, my lord. She is not here."

"What?" He stared at the butler, uncomprehending. "What do you mean, she is not here? Where *is* she?"

The servant hesitated briefly; then his mouth firmed with unhappiness. "She received a letter today, my lord. From someone named Maisey."

James's eyes widened in horror, and he snatched his hat and cane back. "Dear Lord, she has gone back to Dubarry's."

"Nay," Meeks said quickly, following him to the door. When James turned on him, the man seemed to struggle with his conscience, then admitted, "The letter was not sealed. A street urchin brought it. I dropped the note, it fell open, and I just happened to see—"

"You read it," James snapped, unwilling to waste time on the man's excuses. "What did it say?"

Meeks colored slightly, but he straightened and said with dignity, "This Maisey person claimed to know of a club she thought G. W. Clark might be interested in. A men's club."

"Which one?" James prompted.

"The letter did not say. It simply mentioned a club with dastardly goings-on and requested that her ladyship reply as to whether she was interested in the club and when might be a convenient time to investigate it."

"And what was Maggie's answer?" James asked impatiently.

Meeks drew himself up indignantly. "I would not stoop to reading her ladyship's letters."

James frowned. No, he would not expect the man to be so impertinent as to open a sealed letter as Maggie's response clearly would have been.

"But," the butler went on. "A second missive to Lady Margaret also went unsealed. It simply said seven o'clock tonight, and an address. There was a mask with the letter."

"A mask?" James asked suspiciously. What was Maggie up to? "What kind of mask?"

"It was quite distinctive. A teal-and-gold feathered affair."

James digested that, then glanced up sharply. "Do you recall the address in the letter?"

"Of course."

"Good man," he said with relief.

Maggie leaned against the wall of the building, doing her best to look inconspicuous as she watched carriage after carriage stop and disgorge masked individuals and couples in front of the address across the street. The house looked completely normal, no different from any of the other town houses in this district, but if what Maisey hinted at was true, there was more going on than just a masked ball.

Shifting impatiently, she glanced nervously up the street, her eyes searching for any sign of Maisey. The problem was, Maggie wasn't sure for what she was supposed to be looking. Maisey was about Maggie's height, with dirty-blond hair, but if the girl came masked like the others, Maggie wasn't certain she would be able to spot her.

Worse, there was a good possibility that Maisey would not recognize her, either, despite the mask the other girl had sent to make the task easier. The young prostitute would be looking for that mask on a woman, and Maggie was not dressed as a female. She had decided at the last minute to go dress as a man, an idea that had come to her while she searched the attic for shoes to match the gown she'd intended to wear.

Maggie had worn nothing but slippers around Lady Barlow's town house since the fire. She could hardly wear those out of the house, however, and Jean and Nora had mentioned while helping her sift through the chest of Sophie's gowns—retrieved under Lady Barlow's direction—that the attic was stuffed full of all sorts of things, including masks, fans, shoes, and the like. Searching through that treasure trove of stored items, Maggie had come upon a chest filled with male clothing.

The style and size of the boxed garments had convinced her that they were no doubt castoffs from James's youth, and the idea had struck like lightning that she should attend the men's club as a male. She'd had no problem finding appropriate garb in the chest for an evening at a men's club, not to mention a pair of old dress boots that fit nicely, and so her mind had been made up. She tied her hair at her nape, slid it down the back of her shirt, and donned the mask and a top hat.

Fortunately, the mask was rather neutral in style, so it was not unlikely for a man to wear. It also boasted enough feathers and other trinkets to hide the fact that Maggie's hair was long and tied back.

Grimacing, she shifted her legs, glancing around to be sure no one was looking her way, then she gave the back of her breeches a brief tug. This was not the first time that Maggie had camouflaged herself in male dress, but it was not a disguise she often chose when she could avoid it. Binding her breasts was a rather painful procedure, and besides, she wasn't all that comfortable in these tight-fitting breeches. While James had been the same size in his youth, at least length-wise in the legs, he hadn't apparently had any hips. Maggie found the breeches far too snug for comfort across her bottom, especially when compared to the freedom of billowing bloomers and skirts. She found herself plagued by the constant and horrendous urge to tug at the behind of the trousers to draw them away from her skin.

It had not occurred to her while she had donned this brilliant disguise that she was just making matters more difficult, that Maisey would never think to look for a male. All she had been concerned with was that should the scarred man see her slipping away through the garden gate at the back of Lady Barlow's home, he would not recognize her—leaving her safe from that concern for a bit as she investigated this club where dastardly events took place.

Now she realized it had been an incredibly stupid idea. Maisey had sent the mask to aid in identifying Maggie, and she would hardly be looking for it on a man. She might very well not notice Maggie at all tonight.

Heaving out an impatient breath, she peered up the

street, trying to work out how much time had passed since she had left Lady Barlow's. She had made her exit an hour before the appointed time, walking several blocks before feeling it was safe enough to hail a hack. She had planned to be here early. Maggie was always early for appointments. But it surely must be nearly seven o'clock by now. Where was Maisey?

"*Lady Margaret.*"

Maggie gave a start at that hiss from behind her. Turning, she peered into the shadows cast by the awning of the building, barely able to discern a cloaked and masked figure several steps away. "Maisey?" she asked.

Nodding, the girl moved forward to the edge of the shadows. "Why are you dressed as a man? You should have worn a gown."

"I did not think it would matter. Does it?" Maggie asked worriedly.

Maisey hesitated, her eyes moving along the street, then across the road to the house, where yet another masked couple was spilling form their carriage; then she shifted impatiently. "It will have to do. Come."

Turning away, the prostitute led her across the street at a quick clip that didn't slow until they neared the door to the "club." Gesturing for Maggie to wait there, Maisey approached one of the two doorman standing on either side of the entrance a few steps away and held a brief, whispered conversation with him. It concluded with her dropping several coins into his open palm. Then, gesturing for Maggie to follow, the young woman entered the house, hardly glancing at the second doorman.

Offering a weak smile when the man turned his gaze on her, Maggie followed Maisey reluctantly into an entryway. There, another pair was handing over their cloaks to a servant. Maisey whipped off her own, tossed the expensive item onto the already weighed down man, then waited impatiently for Maggie to do the same. She removed her borrowed cape and handed it to the servant with an apologetic expression, then followed her guide and the other couple into a room filled with noise and color.

Maggie's eyes widened behind her mask as she absorbed the multitudes inside. The room was crammed to capacity, and she struggled to push her way through to keep up with Maisey. The masked occupants were both men and women, all talking and crowding together. There wasn't much out of the ordinary here that she could see, however. It was true that everyone seemed to be standing a bit closer than was absolutely proper, but space constraints dictated they had little choice in the matter.

Realizing that Maisey was outstripping her, and afraid she would lose the woman in the crowd, Maggie forced her way through the throng a bit faster, apologizing for her rudeness as she attempted to catch up. She did so just as Maisey started up a set of stairs to a second level, and caught at her arm anxiously. "Where are we going?"

"Upstairs is where all the action is," the girl paused to whisper, then continued on apparently confident Maggie would follow. Which she did, looking back over her shoulder as they went. From above, it was clear that everything wasn't as ordinary as she had first thought. While the majority of people were standing talking in the center of the room, there appeared to be a great deal of inappropriate touching going on. Scanning the edges of the crowd, Maggie discerned the true nature of this gathering. There were couples crammed into all manner of corners and recesses, indulging in the most improper behavior. She'd heard of members of the ton sneaking away into the gardens—shocking as that was!—but copulating against the wall was not acceptable at any of the balls she had ever attended.

"Come on!" Maisey called.

Realizing that she had stopped to gape down at the crowd below the stairs, Maggie turned to see her young guide moving off down the hall. Starting after her, Maggie did her best to ignore the lascivious couples lining the corridor, and hoped fervently that this article was worth this. She felt sullied just being in this place. Briefly she considered fleeing, but then she thought of the fire and the expenses incurred daily to repair her home, and she stiffened her spine. An hour—no, half an hour—and she would surely have the information she needed and be out of here. She assured herself of that with more hope than certainty and moved determinedly forward.

She hadn't taken more than a few steps when a scream from behind a door she was passing brought her to an abrupt halt. It had been a cry of agony, and Maggie felt chills run down her back. Was someone being murdered behind this wooden portal?

"Come on!" Maisey was suddenly at her side, taking her arm and dragging her forward again.

"But it sounded like someone was—"

"Games," the prostitute said in a hiss; then she showed Maggie the back of her head as she dragged her forward. For a moment Maggie felt trepidation race through her. Then, recalling some of the tales the prostitutes at Madame Dubarry's had told her, she forced herself to relax. She had seen for herself the games that Pastor Frances had enjoyed. They were just games, she assured herself silently. Then she frowned. If all this was just some sort of sex club . . . But Maisey had said "dastardly things" happened here.

Confused and unhappy, Maggie sped up until she drew abreast of her short guide. "You said 'dastardly things' happened here. What—"

"You'll see soon enough," the other woman assured her, pausing near the door at the end of the hall and producing a key. After turning it in the lock, she pocketed the item and went through the now open door leaving Maggie to follow. After a quick glance down the hall, Maggie did so. Inside, her gaze moved over the room's odd trappings as Maisey lit a single candle by the bedside, then carried it to the window to stare at the street below.

"What—?"

"Shh," Maisey hissed, then hesitated before setting the candle on the window ledge and walking to the door. "There is a peep hole in that painting on the wall. Through it, you can see the room next door. I'll return shortly."

"But . . ." Maggie started anxiously toward the prostitute, breaking into a run when the girl stepped out into the hall and pulled the door closed. She heard the lock click as she reached it, and she cursed. Maisey certainly liked to lock her in uncomfortable places, she thought with disgust. She twisted the doorknob futilely.

Giving the door an angry kick, she turned and surveyed the chamber. The bed was the only ordinary item in the room. An oddly angled bench with chains on it and an oddly shaped chair with wrist locks made her wonder just what went on here. Her second thought, as she peered at chains dangling from the ceiling and affixed to the walls, and a selection of whips and various other unpleasant-looking items along one wall, was that she probably didn't want to know.

Forcing herself to take a deep breath, she glanced at the painting Maisey said had a peep hole and moved for a better view. It didn't take long for her to realize that the eyes in the rather naughty portrait were hollowed out. Unfortunately, they were a good foot above her head. Moving to the chair with the wrist locks, she dragged it over to position it beneath the painting, then climbed onto it and peered through the eyeholes. A room similarly outfitted to the one she was in was all there was to see. It was empty.

Sighing, she stepped back down off the chair and glanced around, then paced the room, examining each various item therein. When she reached the door, she tried the doorknob again, but it was still locked. On impulse, she knelt and pressed her eye to the keyhole. Despite the fact that the room she was in was at the end of a hall and presented a clear view of its length, there wasn't much to see. The corridor was still crowded with couples indulging in libertine behavior she had barely touched on in those frantic moments in the Ramsey library. She supposed this was quite an education—and more like what she'd expected in Maisey's closet—but not one she really wanted. Maggie was about to straighten from the keyhole when a figure mounting the last few stairs at the end of the passage caught her attention. Surprised, she stared at the man as he moved up the hallway.

He wasn't wearing a mask.

That was what had originally caught her attention, but as he drew closer and his face came into better focus, her

eyes froze on the scar. Sucking in her breath on an
alarmed gasp and shoving instinctively back from the
door, she tumbled from her knees onto her behind. She
stared at the keyhole briefly, as if it were a snake, then just
as quickly returned to her kneeling position. Much to her
horror, she saw as she again peeked outside that the man
was moving straight up the hallway. It seemed she hadn't
given him the slip with her disguise after all. He must
have followed her, had probably just been waiting for
her to be alone! *Dammit!* Where was Maisey?

Realizing that the girl wouldn't return in time, and
probably wouldn't be much help against the brute in
any case, Maggie cursed and leaped to her feet. She
searched frantically around the room for a weapon.

Her gaze flew over whips and chains in agitation; she
somehow didn't see herself wielding any of them with
much success. Still she grabbed the nearest one, then
took an empty candleholder in her other hand for good
measure. Turning grimly to face the door, she readied
herself for battle. Her intrepid stance lasted until she
heard the key in the lock; then Maggie's courage failed
her and she scrambled in a panicked shuffle to the wall
behind the door. Perhaps she might take him by surprise and bash him over the head as he entered.

The door opened, and Maggie reacted out of hysteria
more than anything else. She leaped from her hiding
place with a shriek, which made the intruder turn with
a start. She brought the candleholder down on the side
of his head with all her terrified strength. Much to her
amazement, the man gaped at her, then went down like
a felled tree.

Maggie stared uncomprehendingly at his unconscious
form for a moment, hardly believing it had been so easy,

then regained her scattered wits enough to drop her makeshift weapons and scramble over the man's legs and out the door. She was running at full-tilt, paying no attention to the startled reactions of the people in the hallway in her haste to flee the scene, so that when she suddenly found someone in her path, she smashed blindly into his bulk. With a moan of despair at the delay, she scrabbled to break free of the hands that rose automatically to restrain her.

"Maggie?"

Some of her hysteria slipping away, Maggie focused on the face of the man gawking down at her. Lord Ramsey's wonderfully familiar features took shape.

"James," she said with relief.

His expression immediately turned from shock to anger. Maggie bit her lip, then glanced back the way she had come.

"That man . . ." was as far as she got before she found herself being jerked along the hall by her arm. James was obviously furious, she realized, and peered over her shoulder toward the room where she'd left her attacker. He was beginning to stir. She considered telling James about the man, then decided against it. Scarface was a very strong man—bigger than Lord Ramsey—and she didn't want to see James hurt. Perhaps it was best all around if they simply left well enough alone and got out of there.

She made no protest as James jogged her down the stairs and dragged her through the crowded room to the exit. He had hauled her out of the house and crammed her into his carriage before she recalled that her borrowed cloak was still inside.

Chapter Fifteen

"I . . ." Maggie began in an effort to explain herself as soon as the carriage door shut, enclosing them in darkness and privacy, but James raised a hand to silence her.

"Not *one* word. Not one," he said in a furious hiss. "Or I might very well take you over my knee and . . ." His threat ended on a hiss of air.

Maggie stared, fascinated, at the tic of his eye for a moment, then, deciding she might do better to follow his advice, she turned her head to stare out the window. Neither of them said a word the entire ride back to Lady Barlow's. Maggie watched blindly out the window, her body stiff as she did her best to ignore the glare boring into her across the dark space between herself and Lord Ramsey.

When the carriage came to a halt, Maggie focused her eyes to see that they had arrived. She had hardly deduced their location when James thrust the door open, snatched her hand in his, and bounded out of the coach, hauling her after him. She was barely able to keep her feet as he dragged her to the door, his boots clacking angrily with each step. It was perhaps telling how angry he was that he did not knock or wait for anyone to open the front door of his aunt's town house, but thrust it aside as he had his carriage door. He pulled her inside.

Meeks rushed up as they entered, his eyes widening at the sight of them. He opened his mouth to speak, but James held up his hand as he had done with Maggie and merely sailed into the library with her.

The door slammed behind them as he tugged her across the room toward the fire. Then he paused and glanced around. Maggie wasn't sure what he was looking for, but she'd had just about enough of being lugged around like a horse by its reins. She pulled her hand free, the suddenness of the action probably the only reason she succeeded. James turned on her at once, and Maggie opened her mouth to go on the offensive, but she never managed a word. It seemed James had reached the end of his tether. Grabbing her by the upper arms, he pulled her abruptly against his chest. The action startled Maggie into closing her mouth, which was a darn good thing, since his lips then slammed onto hers with all the finesse of a charging bull. Had her mouth been open, she might have done him injury.

As it was, she winced as the inside of her lips were ground against her teeth in a brutal kiss. Then she began to struggle instinctively against his punishing grasp. James shifted his hold, wrapping one arm around her back, his other hand clasping her head and holding her in place as the kiss changed, becoming less harsh yet more demanding.

Maggie continued to struggle for a moment, then stopped, a gasp of shock escaping her as the arm around her waist shifted. One of James's hands slapped her bottom lightly through the pants she wore, then gently squeezed even as he urged her against him.

James took immediate advantage of her reaction. His tongue slipped inside her open mouth, but while she wasn't fighting him any longer, she didn't respond at once to his kiss. He pulled away and glared at her.

Maggie stared back, knowing that her confusion and a vague sense of hurt at his treatment were evident on her face. It took a moment before he seemed to see past his anger and notice; then he sighed and leaned his forehead against hers, still holding her tightly.

"I have never been so worried or frightened in my life as I was when I realized you were running about on your own. After those accidents, the fire . . . I was so afraid I was going to lose you."

His voice was low and husky. Maggie's eyes widened, her hands relaxing against his chest. The basis of this anger was fear. This was all because he feared losing her! And he had every right to that fear, she realized, recalling the man she'd left unconscious in that awful place. Her heart softening, Maggie slid her arms around James's waist, holding him.

"But you didn't. I am here. I am fine," she whispered.

His eyes opening, James pulled away enough that he could look at her again. Seeing her understanding expression, he managed a crooked smile. "I never want to feel like that again. Please don't go out again on your own like that. I will help you if you need to investigate a story. I—"

"Shhh." Maggie pressed a finger gently to his lips. "I promise never again to investigate a story without at least telling you. It was very foolish of me to go to meet Maisey alone. I should have known better after all that's happened, but I thought that I would be fine if I went in disguise. I was wrong," she added quickly when he would have interrupted. "I see that. And I am sorry I worried you. It will not happen again."

He remained speechless for a moment, staring into her face; then she felt the hand on her derriere move curiously against her bottom. A small smile crossed his lips. "You look rather delectable in men's clothing."

Maggie felt a blush rise from her chest to cover her throat and face, but she remained still in his arms, unresisting when he used the hand on her bottom to urge her lower body tighter against his. She could feel him growing hard against her. His gaze sought hers, and she met it unflinchingly; then his eyes dropped to her lips. She held her breath, letting it out on a disappointed sigh as his gaze traveled up over her face to her hair.

Smiling more devilishly, he reached behind her head and pulled her ponytail out of the back of her shirt, then removed the bit of ribbon she had used to tie it. The pale strands fell free, tumbling around her face and over her shoulders. Maggie remained still as he brushed his fingers through the tousled mane, smoothing it; then he caught her face in his hands and pressed a kiss to her lips.

The kiss started out gentle, James's lips soothing any hurt he might have caused with his earlier brutality, but it did not stay gentle for long. The moment Maggie opened her lips beneath his, kissing him back with innocent fervor, something seemed to ignite within them both. The embrace became consuming, his hands sliding away from her cheeks and beginning to explore her body, moving over the men's clothes she wore with curiosity and determination. One moment they were traveling over her breasts, through the shirt and binding that covered them; then his hands had slid back to her bottom, squeezing and lifting her against him so that his swollen arousal rubbed between her thighs.

Gasping, Maggie threw her arms around his shoulders and pressed herself tighter against him—eagerly, as he was pressing into her. He groaned into her mouth, then began to back her up until she felt the hard edge of Lady Barlow's desk pressing into her behind. Lifting her, gripping her buttocks, he sat her on the desk, then urged her legs apart so that he could step between them. He was still kissing her, his lips and tongue doing things that left her quivering and moaning into his mouth even as she kissed him in return. His hands were busy between them, working at her clothing.

She felt the cravat fall loose, then slide across the back of her neck as he drew it off her, but she hardly paid any attention, easing back slightly at his insistence, uncaring of the inappropriate nature of what he was doing as his hands moved over the front of her clothing. She hardly noticed when he pushed her waistcoat off her shoulders, or when her vest followed—except for a touch of impatience as her arms were briefly forced away from him. All she felt as the cloth slid off her to drop to the floor was relief that she could hold him again. She raised her hands at once to slide her fingers through his silky hair, thrusting her tongue out experimentally to tangle with his.

His fingers slid over her bound breasts, then dropped to tug at her linen shirt. She murmured encouraging sounds into his mouth as he freed her shirt and slid his fingers underneath running them lightly over the quivering muscles of her stomach, then the material she had used to bind her breasts.

Her arms tightened instinctively around him in protest when he suddenly broke away, but when his lips traveled down her throat she sighed gloriously and tipped her head back in delight. He nibbled and suckled at her flesh. She noticed nothing as he found where she had fastened her bindings, undid them, then began to unravel them, drawing the wrap around and around under her loose linen shirt, easing her discomfort with every go.

She moaned her relief into his mouth as the last of the bindings fell away, freeing her tender breasts from their bondage. She almost reached down to rub herself soothingly, but James took care of that, his hands cupping her gently and caressing the irritation away. Her discomfort was quickly replaced by a different feeling entirely. Within moments, Maggie was pressing into his hands, encouraging him to a less soothing touch.

James smiled against her lips, then pulled back and tugged her shirt quickly upward. Maggie felt herself blush as her breasts were entirely bared to him; then he pulled her forward until his lips closed around one erect nipple. She cried out, her modesty forgotten as he suckled and laved the sensitive tip.

Groaning in pleasure, Maggie pushed into the caress, her hands catching in James's hair, enjoying the soft textures as she pressed him closer. When she felt his hand slide down to cup her between the legs, she opened eyes she hadn't realized she'd closed.

Peering down at the cloth of her shirt, which he had let drop over his head to free his hands, she touched his hair through the linen with one trembling hand, then moaned in disappointment when he ducked out from beneath the material. His eyes met hers briefly; then he tugged her top away, attempting to lift it over her head and remove it entirely. The back of the shirt, though, was caught under her bottom where she sat on the desk.

James didn't hesitate; giving up his tugging, he reached for the collar and rent the shirt from collar to hem. Maggie gasped in shock as the garment came open; then she reached out to clasp him by the back of the neck and tug him forward to claim his lips with hers.

She kissed him in just as demanding and hungry a fashion as he usually kissed her, arching her back to thrust her breasts eagerly forward as his hands closed over them. It was madness, and it was delicious, and she ached to feel more of him. Releasing his neck, she felt her way to the front of his cravat, undoing and removing it with an ease that she could not duplicate with the buttons of his waistcoat. Much to her combined relief and disappointment, James's hands slid away from her breasts and moved to help, undoing and shedding first the waistcoat, then his vest with expedience.

Maggie didn't bother freeing his shirt from his breeches; reaching for the collar, she bit at his lower lip, holding him when he broke the kiss and tried to draw away. She slid her hands into the collar, pulling at the material. The garment did not rend as easily as her own, its material resisting, but with a little more force she heard the tear and felt the cloth give, splitting to James's waist. She promptly splayed her hands on his chest, her fingers spreading over his naked skin and nipples. Then she slid her hands around his waist and pressed forward to rub against him, shivering as the hair on his chest brushed her breasts.

He let her play that way briefly, then took over again, his lips mastering her as he urged her body forward slightly on the desk. As his hand slid down to press between her legs, Maggie felt the breath catch in her throat, her body freeze briefly with the shock of the sensations shooting through her. Liquid pooled in her lower abdomen; then James pulled away enough for his hands to work at her breeches.

It wasn't until the front flap of her breeches was undone and falling open, allowing air to brush against the skin of her stomach, that Maggie felt the first stirrings of the impropriety of all of this. His hand slid inside her breeches so swiftly, though, she couldn't catch his wrist in time to stop him. Then, as it brushed against her swollen flesh she wasn't sure she wanted him to stop.

"Oh," she moaned when he removed his hand from between her thighs. It was over, and, shameful as it was to admit, she didn't want it to be. Still she stood resignedly when he urged her to her feet.

Her eyes opened wide as James suddenly knelt before her, his hands catching the waist of her breeches and drawing them down. Maggie gave a strangled cry of embarrassment and instinctively tried to cover herself. James ignored this show of modesty, urging her to lift one leg, then the other so that he could remove the breeches from her legs entirely.

She expected him to stand again then, but he had other ideas. Pushing the trousers away, he glanced up at her with a devilish grin, then caught her by the ankles and tugged them swiftly apart—much as he had that day in his library when he'd dumped her in his chair. There was no chair this time, however, and Maggie was forced to stop trying to cover herself and grab the desk behind her for balance. Her alarm quickly turned to surprise, then trembling anticipation, as James's hands glided up the skin of her legs, tickling and tingling over the flesh of her calves, the backs of her knees, then up to her thighs, where they tightened and tugged, urging her lower body forward.

He pressed a kiss to her lower belly, leaned his forehead there and rubbed it once gently back and forth, then pressed a kiss to the hollow of her hip. Next came the top of her leg, as his hands slid to the inside of her thighs. The first brush of his fingers against her femininity made her buck like a wild horse; her body was assaulted by the same sharp sensations that had overwhelmed her in James's library. She'd forgotten how violent a reaction her body had to his touch. She remembered it quite clearly now. *This* was what had haunted her dreams. *This* had left her trembling and wanting in the mornings when she woke. This was . . .

"Oh, God." She gasped, closing her eyes tightly, her hands catching in James's hair. Her legs tried to close against the sensations he stirred as he probed the center of her excitement.

Apparently expecting that reaction, James caught her thighs. Instead of letting them close, he urged them farther apart. Catching her bottom lip between her teeth, Maggie leaned back, her thighs spread wide now of their own volition. Remembered anticipation flooded her as his head ducked between her legs.

Maggie stopped thinking. Thought was impossible under this assault to her senses. James's lips and teeth sucked and scraped over flesh burning with want. When he inserted one finger gently inside her, she was positive it was what her body was shrieking for. She shifted violently into the caress, her ability to speak reduced to grunts and groans and mindless begging. She wanted . . . She wanted . . .

She *wanted.*

She shifted and arched and ground mindlessly into his touch. As he straightened suddenly before her, his hand still manipulating her flesh, she pulled him to her by the hair, pressing upon him, an open-mouthed, desperate kiss. She raked at his shoulders until his upper body was pressed tightly against hers, naked flesh to naked flesh. Some vague memory of his guiding her hand to his arousal back at Ramsey rose in her mind, along with the feverish thought that perhaps, if she did it again, he might give her what she was aching for.

It was a purely selfish thought, but Maggie didn't particularly care. Sliding a hand between them, she sought and found the rigid length of him through his breeches. She smiled against his mouth when he stiffened. His mouth and hand froze until she squeezed, then ran her hand over the length of his hardness, then his kisses became more like her own desperate devouring.

Maggie didn't really have a clue what she was supposed to be doing, though, so relief washed through her when he brushed her hand aside. She felt his hand moving between them, but didn't realize what he was trying to do until he cursed against her lips, then tugged away to glance down. Following his gaze, she saw that he was trying to undo the buttons of his breeches. She started to reach down to aid him, but he didn't have any patience. Grasping the flap, he tugged violently, snapping most of the buttons and pulling the flap open so that his manhood sprang out.

Maggie's eyes widened incredulously at the size of the member pointing up at her, but then James moved closer, his lips gliding over her brow, down her cheek, and then to her lips. Her response to his kiss was a little less excited than it had previously been. Apparently noting this, James slipped one hand between her legs, obviously trying to rebuild some of that urgency. It didn't take much effort before Maggie was moaning and arching into his touch again. He left off his caresses to pull her a little further forward on the desk, and press her legs apart. Then, he paused.

Confused, Maggie glanced up to see the question in his eyes. He was awaiting permission. Biting her lower lip, she gave a slight nod. That was all he needed. Holding her firmly by the bottom, he plunged into her.

They both froze. For a moment the only sound was their labored breathing; then James lowered his head to glance at her uncertainly. "Are you all right?" he asked.

"Yes." Maggie's voice was slightly strangled, but understandable for all that. His penetration had caused a slight pinching sensation, but it was already gone. Feeling heat rise into her face, she cleared her throat. "You?"

A tiny laugh slipping from his lips, James leaned his forehead against hers and nodded. "Tell me when you are ready to continue."

Maggie hesitated, prepared to say "Right away," then

thought perhaps this would be terribly indelicate. She waited a twelve count before murmuring, "I think it would be all right to continue now, my lord."

She felt James begin to shake, and it took a moment to realize that he was laughing. Scowling, she drew back. "What is so funny?"

"You. Me," he admitted wryly—then all humor was gone from his face and his dark eyes seemed to swallow her. "God, you make me burn."

Maggie felt herself melt; then his mouth descended on hers. It was a hard, branding kiss, and he began to move out of her, then back in. Maggie wasn't impressed with the activity at first. It was pleasant enough, she supposed. At least, it wasn't *un*pleasant—but it did leave her wondering where all the fire and excitement had gone. That thought had barely crossed her mind when James used his hand on her bottom to change the angle of her hips, shifting himself at the same time to add a friction that had been absent.

Maggie gasped. Her earlier excitement returned in full force. Her nails dug unconsciously into the skin of James's shoulders as she arched into him, doing what she could to increase the fire that was building within her. Reaching and striving for the unnamed reward that awaited, Maggie instinctively closed her legs around his hips, her heels digging into his backside, urging him on.

"Oh, God, Maggie, I—" Breaking off that thought, whatever it had been, James reached between them, his hand searching the center of her desire, and Maggie cried out as his touch helped her finally find what she sought. She was so overtaken with the shattering discovery of her pleasure, she was barely aware of the way James suddenly thrust into her—or how he held still, his face contorted in what looked like pain as he gasped her name through gritted teeth.

Maggie was the first to recover. Aware of the echoes of a pulsing throb in her body, she turned her head against James's chest, her hands moving soothingly over his shoulders. He murmured something she couldn't understand where he slumped against her, then turned his head to press a kiss to the side of her throat, his arms tightening possessively around her.

Maggie was a little concerned to see the solemn expression on his face as he straightened. It rather pointed out just what they had indulged in and the possible ramifications. She knew instinctively she wasn't going to like what he said when he opened his mouth to speak, but wasn't any happier that he was cut off by the sudden opening of the library door.

"Really, my lady, I do not think—" Meeks's voice cried out in alarm. Maggie and James both watched in horror as the door opened.

"Nonsense, Meeks. I just want James to tell Lady Wingate here—" Lady Barlow's voice died abruptly as she stepped into the room and caught a glimpse of her nephew and her houseguest.

There was a moment of utter silence; then Lady Wingate—who—Maggie had unfortunately had the pleasure of meeting in previous, much more socially acceptable conditions—stepped around the frozen Lady Barlow and into view.

The old woman was a sweet, dear old friend of Lady Barlow's, one Vivian had known since her youth. She was also blind as a bat. Squinting at the tableau, she adjusted her glasses and tried to make out exactly what she was seeing. "What the devil? Is that you, James?

Who is that with you? And what in heaven's name are you doing on Vivian's desk?"

The woman's screech set everyone in motion at once. James stepped around to try to shield Maggie from view: a poor choice that left him hanging out for the world to see, and left little doubt as to what had been going on. Meanwhile, Maggie had slithered off the desk. Well, once she unstuck her behind from the wooden surface to which she seemed to have become some how adhered, she slithered off, dropping out of sight behind it.

Lady Barlow shook herself out of her own shocked state. She promptly turned to push her dear old friend out of the room. Meeks, always quick to help, muttered unintelligibly, grabbed the door, and tugged it abruptly closed behind himself as he followed the women out.

The room fell silent as James's aunt and her friend departed. James stood frozen for a moment, hands on his hips, his eyes closed against what had just happened, and a miserable sigh slipped from his lips. This was not what he had intended. Hell, he hadn't intended any-thing at all—but if he *had* planned anything, it would not have been this! He could hardly believe he had been caught in such a compromising position. *Dear God!* His brains had apparently gone a-begging. How had he been reduced to this? It was bad enough that he'd allowed his passions to overtake him and had taken Maggie on a writing desk like some rutting bull. But he had done so in his aunt's damned house, with her in the next room, where discovery was almost a certainty. What had he been thinking?

He knew what he had been thinking: he had been thinking of Maggie's silken thighs around him and her small, full breasts in his hands. He had been thinking of her lips soft and warm under his, and her warm, slick flesh wrapped around him. *Dear God, I'm thinking it again*, he realized with dismay, feeling himself swell with desire at the memories dancing through his poor beleaguered mind.

"James!"

Giving a start, he opened his eyes, guilt filling him as he met his aunt's furious gaze. She stood in the open doorway, obviously having returned to chastize him. Closing the door with a snap, she propped her hands on her hips and narrowed her eyes. "Put yourself away, young man, before I put that away for you!"

Brought to the realization that he was standing naked with a rather impressive—if he did say so, himself—erection in plain view, James turned quickly away. He tucked himself inside his breeches and did up the few buttons remaining after his earlier recklessness. That done, he started to turn back, then paused to tuck his shirt into his waistband and smooth his hair. He paused to take a long, deep, steadying breath, then turned to face his aunt's puckered expression.

"I . . ." he began, unsure what to say but ready to try. He needn't have bothered. Aunt Vivian wasn't up to listening to any of the nonsense he might have trotted out.

"I have managed to hustle every last one of my guests out. Where is Maggie?" she asked fiercely. James glanced over his shoulder, frowning when he saw the empty desk. A movement drew his gaze downward, and he spotted her barely covered derriere and ankles sticking out from beneath it. Knowing from experience how cramped and hot she would be, he sighed then stepped around the desk and bent forward to peer into the nook.

Maggie sat curled inside, her knees up, covered by her shirt and her arms. Her head was bowed, her eyes pressed firmly into her linen-obscured knees.

"Maggie?" he called gently. Her only response was to curl up tighter, like a child hiding from an angry nanny. Biting back a smile, James dropped to his haunches and reached out to brush one hand over her elbow. "Come out, love," he said.

Her head shook violently.

James was about to try again when a rustle of material warned him of his aunt's approach. He glanced up to see her expression soften as she saw Maggie, and he felt relief. This was a bad enough situation; he really had no desire to see his aunt blame her for it. It was entirely his fault, after all. She'd been an innocent. He was experienced, skilled, had overwhelmed her with his passion. . . .

His smugness died an abrupt death when his aunt snapped at him. "Get out of the way, James. Leave the girl alone. Haven't you done enough to her?"

Wincing at her sharp tone, he straightened and moved around the desk. His aunt paused to murmur something to Maggie, then followed James, her expression becoming grimmer with each step. He was not at all surprised when she launched her attack.

"So *this* is how you repay her brother for saving your lecherous life?"

"I am marrying her," was all he said.

"I have never been so ashamed in all my born days. That poor— What did you say?"

James nearly smiled at her astonishment, but managed to contain himself and repeated, "I shall marry Maggie, of course."

Aunt Vivian deflated like a sail losing its wind, then raised her head, her nose high. "Yes. Of course."

"A quick marriage would probably be best."

"Dear God, yes," she agreed. "Hazel Wingate is not known for her ability to keep a confidence." Moving toward the door, his aunt announced, "I shall start to make the arrangements. Perhaps you should coax Margaret out from under the desk. I will order a bath sent to her room . . . it should help her feel better."

Lady Barlow sailed out of the room, pulling the door closed behind her. Oddly, James would swear he had spotted a satisfied smile on her lips in that last moment. He frowned over it briefly, then turned to the desk as the chair squeaked, announcing Maggie's emergence from beneath.

Quickly rounding the desk, James took Maggie's hand to help her up, his heart aching when he spied the mortified expression on her face and the dark, rosy flush of humiliation on her skin. She ducked her head. This had been a lousy way to end her first experience in love-making, and he wouldn't have wished it on her for the world. She deserved better. The woman should have had a soft bed beneath her, a wedding ring on her finger, and a slow, passionate seduction. Instead she'd gotten a quick hump against his aunt's desk. He was an animal.

"This is awful."

Those muttered words from Maggie merely added to James's guilt. He pulled her body against his, a hug being the only thing he could think of to soothe her upset. It didn't appear to be working, he realized when she did not melt against him with relief, but stood stiff in his arms, her head shaking repeatedly in denial.

"Maggie," he murmured gently. " 'Tis not as bad as it seems. There will be some gossip, but once the marriage is accomplished, the rumors will die down and—"

"No."

"Yes, they will," he assured her, thinking she didn't believe him.

She pulled away and frowned at him. "I am not marrying you."

James blinked in amazement at her announcement, then, deciding she was too upset to think clearly, again tried to draw her into his arms. "Of course you are, my dear. We—"

"Nay, I am not," she argued, fighting her way out of his embrace. Bending, she snatched up her breeches from where they lay crumpled on the floor. "When my brother asked you to look after me, he hardly meant for you to sacrifice your life to my honor."

"That is a bit melodramatic, is it not?" he chided gently, a touch embarrassed that he couldn't seem to get his eyes off her derriere as she tugged the breeches onto first one leg, then the other. "I am not sacrificing my life. I had to marry sometime, after all."

"Yes, but—"

"And there is always the possibility of a child." Much to his satisfaction, that thought seemed to give her pause. The horrified expression that suffused her face was almost gratifying. That last had definitely been a winning argument. Quite inspired really, he thought.

She turned on him pleadingly. "Can we not wait and see? Perhaps we will be lucky."

James gaped. He already *had* gotten lucky, as far as he was concerned. Glaring at her, he shook his head. "Honestly, Maggie, you are harder on my ego than any woman I have ever met! Most women would be leaping for joy at having to marry me. Hell, many women would have *arranged* for us to be caught as we were, but you—"

James paused, his mind suddenly stuttering over the idea of an arranged scandal. It occurred to him that making love to Maggie with a passel of women in the next room had been the height of stupidity. James was not generally a stupid man. One might almost think he had been hoping to get caught and forced into this marriage. Was it possible he had played such a trick on himself? he wondered in amazement. He shook such thoughts away as Maggie finished doing up her drawers and bent impatiently to collect her waistcoat.

"I do not care what most women would like or want, my lord. You should not be forced into an arrangement to save my reputation. I was hardly fighting you off or crying rape. I was a willing participant in this affair and shall suffer the consequences for it without regret."

"There is no need for anyone to suffer," James snapped. "Good Lord, woman, it is no sacrifice on my part. In case you missed the fact, I quite enjoyed ruining you. I already look forward to being able to enjoy you again, and on a regular basis. In fact, the idea of being able to do so in the comfort of a bed makes me quite eager."

To prove that fact, he grabbed her hand as she tried to shrug into her waistcoat, and drew it down to press against the proof of his claim. Maggie stilled, her eyes widening, surprise on her face.

With her ripped linen shirt gaping open, James could hardly miss the way her nipples hardened. Releasing her hand, he lifted his fingers to catch one nipple between thumb and forefinger and pinched it gently. Maggie closed her eyes and swayed, her fingers tightening on his erection. It was enough to make James forget the situation and pull her into his arms. Catching her by the bottom, he pulled her forward, grinding himself against her.

If it weren't for a knock at the door right then, James very well might have taken her again—standing right there. But the knock made them draw apart.

"Yes?" James snapped as Maggie turned away to don her waistcoat. She began fastening the buttons to hide her torn top.

The door opened, and Meeks warily poked his head inside the room, relief on his face when he saw they were both dressed and behaving. "Lady Barlow asked that I tell you Lady Margaret's bath is ready, and that she would like to see you in the salon at once, my lord."

"Very well, Meeks. Tell her I shall be right there."

Nodding, the butler pulled the door closed, leaving him and Maggie alone again.

"I had best go above stairs," she murmured, moving to the door. James followed her, his eyebrows rising when she paused with her hand on the doorknob. Staring down at the floor, she asked, "Have you considered that you might find someone else you would rather marry? That if you marry me, you may come to regret it?"

"There is *no one* I would rather marry," James assured her with a smile.

She twitched impatiently, then said, "But what if you find someone you could truly love? What if—"

"Love?" James interrupted with a frown. "True love is a fairy tale for children, Maggie. We have friendship and mutual desire, which is the best anyone can realistically expect in a marriage. Actually, 'tis more than most people get. Do not trouble yourself about such nonsense. We will be married. We will get on famously. Now go take your bath."

Shoulders slumping, she opened the door and stepped out of the library. James watched her go with a frown. The woman looked terribly unhappy as she ascended the stairs to find her room and the waiting bath. He had to admit, it wasn't very flattering that the idea of marriage to him should be so unattractive to her.

Chapter Sixteen

Maggie chose the chair in the corner of the library. Cast in shadow, and out of immediate sight of the door, it looked to be a good place to curl up and hide a bit from the madness presently taking over Lady Barlow's home.

It had been a week since she and James had been caught with their drawers down . . . literally.

"Only you, Maggie." She whispered the familiar refrain to herself with a grimace, but had to admit she deserved it. She'd always gotten herself into trouble, and now she'd finally managed to get herself compromised and forced into marriage. She sighed dismally. The last seven days had felt like years. They had been filled with a whirl of fittings and planning: fitting the bridal gown, planning the rushed wedding.

The union was to take place in another two weeks. Lady Barlow had decided on the date. The woman was terribly concerned that their tryst in her library might bear fruit, so she said, and she insisted there be no scandal around the birth of any grand-niece or -nephew. As for the whispers such a rushed wedding would cause, those would die down quickly enough once the vows were said and done. They would be long forgotten by the baby's birth—if there was a baby.

It rankled Maggie that all of this was to protect a child that might not even exist. Well, she supposed, she was being unfair. They were also trying to salvage what they considered to be her endangered reputation. Yet Maggie wasn't as concerned with that as perhaps she should have been. After all, with Frances out of her life, she really hadn't had any prospects. Besides, it was not as if she went anywhere that she might be humiliated by overhearing the titters that being caught in flagrante delicto might cause.

Or, at least, she hadn't previous to this engagement. She thought with irritation about the last week since Lady Barlow and James had decided that he and Maggie should marry. She had found herself being dragged to ball after ball, party after party, as well as various operas and plays. Basically, they went anywhere they might be seen. Lady Barlow had said that it was to show that they had nothing to be ashamed of, as well as to allow the ton to see that she was now under her soon-to-be husband's protection. She would soon be Lady Ramsey.

Maggie's face puckered with annoyance. She could hardly believe that, in the space of such a short time, her life had been turned completely upside down. Everything was changing. Even her relationship with James was different than it had been before. For one thing, whereas he had often visited her and his aunt, spent hours talking, laughing, and playing cards with her before their engagement, since that fateful day they were caught in the library, she hardly saw him at all. She'd had only one chance even to talk to the man since that night, and it had not been about anything she herself had wanted to discuss.

He had started the talk by "requesting" that she discontinue her employment with the *Daily Express*. In fact, he had asked her to write a letter to Mr. Hartwick, informing him that G. W. Clark was retiring and would no longer be available to provide articles. He had then seen to it that Banks delivered the missive. When the butler returned with a rather alarmed note asking for an explanation, begging G. W. to reconsider, James had overseen her apologetic refusal to do either. The odious man had refrained from actually giving orders, but his requests had been little else. Was such the lot of a wife? she wondered miserably.

On the bright side, while they waited for Banks to return from his chore, James had mentioned that her servants would, of course, be incorporated into their household. He had told her that they would be her own private servants, that they would always have a home with them. In fact, he'd intended to move most of them into his town house right away, but Lady Barlow had argued against it. As they were Maggie's own private servants, the matron felt they should remain with their mistress, where they could assist with all the chores necessary for the wedding celebration. Aunt Vivian had told her privately that she knew Maggie's staff were like family to her, and thought she might enjoy the support until the wedding. Maggie was terribly grateful for that thoughtfulness. It comforted her to have Banks and

Mary and the others nearby, and made her feel more at home.

The next subject he had brought up had been the town house of Gerald's. The repairs were nearly finished, he'd informed Maggie, causing a flash of guilt in her for not wondering about the matter herself. He had then suggested she sell the house and invest the proceeds in her own name, assuring her that he intended to leave her the freedom of those funds.

Which was very considerate, really. Maggie supposed she should be happy, or at least content. She knew very well that few women were as fortunate in their marriages as it appeared she was to be. But . . . But . . .

Maggie sighed miserably. She knew she had a lot to be grateful for, but, greedy woman that she was, she wanted more. She wanted a husband who would love and cherish her. She wanted *James* to love and cherish her. She made a face at such foolishness, wondering why the fact that he didn't bothered her so much. After all, it was not as if she loved him, was it? The very question made her tremble where she sat. *Did* she love him? Dear God, surely she hadn't been so foolish as to fall in love with the man?

Forcing herself to take a deep breath, Maggie tried to consider the matter sensibly. She *did like* him. She would admit to that. Even when he was being bossy and overbearing, as he'd been when he kidnapped her, he had acted with the best of intentions and had not been unkind. Then, too, while having her in his power and thinking her a fallen woman, he had not taken advantage of the situation by using her to slake his desires. Well . . . there was that time in the Ramsey library, but that had hardly been "using" her. Maggie herself had actually initiated that kiss when James had hesitated. Perhaps the truth of the matter was that she had seduced him.

That thought gave her pause. Maggie had never really thought of herself as a seductress, but she had pressed that first kiss to his lips and set off that whole heated first exchange. Aye, *she* had seduced *him*. And wasn't that an interesting turn of events? She had seduced him. *Aren't I a wicked girl?* she thought with delight, finding the idea terribly encouraging—in an odd way. If she could seduce James, perhaps there was the possibility that she could make him love her, too.

She was still pondering that when the library door opened, drawing her reluctant attention. James stepped inside and glanced around, and her heart tripped with surprise. She had seen very little of him since the night of their downfall. Lady Barlow, she suspected, was doing her best to keep them apart until they were safely married. Where before James had visited often and long, she'd hardly had a glimpse of him these last few days.

The day he had made her retire G. W. Clark was the only real time they had spent together, and that had been with Lady Barlow present the whole time, negating any possibility of a serious or intimate conversation. Seeing him here now, and without his aunt on his heels, was something of a surprise. Enough of a surprise that Maggie must have made a startled sound or movement, for he glanced her way, his eyes settling warmly upon her.

"There you are." Pushing the door closed, he crossed the room and caught her hand to draw her to her feet. Then he said, "Surely you have a welcoming kiss for the man soon to be your husband?" He didn't leave her time to answer, but instead lowered his head to cover her mouth with his.

It truly was little more than a welcoming kiss, though, a quick brush of his lips over hers, and Maggie felt disappointment rise within her as he started to pull away. She didn't pause to consider why she was disappointed, or admit that she enjoyed his kisses greatly and hungered for more of them, had hungered for them since their first one; she merely reminded herself that she was a seductress. Wasn't she? Hadn't she seduced James in the country—even if unintentionally? Couldn't she do so again?

Eager to test this new side of herself while she still had the courage, Maggie caught the back of James's head with one hand as he tried to pull away. Drawing him back to her, she again pressed her lips over his. James stiffened in surprise as Maggie brushed her mouth over his. Then, when she opened her mouth and ran her tongue along the seam of his closed lips, requesting entrance, he opened at once and the stiffness left him. He took over.

The stiffness in most of his body was gone, she amended with secret glee. The part of him pressing against her belly, however, grew noticeably stiffer, apparently excited by her aggression. He responded in kind.

When she broke the kiss to nip gently at his chin, then trailed little kisses along James's jaw to his ear, as he had done to her, her name slipped from his lips and his arms tightened around her. A moment later, his hands dropped to cup her bottom through her skirts. Maggie reciprocated by clasping his behind, then slid one hand between them and cupped his crotch.

"God, Maggie," he said under his breath, thrusting into her touch. He shook his head as if to clear it. "What are you doing? My sis—"

Maggie silenced him with another kiss, this one deep and passionate. She quickly undid the buttons of the front flap of his breeches, then slid her hand swiftly inside. She found and fondled his erection. He grew farther in her hand, bulging, throbbing, harder. Much to Maggie's surprise, her own excitement grew. She felt in control. Powerful. And she felt herself grow damp with arousal.

Recalling what he had done to her on two occasions now, she ended their kiss and dropped to her knees before him. Finding, licking, and pressing kisses along the length of his shaft, she began an effort to please him as he had done to her. She was kissing the tip of him when James unexpectedly thrust forward. Maggie started to pull back, her mouth opening in surprise, and found herself with a mouthful. The groan it elicited from him made her hesitate; then she drew her head back slightly, her teeth gently grazing the head of his member before she slid her lips forward again, taking in as much of the shaft as she could while she held its base.

The action appeared to have an electrifying effect. James bucked, the words "Maggie, oh, God!" torn from him in tortured gasps. Maggie managed the action two more times before he grasped her upper arms and dragged her back to her feet.

"Did I do something wrong?" she whispered in alarm. James shook his head violently, and she straightened before him.

"No. God, no," he muttered. "It is just that if you do

not stop, I . . . I have been dreaming about you all week and I . . ." Giving up his explanation, he peered about, then steered her behind the chair in which she had been sitting. Pausing there, he claimed her lips with something close to desperation.

Maggie kissed him back just as passionately. This time, when she felt the brush of air making its way up her legs, she didn't need to look down to know he was tugging her skirts up. The image she'd seen at Ramsey of James's dark hand against her pale flesh immediately rose in her mind, and she moaned into his mouth in anticipation, then bit his lower lip lightly in excitement. His hand slid between her thighs to work its magic.

Maggie was so wrapped up in what he was doing, it took her by surprise when his other hand reached down to stop hers as she tried to touch him again. Pulling it away at the same time as he broke their kiss, he grasped her by the waist and turned her to face the back of the chair in which she'd earlier sat. He then urged her to bend forward.

Lifting her skirts, he slid into her from behind. Maggie gasped in surprise. Eyes wide, she held her breath as he filled her, then let that breath out on a long, loud moan. One of his hands moved to cup her breast through her gown, and the other slid under the front of her upraised skirts. It found the center of her pleasure and continued caressing. Her moan turned into little mewls of pleasure and pleading as he began to slide in and out of her, his fingers moving in time with his thrusts.

Digging her fingernails into the upholstery of the chair over which she was bent, Maggie cried out; her body was beginning to shudder and shake. Pleasure ex-

297

ploded through her. She heard James cry out, too. After one last thrust, her body throbbing around him, he collapsed on her back with a groan.

The library door opened. One moment Maggie and James were hanging over the chair panting; the next they were both standing upright, guilt and alarm painting their flushed faces. James slid out of her, and her skirts fell back into place.

"James, where the devil have you gotten to?" Lady Barlow called irritably as she stepped into the room. There was an attractive brunette at her heels. Despite the fact that the woman was not the wizened Lady Wingate, Maggie suffered a definite sense of déjà vu at the situation. James's aunt looked about the room until she spotted them, standing one behind the other, half-hidden by the chair. "Oh, there you are. Sophie wants—"

Lady Barlow paused after only a few steps, her gaze narrowing at their flushed and breathless state. Her eyes widened, and she cried, "Good Lord, not again! What the devil is it with you and libraries that makes you unable to control yourself in them, James? You have always had a passion for books, but really!"

Groaning, Maggie closed her eyes and wished with all her heart that the floor would do her the inestimable favor of opening up and swallowing her whole. She was not at all appreciative of James's sense of humor when a small snort of laughter slid from his lips, blowing against the sensitive skin on the back of her neck. For a moment she considered sliding out from between him and the chair and making her escape, but she wasn't at all sure that the chair was high enough to hide his presently unsheathed state—she was trapped where she was unless she wished it revealed.

Much to her relief, Lady Barlow did not leave her trapped for long. Giving a huff of disgust, the woman turned and made her way back to the door. "Sophie and I will be in the salon. I will expect you immediately, James. I do hope you can keep your hands off the poor girl long enough for her to meet your sister."

The door closed behind the two women with a soft thud, and James heaved a breath of relief. Sliding his arms around Maggie's waist from behind, he nuzzled the top of her head. "I fear she is right. I always have had a passion for libraries. Still, I never realized quite how much pleasure they could afford until I met you."

Caught off guard by the comment, Maggie found herself chuckling, her shoulders relaxing as the tension slipped from them. Covering his hands with her own, she leaned back and tipped her head to smile up at him crookedly. "I do not know if I can face them after getting caught like that again. Your aunt must think me the lowest of creatures."

"You?" He glanced at her with surprise, then shook his head firmly. "Nay. She thinks the world of you. It is me of whom she thinks poorly. I am the seducer of innocents, you see."

"Oh, but I seduced you," Maggie protested earnestly, turning in his arms. James's gaze heated again. "So you did, you little minx." He rubbed his hands up and down her arms, his lips curving in an appreciative smile. "And rather thoroughly at that, too."

Rather pleased with herself, Maggie smiled and leaned against his chest, tucking her head under his chin to enjoy his simple caress. His hands moved over her back in a soothing rhythm. The two of them stood like that for a moment; then James chuckled.

"What a shame we were caught, however. I am quite certain Aunt Viv shall make sure we do not get any more such opportunities. We will be lucky if she doesn't raid the museum for a chastity belt and clap it on you until the wedding."

An amused giggle erupted from Maggie at the thought, and James's arms tightened around her. His voice was a bit irritated as he said, "There is nothing funny about it, madam. In case you hadn't noticed, just holding you like this has left me embarrassingly eager for more. The next two weeks are shaping up to be rather hellish."

Pulling back, Maggie peered down at his breeches, surprised to note that he was indeed bulging with interest. But that didn't surprise her as much as the fact that he was bulging against the cloth of his breeches. He was tucked in and buttoned up, and the only time he could possibly have done that without her noticing was while they had stood facing his aunt. It was no wonder she had worked out what they were doing if he had been busy putting himself away as she approached!

Maggie should have been annoyed with him, but he was gifting her with such a sweetly wry expression, she couldn't seem to muster any irritation.

"Come. My sister is going to love you, and you shall love her, too. The two of you shall no doubt become good friends."

"Your sister probably already hates me," Maggie muttered unhappily as he dragged her toward the door. "She probably thinks me a tart."

"Nonsense. She was caught in rather similar circumstances herself with her husband—before he was her husband," he confided with amusement. "Their wedding was rather rushed as well, you know. It would appear a bit of scandal runs in the family."

A little more than an hour later, Maggie had to admit that James was right. She wouldn't have said that she and Sophie loved each other already, but they certainly got on well enough and had found several interests in common. Maggie rather liked her soon-to-be sister-in-law and hoped it might be mutual. Which was why it was such a shame that this was James's sister. Maggie felt rather in need of a friend just now.

Peering out the window of her room, she watched the activity on the street below with blind eyes. Maggie had enjoyed the visit, despite its embarrassing beginning, and had cut it short only out of consideration for Sophie and Lady Barlow. The two women had an obvious affection for each other, and Maggie had thought to let them visit privately after James excused himself. Maggie couldn't recall the evening's plans exactly at the moment, but supposed they would all either go to a play and a ball, an opera and a soiree, or some other similar combination. This would be another evening on display.

She twitched the drapes at her windows impatiently, her mind returning to the dilemma she'd been considering before her exciting little adventure in the library. Did she love James? The question left her with the beginnings of a headache. Normally she would have taken such a problem to her friend Charlotte to discuss. Unfortunately Charlotte hadn't ventured into London yet. It was early in the season still, and Charlotte's family tended to be one of the last to arrive each year.

Maggie had friends with whom she might have discussed other problems, but Charlotte was the only one with whom she would feel comfortable discussing this personal issue, and in this matter, Maggie wasn't at all sure she would even have felt thoroughly comfortable discussing it with her. Charlotte like Maggie was unmarried, but Charlotte was well-behaved—which Maggie could no longer claim. Nay, perhaps she couldn't have discussed this dilemma with her. What she needed was a more experienced woman, someone married, someone to whom she could talk. Like Sophie.

She discarded the thought as quickly as it came to her. While she hoped that she and Sophie might someday become close enough to discuss such things, it was too early in their friendship yet. Besides, the other girl would be biased in her opinions: James was her brother.

Sighing, Maggie leaned her head against the window, her gaze focusing on an old woman peddling fruit on the street. The shawl covering her head and the hunched way she walked reminded her of the disguise Madame Dubarry had used when she'd come to tell Maggie that someone was impersonating her dead brother. Maggie smiled fondly at the thought of the woman. She supposed it was shocking that she enjoyed a friendship with the brothel owner, but Agatha was the only one who had seen both sides of her: what the world saw, and her secret identity as G. W. Clark. And the older woman never judged her. Which was not how the ton would have reacted, she knew.

"Oh, stuff!" she muttered suddenly, straightening by the window. She could talk to Agatha Dubarry. Aggie would neither be shocked nor biased. She would listen and offer advice born of years of experience. It was such a brilliant idea, and so obvious, that Maggie wondered why she hadn't thought of it before. She would invite Agatha to tea. She hadn't done that in ages—not since before her abduction to the country, anyway.

Moving to the bellpull in the corner, she gave it a tug, knowing it would bring Mary immediately. She would send the girl for stationary and ink and invite Agatha here to Lady Bar—

"Oh," she murmured aloud as she realized that she couldn't possibly invite the woman here. This was not her home. It was one thing to invite the madam to her own house, but she could not possibly invite her here without Lady Barlow's permission. Maggie grimaced. She could just imagine Lady Barlow's reaction to a request to invite a brothel owner to tea. The woman would be scandalized.

Maybe, some part of her reasoned. *Then again, maybe not.* She hadn't been scandalized by Maggie's being G. W. Clark, she considered. Then she shook her head. Writing articles for the *Daily Express* and owning a brothel were not exactly similar degrees of scandal.

Sighing, she gave up the idea with regret, only to glance up in surprise when Mary rushed in. "Yes, m'lady?" the maid asked.

"Oh, never mind." Maggie started to wave the girl away, then paused as her gaze fell on the maid's serviceable gown and the shawl draped over her shoulders. Her cheeks were rosy, she noted, a telltale sign that she had been out to the stables to see her beau, but it was Mary's dress that caught Maggie's attention. The beginnings of an idea were taking root in her mind: perhaps Agatha could not come visit her, but might she possibly slip out to visit Agatha?

"M'lady?"

Maggie gave a start at the maid's uncertain murmur and stiffened. "It is all right, Mary. I was going to write a letter but changed my mind. I am sorry to have troubled you. You may go back to what you were doing."

"Yes, m'lady." The girl was gone as quickly as she had come—no doubt straight back to the stables, Maggie thought. She turned her mind back to her daring thoughts of moments before.

Dared she sneak out and visit Madame Dubarry? Lady Barlow and James would have a fit if she were caught. *If*, she argued with herself, and she had no intention of being caught. She would sneak out now, while James was gone and Lady Barlow was visiting with her niece. She would be back in plenty of time to prepare for their evening outing.

Yes, but there was her assailant to consider. She risked his harming her if he saw through her disguise. *But no one pays attention to servants*, she told herself. She could dress as a servant, slip out the back, and carry a basket as if she were going to market. It was growing rather late for a trip to the market, but not so late that it wasn't possible. Then, too, no one would believe she would dare leave her guard behind and traipse about on her own. Not after the last attack.

Which brought her guard to mind. Maggie frowned. *Jack*. The man who had saved her from the fire was supposed to have taken time to recuperate, but he was . . . well, a man. And everyone knew that men could be stubborn to the point of stupidity when it came to their health. Good Lord, one could never expect them to admit to being human and needing to heal. Fortunately, nothing had arisen to call his claims of health into question. Not that she didn't feel safer with him around. She did, and she had no doubt at all that the man would do more damage to his own hands to protect her if the need arose. She simply didn't understand the male need to take such risks rather than admit to human frailties.

Ah, well, it didn't matter right now. What did was that originally Jack had merely been in the house. He'd been allowed to spend his time in the kitchen or wherever he would be available if there was trouble. But that had been before Maggie's jaunt to the men's club. After that, James had decided Jack needed to follow her around and keep a close eye on her. He now trailed her about like some hulking Cockney angel. Maggie had been forced to promise that she would sit still in the same chair in her room this afternoon simply to get a few minutes' peace and privacy—and she knew Jack had likely stood outside the door, anyway.

The thought made her groan aloud as she recalled what she and James had done earlier—and the noise they had no doubt made doing it. Dear Lord, seduce James she may have done, but she had also apparently given up her sense of decorum. Close proximity to the man obviously did things to her brain, else she would have recalled her guardian's embarrassing presence outside the door then, instead of now, when it was too late. . . .

"Only you, Maggie," she muttered then pushed those thoughts aside. Little could be done about it now, so Maggie considered the problem at hand: how to slip out without her guard knowing. After a moment's thought, she decided that simple prevarication would be easiest.

Taking a deep breath, she gave her hands and arms a shake, then straightened her shoulders and walked calmly to the door. As expected, Jack stood in the hall looking solemn and immovable. Maggie smiled, hoping it was the same expression she usually used and didn't scream, *Hello! I'm about to lie to you!*

She forced herself to say, "I thought I should tell you that I am going to take a nap before tonight's entertainment. You might like to fetch a chair and something to entertain yourself—unless you'd rather go down to the kitchens for a bit of a snack and a beverage?"

"A chair'll do," the large man rumbled, as she expected; then he glanced up the hall with a frown.

"I think there is one in the gallery by the top of the stairs," Maggie suggested, hoping she didn't sound too sweet. She closed the door then, and quickly dropped to peer through the keyhole, relieved to see her guard move off down the hall. She hadn't expected him to take her suggestion of retiring to the kitchens, but his fetching a chair from the gallery also played right into her hands. He could see the top of the stairs from there and would think he could watch for her coming or going.

Of course, Maggie didn't plan to take those stairs. Easing the door open, she watched him walk down the hall. This was the tricky part, and luck would play a large part. She needed to slip out and make her way to the opposite end of the hall *before* he went into the room and returned, which meant she had to creep out into the hall while he was still in it. Fortunately, her room was only two doors from the attic, into which she planned to escape.

Maggie waited until he was halfway to the gallery, saw him glance back once, then decided it was now or never.

She slipped out into the hall. She eased her bedchamber door silently closed, then made a quick dash on tiptoe for the end of the hall. She didn't look back until she had slid through the attic door, then she peered out as she eased it almost closed. Through the crack, she saw Jack glare back as he reached the gallery. Maggie waited until he stepped inside before easing the door shut and making her way up into the attic.

Her previous trip in search of a disguise to meet Maisey had revealed various other bits of clothing, some of which would aid her now. Sophie and James weren't the only ones who had cast-off clothing up here; there were also items of obvious servant quality. Maggie supposed the garments had been outgrown or left behind, but either way they would aid her now.

Once in the attic proper, Maggie cursed her own stupidity for not thinking to bring a candle. Opening the small window at the end of the packed room, allowing the gloomy late-afternoon light in, helped. The window was not very big and the light was rather poor, but it was enough. She was able to quickly find and don what she needed.

Locating a basket that had seen better days, Maggie tossed in some fabric and covered it with a linen shirt so that it appeared full. Next she made her way silently back down the stairs to the hall.

This was another tricky part, of course: getting out of the attic and slipping to the servants' stairs without Jack noticing. Pausing, Maggie eased the door open a crack and peered out into the hall. Her guardian had retrieved a chair, set it outside her door, and now sat twiddling his thumbs in a rather bored fashion. It did not look promising. In fact, as the minutes ticked by and Jack sat glancing alertly about, Maggie began to think she would be stuck on the stairwell forever.

At last, Jack stood, stretched, then walked toward the stairwell. Sucking in a breath, Maggie slid out of the attic stairwell, hurried the few steps to the servants' stairs, and eased through the door. As she carefully slid it closed, she saw Jack peer down the stairs, then turn back and start up the hall once more. Letting out her breath on a sigh, Maggie turned and started carefully down toward the first floor. Her ears straining for the sound of anyone approaching, she managed to make it all the way to the door leading into the kitchen unde-tected. Pausing there, she lifted the shawl hanging over her shoulders and rearranged it to cover her head and shadow her face; then she eased that door open to peek out.

She couldn't believe her luck when she saw how quiet the kitchen was. Lady Barlow's cook and another ser-vant were standing in the cellar just off to the side, dis-cussing something as they looked over the stock, but otherwise the room was momentarily empty. Deciding it was now or never, Maggie pulled her shawl closer around her face, pushed the basket up her arm, and moved quickly out of the stairwell. She was across the room and at the back door before she heard another door open behind her, but she didn't slow down or glance back. Counting on her servant's disguise to pro-tect her, she slipped out of the house and straight through the gardens. She reached the back gate in a hurry, and a moment later she had passed through it to freedom.

Chapter Seventeen

"Lady Margaret!"

"Good afternoon, Agatha." Maggie greeted the older woman with a smile of relief. It had taken a lot of talking to convince the brothel doorman to at least fetch his mistress out to her when he had refused her entrance at the door. She'd had to take on her snootiest attitude and order the man in her most cultured tones to ask Madame Dubarry to come outside.

At least, she thought happily, her disguise was working. This man had obviously been convinced that she was nothing more than a servant.

"Well, come in. . . . My goodness, come in," Madame Dubarry urged, turning to frown at her amazed doorman. "You must never again leave this young woman on the stoop, Ralph. She is always welcome."

"Yes, madame," the flustered man said, his gaze moving over Maggie's face as if he were trying to memorize her as she entered. She offered him an apologetic smile, aware that her disguise had been the problem. No one paid much mind to servants. The fact that she had arrived here unmolested proved that.

"Well, what a delightful surprise," the brothel owner murmured, slipping her arm through Maggie's to steer her along the hall toward her private drawing room. "I haven't heard tell of you since you were here to interview the girls."

"Oh, er, well—"

"Speaking of which," Aggie interrupted Maggie's stammering, "I am sorry about that Frances business. The way you spoke about him led me to think that your emotions were not truly engaged, else I would never have let you find out that way. It wasn't until you disappeared without a word that I considered that you might have cared for him after all, that you'd been hurt by what you saw."

Maggie started to protest, eager to assure her friend that such hadn't been the case, but the older woman continued, "I went around to your house the day after— disguised, of course—but your butler said that you were not in. When I had no word from you after that, I assumed you were angry at me."

The woman fell silent, an uncertain expression on her face as she urged Maggie into one of two chairs by the fire. She took the other for herself.

Once seated, Maggie quickly assured her that she wasn't angry or hurt. She told Agatha the tale of Lord Ramsey mistaking her for Lady X, kidnapping her, and taking her to the country for reformation then her return to London and her adventures since.

Knowing that the brothel owner could hardly be

shocked by any thing, Maggie didn't hold back; she revealed all, sometimes blushing and stammering, but continuing determinedly nonetheless.

Aggie listened entralled, bursting out into gales of laughter at various points, and rolling her eyes or muttering at others.

When Maggie finally finished, both women fell silent, then Aggie sighed gustily. "So you are in love. I could not be happier for you. I really have to tell Lady X about Lord Ramsey thinking you were her—she will get a giggle out of it."

"Are you sure?" Maggie asked with alarm.

Dubarry smiled and nodded. "Yes, of course. It *is* funny, you know. An innocent like you being mistaken for—"

"Nay, not that," Maggie interrupted. "I meant about the love part. Are you sure I am in love?"

Eyes widening, Agatha sat back and contemplated the question with surprise. "Aren't you?"

Maggie bit her lip, and Agatha's expression turned sympathetic. "Is that what is upsetting you? I could tell from your strained expression when I first saw you that something is. . . . I thought perhaps it was that Frances business, but—"

"I have never been in love before," Maggie broke in. "I am not sure if what I am feeling *is* love. And if it is, what should I do?"

"Let us deal with one question at a time," Aggie suggested soothingly. "And that first question would be, Is it love? What were your feelings upon first meeting Lord Ramsey?"

"Fear," Maggie answered honestly. "He was kidnapping me, after all."

Madame Dubarry grinned. "From what you said, you got over that fear in a hurry."

Maggie shrugged. "I learned he was a friend of my brother's. He explained—"

"And you believed him?" she asked with amusement. Maggie blinked.

"My dear, I have known you since your brother's death and been fortunate enough to have your confidence. In all your adventures as G. W. Clark, you were sharp and showed good instincts. You rarely accepted anyone's word for anything. You had sources willing to tell you all sorts of things going on here or there, but you didn't just write about any of those rumors and whispers; you investigated and researched each tale to find the truth for yourself."

"Well, of course I did. That is merely good sense; people lie all the time."

"And so . . . ? Did you investigate Ramsey's claim to be a friend of your brother's? Did you try to verify that he had only your good intentions in mind?"

"No. I tried to escape," Maggie countered.

"Yes, you did," Aggie agreed patiently, "but have you yet investigated whether Ramsey was telling the truth?"

Maggie found herself annoyed by the question. She knew what James was all about. "I didn't have to. Gerald had written about him often. He wrote about both James and Lord Mullin."

"Ah. So you knew of him before the two of you met?"

"Yes, I suppose."

"So what did you know? What did Gerald say?"

Maggie smiled. "Oh, various things. He mentioned that James liked to read and was teased by the others for always having his nose in a book. He said James was clever and honorable, and he told how, when they marched through decimated villages, James was always giving away his food to starving peasants.

"So you liked and respected Lord Ramsey from those tales even before you met the man?"

"Yes, I suppose I did," Maggie admitted.

"And then he kidnapped you and you were irritated with him"—the brothel owner grinned—"but you said you quite enjoyed the conversations and verbal battles the two of you shared."

"Yes."

"And when he kissed you? That first time?"

Maggie squirmed in her seat, her face flushing with embarrassment. "I . . . He made me feel . . . Honestly, Aggie, I do not know if I could tell you my name if you asked right after one of his kisses," she admitted in a rush. "I am quite overwhelmed by passion just from his touch . . . or a light brush of his lips on mine."

"I see. And, liking and respecting him as you do, and as glorious as you find his physical attentions to be, why are you unhappy about marrying him?"

Maggie was silent for a moment, then admitted reluctantly, "I do not want him to marry me simply for honor's sake and later regret it. I do not want him to be unhappy."

"That *is* love, dear," Aggie said gently. "You are more concerned with his happiness than your own."

Maggie digested her friend's words briefly, then made a face. "I am not so altruistic, Agatha. I mean, I do care about his happiness, but it would also be a misery loving and being married to a man who did not love you back."

"What makes you think that he doesn't? It would appear to me he does." Madame Dubarry seemed slightly exasperated.

Maggie's eyes widened. "What makes you think that?"

"Well, my dear, unless the man is a complete idiot, he does seem to have taken an awful risk making love to you in his aunt's library. With a half a dozen guests in the next room, he was rather asking to be caught, wasn't he? And once caught, it was assured that there would be a wedding. . . ."

Rather than feeling pleased, Maggie felt disappointment drop over her. "Yes, but that was my fault. I *seduced* him."

Agatha burst into raucous laughter; then, seeing Maggie's injured expression, reached out to pat her hand. "I am sorry, my dear. I shouldn't laugh, but kissing the man hardly equates to seducing him."

"But—"

"Nay. Listen to me. I have a great deal of experience in these matters," the woman insisted. "The second time, in Lady Barlow's library . . . Well, perhaps *that* was seducing him. But a mere kiss isn't a seduction. Lord Ramsey knew exactly what he was doing that first time, I think. And it is very possible he was partially hoping to get caught."

"Hoping to get caught?" Maggie cried in disbelief. "But, why?"

"Perhaps he hoped for exactly what happened, that the two of you would be forced to marry." When Maggie looked doubtful, she asked, "What would you have said had he proposed?"

"No."

"Why?"

"Well, because I wouldn't want him to marry me simply to fulfill a promise to my brother."

"Of course not, and no intelligent man would expect you to. You see?"

"No."

"This way, you could not say no," Agatha pointed out. "And he was not forced to delve into anything as messy as his own emotions . . . or declarations of feeling that might not be reciprocated."

"You are saying"—Maggie tried to understand—"that you think he loves me but is unready to confess."

"I am saying that *he is a man*. He probably doesn't even know he is in love. By forcing a marriage this way, he delays having to discover it. Men often think that love will weaken them, that somehow the woman they care for has some power over them."

"But I don't," Maggie said.

Agatha smiled mysteriously. "No? And yet just last night, your touch made him entirely forget that his sister had arrived, that he had come to fetch you back to meet her!" The woman seemed amused by Maggie's blush. "You have a good deal of power with Lord Ramsey. But then, so does he with you."

"But if he loves me . . . I mean, my love makes me wary of marrying James. It makes me worry that this is all a mistake. I hesitate only because I wish him happiness. Why is it not affecting him in the same way? He seems quite content to marry me."

Agatha waved the question away. "Oh, well, don't worry about that, my dear. No woman on earth will ever truly understand the way a man thinks. They simply react differently than we do." When Maggie didn't appear satisfied with that last answer, the woman sighed.

"All right. If you wish my explanation on the matter, it is all a matter of confidence."

"Confidence?" Maggie echoed uncertainly.

"Aye. A woman may love, but if she fears the one she loves does not reciprocate her feelings—that perhaps she does not even deserve the gift of his love—she will let him go to another. Men, on the other hand, have more confidence. Should a man fall in love and fear the feeling is not reciprocated, he will tend to believe that he can *make* the woman love him . . . in time. So men hold on tighter. It all has to do with confidence. Have you never noticed that a man will think himself a catch no matter how little he has in the way of looks or wealth? And yet the loveliest woman often believes herself unattractive?"

When Maggie did not appear impressed by her argument, Agatha shook her head. "Never mind. Just trust me on the fact that Lord Ramsey has not reached his advanced age and remained single by giving in to impulse every time he was attracted to some young innocent. He has a reputation for being terribly proper . . . honorable and disciplined. And yet he gave in to you. And he sounds more than happy to marry you, Maggie. I believe he loves you. In time he will tell you so."

Maggie relaxed in her seat with a sigh. She wasn't sure she understood or even agreed with Agatha's opinions on love in general, or Ramsey in particular, but she did feel some of her misgivings replaced by hope. She let the conversation move on to other topics.

The two women enjoyed a companionable visit, but soon Maggie decided she had best return to Lady Barlow's. They were walking toward the front door when she suddenly thought of Maisey and what had happened the other night at the men's club. Pausing, she asked Madame Dubarry if the girl was around.

Agatha looked surprised by the question, but answered readily enough, "Aye. She is probably up in her room."

Maggie nodded, considering asking if the girl could be called down, then changed her mind. "Do you imagine it would be all right if I went up for a moment to speak with her?"

The madam's gaze narrowed on her considering; then she shrugged. "If you like. Though I could call her down here to talk if you wish."

Maggie shook her head; she didn't wish to speak to the younger girl in front of Agatha. "Nay. Thank you, but I will just go up to her room."

Nodding, Agatha turned them back toward the stairs. "I shall walk you up."

Much to her relief, Agatha did not stay when Maisey answered her knock, but left them alone to talk and moved up the hall.

"Could I come inside?" Maggie asked, smiling at the girl.

Shrugging, Maisey stepped aside to allow her entrance. "Ye can if'n ye like, miss, but I don't know what for. I thought we settled about the gowns."

"This isn't regarding the gowns," Maggie explained as she entered the room. The other woman closed the door behind her. "I wanted to explain about the other night."

Maisey looked at her blankly. "The other night?"

"At the club," Maggie prompted, frowning when the girl continued to look confused. "I just wanted to explain why I left without leaving word for you."

"Why ye left?"

Maggie hesitated. The girl truly didn't seem to know what she was talking about! "Why I left the club after you locked me in that room," she added.

Maisey shook her head. "I don't know what ye're talking about. I haven't seen ye since the night ye left through the window."

"What?" Maggie gasped, feeling the air knocked out of her. It was her turn to be left feeling bewildered. "But, you sent me a letter. About the gowns and calling it even."

"Yeah." Maisey nodded slowly, and Maggie felt some relief stretching through her. "Then you mentioned the men's club, offered to meet me. . . ." Maggie trailed off. The girl was shaking her head.

"I didn't say nothin' about no club."

"Yes, you did," Maggie insisted. "And then we met at the club, and you—"

"Ye're daft is what ye are," Maisey interrupted impatiently. "I didn't mention no club and didn't meet you at one."

"But—"

"I think it's time you left," Maisey decided abruptly, eyeing her as if she were mad.

Maggie opened her mouth to argue, but seeing the determined glint in the other woman's eyes, she decided that perhaps leaving was for the best. Maisey was apparently set upon lying, and the only reason she could think of for it was that the girl feared getting in trouble. Which would happen only if she were working with the man who had attacked her. That thought made Maggie remember that the man had unlocked the door. She'd heard him unlock it. Where else could he have gotten the key but from Maisey?

Eyes narrowing on the girl, Maggie decided she would give this information to James to pass on to Mr. Johnstone. He would get to the bottom of the matter. Deciding that the smartest move at that point was to leave, Maggie exited the room without further argument.

There was no sign of Agatha in the hall. Maggie didn't wish to leave without at least saying good-bye, but she had a sudden panicky desire to get back to Lady Barlow's. She was beginning to feel decidedly uneasy.

Hurrying to the stairs, she ran down them and straight for the front door, giving a start when Madame Dubarry's butler appeared to open it for her.

Mumbling her thanks, Maggie slid outside and hurried along the walkway, her feet moving faster with each step. She was in a frenzy to reach the Barlow town house and James. In her rush, Maggie didn't notice the carriage that kept pace with her or the footsteps echoing her own until it was too late. She was crossing the first intersecting street when a carriage turned abruptly before her, the door swung open, and she was grabbed from behind and bundled inside.

At first Maggie was too stunned to resist, but then she heard a shout and the pounding of someone running toward her. She began to struggle. The moment she did, something slammed into her head. She sank into unconsciousness.

James found himself hurrying as he leapt out of his carriage and made his way up the walk to his aunt's front door, and grimaced at his own eagerness. He had been distracted and a tad short-tempered for the last hour as he approved the repairs being done at Maggie's town house. If he were honest with himself, James would admit that he had been short-tempered ever since the night he and Maggie had been caught in the library. The *first* time.

Sighing, he paused and rapped on his aunt's door with his cane. There were several reasons for his moodiness. For one thing, he was a little less than pleased with Maggie's lack of enthusiasm for their upcoming nuptials. It was doing his ego little good. But he had adjusted to that, assuring himself it was caused by her fear of losing the autonomy she had enjoyed since her brother's death. She would relax and settle down with the idea once she realized that he didn't intend to smother her independent nature. He had no intention of doing that; her spirit was one of the things he admired most about her.

James *had* insisted that she give up writing for the *Express*, of course, but that had been out of necessity. Those damned articles were putting her life at risk, and while he had every hope that they would catch the scarfaced man presently trying to kill her, it was doubtful the fellow was the only one out there who would wish G. W. Clark ill. No, her articles were proving far too dangerous, and he was quite sure that her pride would have insisted she keep it up until the wedding had he not insisted straight off that she resign. Yet only pride would have kept her at it, he was sure. She had admitted, herself, that she didn't care for everything she had to do to get information for those articles. And, he rationalized, it was not as if she had a grand passion for the position. She had only been G. W. Clark for a couple months, and had only taken the position up to make extra money after Gerald's death.

Another reason for James's moodiness stemmed from his avoidance of Maggie in what he considered to be a terribly gallant effort to not toss up her skirt at every turn. James loved and respected his Aunt Viv dearly. She had raised him. He was now trying to behave as the gentlemen she'd raised him to be. But he could not do so with Maggie behaving as she had in their last encounter in the library. She easily brought an end to his good behavior with very little effort. So quickly he found his good intentions falling by the wayside. Even now, he couldn't wait to see her again, couldn't wait to be inside her again. To kiss her soft lips, lick her sweet skin, touch her round breasts and . . .

Feeling his body respond to his imaginings, James drew in his wayward thoughts. His concentration was most definitely shot. He had spent every moment since their last scandalous encounter either reliving those passionate moments, or imagining what he wanted to do to her next time. Which had made attending to the repairs of her town house and resolving what to do with her staff rather more difficult than it should have been.

He smiled at the thought of the Wentworth servants. He had spent more time with them than he had with Maggie, herself, of late. Most of her staff were helping out at the town house, and James had come to know them well. Enough to realize that her affection for them was returned tenfold. Every one of the servants was aware of the lengths she had gone to in her determination to keep them all on . . . and every one of them was as loyal as could be because of it. Which, when added to the fact that he knew Maggie would be mis-

erable without them, had moved James to decide that—
no matter what—he was going to see to it that they
went wherever she did. It didn't matter if he already
had a full staff. He was about to have a fuller one.

"My lord!"

He turned his attention from his thoughts to Meeks
as the front door of his aunt's house was opened. The
expression on the man's face echoed the relief that had
been evident in his voice, causing an uneasiness in
James.

"Good afternoon, Meeks," he greeted, stepping into
the house.

"Good afternoon, my lord. Lady Barlow is waiting in
the salon." The man took his hat, cape, and cane, waving him toward the room in question, and James felt his
uneasiness increase. Refraining from questioning the
man, he walked into the salon.

"James!" Lady Barlow turned from her anxious pacing,
rushing to her nephew's side as he entered the room.

James's eyes widened in surprise at such a welcome,
but he smiled and asked, "What is it?"

"Maggie is missing." The blunt announcement
dropped into the silent room like a stone into a pond.

James's smile froze, his face blanching. "What?"

"She is *missing*. She claimed to want to rest before
dinner, but I had a question about her preferences for
the wedding meal, and went to see if she might be
awake, and—" She shook her head unhappily. "She was
not there."

"Where was Jack?" James asked sharply. "He was supposed to be protecting her."

"He was right there, standing guard at her door. He

said that he stood outside it since she went in. She had to have left out of her window. It is the only way. I have had the servants search the entire house, but she simply isn't here."

"Isn't here?" James echoed with disbelief.

"No. I told Meeks to send servants to both you and Mr. Johnstone to make you aware of the matter."

"I wasn't home. I just came from . . . I didn't get the message," James said dazedly.

"I did."

Lady Barlow and James both turned to the door as Johnstone strode forward, his expression grim.

"I have already put several men out to search for her," the runner announced. His gaze went to Lady Barlow and he added, "But it might help if we had some idea where to look. Did you question the servants, ask if she said anything to anyone about going somewhere?"

"Yes. No one seems to have any idea where she might be."

They were all speechless for a time, then James said in a bewildered voice, "She promised me that she would not go out alone again after the incident at the club."

Johnstone offered a sympathetic grimace. "Perhaps she didn't. Is anyone else missing?"

Lady Barlow's eyes widened at the question. "Banks!"

"Banks?" James repeated. His aunt nodded. "Meeks mentioned that he could not find Banks, either. And it seems to me that when we were riding back to town from Ramsey, Maggie mentioned that Banks often accompanied her when she investigated her stories."

James stiffened at the suggestion. "She does not do those anymore. She retired."

Before Lady Barlow could answer, Meeks appeared at

the door to the salon, a concerned expression on his face.

"What is it, man?" she asked.

"A boy, my lady. At the door. He insists that he has a message for his lordship."

James hesitated briefly; thinking—hoping—that it might be from Maggie, he hurried out into the hall. A boy of perhaps five or six years waited nervously by the front door.

"Who is the message from, boy?" he barked, looming over the child.

The child's eyes widened fearfully, then darted nervously around as if in search of an escape route.

"Well? Have you been struck dumb? Who is the message from?" he snapped.

"I . . . I . . ." Dismay spread across his young face; then the boy wailed, "I can't remember."

"What? Look, lad, I do not have time to—"

"Perhaps if ye were not screaming at the lad, he could remember." Johnstone came up behind James. "Ye're scaring him."

Urging his employer to the side, the runner dropped to his haunches before the street urchin and offered him a warm smile. "Don't worry about him, lad. He's just a bit worried about his lady. Now, if ye can recall the message ye were to bring, ye can have this." Johnstone produced a shiny coin from a pocket and waved it. The boy watched it move from side to side before his eyes as if mesmerized, then blurted, "The lady. The bloke said to tell ye that 'e followed the lady."

"Who did?"

"Er." The boy frowned, his face screwing up as he tried to recall the name he had been given. "I can't remember, but 'e was a tall feller. Old. Stern-like."

"Banks?" James asked sharply.

"Aye, 'at's his name, guv'nor," the boy said, brightening. " 'E said as 'e 'ad followed the lady and sent me to get ye, and . . ." His face flushed slightly, and he admitted unhappily, "I can't remember the rest. . . . Somethin' about a man with a scar."

James paled, but asked, "Can you lead us back to him?"

"Sure, m' lord."

"Good lad." He sighed, patting the boy's shoulder, then turned him toward the door. Shouting for his driver, knowing the man would be in the kitchens, where he always waited while James visited his aunt and Maggie, James prepared to go and rescue Maggie.

Chapter Eighteen

Only you, Maggie . . .

The words echoed through her head as Margaret touched a hand to her sore head and slowly sat up. It occurred to her that she found herself awakening with headaches a lot lately; it was becoming rather de rigueur. Frowning, she tried to see through the inky blackness surrounding her and determine where she was, but the darkness was absolute. She could not see a thing.

Lifting a hand, she felt her face, briefly hoping that her cape was covering it and blinding her as it had in James's carriage, but she was disappointed. Her hands and feet were unbound, her face uncovered. She was simply in a room devoid of light.

Or she had been hit so hard she was blinded, she considered. The thought scared her so much that when the door opened and light suddenly spilled into the room, she was almost grateful for it. Almost. The pain it elicited in her head was rather unbearable, however, so she was a little less thankful than she might have been. She scrambled to her feet and confronted the mis-shapen hulk that entered her prison, cast in shadow as he was by the light at his back.

At first, Maggie thought her poor eyes were playing tricks, for surely no one could be shaped that way. Then the hulk paused several feet away and bent at the waist. He hefted something off of what turned out to be his shoulders, and Maggie understood. Her gaze dropped to the burden the man had just deposited, and a gasp slipped from her lips at the sight. It was a bruised and unconscious Banks.

The hulk turned away, and Maggie stepped forward, her fists balling at her sides. "Who are you? Why are you doing this?"

When he merely ignored her and turned to leave, she took another step forward, her eyes desperately search-ing her cell for a weapon. "What is all this about? What have I done?"

Pausing in the lit hallway, the man turned and arched an eyebrow at her. "You know why."

"No. I don't. I haven't a clue," Maggie said honestly. The man stared at her silently for a moment, studying her face as if determining whether she was telling the truth, she supposed. After a moment he appeared con-vinced, but it didn't move him to explain. Giving a small shrug, he spun back to the door.

"She'll maybe explain when she comes," was all he said. Then he closed the door.

"She? She who?" Maggie called, stumbling forward to fall against the door as the lock clicked into place.

"Who?" she shrieked furiously, pounding her balled-up fists against the wood.

It was a passing fury, gone as quickly as it had erupted, leaving her to press her face to the cool surface as tears pooled in her eyes. They spilled over to trail down her face. "Who?"

She stayed there, wallowing in self-pity and frustration, until a muffled moan from Banks drew her attention. Sniffing, Maggie wiped her face with the back of one hand, then turned to move cautiously back through the darkness. When her foot brushed up against some part of him, she knelt and felt around to determine his position on the ground. She eased down next to the man and drew his head into her lap.

Murmuring reassuring words and phrases, she brushed the hair away from his face and waited for him to regain consciousness. This man had been a part of her life from the time she was born. He had been her butler, her friend, and sometimes just a grouchy old curmudgeon. He used to sit with her and talk at night after Gerald died, keeping her company in those sad, lonely hours when her mind would have turned to morbid mourning over her brother. She loved him.

She had neglected their friendship somewhat since James had come into her life, and had no idea how he had come to be here unless he had followed her here without her knowledge. She wouldn't put it past him. He'd sworn to keep her safe after Gerald's death, and he had now been hurt in the attempt.

"My lady?" His voice quavered with age and weakness.

Maggie stilled at those rusty words, her hands stiffening on his face. "Banks? Are you awake?"

"Aye." The word was almost a groan. Obviously the man was awake, and regretting it. Which answered the question she had been about to ask. He apparently had a headache, too.

"Where . . ." he asked, sounding a bit cranky.

Maggie smiled, affection rising up in her for the old domestic. "I do not know. An old abandoned building, I think." She peered around fretfully, trying to make out something—anything—in the blackness that pressed down on them from all around.

"An old abandoned house near the docks," Banks decided in a pained voice, and Maggie glanced down, forgetting she wouldn't be able to see him.

"Are we? How do you know that?"

"I . . ." He shifted, and his weight was removed from her lap. The groan that followed sounded near her ear, and she supposed he had sat up beside her. He gasped, "I followed you."

"You did?"

"Aye. I saw you sneak out of Lady Barlow's. I trailed you to Madame Dubarry's, waited, and started to follow you home when you were snatched off the street into that carriage."

"You were the one who shouted when I was grabbed," she realized.

"Yes. I tried to get to you, but I wasn't fast enough. I am getting *old*." The word was said bitterly, and Maggie reached out in the darkness until she found the butler's hand. She squeezed his cold, wrinkled fingers gently. That drew another sigh from the man, and he continued, "I couldn't get there quickly enough. I hailed a hack and followed, but we were a ways back. Once I saw which building they took you into, I wanted to go get help, but was afraid that by the time we got back it might be too late. I paid a boy to fetch Lord Ramsey, then tried poking around, thinking that if I could just figure out where they were holding you, I might be able to break you out and . . ." His voice broke, and he was silent for a moment. "I guess in my excitement I forgot how old I am. Instead of finding and rescuing you, I ran into that scarred fellow. Next thing I knew, I was seeing lights. I am sorry."

"What for?" Maggie asked. "I am glad to have you here, and to know help is on the way."

"Aye. But no doubt finding me has warned that animal that help is on the way. It will make a rescue harder."

Maggie had opened her mouth to reassure him, when the door suddenly opened again. Light splashed into the room, bright and stabbing. Maggie shielded her eyes with one hand, blinking rapidly and hoping they would adjust. Footsteps and a shadow, then brighter light, told her someone was entering the room and bringing a lantern with him.

It seemed their time had run out.

Feeling extremely vulnerable on the floor, Maggie got shakily to her feet. She forced her eyes to open, determined to face her enemies.

"You are sure this is the right place?" James asked, peering about the deserted buildings with a frown.

Robbie—they had learned that was the boy's name—nodded solemnly. "Aye, m'lord. I live right over there, and I was playing with me mates when that old fellow waved me over."

James felt himself grimace as he took in the length of

street. He found it hard to believe that anyone could live in these decrepit and deserted-looking structures. James decided he would visit this lad's parents after he rescued Maggie and see if he could find jobs for them.

Perhaps at Ramsey. The boy was too thin and pale by half; some time in the country would be good for him. James had to rescue Maggie first, though. He must not focus on anything but succeeding at that task.

"I don't see this Banks fellow anywhere," Johnstone said.

James scowled. He had been waiting and watching for the butler, expecting him to step out into the street and hail them. "Neither do I," he said. His gaze dropped to the boy. "Where was he when he waved you over?"

"Right there." The child pointed at the building their carriage had stopped before, and James scanned every nook and shadow hopefully before admitting to himself that the man wasn't to be found. He only hoped that didn't mean that they had moved and the domestic had followed.

"Which of the buildings was he watching? Could you tell?" James asked.

Robbie hesitated, then scrambled off the bench seat and made his way through the legs of the men filling the coach. He peered out the window at the buildings opposite where he claimed Banks had been. His face scrunched up in concentration as he considered the matter.

"I think he was watching that one," he decided at last, and James leaned across Johnstone to look out the window at the building in question.

"I don't suppose ye saw a woman bein' dragged into

it before ye noticed the old man, did ye?" Johnstone asked hopefully.

They all sighed in disappointment when the lad shook his head. "I just come out to play when the man nipped me."

"All right, Robbie," James said grimly, reaching into his pocket. "Take this, and go on home now. And thank you for your help."

Robbie's young eyes brightened at the sight of the coin held out; then he snatched it up. Gasping a thanks, he scrambled out of the door James opened.

"What do you want to do, m'lord?" Johnstone asked quietly.

James pulled the door closed again. "I think we have to check all three buildings: the one the boy pointed out, and the ones on either side. She could be in any of them."

Johnstone nodded, his glance moving over the three other runners with them. "Jack, you and Bob take the house on the left; Jimmy and meself will take the middle, and m'lord—"

"No. I take the middle house," James said firmly.

Johnstone hesitated, then nodded. Glancing at the youngest of the group, he said, "Jimmy, ye'll have to take the house on the right on your own. I'll accompany his lordship."

"No," James said again, frowning at the nervous Jimmy. The boy was young and obviously the least experienced. If James was wrong and the middle building wasn't where Maggie was, if she was in the building on the right, he didn't want this fidgety pup going in on his own and possibly getting her killed. "You go with Jimmy. I can manage on my own."

"Oh, m'lord, I don't think . . ." Johnstone began, but James didn't stay to listen. Opening the carriage door, he stepped out and moved toward the building in the center, his heart pounding with rage and fear: rage that someone had dared to touch what was his, and fear that he would be too late to save her.

Maggie had thought that seeing the "she" behind these attacks would clear matters up. Much to her consternation, however, the woman hanging the lamp from the hook by the door was a complete stranger.

Maggie forced herself to look closer, sure she was missing something. Her eyes slowly absorbed the generous figure in the red dress, the blond hair piled on the woman's head, little curls free to frame her pretty face, but it didn't help. Maggie had no clue who she was.

"Who *are* you?" she asked quietly.

The blonde turned to survey her captives. Her eyebrows rose with amusement. "Come now; you don't really expect me to believe that you do not know who I am? Not the famed G. W. Clark."

Maggie stiffened, her blood running cold. "I fear you have me at a disadvantage. It also seems that you have more to blackmail me with than I have on you. I haven't a clue who you are." She thought that last bit a touch of subtle brilliance. Perhaps it would give the woman the idea of blackmailing her rather than killing her, as she feared was her captor's ultimate objective.

The woman's eyes narrowed as if suspecting a trick. "You do not recall me?"

When Maggie shook her head, the blonde's mouth twisted with disbelief. "Think! Think hard."

Maggie stared at her silently, still shaking her head until a memory exploded in her mind. Just a flash, like a bolt of lightning quickly there and just as quickly gone, but her head slowed its shaking. The woman smiled.

"You *do* remember."

Maggie hesitated, then asked uncertainly, "Madame Dubarry's? In the room I climbed into? I was putting on Maisey's mask. You were on the bed."

"There you are!" The woman smiled brightly, but Maggie still didn't understand.

"I am sorry. I saw you in Lady Dubarry's, I think. All right. Briefly, when I was trying to escape . . . but I still do not see what this is all about."

"Yes, you do. You know *exactly* what this is all about. And so do I. How long until I would have opened the *Daily Express* to find the article?"

"The article on what?" Maggie asked in amazement. "Mr. Hartwick has already published my article on the interviews I did with you women at Dubarry's."

The blonde hesitated, then frowned. "You really do not know."

It wasn't a question, rather an amazed realization the woman was voicing aloud, and Maggie felt a touch of hope tingle through her. This was all a mistake. They would let her and Banks go, because this was all a huge mistake.

"What were you doing in my room that night?"

"I climbed out of Maisey's room via the window," Maggie answered. "I'd traded my gown in exchange for hers and information on which way to go to avoid running into anyone else. She said Lady X and Lord Hastings were in the room on one side, but the room on the other was empty. She said the left was the empty room and I went that way, only to recognize my mistake when I reached that room and found it occupied. I realized then that she must have meant *her* left. I had gone to *my* left, but she had been facing me through the window and her left would have been my right, so I had to turn and go back the other way. Unfortunately, by the time I made it to the right window, you were in there. Though I didn't realize that until I stopped to put on my mask and glimpsed you."

"Dear God." The woman sagged like wet cloth. "You really did not know. All this time, all this fear and . . . It was a mistake. Just a terrible, horrible mistake, and all because Maisey actually told you the right way."

"The right way?" Maggie was totally bemused. She pushed the feeling aside. What did the explanation matter? She just wanted out of here.

Waiting in that dark prison with Banks, Margaret hadn't dared reveal her fear that she might be living her last moments. That, perhaps he was, too, thanks to his loyalty to her. She had kept those thoughts to herself and suffered with them.

It wasn't death itself that frightened her, so much as the idea of never seeing James again. That very possibility caused her unbearable anguish. Now, she felt hope spring to life within her. If this was all a mistake, she might yet live to see him, might hold him in her arms and be sheltered by him once more. Trembling with this new possibility, Maggie asked, "Will you let us go?"

A bewildered expression crossed her captor's face. She seemed to struggle briefly, then shook her head unhappily. "Nay. I cannot."

"What?" Maggie stared at her in frustration. "But—"

"You could still write about all this," the woman interrupted quietly. "If you had nothing to write about before, you do now."

"No, I don't. Besides, I couldn't if I did. My fiancé has forbidden me to write as G. W. Clark anymore." Maggie almost rolled her eyes at her own words. She sounded so plaintive, like a child begging. . . . But she was begging—for her life and for Banks's.

"I am sorry," the woman said, and Maggie almost believed her. "But I cannot risk your telling."

"Telling *what?*" Maggie snapped in frustration. "I know what you look like but not who you are."

"You know I am one of Aggie's girls, and that I kidnapped you and have tried to have you removed several times," the woman said patiently.

"I will not tell," Maggie promised. Her blood was like ice in her veins as she watched a sad expression come to the other woman's face. "I wish I could believe that."

"You can," Maggie assured her. It was no use; the blonde raised a gun. Maggie's thought then was to stall as long as she could, hoping the boy Banks had paid would bring James here in time. Or, failing that, that some plan would come to her mind. "All right. At least tell me why I am dying. I deserve to know that much. Who are you?"

"I am nobody."

Maggie blinked. "What?"

"I am nobody," the woman repeated. "My name is Elizabeth Drake. I was an actress, and not a very successful one. Then I had this idea to don a mask and set myself up at Madame Dubarry's . . . or some other establishment. Always in a mask. That would lend me mystery, and mystery is a powerful aphrodisiac."

"Lady X," Maggie murmured, understanding. She never should have doubled back that night on the ledge of the brothel, at least not to avoid Lady X. She had gone the right way after all. The first room was the one that was supposed to be empty. Maisey had been in error about its occupancy.

"Yes," the blonde acknowledged.

"They say you are a lady of nobility."

"That was part of my plan. I dropped a hint or two with my first few customers. They thought what I hoped, and were quick to spread the rumors; a lady of nobility selling her body in disguise. Being naughty is as much an aphrodisiac as being mysterious. The men came in droves, reaching deep in their pockets to have just a half hour with me, hoping to figure out who I was. As Lady X I can command ridiculous sums, and often do not even have to do much to earn it. Most of them just want to talk to me in the hopes of discovering my identity—which member of the ton has fallen so low."

"Brilliant," Maggie complimented with unfeigned admiration. "As a woman who has had to make her way in the world, I admire the brilliance of your plan."

"Yes. I believe you do." Regret crossed the blonde's features. "If things had been different, I think we could even have been friends. I know you are not a snob about such things. You are friends with Agatha, after all."

"It was you at the men's club, not Maisey," Maggie realized, recalling what she should have noticed at the time. Maisey was about Maggie's own height, but the woman she had thought was Maisey that night—the woman who had locked her in the room—had been several inches shorter.

"Yes," she admitted with irritation. "I expected you to come dressed as a woman, but you dressed as a man and gave Bull the slip." Her aggravation turned to amusement. "I was livid when you arrived without him on your tail. I paid the doorman to go to my carriage and tell my driver to take him to where Bull was watching Lady Barlow's residence, and fetch him. Then I locked you in the room until he returned. It should have been easy. I did not expect you to knock him out and escape," she added dryly.

"How did you manage the letter she sent?" Maggie asked, wondering what the devil was taking James so long. "Maisey said she wrote that letter, and that there was nothing in it about meeting at a men's club. Was she lying? Did you pay her to help you?"

"I did not have to." Lady X shrugged and explained, "Maisey cannot write. I offered to write it for her."

"Ahh." The sound came out on a gust of air. She should have thought to ask. It should have been obvious the prostitute probably wouldn't have that skill. Very few of the working class did. For someone who liked to claim that she had an investigative mind, Maggie really had let a lot of details slip by.

"And how did you manage today?"

In the process of raising her gun again, Lady X lowered it once more and tilted her head in confusion. "Today?"

"I presume my disguising myself as a servant worked, else your man there would have grabbed me on the way to Dubarry's rather than on the way back. I trust he was still skulking around looking for his opportunity?"

"Yes." The blonde nodded slowly. "I have had him watching Lady Barlow's since he failed to take care of you in that fire. Your disguise did work. But there are no secrets at Aggie's, and the doorman, Ralph, was rather distraught at being reprimanded for not showing you in immediately. I was in the kitchens and heard him telling Cook about it."

"And you sent someone to fetch . . ." Maggie gestured to the scarred man, her gaze moving slowly over his blank face. There was no sign of mercy there; if anything, he appeared to be looking at her with deep dislike. She could only think that was because she had survived his various attacks and made him look bad.

"Yes." There came a click as Elizabeth Drake cocked her gun, and Maggie's attention was drawn away from such trivialities to the matter at hand: her death. She stared wide-eyed at the barrel of the pistol, her mind gone blank of any way to delay any longer. The barrel seemed to grow, filling her entire vision. She couldn't believe this was the last thing she would see in her life, the black hole at the end of a gun. And all because of poor directions.

A soft thump drew Maggie's eyes from the gun to the hallway beyond the door. She saw the shadow of a crouching figure cast on the opposite wall from the light in the room next door, and knew at once that it was James.

"What was—" Lady X didn't get to finish the question. Overcome with panic that James might be caught, Maggie leapt forward and grabbed the cocked pistol. It was an instinctive action, a desperate attempt to save Banks, James, and herself . . . and a wholly stupid move. A shot rang out, deafening her, and Maggie felt as if some invisible tree trunk had hit her in the chest to throw her backward.

"My lady!" Banks cried.

She saw James lunge through the doorway as her back slammed into the wall. Their shocked gazes met, then her legs seemed to lose their strength. Maggie began to slide toward the floor. Her last thought was that he looked terribly pale, and she wished she'd had the chance to tell him she loved him.

Chapter Nineteen

James moved carefully toward the front of the building and the stairs waiting there. The first floor had a stench he didn't want to identify, and was littered with various bits of rubbish. It had also proven to be empty. He was beginning to suspect that he had chosen the wrong building and that Maggie, if she was anywhere on this block, would prove to be somewhere else. This building appeared empty and was as silent as a tomb.

He shuddered at the thought, then pushed it away. She wasn't here, he assured himself. He would not believe that her death was the reason this place felt so empty and cold. Maggie was alive. He would sense it if she were gone. The world would seem different, he was sure. It certainly had seemed different since she had entered his life.

James paused at the base of the stairs and peered up into the yawning darkness. He was really starting to think that Maggie was in one of the other two buildings and, for a minute, he considered giving up on this one and going to join the others. Then he changed his mind. He should check this building out, at least. Johnstone and his men would check the others, and he couldn't not search here, simply because of a hunch. It was just that he wanted to be the one to find Maggie, and he had a dreadful feeling that time was running out. She was in great danger. If the man who had attacked her and set her town house on fire was the same one who had her now, he would kill her; James didn't doubt that for a minute.

It was better to do a thorough check, then he could go join Johnstone and young Jimmy in the next building. With that decided, he started up the steps, walking as close to the wall as he could to avoid too much creaking of the stairs.

As he reached the last couple of steps and was able to view the long hallway at the end of it, he spotted a light. It spilled out of two rooms at the end of the long, dark corridor. James's heart squeezed painfully, then started beating at an accelerated rate. He hesitated only briefly, his hand tightening around the dueling pistol he'd taken from his aunt's library. Drawing some comfort from it, he straightened his shoulders and went determinedly onward.

He was halfway down the hall before he heard the voices. They were drifting from one of the lighted rooms ahead, and he couldn't make out what was being said. Still, he recognized one of the voices as Maggie's. He moved a little more swiftly while still trying to creep as silently as possible.

He paused at one side of the first door, took a breath,

then eased around the frame for a quick peek inside. When he saw that it was empty, a beat-up chair and small rickety table the only furnishings, he relaxed. The light came from a lantern on the table, which also held a deck of cards, one dented metal cup, and a half-empty bottle of something. James supposed this was where Maggie's abductor waited. The single cup suggested there was only one man, probably the scar-faced man. Which was perfect. James would be more than happy to deal with that animal. He had been eager to meet that bastard since seeing Maggie's bruised and battered face after the fire. He wanted to return the favor and wouldn't pass up the opportunity to kill the man responsible.

His gaze raked over the table again as he listened to the murmur of voices from the next room. He couldn't hear what was being said, but the calm tones made him think that there was still time. Maybe he would hear a hint as to what to expect before he burst in to save Maggie. He wanted to be well prepared when he did so, as he had no desire to get Maggie killed by making a mistake.

The room had little else to tell. The single chair and cup suggested a single guard. The cards suggested the man had been waiting for someone—perhaps whoever had hired him. James wouldn't mind getting his hands on that person either, he decided. Easing back out of the room, he crept to the side of the next open door. His ears strained to make out the words being spoken.

"And you sent him to fetch . . ."

That was definitely Maggie speaking. James breathed a sigh of relief at the calm, strong tone of her voice. She didn't sound injured or weak, or even scared, he thought with relief. But then he heard the answering voice say, "Yes," and he stiffened. It was a woman answering her!

In all the time he'd had Johnstone looking into this mess and who might be after Maggie, he'd never considered that a woman might be involved. He'd assumed it must be one of the men she had written about, someone who had been embarrassed or ruined by one of her articles. He had never even dreamed a woman would be responsible!

James was so startled by the sound of the woman's voice that his arm jerked, the pistol he held bumping against the wall. It was the smallest sound, but seemed loud in the silence that had just fallen.

"What was—" he heard the female begin sharply; then there was a scuffling, promptly followed by a gunshot. That sound made him freeze, but the horrified shriek of "My lady!" that came directly afterward sent blood rushing through him. Horrified, James swung into the room, his pistol at the ready.

The first thing he saw were the backs of two people— a large, wide shouldered man and a petite, cloaked woman—but beyond them he caught his first glimpse of Maggie. What he saw both enraged and terrified him. She was in the process of falling backward, her pale face filled with shock and pain as blood squirted through her fingers from her chest. He watched in horror as she slid down the wall, then drove his gaze back to the couple standing between them. He had expected the man to have the gun, so he was surprised when he realized the woman held it, but that didn't give him pause for long.

Striding forward, James grabbed the weapon from her

startled hands. He swung then to plow it into the face of the man. Taken by surprise, the ape stumbled backward. James pursued him, his fists flying, the heavy pistols he held inflicting more damage than did his knuckles. He didn't stop until the man was unconscious.

Chest heaving, James straightened and turned to confront the woman—only to find that she had slipped out while he'd been busy with her compatriot. He took a step toward the door, but paused when a moan drew his attention to the floor. Banks sat holding his mistress close, supporting her with one arm, the other hand pressed against her wound as if he were trying to keep more blood from spilling out into the pool already growing on the dirty wooden floor.

"Please don't die, my lady." The butler moaned, tears streaking down his old face. He rocked her gently.

Changing direction at once, James moved to kneel beside them. Banks raised sorrowful eyes to him. "She is bleeding badly, my lord. Very badly. I fear she isn't going to make it."

"The hell she won't," James answered. Scooping her into his arms, he stood and turned to the door, leaving the old man to find his feet on his own. He moved down the hall with her quickly, Banks scrambling after them, running to catch up, and promptly applying pressure to Maggie's wound from the side as he accompanied them down the stairs. Despite the awkwardness it caused in trying to descend, James didn't make him stop. He doubted the action was doing much good, but the man obviously needed to feel he was doing something.

He hardly even cared when he spotted Johnstone approaching, the woman who'd shot Maggie firmly gripped in his hand.

"What do ye want me to do with her, m'lord?" he asked as James hurried forward.

"Wring her bloody neck," he said in a cold snarl.

Johnstone jerked to a stop in shock as he recognized Maggie's pale face, then saw how she was bleeding. Alarm covered his face, and he dragged the blonde along as he followed them to the coach. "What happened?"

"That bitch shot Maggie," James answered through gritted teeth. They reached his carriage. "Her man, the scarred bastard, is upstairs. He is unconscious right now, but probably won't be for long."

"Jack!" Johnstone shouted, bringing the other man running.

"Yes sir?"

"The scarred man's upstairs. Go get him." Johnstone turned back as Crowch opened the carriage door. The driver had scrambled down from his perch on first seeing their approach, and now he held the door open as James got inside. Ramsey did his best not to jar Maggie as he did, but it was impossible not to altogether, and he winced at every little moan of pain that slipped from her lips as he settled her on his lap.

"Get us to Lord Mullin's, Crowch," he ordered. Banks clambered in after him and returned to applying pressure to her wound.

"Straightaway, m'lord," the coachman assured him, slamming the door. The carriage swayed as he hurried back up onto his seat; then the vehicle was off, leaving Johnstone to watch them go.

Crowch rode the horses full-out, careening wildly through the narrow streets in a way that would have alarmed James if Maggie weren't growing paler with each passing moment. He stared at her face, unaware that he was alternately cursing God for letting this happen and praying to him to save her. And he was begging Maggie not to die.

When the carriage at last stopped, James waited impatiently for Banks to push the door open, then scrambled out. He led the way to the door of Robert's town house, paused there, and, hands full, began kicking it. Using his free hand, Banks promptly added his imperious knock while Crowch began shouting, "Here! Here!" through his cupped hands at the windows above. Between the three of them, they were causing enough racket to disturb the whole street, and much to James's annoyance other doors began to open while Robert's stayed closed.

"It is about bloody damned time!" he said in a snarl when the door finally opened to reveal a startled and slightly annoyed butler. Furious that it had taken the man so long to answer, he pushed forward, forcing the servant back into the hall.

"What is it, Mills?"

James turned at that voice, peering over the butler's shoulder to see Lord Mullin himself standing in a room off the entry. Relief rushing through him, Ramsey quickly moved toward his friend, Banks stumbling to keep up.

"James!" Robert recognized him with obvious surprise then glanced down at Maggie whom James held in his arms. "What? Dear God, what has happened?"

"She's been shot," he answered tightly.

Robert brushed Banks's hand away and lifted the blood-soaked cloth that was pressed to her wound. James had known it was bad—the amount of blood had told him so—but the way Robert blanched confirmed his fears. He felt his heart shrivel.

"Get her upstairs," the younger nobleman ordered, replacing Maggie's bandage. "Show them to the spare room, Mills, I'll collect my things."

James followed the servant silently, his eyes shifting back and forth between Maggie's pale face and where he was going. The clomp of footsteps on the stairs behind him signaled that Banks and probably Crowch were following, though he couldn't fathom why. They would be of little use here. He would be useless, too, he knew. Only Robert could help. There was nothing he could do for her now.

But then, he had been little use to her since they'd met, he berated himself. *Look after my sister*, was all Gerald had asked in exchange for James's life . . . and James had failed him. Miserably.

First he had mistaken the woman for a prostitute. A terribly stupid mistake. Foolish. Idiotic. Who could believe sweet, innocent Maggie a ladybird? Only an idiot like himself. Then he had failed time after time to keep her safe. True, he had managed to pull her out from in front of one carriage, but he hadn't managed to draw her from harm's way. He hadn't saved her from being pushed in front of the second crash, or from having her hat shot, or from the fire. Dear Lord, he hadn't even protected her from himself, taking her there in his aunt's library as if she were some common strumpet. And not just once, but twice! Gerald had entrusted him with his sister. He had been foolish.

And now he hadn't protected her at this most critical moment. He had stood just feet away and let her get shot. If he had moved more swiftly, acted more quickly . . .

"You can lay her down, my lord."

James stopped his self-recriminations long enough to notice that they had reached a bedroom, and that Mills had spread a rough woolen blanket over the bed. Even now, he was brushing out the last few wrinkles so that Maggie could be laid upon it. James scowled at the sight of the prickly-looking material. "Get that off. She will lie on the sheets."

"It is to save the linens from the blood, my lord," the man explained. "Once Lord Mullin has cleaned and sewed up the wound—"

"Get it off!" he roared. "I shall replace the damn linens, and the damned bed, too, if I have to, but she shall not spend her last moments on that damn piece of—"

"Do as his lordship asks and take it off, Mills."

James paused midsentence, and glanced over his shoulder. Lord Mullin entered the room, his hands full of implements. He was followed by two more servants, one carrying fresh white bandages, the other dragging a bucket of steaming water.

"Lay her down, please."

At Robert's order, James turned back to the bed. Mills had whisked the ratty woolen blanket away and was now tugging the clean top linens down on the bed. Seeing the fresh white bottom linen for her to lie on, James grunted in satisfaction and laid Maggie down. He hesitated, then knelt at the bedside, taking Margaret's small hand in his own.

The doctor moved around the bed to the other side. He paused to murmur something in the ear of his butler, then tentatively lifted away the blood-soaked cloth to get a second look at Maggie's wound.

"Well?" James asked anxiously.

"I shall have to cut her gown away." Robert lifted his head, looking around at the hovering servant. "Do you wish your men to remain?"

James turned to scowl at Banks and Crowch. The two men immediately scuttled to the door, though Banks moved more reluctantly than the driver. Satisfied, James glanced back as Robert began cutting away Maggie's gown. He started at the neckline, working downward in a curved pattern that left nearly half her chest bare. Maggie moaned as he pulled the material away, that little action alone seeming to pain her. The sound drew James's eyes to her face, and he felt his heart stop beating in his chest when he saw that her eyelashes were fluttering. Then he felt her hand twitch, and he held it a little tighter. She had been so silent and still since he had lifted her, he had almost feared her already dead. These new signs, terrifying as they were, were also encouraging.

He peered at her face hopefully and whispered, "Maggie?"

Her eyelashes fluttered once again before opening. They remained open this time. "James?"

She seemed confused, and James squeezed her hand, then rubbed his thumb over her small fingers. He frowned at how cold they were. "Yes. I have brought you to Robert. He will heal you, love."

If she understood him, she didn't show it. Her eyes began to slip wearily closed; then she forced them open again as if remembering something of importance.

"James," she said softly, trying to sit up. Both he and Lord Mullin pressed her back down.

"Rest. Save your strength," Robert urged quietly.

"What, Maggie? Don't talk. Save your strength. What is it?" James murmured. Picking up her hand, he pressed it flat to his face, trying to warm the cold flesh. He wasn't even aware that he was contradicting himself, urging her to rest while asking what she wanted to say. All he could think was that she was as cold as death, and that he was losing her.

"But . . . have to . . . tell you," she got out breathlessly, then winced and sucked in a breath. Pain knifed across her face as Mullin began to probe gently at her wound.

"You're hurting her!" James shouted.

"Yes, I am," Robert said quietly, then spoke to Maggie and not him as he said, "And I am sorry for that, Margaret. But I have to get the ball out and clean the wound. It will hurt a great deal. Mills is bringing something to ease your pain, but I fear I can't wait. You have already lost a lot of blood."

"Yes." Maggie managed a grimace of a smile, then closed her eyes briefly and said, "I just . . . have . . . to tell . . ."

"Maggie." James almost moaned her name, agonizing over the pain she was suffering. He dropped his head, desperately squeezing her hand.

"I love . . . you," she managed to get out. Her voice was faint, but James heard her declaration for all that. Tears welled in his eyes, stupefying him. He hadn't cried since his parents' deaths. Shocked, he squeezed her hand and, wiping away his tears, he lifted his face.

"Mag—" Her name died in his throat as she squeezed his hand viciously and cried out. In the next moment, her grip loosened and her body relaxed, too. She fell silent.

"What have you done?" James roared, rearing to his feet.

He was about to rush around the bed and throttle Robert when a hand fell on his shoulder to stop him. James turned to see Mills standing behind him, a pitying expression on his face and a glass in his free hand. A bottle of some medicinal was caught between his arm and chest.

"She has just fainted," Robert assured him. Glancing up to nod toward the glass the butler was holding out, he said, "Now drink some of that down and go pray."

"Pray?"

"Yes, pray. She'll need it," Robert said grimly as he continued to work.

James downed a good portion of the drink Mills had poured him. His hand clenched on the glass as he lowered it, his expression turning hard. There was so much blood. She was so pale. He couldn't lose her. "You are the one who had best pray. If you let her die, I—"

James paused as Robert raised his head. He blinked in confusion, unable to believe he had been about to threaten his friend. He was obviously losing his head. Which was nothing new around Maggie.

"You have it bad, my friend," the other man announced almost mournfully. Then he turned from James's tortured face to Maggie's wound.

Ramsey winced as the other man worked, grateful now that Maggie was not conscious to feel anything. "*I* have it? What? I am not the sick one."

"Yes, you are. Lovesick. I wondered before, but this is one of the worst cases I have ever seen. You have it bad." Glancing up to see his friend staring at him blankly, Robert explained, "You love her, James. It's why you're acting like such an unbearable ass. You weren't even this

352

bad when I was working on Gerald. Now get the hell out of here and go finish that drink so that I can work on her—else you'll be loving a corpse."

James stood frozen for a minute, then staggered away from the bed when Mills urged him toward the door. His head was reeling. Was this love? Was that what this panic was? If so, the books lied. Love was not a happy, joyful feeling that made everything seem lovely; it hurt like hell and turned one into a panicked ninny. *Damn*. Love wasn't heaven; it was hell.

A moan from the bed made him pause at the door. He turned back, despite Mills's best efforts at keeping him from doing so. He couldn't leave Maggie. She needed him.

For once, Maggie found herself waking up without a headache. Unfortunately, her chest was paining her instead. Every breath seemed an effort, but she agonizingly opened her eyes, gritting her teeth as she tried to bring the room into focus. When she was finally able to make anything out, all she could do was blink in confusion. She didn't recognize the room at all. This wasn't her bedroom in her town house, she knew. And neither was it the chamber she had been given at Lady Barlow's.

She was in a small, bright yellow room, lying in a narrow bed she had never before seen. Her gaze slid over the pleasant furnishings, and she tried to puzzle out what had happened. She was still doing so when the door to the room opened moments later, and Lord Mullin stepped into the room.

"My lord." She tried to greet him, but her mouth and throat seemed terribly dry. She was unable to do naught but mouth the words.

"Ah. You are awake, I see," Robert murmured, moving to her bedside and pressing a warm hand to her forehead. "And completely fever-free."

Maggie's eyebrows rose at the combination of satisfaction and relief in his voice, but he noticed neither as he picked up a mug from a nearby table and seated himself on the side of the bed; he then helped her sit up enough to sip from it. It wasn't worth the effort, Maggie decided as pain shot through her chest. Still, she dutifully took another sip of the liquid when he pressed her, enough to wet her mouth and throat. She was thankful when Robert allowed her to lie back down again, and she sighed in relief as the pain in her chest eased.

"I imagine you feel just awful," he commented, moving to replace the mug on the table. He turned back in time to see Maggie nod. "Well, you are very very lucky to feel anything. You nearly died, Margaret. If James had not gotten you here so quickly . . ." He shook his head to finish the sentence, but Maggie understood well enough. She would have died. His words had the beneficial effect of reminding her what had brought her here. She quite suddenly recalled the dark room, the scar-faced man, Banks, and Lady X. She also vividly recalled the moment when Lady X had shot her. It was a most unpleasant memory.

She also recalled opening her eyes to find James's worried face hovering over her. She remembered being surrounded by yellow, hearing his soothing voice telling her everything would be all right. Or had that been a dream? she wondered now. His voice had seemed . . . different. It had been full of something, some emotion she had never heard from him.

"Where . . . ?" she croaked, unable to finish.

Fortunately, Robert understood. He smiled wryly before answering: "I had to throw him out."

She felt shock at that pronouncement, and it must have been evident. Robert nodded and said conversationally, "James was quite devoted. He didn't leave your side from the moment he brought you here. He held your hand throughout my work on you, then bathed you during your four days of fever—neither eating nor sleeping until your temperature lowered and the danger passed. That was last night," he added. "Of course, James was quite disruptive in his . . . attempts to help."

"Disruptive?" Maggie mouthed.

Robert made a face then explained, "He shouted a lot." When she shook her head in disbelief at that news, Lord Mullin assured her, "Yes, he did. He bellowed at me for—as he put it—'butchering you.' Also for not healing you faster and for being . . . I believe it was a *bloodletting quack*—though I don't know why he said that; he knows that I do not agree with bloodletting."

Maggie offered an apologetic expression, but Robert wasn't finished.

"He also yelled at Mills, my butler, for being slow and lazy, at Crowch and Banks for being useless, and at you for daring to almost die on him. And he cursed Heaven too, a couple times, I believe." He grinned at Maggie's dismayed expression and patted her hand reassuringly. "He wasn't always rational. But four days without sleep or food will do that to a person. I finally had to send him home with instructions to rest and eat. I assured him I would not let him back until he had done both."

Maggie relaxed somewhat. Then Robert added, "He loves you very much."

Her first reaction was shock. It was quickly followed by hope, then doubt, then fear, and finally simple confusion as to why he would tell her something like that, and in such grim tones.

"Why . . ." she croaked, grateful when Robert once again finished the question for her.

"Why am I telling you this?" he asked. When she nodded, he sighed and admitted, "Because he didn't take it at all well when I pointed it out to him."

"You pointed it out?" she began, noting with distraction that her voice was becoming stronger.

Robert noticed it, too, and he smiled even as he saved her from speaking further by explaining, "Oh, yes; I told him that he loves you. It is rather obvious for anyone with eyes. However, he apparently wasn't ready for the knowledge, and he isn't taking it at all well. I am not sure why. I do know that he took his parents' loss poorly and has seemed to try to keep a protective distance between himself and others since then, but . . ." He shrugged and shook his head. "Anyway, he has been a bear ever since." The young nobleman looked at her with wry amusement. "Hence the reason I had him leave."

Seeing the unhappy look on her face, he patted Maggie's hand. "I thought it best to warn you up front. He wasn't ready to have such feelings thrust in his face, and I fear this moodiness shall continue until he comes to terms with them. And since he certainly won't reveal his love for you until he does . . . Well, I hoped this chat would make married life a bit easier for you to bear until then."

When she merely stared at him, her thoughts in turmoil, Robert announced, "I think it is time I take a look at your wound and change your bandages."

Maggie ignored him as he set to work, her thoughts still in an uproar. She tried to sort out all he had just said. None of it made any sense and she hoped briefly that she was still feverish and imagining this entire conversation. A stab of pain as Lord Mullin lifted the last of her bandages away and poked at her stitches convinced her otherwise. She was awake, all right. But she was having trouble accepting what Robert had said, and all it meant. She had just been told that the man she loved, loved her in return. *By his friend.*

"Only you, Maggie," she breathed, unsure whether to laugh or cry.

"What was that?" Lord Mullin glanced at her in question. When she merely shook her head and waved one hand in a vague gesture, he shrugged and went back to work. Maggie was left to her thoughts. How could James possibly not know he loved her until Robert told him so? That was preposterous! Until she recalled that it had taken a talk with Agatha to straighten out her own confused feelings.

All right, she reasoned, so it wasn't preposterous that he too had needed someone to clarify his thoughts, but his being reputedly miserable about it?

Well, that wasn't so ridiculous either, she decided, recalling her own misery when she'd realized she loved James and felt sure he did not love her back. . . . Perhaps his unhappiness was caused by the same thing. All she needed to do was tell him that she loved him, too, and everything would be fine. They would be happy. Her gaze flickered to Robert. "I love him, too."

"Yes, I know," he said. Robert finished cleaning her wound and began to replace her bandages. "You told him while I was first tending to you. By the way, you are doing very well. The ball missed all your vital organs. There was a lot of blood loss, but very little real damage." He glanced up and looked her in the eye. "I suppose I should tell you that Lady X and her accomplice have already been before the magistrate. They won't be bothering you—or anyone else—anymore."

Maggie nodded at that news, happy to hear it, but really more concerned with what he had said before that. "Did you say that I told him that I love him?"

"Yes," Mullin answered distractedly as he finished with her bandages. Then he offered a smile. "You are mending very well. Which means that, in a day or so, we should be able to move you back to Lady Barlow's. That ought to please James. Mind you, the house staff would probably wish it sooner. His hanging about, acting like a wolf with an injured paw, growling about this and that every few minutes, has rather put them all on edge. The sooner it is safe to pack you off to Lady Barlow's, the better. Not that your company isn't delightful," he added to soften his words.

"He's back, m'lord!"

Maggie and Robert both turned to the door. A servant stood there wringing her hands.

"Already?" Lord Mullin rose with a frown.

"Yes. Mills sent me to warn you the moment he saw the coach pull up."

"Very well." Robert sighed then glanced down at Maggie with a tired smile. "It would seem Lord Ramsey has finished resting. Let us hope his mood has improved."

Chapter Twenty

"Do you, Lady Margaret Wentworth, take this man . . ." The rest of the cleric's words faded into a drone as Maggie's mind started to swim.

What was she doing? How could she marry James? Was she willing to spend the rest of her life tied to a man she loved desperately, but who felt nothing for her? Or, at least, a man who could not express the feelings he had?

Turning, she glanced over the guests at the wedding, her gaze finding Lord Mullin. The man had saved both her life and her sanity—at least up to this point. His calm, steady manner and words were the only thing, that had gotten her this far. His insistence that James loved her had helped her heal, and had kept her from calling off the wedding each time James acted as if this union were purely a matter of honor. And he'd done so many times. He had barely spoken to her since her recovery.

Of course, he had not been shouting or stomping about, either. She could have borne that. But he had been cold. He didn't seem to want her anymore—not physically, at least—and that worried her more than anything. Their passion had brought them together, and to feel its absence . . . In James's passion, she had been able to find hope that he cared for her. But he hadn't touched her since before she'd been shot. He'd even seemed to avoid her.

No, she supposed she didn't believe Lord Mullin's claims anymore. She didn't think James loved her; he didn't even seem to like her. His cold and reticent behavior these last two weeks seemed to indicate that clearly enough. If anything, he appeared to loathe her now.

What had caused this? Had it been her confession of her feelings? Perhaps it was all right for him to like and lust after her as long as her emotions were not engaged. Perhaps he was trying to let her know not to expect her feelings to be reciprocated. Would he treat her thusly for the rest of their lives? she wondered miserably. Could she bear it if he did?

"Lady Wentworth?"

Maggie peered up blankly at the minister, aware that she had missed her cue.

"You are supposed to say, 'I do,' " James prompted. Maggie turned her eyes to his implacable expression. He did not look like a happy man. He looked stiff and cold and as if he wished himself anywhere but here with her. If she said yes, she would be consigning him to a lifetime of what he considered to be hell. And herself, too.

"No." She didn't realize the word had slipped from her lips until James's expression changed to one of shock. He looked as if she'd hit him between the eyes with a mallet.

"What?" he squawked disbelievingly. The word was echoed in horror by his aunt and all of Maggie's servants.

"I said, no," she repeated. A calm quiet replaced the fear and confusion of moments before. She was doing the right thing. She knew that. "I will not marry you, James. Not when it is going to make you miserable."

Turning away, she started back up the aisle toward the church's exit, refusing to look at the shocked guests rising from the pews.

"My lady!" Banks was the first to break out of his shock and move after her. His alarm was obvious as he hurried to her side, pleading, "Oh, do reconsider, my lady. Are you sure about this? Think of the future."

"I *am* thinking of the future," she answered sympathetically. The servant was worrying over their economic forecast, but there was so much more at stake. This once, she needed to look out for herself as well as her servants. "We shall buy a smaller home, big enough for everyone, but less expensive than the house Gerald left me. We will be fine."

"Sit down!" James suddenly roared. Maggie paused and swung around in surprise. It wasn't till she saw the way he was glaring at their guests that she realized he hadn't been speaking to her.

"All of you! Sit down! This wedding is not over," he shouted. As soon as everyone had retaken his seat, James started up the aisle toward Maggie, scowling furiously. Pausing before her, he struggled briefly until he managed a less angry expression. His voice was reasonable as he said, "Maggie, what is it that you think you are doing? You cannot refuse—"

"I just did," she interrupted quietly.

"Yes, she did," one of the nearby guests said, the comment particularly loud in the silence. A wave of murmured agreement followed.

James turned a fierce glare on the crowd until they fell silent; then, managing to school his face into something approximating calm, he once more faced Maggie. "Think of the scandal," he implored.

Maggie did. Briefly. She was hardly aware of her foot tapping as she considered. In the end, the answer seemed easy enough. Yes. People would talk. They would whisper and twitter and so on, but if she moved to the country as she planned, all would be forgotten soon enough. Well, perhaps not so soon, but hopefully sooner than her death . . . which was how long she would suffer the misery of being married to someone who didn't love her. Straightening, she said with feigned cheer, "What is another scandal, more or less? Give them ten or fifteen years and no one will remember my name."

The comment sent another wave of whispers through the church, some agreeing that ten or fifteen years should be enough to forget the scandal, and others disagreeing. It seemed about half and half, she noted before James burst out frantically, "But we have been together! You could be with child!"

"Oh, that was grand of you to announce," Maggie snapped. It didn't look as though things would be forgotten in ten years, after all. The entire church was now talking excitedly.

"Maggie—"

"No!" she snapped. The crowd went silent again, eager to hear what came next. "I have said no and I meant it."

Spinning on her heel, she started for the door again. Banks was steadfast by her side, and the rest of her staff slipped out of the pews to march toward the back of the church in a little parade. Their show of support was heartening, and Maggie could have hugged every single one of them. She didn't see Lady Barlow give up her startled state and rush out of the front pew to hurry toward James, but she did hear her when the woman barked, "Do something, James! She is leaving!"

"You said you loved me!" he called out.

It wasn't the words so much as the betrayed sound of his voice that made Maggie pause. The murmurs in the church had grown ridiculously loud. Closing her eyes, she took a deep breath then made herself face him once more. The murmuring died at once, the air growing tense with anticipation.

"I do love you," she admitted softly, flushing at the oohs and ahhs exhaled by their guests.

"Then . . ."

James took a step forward, but she raised her hand to stop him and continued, "And that is why I will not marry you. I will not marry someone I love when the very idea of it is making him miserable."

"Who is miserable?" he asked with surprise. "I am not miserable."

"Oh, James," Lady Barlow piped up at his lame response. "I think she is referring to how cold and grumpy you have been of late."

"Aye, you been miserable lately," one guest said.

363

"These last few weeks at least," another agreed.

Lord Mullin stood up. "You tore a strip off your driver the other day, right in front of the club, and you never treat your servants poorly. Aye, you've acted miserable, all right, James." Robert gave Maggie an apologetic glance.

"Oh, do shut up!" James glared at his friend, then turned back to Maggie with a sigh.

"Well, perhaps I have been out of sorts of late," he admitted reluctantly. A series of snorts rose among the guests, but James steadfastly ignored them. "It is not because of this wedding, though. Or because you love me. I am glad you love me. That isn't what has made me so unhappy."

"Then what has?" Maggie asked desperately. She watched a battle take place on his features. When at last it ceased and he merely looked at her helplessly, she felt disappointment tug at her. She turned toward the door again. She had managed only one step when he blurted, "Because I love you, too!"

"He loves you, my lady!" Banks called hopefully to where Maggie had stopped again.

"Harrumph. It's not decent to love your wife," a woman to Maggie's right said staunchly. "Good thing she isn't marrying him."

"Oh, do shut up so we can hear her," someone else snapped at the unhappy-sounding woman.

Maggie turned toward James, her confusion clear. "You are miserable because you love me?" she asked. Robert's words came to mind, but still she didn't understand.

"No," James answered unhappily. He moved forward until they were standing nose-to-nose. "I am not miserable because I love you; I am miserable because of how it makes me feel."

Maggie tipped her head, annoyed and bewildered. "How does it make you feel?"

"It hurts and it scares me," he admitted in a soft voice. His aunt and Maggie's servants crowded closer to hear. "I cannot control or protect you, Maggie. You do what you will, when you will. When I nearly lost you, and I saw my life spreading out before me so barren without you, I—"

"What the hell is he jabbering on about?" an older gentleman asked grouchily.

Maggie glared at the rude man, then was taken somewhat by surprise when a flushed James suddenly took her arm and dragged her toward the exit. Over his shoulder he called, "Wait here. We shall return momentarily."

Much to her surprise, he didn't stop once they were out of the church, instead he continuing on until they reached his coach. Waving away the temporary servant hired to watch the horses while Crowch attended the wedding, James opened the carriage door himself and helped her inside. He followed.

"This is not perhaps the best place to talk, but at least it offers a modicum of privacy," he said. Pulling the carriage door closed, he settled on the bench seat across from her.

"I—" Maggie began, but he held up a hand to silence her.

"No. Let me start," he said. Tugging at his cravat impatiently, he took a deep breath and dove in. "Maggie, I have been a complete ass these last two weeks. I love you. I realized it at Robert's after you were shot."

"Well, Robert told me that he told you that you loved me."

"Yes, he did. But he didn't have to. Not really," he added when she looked doubtful. Heaving out a breath, he confessed, "Maggie, I was half in love with you before we ever met. I think good old Robert was, too."

Maggie's eyes widened. "The letters?"

"Yes. Your letters. Gerald read them to us every time he got one. He told us a lot about you, too, of course, but through your letters we heard your voice and got to know you. You lifted us out of that blood- and muck-filled world and brought life and light with you. I couldn't wait to meet you when I returned. I was actually eager to keep my vow to look out for you. I would have done it even had he not asked me."

He grimaced slightly at himself, then said, "You see, that day you were shot, when you told me that you loved me, I opened my mouth to say it back, but then Robert started to work on you. You cried out and fainted, and I didn't have to say anything. If I had spoken, I might have convinced myself that I was just repeating the words to be polite. I'm not very . . . good at *feeling*. But I didn't have to speak. Unfortunately, Robert didn't let me off the hook. He saw how I truly felt." James sighed. "He saw that I truly love you. But what he doesn't know is *why* I love you."

"Why?" Maggie echoed, almost afraid she was dreaming.

"Yes, darling. Why. You see, I love you because of everything you were in those letters, but I love you also because of the exuberance with which you live your life. I love you because you care for your servants more than you care for yourself. I love you because you do what you believe, and go where you need to go to do what you have to do. But loving you for those reasons— you're not someone who's easy to love, Maggie. You have a wild streak. The way you live is dangerous. When I saw you lying in that bed, when I truly believed you were going to die on me, I felt such pain that . . . well, I haven't felt it since my parents died."

He looked up, and she felt herself melt in the heat of his stare. "When your brother died in my arms, it almost killed me. He was such a dear friend. I admired and loved him. But you, Maggie, have come to mean so much more than he ever did. I knew that your death would tear me apart. Losing you would hurt so—"

"But you *didn't* lose me," Maggie interrupted. She shifted from her bench seat to his, patting his leg soothingly. "I survived."

"This time," he agreed. "But I will lose you someday. I must. Either I will die or you will, and that has been tormenting me these past two weeks."

"But—"

"No, let me finish," he said quickly. "That is why I have been such an ass. But I haven't been thinking clearly at all." He laughed suddenly, self-mocking. "Obviously. Because when you said no to marrying me just now, I realized what I was doing: instead of protecting myself with my foolish behavior, I was simply causing myself to lose you even sooner than was necessary."

Taking her hands in his, he pressed a kiss to each. "An intelligent man would enjoy the time we have together, cherish every moment with you, and not waste whatever time we have on fearing the future. I haven't been a very intelligent man, Maggie, but I vow here and now that if you marry me today, I will return to being the intelligent man I used to think I was. I'll spend the rest of my life doing everything in my power to make you happy."

"Oh, James," Maggie breathed, tears welling in her eyes. "I love you and always will."

"Even when I am stomping around, grumpy and miserable?" He asked the question with gentle humor, but Maggie caught the uncertainty that flashed in his eyes.

His uncertainty should not have surprised her; his misery and grumpiness were the reasons she had just refused to marry him. Still, Maggie found herself startled by the sign of his vulnerability. Cupping his face in her hands she put all the sincerity she possessed into her words as she said, "Yes, my lord. I shall love you always no matter how grumpy and miserable you occasionally get . . . I shall just remind myself that it is caused by fear." She broke the solemn moment with a grin and added, "Then I shall remind you. That should jolly you out of the mood at once."

"Aye, it should," he admitted wryly, then chuckled and pulled her into an embrace. Hugging her close, he sighed into her hair then said, "And I love you, and always shall." Maggie was about to pull back to kiss him when he added, "Despite the fact that you tend to act without thinking, and are always managing to get yourself into trouble."

She drew back abruptly, but rather than kiss him she offered an indignant glare. "I am not always getting myself into trouble!"

"No?" It was his turn to grin. "Who is it who was kidnapped from a brothel some weeks back?"

"*You* were the one who did the kidnapping!" she exclaimed hotly.

"Ah . . . so I was. But then you nearly got run down by that scar-faced man."

She glared at him, and he continued, "And who is it who got shot while—"

"Trying to save her future husband from being discovered and shot?" Maggie finished archly.

James stilled. "Banks said he thought that was what you were trying to do. I had hoped he was wrong."

"Why ever would you hope that?" Maggie asked in amazement.

"Ah, Maggie. Had you died trying to save me . . ." Anguish washed over his face and Maggie felt tears well in her eyes again as he said, "I must thank you for what you did, but if you ever do it again, I swear I shall—"

"My lord?"

James scowled at the interruption. "What?"

"Do please shut up and kiss me."

His scowl faded slowly, then he bent to press a kiss to her lips. It started as a sweet kiss, a gentle brush of lips to celebrate their love, but as always happened between them, it soon became a desperate, all-encompassing embrace that left them both panting.

"Oh, I have missed you," Maggie gasped as his lips slid along her jaw and started down her neck.

James mumbled something of an agreement, then tugged impatiently at the collar of her wedding gown. Irritably he asked, "Why do they make women's clothing so damned restrictive?"

"To prevent men from doing exactly this!" Maggie laughed breathlessly, then groaned as he finally managed to get one breast free of her gown. He suckled it relentlessly. "Oh, James. Oh, oh, oh, *James!*" She squealed suddenly, pulling away as she recalled where they were.

"We are supposed to be getting married today," she reminded him, tugging fretfully at her gown, trying to get covered back up.

"We are supposed to be consummating the marriage today, too," he said in the velvety voice that always made her tingle. He began tugging at the skirt of her gown, now, trying to find the hem line to get under it.

"Yes, but I think you have it in the wrong order," Maggie pointed out with a laugh, pleased to see that the passion was back. "Do you not think we should—"

He silenced her by covering her mouth in a kiss that curled her toes. When he added to his persuasion by sliding his hand up under her skirt, Maggie gave up her arguments and melted into him.

The guests could wait a little bit longer.

"Well?"

Lady Barlow glanced from the carriage she was watching outside the church, to the woman who came to stand beside her. Agatha Dubarry. Maggie had insisted on inviting her friend, the brothel owner, and been terribly surprised when neither James nor Lady Barlow had argued. Vivian saw now that it was the right decision. The woman was dressed in a prim pink gown, her face free of makeup, and her brassy red hair was hidden by a wig. No one would recognize her.

"Ah," the madam said, noting the way the carriage was rocking. "They have made up."

"Yes. It would seem so," Vivian agreed, turning her attention back to the moving vehicle. "At least they're not in the library."

Agatha chuckled softly and when Lady Barlow looked over in surprise, the woman admitted, "Maggie told me all about Lord Ramsey's love of books."

"Hmm. Love of books, love on books, love among books," she counted off humorously, then glanced over her shoulder at the wedding guests. They were all peering curiously toward them. "I suppose we should tell these people that the wedding is still on. Do you think James and Maggie will be much longer?"

Agatha squinted at the carriage, pursed her lips and shook her head. "Nay. It has been two weeks since they have been together. Besides, by the way the carriage is moving, I am guessing that things are coming to a climax."

"I hope for Maggie's sake it is two," Vivian murmured.

Agatha glanced in shock at her, then burst out laughing. When she had regained herself, she took Vivian's arm, and the two started back into the church. The brothel owner said, "Why, Lady Barlow, Maggie never mentioned what a witty woman you are. I do believe we could be friends."

"That is more than possible," the noblewoman allowed with a smile. "And please, call me Vivian."